Delilah

Enjoy!

Cat x H

Delilah

Cat Hextall

G.C.Butt Publishing
2017

First Printing: 2017

ISBN 978-1-326-85329-7

Copyright © G. C. Butt 2017

G.C.Butt Publishing

gcbuttpublishing@gmail.com

Cover photography © Rob Kerr 2017

www.rob-kerr.co.uk

This book is dedicated to all those who work with disaffected young people: the social workers, family resource workers, youth workers, residential care staff and magnificent multi-agency teams to name a few, plus the plethora of teachers, tutors, mentors and support staff who work in alternative education.

And to Kitty Hextall, the Nana I never knew, but whose name grows comfortable as a hug around my shoulders and to the link between us, the wise and wonderful woman who is, my mum.

1

Delilah lay still, listening. The scratching outside her window, she knew, was a piece of loose guttering. It was a comforting, familiar noise, unless it was windy, and then it kept her awake. She tuned in to the drip of the tap in the bathroom and the laboured hum of the fridge downstairs, straining her ears for any human sound. There was nothing. No creaking of bedsprings or snoring from the bedroom next door, no low moans from the bathroom. She would hear if the tv in the living room was on.

Still cautious, Delilah reached out for the coat by the side of the bed and dragged it under the duvet to warm up. The gas had run out yesterday morning and it was colder inside the house than outside. No wonder the bloke was pissed off and shouting last night, saying he wouldn't be able to find his cock if he stayed. Delilah didn't quite get that, but was glad when they left. Maybe her mum would top the gas card up on her way home today.

She was about to get up when the knocking on the front door started; quiet at first, then louder, more insistent. Delilah shot back under the duvet. Was it locked? The chain wasn't on. Then it stopped. Not the loan man then – he'd hammer away for half an hour sometimes and yell through the letterbox. She crawled over to the window on her hands and knees, careful not to lift her head above the sill. One curtain was covering her mattress and the other hung, limp and ineffective, from the three hooks left on the pole.

It was Saturday. There was too much going on outside to distinguish footsteps, amongst traffic noise and the kids screaming further up the road. Should she risk a look? At least a minute had

1

elapsed since the last knock and she wanted to see who it was before they disappeared.

'Delilah? Are you there?'

Right under her window. Becky, the-nosy-fucking-bitch social worker. Scowling, Delilah slumped against the wall and wrapped her arms around her knees. Becky was the last person she wanted to see.

'Delilah? Cleo?'

Cleo. Only Becky and new people called her mum 'Cleo'. Everyone else just called her Kelly, like they always had. The change of image had only lasted as long as the two grand from the scratch card – just over three weeks - but for some reason, her mum kept using the stupid name. Oh for fuck's sake, go *away*, Becky.

'If you're after Kelly, she went off last night. Not seen her this morning.'

Oh shit, it was Shona, next door.

'Oh, er...was Delilah with her?'

'No.'

'Do you know where Delilah is?'

'No.'

That was more like it. Shona might be a soft old hippy, but she wasn't stupid. Delilah didn't move, but could picture the scene: Becky, smiling, thinking she looked friendly but doing that weird thing with her nose, like she'd found shit on her shoe; Shona, realising it was Social Services, backing away from the fence. Social Services were as bad as the pigs – they all talked to each other.

'Are you friendly with Cleo?'

'Not really, not any more. Got to go, the dog needs feeding.'

Ha. She didn't even have a dog. A door banged, so Shona must have escaped. Perhaps now Becky would leave and she could get on with her day. She wanted a fag, badly, and was crossing to the door on her hands and knees when a sharp rap from downstairs made her jump. It sounded like the letterbox. Delilah waited, cold now. The annoying twitch under her bottom lip kicked in, but made her angry at the same time. She wasn't going to cry today.

After pulling on an extra jumper and her coat, she crept out onto the landing, but could see the closed letterbox from the top of the stairs. Becky wasn't spying, she'd just posted something. Ignoring the envelope on the floor, Delilah went into the living room. There was an ashtray on the table and another on the window sill, but every nub was smoked down to the orange filter. The kitchen held a nice surprise - a whole Superking, with a sachet of Nescafe next to it. Her mum hadn't forgotten after all.

Smiling, Delilah put the kettle on and lit the fag. She'd have a coffee and then see if Jono was in. Weekends were great, there was no need to watch out for the School Attendance Officer. She was rinsing a mug in cold water when the electric went off. It wasn't scary - it happened all the time - but the kettle hadn't boiled. The coffee tasted crap, especially with no sugar, but was hot enough to warm her insides and her hands around the mug. Rooting through the various letters and papers on top of the microwave, Delilah was disappointed to find both the gas and electric cards. The cold was bad enough, but it was the 4th of December and the house would be dark by late afternoon.

Breakfast was the most important thing on her mind right now though, so she left by the back door, avoiding any awkward questions from Shona. It was a ten minute walk to Jono's house and Delilah was not surprised to see the curtains closed. 10am was a bit early for a guy who often stayed up gaming all night. It was an age before he answered the door and then it only opened a crack.

'Hey Dee. You alright?'

'Yeah. I was just going to hang out, make you some toast.'

'I've got no bread and it's...um...not a good time. Can you come back later? P'raps tomorrow?'

'Oh. Right. Whatever.'

She turned away, her mouth twisting.

'Dee?' he called after her.

Delilah didn't turn around. She was cold, hungry and didn't want to think about the possibility of Jono having a visitor. He sometimes called her his 'little sis', but she didn't think of him as a brother and planned to change things when she got to 16. Of course, he'd have other girlfriends before then, but she didn't want to meet them. Where now? She wanted another fag.

Walking up the main road, Delilah watched two bitchy-looking girls going into the new nail salon. She couldn't imagine having that much money, but was soon distracted by a food opportunity. The woman with a pushchair and toddler in front of her had gone into the corner shop and would provide a good screen. She followed them in, grabbed a bag of crisps from the stand just inside the door and slipped out again. No-one noticed. Result. Except the crisps were cheese and onion flavour, which she didn't really like.

She ate them on a bench in the park, hoping someone with a fag would walk past. No-one did, just a man walking his dog and some little kids on the swings, who all ignored her. After half an hour she was shivering and when she checked the time on her phone, noticed the battery was on its last bar. There were no messages. So what if Shona grilled her, at least it would be warm in her kitchen. Shoving her hands into her pockets, Delilah headed home.

The envelope was still lying on the floor by the front door. She picked it up and noticed her name was on the front, but tossed it onto the settee anyway. Her phone was now bleeping with an urgent tone and she didn't want to miss a call from her mum. Taking the charger from the kitchen, she went next door.

~ ~ ~

Shona recognised the dark head through the frosted glass and sighed. She didn't want Delilah around if Social Services were on her case, but neither could she leave her standing in the cold. Where the hell was her bloody mother? She opened the door.

'Morning. Everything ok?'

'Alright. Can I come in and charge my phone?'

Sighing again, Shona stepped back to let her in, scanning the street for any watchers and seeing nothing unfamiliar.

4

'Someone was looking for you this morning.'

'Yeah, I know.'

'So who was it?'

'Social worker.'

Delilah didn't look at her and Shona didn't push it. She knew better than to interfere and didn't have the resources to anyway. The girl went straight to the socket over the worktop, eying Shona's toast as she passed.

'Do you want some toast?'

'Cool, thanks.'

Great. She'd have to go and buy more bread for later now, but the poor thing was stick thin.

'Just butter I'm afraid – I've run out of jam.'

'Fine.'

It wasn't fine at all. Shona was sailing close to the wind already and didn't need Social Services poking their nose in now. A few years ago, maybe, when she could have done with some help with Paulie, but definitely not now. Why did a teenager want to hang out with an old bag like her anyway, didn't she have any friends?

'So what are you up to today? Saturday was always my favourite day of the week.'

Delilah shrugged.

'Nothing much. Can't even watch telly with no electric.'

'What about Chelsea, I thought you and she were big friends?'

'She's a stupid cow.'

'Oh'.

It was more likely that Chelsea's mother – a loud, hard woman, but one who loved her children – had put a stop to the friendship. Kelly, or 'Cleo' as she was now supposedly called, was a disgrace and had headed further downhill over the last few months. Shona had to admit, she wouldn't want any daughter of hers having contact with her. Folks on this estate were tolerant, but there were limits.

She shook her head. It was difficult to maintain a foothold in normality, but you shouldn't stop trying. She couldn't play the Good Samaritan today though. Delilah saw too much of life already and Shona didn't want her meeting the visitors due at

5

lunch time. They were new guys; hard men, large scale dealers she'd been forced to go to when demand increased.

'Tell you what, why don't you have an hour in front of my telly and I'll bring you some toast and a cup of tea through? I need to have a clear up in here and you're better off out of the way. I've got people coming in a bit though, so you'll have to be gone by lunchtime.'

'Alright. Thanks.'

Delilah slid past her and into the living room. It was difficult not to pull a face as she passed, for the girl – or her clothes – smelled terrible. Shona didn't think Delilah would appreciate the offer of a shower or use of the washing machine however. She would give that can of worms some thought, but a more pressing dilemma was tobacco.

It wasn't right to encourage kids to smoke, yet she could see Delilah working through the ashtray on the coffee table – surely it was worse to let her smoke someone else's tar-soaked fag-ends? She went in and put a pouch of tobacco down next to the tea and toast.

'Delilah, you're going to wreck your lungs before you're even old enough to smoke. At least roll yourself a fresh one.'

Delilah grinned up at her and Shona shook her head. If only her Paulie was so easily pleased, but how sad that it took nicotine to inspire a smile. Kelly had no idea how lucky she was, or what she was doing to her daughter.

~ ~ ~

The afternoon dragged. No-one was about and Delilah moved between the park and the house, checking her phone every ten minutes. There was no message from her mum and Jono's curtains were still closed when she walked through the estate. He'd sent her a text asking if she was ok, but she didn't have any credit to reply.

By 6 o'clock her belly was rumbling again and she was heading back to Jono's for another curtain check, when Doogie and his crew came tumbling out of an alley in front of her. Shit. It was dark now and people around here locked their doors when they heard shouting in the street. She turned to run, but it was too late.

'Heeey, Delilah!'

She forced her legs to remain still. This lot were like dogs and worked in a pack, loving the chase. If she tried to leg it, she'd be running all night.

'Looking for a bit of business? I'll give you a fiver for a blow job,' Doogie said.

The lads all laughed, but the three girls with them stared daggers at her.

'Nah, your nob stinks.'

'And you don't? You dirty fucking tramp.'

That was Stacey, Doogie's girlfriend. She was worse than any gang of lads. Delilah said nothing, but started to back away.

'Where are you going? It's Saturday night, time for a party,' Doogie said, grinning now, excited by the prospect of a bit of action.

'Got other places to be.'

'Better places than hanging out with us? I doubt it.'

They were only a few feet away now, spreading out, blocking her escape.

'They're expecting me. They'll come to find me.'

'Who will? You haven't got any friends, Delilah,' Stacey said, as she moved closer, circling to get behind her.

Delilah felt a sharp pain at the back of her knee and dropped to the floor. That was it, she was finished now. A hand grabbed her hair, yanking her head back, but it let go just as quickly.

'Eugh, gross! She's all greasy!'

Panting with fear, Delilah tried to get to her feet.

'Don't get up, you were in the perfect position.' Doogie said, pushing her back down to the ground. 'Stop being such a girl and grab her hair, Stace.'

'You're not coming near me if you let her suck you off. I don't want any STDs.'

'Don't worry, she's going to suck Mark off and we're going to watch. He's too desperate to care what he catches.'

Stacey giggled. Bile rose in Delilah's throat as she watched a big fat lad move forward, a bubble of spit bursting over his lips as his mouth widened into a leer. She couldn't. She'd rather die. The grip on her hair tightened again, pulling her head back, stretching her throat.

'Oi! What the bloody hell's going on?'

It was a man's voice, shouting from down the road. A dog barked and the mood changed.

'It's that psycho biker,' Stacey hissed. 'He'll let the dog go, he's done it before.'

'Split.'

Doogie issued the order and they all obeyed, but not before Stacey had buried her bony knee in Delilah's back and delivered a hard slap to her left cheek that knocked her flat. One of her rings had torn the skin and Delilah could feel blood trickling down her face, but she was more bothered about the huge alsatian that was bounding down the road towards her. She rolled in the gravel and got to her feet, casting a quick glance at the man running behind his dog, before making for the alley on the opposite side. He was shouting, at his dog and at her, but she wasn't going to stop now.

~ ~ ~

The session was in full swing and Shona was in the kitchen, making the fourth round of tea and coffee. Half the delivery was already sold and she was expecting several more people later. There was a tap on the door; probably Jim, who was late this evening. Her heart sank when she opened it.

'Delilah, this isn't a good time.'

'Sorry.'

The girl was staring at her shoes and Shona couldn't see her face through the mop of black hair.

'What are you after?'

What she wasn't in need of would be a more relevant question. Food, money and a responsible parent for starters, but Shona was not in a position to provide for her.

'Can I borrow a tenner?'

8

Borrow? How the hell would she pay it back? The wad of notes in her pocket burned into Shona's leg, but that wasn't spare cash; every penny, and more, was already accounted for.

'What for?' She looked through the window and saw the neighbouring house was in darkness. 'Is your mum back yet?'

'No'

So there was still no food and no electric. Oh, that stupid, stupid woman. Think, think.

'Look, I can't give you any money, but sit there for a second.' She ushered Delilah towards a chair at the kitchen table. God damn it, she didn't need this right now. She re-filled the kettle. 'I'll make you a picnic. Is your heating still on?'

'No.'

Oh, for pity's sake, it was freezing. What should she do? There was no way Delilah could stay. Someone shouted 'we're dying of thirst in here' from the living room. Shona put eleven steaming mugs on a tray and carried them through, noting on her return that, although Delilah didn't seem to have moved, the half-smoked spliff on the kitchen table was gone. Little bugger.

She took a flask from the cupboard and spooned coffee and sugar into it. The boiling kettle gave her an idea and she went upstairs to the airing cupboard, relieved to find a couple of old hot water bottles. Coming back down the stairs, she heard another knock at the kitchen door. Oh please, let it be Jim and not the others who were due. In the kitchen, Delilah had retreated into the corner and Shona decided to risk letting whoever it was in.

'Jim! Thank God it's you.'

'Why, who're you expecting?' Jim asked, dumping two carrier bags on the table.

He did a double-take when he spotted Delilah, the frown on his face bringing his eyebrows down towards his full beard in a look that would be comical, if he wasn't so huge and intimidating.

'No-one special, it's just...' Shona waved a hand towards Delilah. 'Go on through, I'll bring you a tea.'

The kettle snapped off and Shona busied herself filling the flask and hot water bottles. She took a packet of sausage rolls from the fridge, shoved the lot into a shopping bag and almost dropped it when she turned around. Jim and Delilah were staring at each other across the kitchen. The girl's left cheek was cut, a trickle of dried blood crusted beneath it, but she was glaring black at Jim with fierce blue eyes. There was no denying she had guts.

'What happened to your face?'

Delilah shrugged. It was Jim who answered.

'I reckon this one got into a bit of bother earlier. Ran into that shit Doogie and his cronies. Crank saved the day though.'

'Really? Is his leg better?'

'Seems so.'

Delilah said nothing and there was a long pause. Deciding to ignore the impasse, Shona took a tube of antiseptic cream and a couple of candles from a drawer, added them to the bag and then held it out. Delilah stood up and took if from her.

'What's this, a midnight feast?' Jim asked.

'Something like that,' Shona said. 'Get that face cleaned up before you do anything else though, Dee.'

Delilah nodded, but recoiled when Jim held out an arm to block her exit.

'Hang on a minute.' He dug around in one of his carrier bags and pulled out a shop-bought cake. 'Add this to your stash.'

Delilah's 'thanks' was barely above a whisper, as she slipped around Jim to make her exit. With one foot out of the door, she paused and turned around.

'Is Crank your dog?'

'Yeah, and you owe him a fuss next time you see him.'

'Alright.'

And Delilah was gone. Shona hoped she'd done enough, but what more *could* she do? She would check on her in the morning.

'She's an interesting one,' Jim said.

'Hmmn, more interesting than a child should be. We'll talk another time though, I need to get back in there.'

Jim followed her through to the living room and Shona tried to push all thought of Delilah from her mind.

~ ~ ~

10

Once the door was locked and chained behind her, Delilah lit one of the candles and took the bag up to her bedroom. She fetched her mum's duvet, threw it on top of her own and then shoved the hot water bottles underneath them. They were weird, floppy things, but would be awesome to snuggle up to. She laid out the flask and food by her bed and extracted the rather squashed spliff from her pocket. All she needed now was an ashtray.

Going back downstairs to the living room, Delilah decided she liked candles - the light made things seem magical. She tipped one ashtray into another and was about to return to her feast when she saw the envelope on the settee. She stared at it for a second and then tucked it under her arm.

Having eaten the sausage rolls, Delilah poured a cup of coffee and picked up the cake in its plastic case, turning it around in her hands. That Jim bloke seemed alright. She put the cake down and lit the spliff instead, rearranging cake and candle until the chocolate icing on the top glowed. The envelope drew her attention again and Delilah opened it, with some reluctance.

It was a card, with a picture of the sky and a field and some rocks on the front. Inside it read:

Dear Delilah. Happy Birthday! Hope you have a lovely day. Call me whenever you want to. Becky

Huh. A fiver would have been a lot more useful than the business card that fell out. Still, she had a birthday cake - her first ever - and now she was 14, it would only be two more years until she and Jono could be together. She tossed the card aside and wormed her way into the warm cocoon of duvets without bothering to get undressed. The cold pinched at her face, but Delilah lay watching her cake sparkle in the candlelight until her eyes closed of their own accord.

2

Shona had knocked twice and was about to try once more when she realised it was a waste of effort. What a fool, although she'd only had a few hours' sleep and was still stoned from last night.

'Delilah? It's me, Shona,' she shouted up at the nearest window.

A face appeared and then disappeared. Shona heard running feet on the stairs inside, followed by the rattle and snick of metal on metal. At least the house was pretty secure. When Delilah finally opened the door, Shona burst out laughing.

'Well I came to offer you breakfast, but it looks like you've already had it.'

Delilah's grin made her look like a medieval peasant – her teeth were as coated in chocolate as her face.

'Awesome cake,' she said.

'Do you want some toast to balance out the sugar?'

'Thanks. I'll fetch my phone.'

'Come round when you're ready.'

It was less than a minute before Delilah joined her in the kitchen. Shona noticed that she had wiped, not washed, her face. There was still a light smear of chocolate down both pale cheeks.

'If there's no hot water at yours, you're welcome to a shower here you know,' she said. 'Tea or coffee then?'

'Nah, I'm alright. I'll have a tea, two sugars.'

Delilah sniffed and wiped her sleeve across her nose, leaving a new, horizontal smear of chocolate across her face. Shona rinsed a dishcloth in warm water.

'Catch!' she said, lobbing it at Delilah's head. 'Your face is still plastered in cake.'

The girl pulled a face as she caught the dripping cloth, but was vigorous, if not very efficient, in her use of it.

'Where's Paulie?' she asked. 'I haven't seen him in weeks.'

The smile dropped from Shona's face. She didn't want to examine the feeling in her stomach. It could be fear, revulsion, or a whole host of other negative emotions, none of which a mother should feel for her son.

'He's away. He got some cash work with a roofing company and they've got some big contract up in Newcastle.'

The words tasted sour on her tongue and even Delilah looked sceptical.

'You got those guys off his back though?'

'Yes, yes I did.'

Off his back and onto mine, with interest.

'But I saw them here last week.'

'Yes. Paulie owed them a lot of money and I couldn't pay it all. They'll be hanging around for a while yet, but don't worry - they're only coming to collect, like the loan man.'

Delilah went quiet at the mention of the loan man and Shona's thoughts jostled to take precedence. Paulie had been working, but was only supposed to be in Newcastle for ten days. He'd gone three weeks ago and she'd heard nothing from him. There was a small chance that the contract had been extended, or he might have had an accident and be injured in hospital, but he was probably smashed out of his mind in some drug den. She could only hope he wasn't in too much trouble.

'Shall I put some toast on?' Delilah said.

'What?' Shona fought to drag her mind back to the present. 'Oh, yes, you do that. Have you heard from your mum yet?'

'Yeah, she's coming back tonight. Her new boyfriend wanted her to stay for the whole weekend.'

Charming. Shona hoped it had at least been a profitable few days. She put mugs of tea on the table and passed Delilah a plate for the toast, which she was buttering on the worktop.

'So what are you up to today?'

14

'I'm going to see Jono. He's my best friend.'

'How come I've never met him?'

'He doesn't come on to the estate and he couldn't come to our house anyway.'

That didn't sound good. Unless he was just a snob...but then, why would he be hanging around with a grubby kid whose life was going down the pan?

'How old is he?' she asked, keeping her tone casual.

Delilah didn't answer. Her phone had buzzed and she was squinting at the screen, running a finger along the lines of text. After a full minute she looked up, eyes shining.

'I've gotta go. Jono's cooking breakfast, with bacon and everything. Oh, and he's 28. Thanks for the tea.'

'But...'

Delilah was gone, without a backward glance. Whoever this Jono was, he seemed to make Delilah happy and it was good to know someone was giving her decent food. But was he really that nice? There were so many horror stories these days. She'd ask a few more questions when there was an opportunity.

Thankful she didn't have to eat any of the finger-marked toast, swimming in a sea of butter, Shona dropped it into the bin and washed up the few pots. She hoped there wouldn't be too many callers today. The increased business was horrendous to deal with, but the interest on her loan was spiralling out of control and there was no other way of paying off Paulie's debts.

She finished clearing up the living room and was weighing out a few bags when someone started hammering on the locked door. Shona's heart lurched in her chest. Police? She swept everything into a drawer and lit some incense, while the hammering continued. Should she let them in, or hide in the bathroom?

'Mum. MUM! Open the fucking door.'

Speak of the devil. She opened the door.

'Hello, stranger,' she said, and tried to smile.

Paulie pushed past her into the kitchen.

'About fucking time. Got any weed?'

15

Hi Mum. Great to see you. Sorry I haven't been in touch. Shona took one of the bags from the drawer and threw it on the table.

'Bit early, isn't it?'

'Look who's talking.' He sneered at her and started putting a joint together on the table. 'I need some money. Two Geordie gorillas are going to break my spine if I don't give them £700 by the end of the day.'

'How are they going to break your spine from over a hundred miles away?'

'They're not, they're here.'

'What?!'

Shona yanked the blind aside and stared out onto the street. It looked quiet.

'Not *here*. I left them in a cafe, but you've got to sort me some money out.'

'Paulie, I don't have any money. I'm still trying to pay off your last drugs bill.'

'Bullshit. I bet you had a session last night. You've got at least a few hundred stashed in here somewhere, I know you have.'

'But the new dealers lay it on. That money's theirs, to pay for the weed I've already sold, and the loan man's coming tomorrow too. I'm at my limit Paulie – it's my spine that'll be broken if I give you that.'

He lit the joint and stood up, his eyes wild, his hands shaking. Shona felt the first stirrings of fear. What if he'd moved on from cocaine? What if he was taking crack, or smack, or even meth? He used to get violent enough on speed. But he wouldn't hurt her, would he? Not his own mother.

'So you're not going to help me? You're going to let those bastards put me in hospital?'

'I can't, Paulie. It's not just the dealers and the loan man; I borrowed off everyone to raise that last two grand. I've nowhere left to turn.'

Slap. The shock was so deep that the pain didn't register for several seconds. Then her cheek began to burn and sting.

'You fucking bitch! Call yourself a mother?'

16

Slap.

'It's your fault I'm on fucking drugs in the first place!'

He was crazy, insane with anger, his eyes terrifying and inhuman. The hand rose for a third strike and Shona groped behind her for a knife, a mug, anything with which to defend herself. The action incensed him further.

'Now what, you're going to fucking stab me?!'

This time it was a punch, a hard hook to her jaw. Shona felt herself falling, spinning in slow motion. It was almost surreal. There was a sharp impact against the back of her head before she hit the floor. The darkness was warm and soft. There were noises above her; crashes, bangs, someone shouting, but it was all a long way away. Easier to sleep.

~ ~ ~

Delilah heard the loud wolf whistle and looked up to see which of the local tarts was passing. There was no-one in the street before her. She stopped and looked back over her shoulder. A balding man with swept-over hair and a dodgy anorak was leaving the pizza place, but he wouldn't interest anyone.

'Hey! Delilah! Come here before I sing to you,' a voice called.

She back-tracked a few paces and stuck her head into the chip shop.

'Don't you fucking dare, Nic,' she said, glaring at the handsome Greek behind the counter.

He laughed, lifted one arm and put the other on his stomach.

'Why, why, why...'

'Nic!' Delilah yelled and rushed inside.

'Ok, ok I'm sorry.' Nic backed away and grinned at her. 'How are you anyway? You're looking different, very beautiful this evening.'

Delilah hung her head, not sure what to say and unable to fight off a shy smile.

'I was alright til you started singing at me,' she said, trying hard to frown.

'Everyone should sing. It's good for your insides. You should try it.'

'Huh.'

She and Chelsea used to sing along to CDs in Chelsea's bedroom. Now there was no CD player and she felt stupid singing on her own anyway.

'I've cooked an extra fish by mistake. Do you want it?'

'Got no money.'

'It's free, on the house, a beautiful fish for a beautiful young lady.'

This time Delilah blushed and could think of nothing to say. She scowled to cover her embarrassment, but Nic laughed again and wrapped the fish in paper.

'Enjoy,' he said, passing her the warm parcel and a can of lemonade.

'Thanks.'

Delilah left before the stupid smile could take hold again. She wasn't beautiful; all she'd done was wash her hair, although it did feel different. It moved when she walked instead of sticking to her head and didn't itch anymore.

She sat on the war memorial to eat the fish. You could see anyone coming, so there'd be time to get away if Doogie turned up. The fish got a bit chewy towards the tail and Delilah left the last bit in the paper. It was her third meal of the day and she wasn't that hungry, just in dire need of a fag. That was the only thing with Jono – he didn't smoke.

He did cook her an amazing breakfast though and apart from the shower thing, it had been a good day. She'd wanted to die when he took her breakfast plate away and said 'Dee, if you're staying, you need a shower.' They argued then, but Jono always won arguments and it was alright in the end. His bathroom was huge and clean, with shiny tiles and a walk-in shower. There was as much hot water as you wanted and Delilah had stayed in there for almost an hour.

She'd freaked when he fished her clothes off the bathroom floor with the window hook, but he'd thrown some trackies and a jumper in for her. When he returned her clothes later, they were clean and warm and smelled nice. He didn't make a big thing of it afterwards, just asked which computer game he was going to beat her at. The monitor was massive; the biggest screen Delilah had ever seen, apart from once when she went to the cinema for Chelsea's birthday. Jono had all the best gaming gear and three different computers. He was loaded.

Something moved in her peripheral vision and Delilah snapped out of her daydream. It was a dog, a big, shaggy dog, which spotted her at the same time and barked. Before she had time to get to her feet, there was a low whistle and the dog turned and ran back down the street to her left, towards a large moving shadow that morphed into a large bearded man, when he passed under a street light.

'Jim!'

She hadn't meant to say it out loud. She didn't even know him, but had been thinking about Jim a lot since yesterday. He'd saved her from Doogie *and* given her a cake.

'Is that young Delilah? What're you doing out here in the dark?'

'Nothing.' Jim was close now and although Crank stayed at his side, Delilah could see him sniffing towards the remains of her dinner. 'Does Crank eat fish?'

'Crank eats most things, given the chance. Hold it out on the palm of your hand. He's a gentle old thing really, but don't tell anyone.'

Having looked up at Jim for approval, Crank took the lump of batter with great care and Delilah watched him eat, unaware that she was smiling. He licked his lips and sat on his haunches, looking back at her and thumping his tail on the ground twice.

'Give him a fuss if you want. I think he likes you.'

Delilah reached out towards the thick fur of his shoulder and Crank took a step closer, licking her other hand, which had presented him with the fish. She giggled and her tentative strokes progressed to firmer scratches, making Crank squirm with pleasure.

'He'll stand that all night, but it's too bloody cold for hanging around. Isn't it time you were home anyway? Me and Crank can walk you back and call in on Shona.'

Delilah shrugged. Her mum hadn't texted again since this morning, but she might be back, although she'd said she wasn't leaving til the bloke paid up. It made sense. There was no money on Thursday or Friday and the next benefit day wasn't until Wednesday. There'd be no gas or electric unless the man paid.

'Alright.'

She was uncomfortable at first, but Jim didn't try to make conversation and soon slowed his pace to accommodate her shorter legs. They walked with Crank between them, and every so often the dog would look up and smile at her with his eyes. Delilah had always wanted a dog, and one like Crank would be perfect. No-one would dare give her any shit. He'd be better than a hot water bottle at night and she could tell him all her secrets.

As they turned onto her street, Delilah could see her house was in darkness, but so was Shona's, which was creepy. Shona hardly went anywhere, except to the shop. It made it awkward. She didn't know what to say to Jim.

'Is your mum not in?' he said, looking from one dark shell to the other.

'Nah, but it's alright, she'll be back later.'

'Hmmn.'

He stood there, pulling a hand through his beard. She wasn't going to ask him in. That would be...weird. Delilah bent down to pat Crank, uncomfortable again.

'Bye Crank.' She glanced up at Jim, but his back was to the streetlight and his face was masked by shadow. 'Er, see ya,' she said and walked up the path to the front door.

She got her key out and threw a last look over her shoulder. Jim hadn't gone very far and as she watched, he stopped walking and said something to Crank. She hoped he wasn't some freak just pretending to be nice. Not all the people who went to Shona's were sound. Thinking of Shona made her look across at the neighbouring house and a cold shiver washed over her. From this angle, Delilah could see the back door was wide open.

~ ~ ~

20

Jim was not happy. It wasn't right, leaving a young girl like that alone in a cold dark house. It was early evening and there was no guarantee the mother would show up. Shona had explained a few things about her former friend the previous evening. A good-time girl, ruined by alcoholism and sunk to the point of blatant prostitution. He wasn't a fan of Social Services in general, but maybe this was where they had a role to play. He stopped and looked down at Crank.

'What are we going to do eh, boy? Delilah can't come home with us – people make assumptions when you've been inside. Don't think I'd be considered an appropriate adult.'

And where was Shona? Since that little prick Paulie had brought a whole load of shit down on her head, she didn't go anywhere. He took a few more slow steps.

'Jim. JIM!'

Delilah's cry was full of fear. Jim turned and ran back towards the dark houses, heading for Delilah's gate and then changing direction as her pale face became visible, leaning over the fence by Shona's back door. He charged up the path and Delilah jumped over to meet him, hanging back to let him go in first. He hit the light switch and saw the kitchen was in chaos. All the drawers had been pulled out and all the cupboards emptied, their contents strewn across the worktops and floor.

There was a tug on his sleeve and Jim turned towards Delilah, who had gone to his left. The dresser by the kitchen table had suffered a similar fate, but Delilah was pointing towards the floor. Shona lay, half under the table, her hair matted with blood and the carpet stained dark around her head. The one eye he could see was black and swollen and her waxy cheeks were tinged with blue.

'Call an ambulance Delilah. Use Shona's landline and dial 999, *now*.'

He dropped to his knees and put a hand over Shona's nose and mouth, trying to find a pulse in her neck with the other. Her skin was cold, but there was a faint warmth against his palm. Looking up, he saw Delilah clutching the phone, her eyes wide with terror.

'She's alive. You're doing great. I'm going to fetch a quilt.' He stood up, reached out to shut the door and saw a patient Crank still sitting outside. 'In here lad. Sit. Stay.'

He took the stairs two at a time and threw open the first door on the landing, finding Shona's bedroom. He bundled the duvet up and raced back down to the kitchen, listening to Delilah's garbled explanation of the situation as he pulled off his leather jacket and jumper. Poor bloody kid. God knows what they'd be thinking at the other end.

Jim lay on the floor beside Shona and spooned against her as best he could, then pulled the duvet over them both. He daren't try and move her - the head injury looked serious – but he could keep her warm. Delilah had gone quiet on the other side of the kitchen.

'You alright over there? Have they asked you to stay on the line?'

'Yeah.'

Her voice was barely above a whisper.

'They'll only be a few minutes and Shona's still breathing. Why don't you come and sit over here and keep Crank calm, he's getting a bit nervous.'

The dog whined on cue and tried to lick Shona's forehead. Jim pushed him away with a pat and watched Delilah move towards the chair on the other side of Shona. There was a smear of blood on the corner of the seat. So maybe Shona had been pushed and not hit, but then the place had obviously been turned over. A nasty thought struck him.

'Do you know Paulie?' he asked and Delilah nodded. 'Have you seen him recently?'

She shook her head and when he frowned said,

'I asked this morning. Shona said he was in Newcastle.'

'Right.'

There was a tense silence and Jim felt oddly vulnerable, lying on the floor with Delilah perched on the chair, staring down at him. Her face was almost as white as Shona's. Although her eyes were dry, they were full of fear and a tremor was wrinkling her small chin.

'It'll be ok,' he said, but even as his lips closed, realisation hit his stomach as a physical blow.

This wasn't going to be ok at all. Delilah stared down at him and said nothing. Jim lay still, his mind racing, but could think of no way of helping her out. The 999 call-handler would have alerted the police too and if her useless mother didn't turn up in the next ten minutes, Delilah was done for. They could make Shona's recuperation a little easier however. He'd have to swap places with Crank for a minute and pray that the kid was as cool as she seemed.

The police got there before the ambulance. One of the two men went straight outside to make a call and when he returned, the inquiries of him became heavy and personal, but they backed off when the paramedics arrived. Delilah was not easing their suspicions by crouching in a corner, her arms wrapped around Crank, refusing to look at them, never mind answer their questions. They were wary at present, but she wouldn't stand a chance when a female officer turned up.

Jim got to his feet and threw the duvet in the corner, his heart heavy. They'd have done a background check by now and he'd be Suspect Number One. A 6'6" bearded biker, with tattoos and a serious criminal record, including several assaults and a long stretch for GBH. Delilah's name would no doubt bring up a link to Social Services and the woman Shona said was snooping around yesterday would now have the excuse to take Delilah into care. Perhaps it was more of a reason than an excuse, as that selfish slut of a mother still hadn't appeared.

The paramedics carried Shona away on a stretcher and were replaced by two more cops; an older bloke, who introduced himself as Detective Inspector McGrath, and a female Detective Constable. Jim wondered whether CID were there because of him, Delilah's involvement, or the severity of the assault.

'Shall we go through to the living room,' McGrath said, with no lift of question in his voice.

Jim went first and leaned against the fireplace. Delilah followed and stood close by his side, holding on to his sleeve with one hand

23

and the fireplace with the other. Crank sat between their feet. The three cops who followed them in could hardly use the low settee and so stood awkwardly in the narrow gap between it and the coffee table. McGrath looked at Delilah and raised an eyebrow, but decided to address Jim.

'So, you two found the injured woman about twenty minutes ago, having checked on her because the door was open and the lights were out.'

'Yes.'

'And the place is exactly as you found it – you haven't moved or touched anything.'

'Well, obviously Delilah used the phone and I fetched a duvet and cleared some space on the floor. We've been around the kitchen a bit.'

The fingers on his arm squeezed a little tighter. *Play it cool girl, or this goddamned mess will get a whole lot messier.*

'You're a friend of the injured woman, who lives alone, and visit regularly on a....social basis.'

'Yes.'

'And what is your relationship with Delilah?'

Delilah's fingers withdrew and she crossed her arms, glaring at the questioner. Cute, but not helpful. McGrath raised both of his eyebrows this time. He wouldn't believe they'd only met the previous day and Jim could not begin to describe the odd, if entirely platonic, bond that had sprung up between them.

'We just know each other. She lives next door and visits Shona, so I see her sometimes.'

'Do you know her mum, too?'

Fuck, shit, damn and bollocks.

'She's not around all that much.'

He could see in his peripheral vision that Delilah had turned her face to look at him, but he didn't return her gaze, not wanting to see the hurt or accusation in her eyes.

'But you do know her?'

'Not to speak to, but what's this got to do with Shona?'

The female DC spoke then.

'It's us who get to ask the questions, you know that.'

Her tone was light, her expression wasn't. The young response cop, who was first on the scene, looked much more confident now and smirked. Jim stared back at him for a moment, but forced himself to look away. Whatever else, he had to keep his temper. McGrath tried another tack.

'It doesn't look like the victim, Shona, had much worth stealing, or that the attacker went beyond the kitchen. Do you think you disturbed them? Did you see anyone leaving the scene?'

'No, I think they were long gone,' Jim said, wishing he was glad to get back to the real issue, but seeing a whole host of further complications rise before him. 'The house was cold and Shona's been lying there for hours – the blood on her head and the carpet is dry.'

'So, as a frequent visitor, can you think of anything the attacker might have been looking for? Drugs, maybe? Money?'

'I've no idea. Shona struggles for money, but she might have some family jewels somewhere, or a valuable heirloom or something. I don't know about those kind of things.'

'Does Shona have any children?'

'A son, Paulie.'

Who has a series of drugs convictions and is a little shit. Christ Almighty, how should he play this? Rescue – depending on the point of view – came in the form of a woman who, judging by Delilah's reaction of dropping to the floor and wrapping her arms around Crank again, was probably the social worker. She came striding forward when she spotted Delilah, but stopped when Crank began a low growl in his throat.

'Sorry,' Jim said. 'There's a few too many folk in here for him.'

The woman didn't appear nervous and looked around, assessing the situation. To his surprise, she nodded.

'I sympathise with him entirely.' She moved closer to the DI and held out a hand, which McGrath took. 'I'm Becky Stocks, Delilah's social worker. I hope you haven't been trying to question her without an appropriate adult present?'

McGrath started to shake his head, but the young cop chipped in.

'Don't worry, Delilah's not been talking to anybody.'

The woman gave him a sharp look, but seemed more concerned by the immediate welfare of her charge.

'Hi Delilah. I know I'm the last person you want to see right now and you've had a horrible night, but I'm afraid it's about to get worse.'

That was a brave statement and Jim looked down at Delilah to see how she would respond. Her face was screwed up in a scowl of such intensity it was almost comical, but she lifted her eyes to look at Becky.

'Your mum isn't in. I suspect she hasn't been home since I called in yesterday morning. Am I right?'

Delilah did not reply, but dropped her eyes again and squeezed Crank even tighter. It said enough.

'As soon as she gets in touch we can review the situation, but until then, I need you to be somewhere safe and warm, with plenty of food.'

As Delilah's gaze transferred from the floor to Jim's leg, his guts twisted. Becky must have seen the shift too.

'I'm going to take you to a place like a care home, but it's not permanent, I promise. You're not actually allowed to stay there more than three months.'

'NO!'

Delilah grabbed the poker from the hearth and let go of Crank, backing into the corner of the room. McGrath raised his hands in a peaceable gesture, but the young cop dropped his to the baton on his belt.

'Put the poker down girl. You're not daft enough to take on odds like this, surely,' Jim said.

He spoke calmly, but felt more fear than he'd ever experienced. The poker wavered but did not drop and the police began murmuring among themselves. Becky opened her mouth to speak, but Jim raised a hand.

'Can I just ask you, will it be ok to give you my number and maybe have yours? I can keep Delilah up to date on how Shona's doing then.' He turned to Delilah. 'You can come and see her yourself, as soon as she's out of hospital – you won't be locked up.'

'Of course that's ok and this man is right, Delilah; it's a home, not a prison.'

The poker drooped until its point was just above the coffee table and Jim saw the stance of the two detectives ease, but the uniformed idiot was eager for action, impatient, unsympathetic. He stepped forward and reached for the poker, which Delilah swung upwards. It grazed the bottom of his chin and he fumbled for a second, before squirting CS gas in her face.

The other two leaped forward, Jim thought to restrain their colleague, but then Delilah turned into a wild animal and it took all three of them to pin her down. She disappeared behind writhing bodies and Jim's vision blurred red, heat flooding into his chest. Crank's bark of distress pierced his rage, only just in time. Fighting to regain control of his raised arms, Jim lowered them slowly, moving to pull Crank out of the way, instead of dragging the nearest copper off the struggling young girl.

The noise Delilah made as they man-handled her out of the door, her head forced down, her arms locked behind her back, would haunt him forever. It wasn't a scream, it was a primal sound; a muted roar of pain, rage and fear.

3

Becky let herself in quietly. The lights were on, but there was no sound of the tv or radio. Simon must have gone to bed. She sighed – he'd be grumpy in the morning, perhaps even angry still. But she wasn't obsessive, she just cared; he'd care if he worked with her for a day or two and interacted with real people instead of playing with figures on a computer. No, that wasn't fair. They achieved a good balance between them and she needed reminding that there was more to life than her caseload.

She went into the kitchen and flicked the kettle on, then flicked it off again and opened the fridge. This kind of night warranted wine, Sunday or not. She felt drained, exhausted even, but the evening's events kept tumbling through her mind in random order, throwing up questions as they passed. Where was Cleo? How long had she been gone? Who had beaten up the neighbour? Had Delilah seen anything? Would she cope in the Assessment Centre? Would the police press charges? Becky thought not. The older policeman, McGrath, had been almost apologetic.

The image that returned with the most frequency was that of the gigantic biker bloke. In spite of the leather jacket and beard, she had seen the tattoos that crawled up his neck and the police intimated there was information she needed to know about him. But that look, the way he had watched when the police piled in and pinned Delilah down. She had feared he would go to her rescue, but the arms that lifted froze stiff, his hands curling into impotent fists. Becky shivered – that would have been a bloodbath – but she had shouted her works' mobile number to him on the way out.

By the time she was in the shower, her thoughts were focussed on Delilah. The poor child had been hysterical and only a warning that they would resort to injecting her with a sedative had stilled her struggles. Becky hoped she would make it to the unit and not be stuck in a cell overnight. Thank God she'd already done all the prep work. The first job tomorrow – at around 10 o'clock - would be leaving a letter for Cleo, informing her of the situation. She deserved a late start after losing this evening.

The work mobile rang at 7:15am. Becky grabbed it on the second ring, but not before Simon threw back the covers, snatched his dressing gown from the chair, and stalked off to the bathroom. She answered and listened to the apologetic explanation of the Relief Manager of the Assessment Centre. Delilah had absconded sometime in the night. They had no idea where she was, but had reported her to the police as a missing person.

Washed and dressed, Becky went downstairs and found Simon eating cereal and watching breakfast television.

'Sorry about the early start,' she said, walking past him to the kettle.

'It's only fifteen minutes early, don't worry about it.'

But he didn't look at her or say good morning. She didn't want to explain that her efforts of last night had all gone down the pan.

'I'll be home in good time tonight. We could go to Ikea and have a look for office furniture.'

'Why say it? Let's just see, eh? If we don't bother making plans, then I can't be disappointed.'

Becky made herself a coffee in silence, gritting her teeth. It drove her mad, his way of saying all the right things, but in a way that made it clear he believed her to be wrong or unreasonable. But then, what did she want - shouting and tears over breakfast?

She took her coffee and a banana into the living room and opened up her work laptop, knocking together a brief report and timeline of last night's events and emailing it to her manager. The letter to Cleo would have to wait until she got in to work – she could hardly say 'your daughter is in the care of the local authority' when she didn't know where Delilah was. The police might have

30

been to the house to check if she was there though and what if Cleo was home? She'd better get moving.

'See you later. Have a good day.'

Becky jumped as Simon kissed her cheek and he withdrew again.

'Sorry, I didn't hear you come in,' she said.

'No, I can see you're busy. I'm off anyway.'

'But...'

'Gotta dash,' he called from the hall and then the front door slammed.

She looked at the clock on the computer: 08:12. He never left before half past. This overspill wouldn't last long though. Things wouldn't be so crazy when she'd got Delilah settled – she was on top of the rest of her case-load. Soon, she'd be able to give time to Simon, and fitting out their little home office, and planning Christmas, and having his parents to stay for a weekend. Once Delilah was sorted.

Ten minutes later she was on her way to work, the long way round, via the awful estate where Delilah lived. Driving up the quiet street she had visited less than twelve hours ago, Becky kicked herself for following the impulsive notion. Delilah was good at hiding and even if she did find her, it wasn't wise to confront the girl alone after the awful scene last night. It was a waste of time. But she felt a thrill in her chest as she rounded a slight bend and saw the kitchen light in Delilah's house was on.

She pulled over, unsure what to do. A slight figure appeared at the window. Was it Delilah? Three seconds later, the front door burst open and Cleo staggered down the path towards her, dressed for a Saturday night on the town, but with tangled hair, stained clothes and a face ravaged and ghastly in its fury.

'You fucking, intref...interfr...stuck up fucking bitch! Where's Delilah? Where's my fucking daughter?'

Becky stared at the spectre, unable to think coherently, then Cleo reached the car and started smashing her fist against the glass, three inches from her head.

~ ~ ~

31

Jim thought the pounding was in his head, but when Crank added his voice to the thuds, he realised it was the door. He sat up and looked at the clock: 8:24. He'd still been drinking whisky at 6am and must stink of it. No way that was the postman either. He peered through the gap in the curtains and saw a squad car outside. Christ Almighty, what was this? He had an appointment at the station later, but was in no state for questioning now.

'Alright!' he shouted. 'I'm coming.'

He flicked the bolt off the door and pulled it open. The two unfamiliar cops outside - one man, one woman – both took a step backwards.

'Yes?' Jim said.

'We're looking for a missing child,' the woman said, regaining her composure faster than her partner, who looked like a child himself and was staring at Jim with wide eyes. 'We believe she's known to you and need to know if you've seen her.'

Jim sighed and shook his head. Delilah. How could one scrawny kid bring so much shit down on his head?

'Lost her already then? She hasn't been here – I haven't seen her since your lot dragged her off last night.'

'Do you mind if we come in and just double-check? We can cross you off the list then.'

He did mind. There was a bag of weed on the settee, a nailed baseball bat behind the door and a bike engine of dubious origin on his kitchen table. He was about to say that it was inconvenient, that they could come back with a warrant later, but then they would assume he had plenty to hide and their interest would be relentless. The pause was stretching out too long. The male cop spoke for the first time.

'We can come back with a warrant later.'

'Or you can let us have a quick look now,' the woman said, giving him a nudge that would have amused Jim at another time. 'We're only interested in finding Delilah, nothing else.'

Yeah right. But he had no choice. Pulling the door open at least hid the bat from immediate view and Jim decided to take the policewoman at her word. He tipped a cushion over to cover the bag of weed and installed Crank on the settee before inviting them in.

'It's a two-up, two-down, with a shed out back. The dog won't hurt you. Knock yourselves out,' he said.

After a brief, muttered discussion, the woman went up the stairs alone, while the man hovered, casting him a nervous smile. Jim reached for a padded jacket that he'd thrown over the end of the stairs and hung it over the bat behind him. It was the best he could do. The woman reappeared on the landing.

'All clear up there,' she said and smiled at him. It was a nice smile, a disarming smile. 'Is the shed locked?'

'Yeah. The key's on the rack under the kitchen cupboard. Help yourself.'

'Thanks.'

She went through to the kitchen and the policeman gave Jim another nervous smile. When his radio crackled he leapt on the diversion and going to the furthest corner of the room, turned away for privacy.

'Charlie Hotel India 5 Golf. Go ahead.'

He was concentrating on the response, so Jim took the opportunity to lob the bat up the stairs and onto the landing.

'Right. On our way.' The guy moved to the kitchen doorway. 'Kath! There's an assault kicking off on Byron Street. We need to go, right now.'

They were heading out of the door within seconds. The woman, Kath, paused when level with him.

'Thanks,' she said and gave him the shed keys. 'You're all clear. We had to check, it was nothing personal.'

She gave him that smile again and was gone. Perhaps they weren't all so bad. But Byron Street was where Shona and Delilah lived and Jim doubted it was coincidence. He pulled on his boots and jacket.

'Walk!'

Crank jumped off the settee and followed him outside. There were two footpaths that cut through to Byron St. Jim peered out of the second with caution, but the police were too busy wrestling with a screeching, foul-mouthed hag to notice him. Two squad cars were slewed across the road either side of a small Renault, which was parked outside Delilah's house. Was *that* Delilah's mother?

A woman got out of the Renault, inspiring a fresh torrent of abuse from the hag and he recognised her as the social worker from last night. She must put some hours in. Shona's windows were all dark, so Jim reversed his steps and took Crank across the fields and out of the way. He had to plan the statement he was going to give. He hoped Delilah hadn't cracked and told the police about their efforts in Shona's kitchen. The last thing Shona needed, if she wasn't seriously injured, was a charge for dealing.

~ ~ ~

Delilah squatted in the stinking darkness, knees under her chin, face buried in her jumper to stop herself gagging with every in-breath. How long had she been in here, two hours? Three? She couldn't take it much longer and was both hungry and dying for a drink to wash away the bitter taste of bile in her throat. Her arm stung where she'd caught it on the broken glass and she raised it to her face again. Her jumper was sticky, but no longer wet. At least she wasn't going to bleed to death.

The longer she waited, the less sure of her plan she became. This was what she'd always promised not to do and he might fall out with her forever. But, she was desperate. And scared. She couldn't go back to that place, not without killing the bitches who'd broken her phone. A text came from her mum last night, but she hadn't even finished reading it when they snatched it from her, throwing it to each other, laughing because it was big and heavy, stamping on it when she spat at them.

There was a noise, not too far away. Delilah held her breath and strained her ears. Was it the back door? Yes. He would be circling the yard, warming up for his morning practice. She straightened her legs and pushed upwards, hearing a cry of alarm and then seeing his horrified face, mouth open in shock.

'Holy shit! What the... You're covered in blood! Oh shit,' Jono said.

34

Delilah pulled herself out of the wheelie bin, taking great gulps of fresh air.

'Sorry Jono, I'm really sorry.'

He shook his head, bewildered.

'Why? What have you done? Is that your blood? Oh God, Delilah.'

'Shhh!'

She circled him and then shot to the back door.

'What the hell are you playing at?'

'I need to come in for a bit.'

'Clearly, but why were you hiding? And we agreed, not in school-time.'

'I know. Please just shut up and come inside.'

Jono didn't look happy, but followed her back into the kitchen. He glared at her for a minute, but his eyes began to stray across her face, down her body and Delilah watched the lines in his forehead soften and his cheeks go pale.

'Where are you bleeding?

She pulled her left arm from the sleeve of her jumper with care and then yanked the whole thing over her head. The skin was caked in blood and there was a deep and jagged cut below her shoulder.

'It doesn't hurt that much.'

'But your legs....' Jono moved towards her and sniffed. 'Right, so that's bolognaise sauce, not blood. I can't think of anywhere more stupid to hide with an open wound than a filthy bin. Are you mad? It's probably infected already.'

Delilah struggled not to rise at being called stupid, but at least he hadn't kicked her out yet.

'Anywhere else? What about your face?'

She touched her cheek and found it crusty.

'It's from my arm. It was dark, so I was checking if it was still bleeding. I didn't want to die in your bin.'

Jono's mouth twitched.

'No, that would have thrown up some awkward questions.' He shook his head and sighed. 'Go and have a shower and scrub that arm with as much soap as you can bear, but chuck your clothes outside the door first – you absolutely stink.'

When she glanced in the bathroom mirror, Delilah was shocked herself. No wonder Jono had yelled when she came out of the bin. One side of her face was dark with blood and looked gross. There were two strands of spaghetti in her hair and a slice of cooked onion stuck to her chin. She stripped her clothes off and threw them out into the hall.

The hot water stung and when she got soap in the cut it made her cry out with pain, but Jono just shouted that she must be doing it right, so she rubbed harder. There was a tracksuit on the floor when she got out. She had to roll the arms and legs up into fat sausages, but it was warm and snugly. The smell of toast from the kitchen made her belly growl.

She dumped the towel on the floor and went through, hoping Jono wouldn't start moaning straight away. He wanted to, she could tell, but he just said 'You look better' and then watched her eat the toast in silence.

Delilah toyed with the last piece for so long, that Jono took her plate away in the end.

'Come on then. Why are you here and what happened to your arm?'

Delilah scowled at the table, but she had to tell him.

'Shona got beaten up, so we had to call an ambulance. Then the fucking pigs tried to put me in a home, so I smashed a window and ran off.'

He didn't reply and was silent for so long that she looked up. Jono was staring at the table too, his head in his hands.

'There were two total bitches in there and I didn't even see the others. They laughed at me and broke my phone. I think Mum's back, but I can't read the text and the pigs'll be looking for me at my house.'

He still said nothing, didn't move, didn't look up.

'Say something then. You're not going to grass on me, are you?'

Now Jono groaned. He was being weird. It was freaking her out.

'Jono!'

'Look, Dee, that's awful. More than awful, it's absolutely shit and I'm really sorry you're having such a bad time.'

'But I can't stay here.'

'You know that, I've explained it over and over. They won't let you.'

'They don't know. Nobody knows I'm here.'

'They will. The police are clever like that.'

Her eyes and throat hurt and Delilah took a vicious swipe at the stupid tears that started running down her face. She pushed her chair back from the table.

'Fine. I'll go. Give me my clothes back.'

'I can't, they're in the washer. Don't get all mardy, just give me a minute to think, will you?' Delilah folded her arms and sat back down. 'Did you go to bed at all last night?'

She shook her head.

'Well why don't you have a kip and I'll come up with a plan.'

'Promise you won't phone the pigs?'

'Promise. Not without telling you, anyway.'

She narrowed her eyes, but Jono didn't break promises. She got up and went towards the settee.

'Not there, go and get in my bed.'

Even better. She went through to his bedroom and climbed into the huge bed without taking off the tracksuit. It smelled of Jono. Delilah buried her face in the duvet and wished harder than ever that she was just a little bit older. It wasn't fair. They could be happy, she could look after him. Why did everyone have to stick their noses in and spoil everything?

~ ~ ~

Sometimes, it was good to be wrong. Shona was pleased that the God thing proved to be just as everyone said; so pleased, it made her smile. That was not so good. It made her left eye hurt. There shouldn't be pain in heaven. Although it wasn't bad pain, not like childbirth. Childbirth hurt more than anything, inside and outside. The cloud wobbled. She didn't have a safety belt, there was nothing holding her on, she might fall off it, or through it, and go plunging down to...earth?

Or was that hell down there? It might just be a temporary cloud, a kind of halfway house. It made more sense. She didn't really deserve to be in heaven, because...something to do with childbirth. Had she done it wrong? Not pushed hard enough? The cloud wobbled again, but now there were angels, three angels. One was pointing at something. Was it Jesus? Was the baby Jesus here? Or were they pointing down to hell? Had they decided she was in the wrong place after all?

No. There were flowers. Another angel was bringing her flowers to welcome her into heaven. As they came close, the colours spun and fractured. It was beautiful. She *was* in heaven. Everything was alright. She could sleep again.

The sterile hospital smell cut through the morphine when she next woke and the pain in her head was detached, but very real. There was still something pleasant though, a beautiful scent, her favourite scent, freesias. Shona turned her head with care and saw them lying on a cabinet beside her. Who on earth would buy her flowers? Further questions superimposed themselves with devastating speed. How long had she been in here? Where was Paulie? Who had brought her here? Were the police involved?

A nurse appeared and smiled at her.

'You're awake Shona, that's good. Do you know where you are?'

'No.'

'This is the City Hospital and it's Monday.' Monday. She'd only been in for one night then. 'Is your head hurting?'

'Yes, but who are the flowers from?'

'He says he's a friend of yours. Jim? He's in the waiting area actually, do you want to see him? He hasn't been allowed through yet.'

'Oh yes, yes please.'

Thank God for Jim. He must have found her and brought her here. But had he seen Paulie? The nurse left and she waited, still anxious, but with less panic. The curtains moved aside and Jim stooped under the rail supporting them.

'Oh Jim, I'm so pleased to see you.'

He gave her a tight smile and squeezed her hand.

'It's bloody good to see you awake. I thought you might have bust your skull.'

'I don't think so. I've not talked to a doctor yet.'

'You will in a minute. Visiting's nearly over.'

'Have you been waiting the whole time?'

'It doesn't matter. Shona, do you know who did this to you?'

Her eyes slid away. She couldn't answer that, or look at him, but if she didn't he might guess.

'No,' she said in a small voice, forcing herself to return his intense gaze. 'Did you find me?'

'Me and Delilah, but we had to call an ambulance and the police came too.'

Her stomach clamped into a ball.

'What happened?'

Jim pulled out a chair and sat down, bending close to her ear.

'We tidied up before they got there, but there wasn't much to sort. Looks like someone's cleared you out – cash and blow. They were suspicious though and they called Social Services too. Delilah got dragged off.'

'Oh no! So what's happening now?'

'Well, right now I'm a likely suspect for having battered you and Delilah's legged it from wherever they were keeping her. They came looking for her this morning.'

'I'm so sorry.'

'Hey, it's not your fault.'

A nurse put her head between the curtains and made them both jump.

'Five more minutes.'

She vanished again and there was a pause. Please don't ask about Paulie, please, please.

'Don't suppose you've any idea where Delilah might be?'

Not what she was expecting.

'Um, not really. I don't see that much of her, only when sodding Kelly goes A.W.O.L.' She tried to think back, remember where Delilah had been going yesterday. Jerry, Jenny, no... 'Jono. She said she was going to see Jono yesterday.'

'From the estate?'

No, not the estate, the whole conversation returned.

'No. It sounds a bit strange…she said he doesn't come onto the estate, but he's got a house in the village. I don't know anything more I'm afraid.'

'Alright. It's something if she's got a friend, but how old is he?'

'I think she said he's 28.'

The noise of scraping chairs and multiple goodbyes was increasing around them. It was a relief that Jim couldn't ask her more questions yet, but she felt awful that he was mixed up in her bad business.

'Thank you, for coming and for sorting things out. Hopefully I'll be out soon, maybe even today.'

'Don't rush it. I'll come back tomorrow if you're not at home. You need to worry about getting better and nothing else. I'll pass on the info about Jono.'

He stood up, just as a nurse came in to evict him. Shona was both sorry and glad about his departure. She hated lying, but the thought of him discovering that Paulie beat her up was far more terrifying than the police being involved. The doctor would be doing his rounds now, so she didn't have long to get her story straight. What could she say?

~ ~ ~

Jim walked straight past the bus stop without noticing it and by the time he came out of his reverie, a mile further on, it was only another two miles home. The see-saw in his head levelled and he took out his phone, calling the number under 'SW' and hoping he'd put it in correctly last night. It rang twice.

'Becky Stocks'.

Her voice was eager, almost breathless.

'It's Jim, the man from...'

40

'Yes, I remember. Do you have any news?'

He was going to ask her that question, but obviously not.

'Not much. Shona, that's the neighbour who was attacked, says Delilah was talking about a friend called 'Jono'. All she said was that he's 28 and doesn't live on the estate. He can't be too far away though, cos she goes everywhere on foot.'

'I'll get the police onto it.' She paused and Jim could hear her scribbling. 'Hey, does that mean Shona's ok?'

'She's in hospital, but conscious and lucid. I don't think she's done any permanent damage.'

'Good. There are too many disasters rolled into one here. Thank you very much for calling, Jim.'

'No problem.'

He hung up and stopped walking to roll a fag. She didn't sound much like a social worker, in fact, he'd have to say she was pretty nice. Perhaps most of them were, if it wasn't your life they were messing with.

4

As he rolled over for what must be the hundredth time on Monday night, Detective Inspector Andrew McGrath's wife moaned a little in her sleep. He looked at the digital clock on his bedside table: 5:03am. He had to be in for 7am anyway, might as well get up and not disturb her any further. It wouldn't hurt to be in early. Everything was muddled with this damned case, not least his bloody head.

That feral girl should have moved over to Child Protection, but there was still a link with the assault and possible burglary. He'd only attended the call because the initial report sounded like a potential murder and the circumstances rather complex. Now he wanted to stay involved.

He slid out of bed and padded to the bathroom, questioning his own objectivity as he shaved with slow, methodical strokes. He didn't think Delilah guilty of anything, beyond making an unfortunate discovery. But then, he couldn't rule it out and the link was not so tenuous. Why was she haunting his thoughts? He dealt with dozens of abusive teenagers every week, although he didn't think it was the standard 'giving a finger to the system' in her case. She had been terrified. Hard, but truly terrified.

He lifted his chin to gain access to his throat, reaching the same angle it had taken to look up at that huge biker bloke. Now he *was* terrifying, but the girl wasn't scared of him. If McGrath was honest, he'd felt a rush of real fear when the idiot rookie dived in. If the biker had gone to Delilah's defence, they'd all be in hospital - he'd seen the file. It would take more than a squirt of CS gas to stop

Jim Travis and the guy couldn't have any love for the police with his history. Yet he was trying to help.

McGrath didn't believe the 'girl-next-door' story, there was something that didn't ring true, but his suspicions were becoming less sinister. As a non-smoker, the stench of stale tobacco and cannabis had hit him the moment he stepped inside the property. It was more than likely a drugs theft gone wrong. The increasing number of calls they were attending that involved stolen cannabis plants and expensive hydroponic equipment was a source of ironic amusement. The issue must be widespread, as he assumed that the vast majority of growers and dealers were not stupid enough to report their own business to the police.

Forty minutes later he was sitting at his desk reviewing developments. Shona's statement read like the opening of an amateur crime novel and there was a note from the PC who had taken it, saying she doubted its validity. The lead on Delilah's whereabouts proved more promising. There were only five 'Jonathans' of the right age living within a two mile radius of the estate. Two of those were married with young children and another was out of the country. Warrants had been issued to search the houses of the remaining two. McGrath opted to lead the team visiting Jonathan Upton, 28, who lived alone in a bungalow just off the main road.

The cars were almost noiseless on the tarmac drive, with no lights or sirens to herald their coming. Half-digested cereal moved uneasily in McGrath's stomach as he approached the house. There was something odd, even clinical about the property, although Jonathan Upton had nothing in the way of a record. He couldn't imagine Delilah in this setting, it was too sterile and ordered. Pushing thoughts of social scientists and medical experiments out of his head, McGrath raised his fist to knock and was perturbed when the door began to open before he'd made contact.

He stepped back, chilled and momentarily confused by the widening view of a blank wall.

'Good morning.'

It was said in a whisper. A man in a wheelchair was shooing him back down the ramp. McGrath felt foolish and backed away, preparing apologies. They weren't necessary.

'Delilah's here, but she's asleep.' He was still whispering. 'Please don't go rushing in and frighten her. Is her social worker with you?'

McGrath was struggling to throw off his preconceptions. This situation just got more bizarre.

'Jonathan Upton?'

'Yes, sorry.'

The man held out his hand and McGrath took it, tried not to be surprised by the firm grip, tried to look Jonathan Upton in the eye. His two colleagues stood to one side, awkward and unsure.

'Jill, get the social worker here. Her name's Becky Stocks, they've got her direct number at the station. Chris, go around the back, make sure Delilah doesn't make a dash for it.'

They moved away and McGrath looked back at 'Jono'.

'How long has Delilah been here?'

'She turned up yesterday. Hid in my wheelie bin and hopped over me when I opened the back door.' He frowned. 'She was in a real state, bleeding from a gash on her arm and falling over with tiredness. She wouldn't take advantage like that unless she was desperate, we're quite good friends.'

McGrath opened his mouth and shut it again. No less likely than a 6'6", 57-year old ex-con, he supposed.

'You should have called us.'

'I know. I was planning to today, but I didn't want Dee to run off and I can't stop her.' He lifted his hands in a helpless gesture, but McGrath suspected it wasn't a card he played often. 'I thought it best to keep her safe while I talked her round. She's got nowhere else to go.'

'How much time does she spend with you?'

Was that a relevant question? Maybe not, but McGrath wanted to know more about this girl and her strange choice of friends.

'She comes over most weekends. Not in school time though, we sorted that out in the end.'

Jonathan shivered. He was only wearing a sweater and must be freezing, but it would be poor procedure to let him go back inside, when he could barricade himself and the girl in. Unlikely, but possible.

'Do you think we could go inside without waking her? Just you and me.'

Jonathan shrugged, but he reversed his chair up the ramp. Having asked Jill to wait outside for the social worker, McGrath followed. The house was clean and tidy, the wide hallway and open-plan layout giving it an airy and spacious feel. In silence, Jonathan indicated the settee. About to decline the offer, McGrath realised there were no doors separating them from the other rooms and kept his mouth shut.

He leaned one hip against the low breakfast bar and watched Jonathan fill the kettle, set out mugs, distribute tea bags; it was fascinating to see how he manoeuvred the chair with confidence and ease. He smiled, impressed, but when Jonathan spun to face him and pointed at his legs, McGrath realised he was blocking the path to the fridge and also understood the earlier request to sit down. It wasn't courtesy – he was in the bloody way.

Retreating to the settee, McGrath felt an unfamiliar heat in his face. He regarded himself as a thoughtful man, but had not only missed an obvious hint, but then treated this young man like some interesting spectacle in a freak show. Wow, the cripple could make tea! In his own home, in which he seemed to live with perfect independence. How crass. A loud *thunk* made him look over at the kitchen area. Jonathan was wincing at the fridge.

'Sprung door,' he said in a loud whisper and began pouring milk into the mugs.

McGrath turned back towards the bedroom doorway and she was there, swamped by an over-sized tracksuit, her thick mop of black hair tousled, bright blue eyes staring right into him. He stared back, taken by surprise and speechless for a moment. Why did he feel like a schoolboy caught smoking?

'Hello Delilah.'

She frowned and without taking her eyes off him, said,

'Jono, you promised.'

'Not me, Guv,' he called, still stirring sugar into the teas. 'I'll make you a coffee, but go and get dressed first, eh? Your clothes are clean and on the bathroom radiator.'

The frown deepened before she retreated to the bathroom. McGrath stood up.

'I'll take those out to the others,' he said to Jonathan. 'And thank you for being so considerate. I'd like to come back in and have a talk to Delilah.'

'I'll see what I can do, and it's Jono.'

'Right, Jono.'

He went back to the door, called Jill over and explained the situation in a low voice.

'Social worker's going to be an hour,' Jill said, taking the two mugs from him. 'She's in a Case Conference or something.'

'That's fine, I want to talk to the girl first anyway. There's no point dragging her away again or we'll only be camped out somewhere else tomorrow. I'd like you to stay in position for a while, just in case, but if she does run then don't use force to stop her. Delilah's done nothing wrong, beyond breaking a window.'

When he returned to the lounge, Jono and Delilah were deep in conversation and didn't notice his presence. Delilah was squatting on the floor, in a similar pose to when he had first seen her and Jono was leaning forward, holding both her hands in his.

'You can't keep running, Dee,' he was saying. 'I had to find another way, so you can too.'

She looked up at him, her eyes full of tears and her mouth screwed up in anger, but as she met his gaze the lines softened and a slow smile spread across her face. It was the most beautiful thing McGrath had ever seen.

~ ~ ~

Becky made as swift an exit as possible from the Case Conference and dashed back to her office.

'Steady on,' Bill said. 'I told them you'd be an hour and that was only twenty minutes ago. You've got plenty of time.'

'They'll end up restraining her, they'll make it worse.'

'Maybe not. It's McGrath and he's alright.'

McGrath had been there on Sunday night and look how that had ended. Becky was not reassured. She found Cleo's number and dialled.

'Bill, how busy are you this morning?' she said, listening to the phone ring at the other end.

'Very. One of mine trashed their new foster placement last night.'

Shit. Cleo wasn't answering, but there was no way she was going to the house on her own again. If she pressed charges for yesterday's assault, the case would be given to someone else, but if she was attacked again - having refused to press charges - there would be little sympathy. She thought about calling Jim, but that wouldn't be appropriate. Taking her car keys from the drawer, Becky said,

'Wish me luck.'

'Have you got her somewhere else sorted?'

'Yes, Sunny Bank. There are only two other kids there at the moment.'

'Good luck.'

There was a policewoman waiting on the drive, who brought her up to speed. McGrath had been in there for almost an hour, with Delilah and this Jono character. Who *was* he anyway? The relationship with Jim made more sense and Becky was beginning to think that she knew very little about Delilah McClafferty. She walked up the ramp and knocked on the front door.

Jono – she assumed it was Jono – answered. He looked every one of his 28 years, but was handsome and clean-shaven, with short blond hair. His upper body was strong and well-muscled, though his legs were thin and angled to one side in the wheelchair. He smiled at her.

'Are you Dee's social worker?'

'Yes.' She held out her hand, which he took in a warm, firm grip. 'Becky Stocks.'

'I'm Jono.' He smiled again and kept hold of her hand. 'From Dee's description, I thought you'd be 50-something, in a twin-set and pearls.'

'I'm pleased to disappoint. How's Delilah?'

'Just onto Celtic history with DI McGrath and more interested than she'd like to be.'

Becky laughed, but felt a little hurt; Delilah was always monosyllabic with her and only answered direct questions.

'If that's the case, then I'll leave them to it for a few minutes. Could you tell her I'm here and give me a shout when she's ready to talk?'

'Sure.'

He shut the door and Becky hurried back down the drive, walking twenty yards up the street before lighting a cigarette. She'd been doing well with cutting down, but it had been a hectic morning and she was desperate for this to go well. Inhaling deeply, she turned and looked at the house over the neighbouring hedge. It was certainly on the nice side of the village. How on earth had these two got together? The work mobile in her bag rang. Seeing it was Bill, she answered.

'What's up?'

'I think I've just taken a call from Cleo McClafferty. She's not making much sense and sounds rather intoxicated. I told her we'd found Delilah and she said 'about fucking time', but I have no idea what else she said.'

'Alright, thanks Bill'.

She took a last drag of the cigarette and threw it down the nearest drain. A mint and a squirt of perfume and she was ready. Ish. If Delilah was talking to a policeman, then they ought to be able to manage a constructive conversation.

Becky turned into the drive and saw Jono in the doorway of the house. Oops. He lifted his nose towards her when she got close and gave a half-smile, but made no comment.

'I'm just sticking the kettle back on. Do you want a tea or coffee?' he asked as she followed him down the hall.

'I'm fine thanks,' Becky said, looking around at his living space and hoping Delilah saw this as more representative of 'normality' than the filthy wreck she and her mother lived in.

McGrath was sitting on the settee, but stood up as she walked into view.

'Where's Delilah?'

'Just gone into the bedroom for a smoke,' he said. 'Probably to escape my tedious history lessons.'

He smiled and Becky relaxed a little. It was a strange situation, but if McGrath was comfortable then she need not worry. There seemed to be no issue with Jono harbouring a minor. She went over to sit next to McGrath and saw the first problem - they couldn't line up like sparrows, talking to the wall - but Jono opened a large cupboard beneath the vast tv screen and pulled out a bean-bag.

'You can sit here,' he said.

Becky frowned at the suggestion, but realised he was looking over her head. She stopped herself turning around and waited, the hairs on the back of her neck telling her that she was under observation. It was an hour-long minute before Delilah walked around the settee and sank slowly into the bean-bag. She was calm and quiet, but her eyes blazed defiance, flitting between the two people facing her.

'Hello,' Becky said. 'I'm glad you're safe, you had me worried yesterday.'

A shade of scorn coloured the defiance, but the girl said nothing. Becky's eyes dropped to the white gauze taped to Delilah's arm.

'The window took some revenge then. Are you sure it doesn't need stitches?'

The gaze didn't drop, but Delilah's chin tilted towards Jono.

'It's a good 'un,' he said, 'but it's stopped bleeding and looks clean. No thanks to Dee's sojourn in my wheelie bin. It's worth letting a doctor have a look though and a stitch or two might prevent a wicked scar.'

Delilah shrugged, but Becky suspected that she would take any advice given by Jono. She was looking forward to a private talk with him, but the pleasantries had to end - she didn't get paid for sitting and drinking tea.

'So, I'll lay the situation out as best I can. Just say if you have any questions and I'll explain a few more bits and bobs at the end. Alright?'

Delilah just stared at her, but it was the closest thing to acquiescence that Becky had experienced so far.

'Ok, so the Assessment Centre didn't work and I'm not going to suggest you go back there. Those who broke your phone have been punished, but if you want to press charges through the police as well, you can.'

A single lateral movement was near enough to a shake of the head.

'The good news is, that because you're in care, you get a clothing allowance and pocket money, we can even go shopping for a new phone this afternoon, but I do need to set some other things up first.'

Silence. So far, so good.

'There's a small home, about three miles away, with just two other young people living there, both older than you and both boys. There's a room that's been redecorated and it's now yours, but the important bit is the word 'home'. I know you have a home and you don't want to leave it, but there's no longer any choice. It's not even my decision.'

Delilah still said nothing. It was like swimming through soup and Becky was tiring already.

'Is that Sunny Bank?' McGrath asked, and when Becky nodded, added 'Decent folks there.'

Delilah's gaze moved to him for a moment, but she didn't speak.

'Your mother is back and knows you're safe.'

The ripples from that fat little pebble worked a change on the girl's face and Becky watched a range of emotions move across it. She waited and silently thanked McGrath and Jono for their reticence. It was time Delilah contributed to the conversation.

'What did she say?' she asked at last.

Becky was not sure if the angry lines on Delilah's forehead were inspired by her for forcing the question, or prompted by the errant parent who had dropped her in this situation. Probably both. But how should she answer? The truth wouldn't cut it in this case. The last line from Cleo had been 'I'll find you and tear your fucking eyes out, you snooty fucking, frigid, stuck-up cunt,' which had come just after 'Open the door or I'll smash your fucking windscreen and slit your throat.' Neither would be appropriate.

'Um, she was angry that you'd been taken away and wanted to see you.'

'So why can't I go home, now she's back?'

Becky met the defiant glare and tried to think. Delilah, more than anyone, would know her mother had 'issues', it was how to identify them as unacceptable without offending her.

'You know that your mum has a few problems.' Stop being bloody trite, it won't wash. 'Delilah, I think that she's an alcoholic and when people become addicted to something, then that thing becomes the most important thing in their life. More important than washing, eating, making sure there's gas and electricity. Because you're not 18 yet, it's my job to make sure you have food and clothes and a safe place to live. The only way I can do that is by asking someone else to care for you.'

Delilah was staring at her shoes, but listening.

'It isn't a prison or a punishment, you can still go out and see the people you want to, you can still spend time with your mum, but I need to know that your basic needs are being met.'

'Sounds good to me, Dee,' Jono said.

'Do you mind if I stick my oar in again?' McGrath asked.

'Not at all,' Becky said, and then blushed when she realised he was talking to Delilah.

When he didn't speak, Delilah looked up, but McGrath was employing his own tactics and waited for her to respond. Her jaw clenched, her foot began a tiny, repetitive movement, but eventually Delilah said,

'What?'

'There are a few things I want to say, so sorry in advance for going on. You're not in any trouble now and it may not feel like it, but people *are* trying to help you. They have to, it's their job to, and if they don't do their jobs then they get into trouble themselves.

That's why I'm here and there are two more coppers outside, because it's the law. It's the law, not a person, which says you have to live somewhere you don't want to. But there comes a point when you will be breaking the law - if you smash any more windows, if you threaten anybody, if you have to steal food because you're hungry. Make this work for you Delilah, before it's too late and you end up on the wrong side of the law.'

Wow. It would take her a whole evening to prepare a speech like that. Delilah's eyes lost some of their suspicion, but her frown deepened.

'So it's temporary...not like, forever. If Mum sorts herself out, I can move back home.'

Becky's mouth formed the 'y' of 'yes'. It was an easy fix when Delilah was on the point of compliance, but the word stuck in her throat. It wasn't true and the thing she needed more than anything was Delilah's trust.

'Technically, you're right. It will be a temporary arrangement, you can move into independent accommodation when you're 16. But I'm going to be honest with you Delilah; I don't think your mum *will* manage to sort herself out soon enough to look after you again while you're still classed as a 'child'.'

Becky resisted the urge to cross her fingers and waited, watching Delilah's face.

~ ~ ~

Why did they all have to stare at her? It was impossible to think. She knew what McGrath's little speech was supposed to mean though – better to live in some shitty care home than a prison cell. She couldn't even go to Shona for help any more. Jono was smiling at her, his eyebrows raised. He obviously thought it was a good idea, but *two years?* She looked back at Becky.

'When will I get to see Mum, if I come with you?'

'In a week or two, if she'll speak to me and arrange a visit.'

'And we can get a phone first? Before I have to go to this...*home*?'

'Yes.'

Delilah took a deep breath. She wanted to cry very badly, but nothing, especially not crying, was going to fix this.

'Alright then.'

Jono reached over and squeezed her arm. It was nice that he wanted to touch her for once, but it just made her want to cry more. She yanked her arm away.

'You're just happy cos you won't have to bother about me any more.'

She stood up and kicked the bean bag, but it just flopped over to one side. Stupid, saggy thing.

'Oh really?' Jono said behind her. 'Well I'll prove you wrong by inviting you for dinner on Saturday.'

Delilah spun around and caught Becky pulling a face.

'You said I could still see my friends!' she shouted and it was only McGrath raising his hand that stopped her from slapping the stupid bitch.

Jono said 'sorry' to no-one in particular and looked sheepish. Becky lifted both of her hands and screwed her face up further.

'I'm not saying no,' she said, 'just give me a minute.'

Delilah glared at her for the whole minute. And then another minute. It couldn't be that hard – was she allowed to see Jono or not?   McGrath coughed quietly and looked uncomfortable, shuffling forward on the settee until he was perched on the edge.

'Um, I was going to leave this for another time, but perhaps there's no time like the present after all,' he said, rubbing his palms together. 'You see, while it's obvious to us that you two are just friends Delilah, both Becky and I will be asked lots of questions when we get back to our offices. It's not that usual for a 14 year old and a 28 year old to be friends and, particularly when a young person is in care, people are very cautious about...unusual relationships.'

'We're not shagging, if that's what you mean.'

Jono grinned and even Becky smiled. What was so fucking funny? Wasn't that what they were on about? McGrath's mouth was a weird shape, but at least he wasn't laughing at her. Delilah concentrated on him.

'Isn't that what you wanted to know? Jono's dead straight. He said he wouldn't even kiss a girl until she was 16.'

There was a pause and now they all looked thoughtful. What was the pissing problem?

'Dee, will you sit down a minute?' Jono said.

'Why?'

'Because I need to say something, but I don't want you to go nuts. You are going to be horribly embarrassed though and probably hate me for a bit.'

'I wouldn't hate you.'

Jono winced.

'You might. But I do need to explain this and I need to do it in front of these people.'

Delilah shrugged, but returned to the beanbag and began picking at the dried mud on her shoes.

'You remember you brought your friend Chelsea round here once?' Delilah nodded, but didn't say anything. 'Well I actually saw her again, a few weeks later.'

This time, Delilah looked up. What had that two-faced cow wanted with Jono? He was *her* friend.

'How?'

'She came here. She wanted to talk to me, to ask me if something was true.'

It was cold at first, like ice down her back and in her stomach. But then she was hot, boiling all over, but especially her face. She was going to murder Chelsea if...

'Apparently you told her that we would be getting married when you turned 16.'

The tightness in her guts eased, just a fraction. At least Chelsea hadn't asked about the nob ring. Delilah had gone on and on at Jono, for weeks, to explain how he could still have sex.

'Now whether we know that there's nothing going on between us, and these people know that nothing's going on, if you went and said that to anybody else, they'd stop you coming here immediately. Do you get that?'

Delilah nodded into her chest. She could hear McGrath and Becky murmuring to each other, but was too mortified to lift her head, never mind challenge them. It was McGrath who spoke next.

'Sorry for whispering, but this really is quite complicated. However, we're happy that there's no inappropriate relationship. If I can just ask you to state that there never has been and never will be any kind of sexual activity between you, then there's no reason you shouldn't have pre-planned visits. Your carers will need to know where you are though Delilah.'

Jono raised his right hand and looked serious, although Delilah could see a kink at the corner of his mouth.

'There never has been, or will be, any sexual activity between me and Delilah.'

'Yeah, the same,' she said quickly, looking at McGrath and then Becky.

Becky smiled.

'Alright then. Well if we're going to get you a phone before visiting Sunny Bank, then we need to get going pretty soon. Have you got a bag or a coat?'

Delilah's stomach tightened again and she retreated a few steps. It was easy talking about things, but she didn't want to leave right now.

'Stick your shoes on Dee and I'll write my mobile number down for you,' Jono said, spinning his chair around and talking over his shoulder. 'Text me as soon as you get your new phone sorted and I'll ring you tonight, when you're settled in this freshly redecorated room of yours.'

Becky and McGrath both stood up and Delilah stumbled off to the bedroom to fetch her boots. It was really happening, even Jono couldn't help. There was nothing she could do to stop it.

~ ~ ~

Jono shook McGrath's hand and watched from the door as he walked down the drive, calling the other officers to follow him. What a crazy experience…and not one he wanted to repeat anytime soon. He could not banish the image of a filthy, blood and bolognaise-spattered Delilah rising from his wheelie bin, poor kid.

He glanced at his Play Station, but didn't feel up to the laddish banter that would accompany any gaming. What he'd really like to do was go out for a run, push himself until all his thoughts were focussed on his burning legs and lungs. *Fat fucking chance.*

Scowling, Jono picked up the tv remote, flicking through channels until he found an action movie he'd not yet seen. When his phone buzzed, he found he'd been staring at the wall above the screen for an hour, without even noticing that the sound wasn't on. Two figures made an impossible leap from a burning boat and Jono wondered if an appropriate soundtrack would make it seem less ridiculous. He sighed and opened the text.

hi got a Samsung its pritty smart txt u wen im in my room D

He half smiled. Delilah was obviously pleased with her new phone, but he didn't doubt that she was still giving that social worker hell. He sent a quick reply.

Cool. Hope you said thank you... ;o)

He dropped the phone onto his lap and headed for the bedroom, leaving the tv on silent. The next text came in less than a minute.

it woz her folt my other fone got broke

Jono shook his head, both at her stubbornness and appalling spelling. Maybe he ought to start sending grammatically correct texts, as she hardly ever made it to school.

It wasn't her fault. It was some idiot kid who smashed your phone, not Becky. Give her a break. 'Thank you' won't be the hardest thing you've had to say today. I'll speak to you later. Can't wait to hear about your room! J

She wouldn't reply to that one in a hurry. He threw the phone onto his dressing table and picked up the window hook. It reeked of fags in here, but he hadn't had the heart to make Delilah go outside. The bed covers were a tangled mess and talcum powder was strewn across the carpet and shoe shelf. Delilah had never encountered talcum powder before and Jono laughed when he remembered her appearance, having covered herself in it from head to foot. He made a mental note to buy her a tub as a moving in present.

It took him another hour to restore the room to its usual, clean and tidy state. It was quite amazing, that she could wreak such devastation in such a short space of time, but he didn't resent it. A prolonged stay would doubtless have driven him insane, but the house now seemed empty and lifeless without Delilah.

~ ~ ~

The one called Josh didn't even look at her when Becky tried to introduce him. He just shuffled on the settee, said 'whatever' and carried on messing with his phone. That was fine with Delilah. Better than she'd dared hope for in fact. The lounge door opened and another lad came in. He was tall and geeky-looking, with big brown glasses.

'H..hello,' he said, pulling a stupid grin and holding out his hand.

Delilah looked at it and noticed his sleeve was way too short. She folded her arms and shoved her own hands under her armpits, dropping her gaze to the floor and noticing on the way that his trousers were also too short, leaving his cheap, shitty trainers exposed. They were definitely trousers and not jeans or trackies.

'Delilah, this is Robert,' Becky said, but she was interrupted by geek-boy.

'N..no, n..no-one really c..c..calls me that. My n..name's Blink.'

Delilah looked up and saw why. 'Blink' was still smiling, but his eyes didn't stay open for more than one or two seconds between bouts of rapid blinking. When he looked back at Delilah and found her studying him, it got worse. He still made another attempt at conversation.

'A..are you m..m..moving in here?'

Delilah looked away again, shrugging, but saying nothing. Becky answered for her.

'Yes, Delilah's moving in today. It's nice of you to make her feel welcome, but she's going to be a bit shy to start with.'

'I've been here for over two years, but I can remember being really scared on my first day too,' Blink said.

'I'm not scared,' Delilah growled. 'I can look after myself.' *Especially if I don't make friends with nobs like you.*

58

She felt a bit mean, but Doogie would make mincemeat of Blink and there would be lads like Doogie around here too. She needed to keep her head down and stay out of everybody's way. If there were just these two to deal with, it might not be as hard as she'd thought. Blink started to tell her where his room was, but Josh shouted at him to stop prattling and fuck off back to it, which he did.

There were more introductions, to Julie, one of the managers at the home, some other woman and a bearded man who were going to be her key-workers. She would meet another bloke called Derek, her third key-worker, tomorrow. Delilah didn't really care. She just wanted to go to her room and be left alone to talk to Jono. Julie started on about house rules and Delilah thought she would have to give in and leg it, but Julie just said they were all written on a poster on her wall.

'What about smoking?' Becky asked. 'I'm afraid Delilah has quite a habit.'

Delilah tuned back in. This was important.

'Well we don't condone smoking and the entire building is a no-smoking zone,' Julie said. 'Staff will not buy cigarettes or tobacco for young people and levels of smoking will be monitored and recorded. Appropriate referrals will be made to ensure that support with any smoking, drug or alcohol issues is available. However, we realise that smoking is a difficult habit to break and if Delilah manages to obtain cigarettes, then she will be allowed to smoke them in the garden.'

If the window in her room was a wide opener, then that rule would go straight out of it, but Delilah was satisfied that she wouldn't get too much grief about smoking. She couldn't cope with any more pointless chat though.

'Can I go to my room now?' she said, to no one in particular.

When nobody answered, she looked up at Becky, whose smile was a bit too wide.

'Yes, if you're ok and don't have any more questions,' she said. 'I'll talk to Julie about someone taking you shopping tomorrow for new clothes and shoes. My number is in your phone, you can call me if you want to. I'll send your mum's number over as soon as I can.'

Delilah nodded. The bearded man stepped forward and said that her room was upstairs and he'd show her which one it was. She followed him to the bottom of the stairs and then paused. Jono's text ground around her brain like gravel. He would ask later if she'd said thank you to Becky, who she knew was still watching from behind her.

Turning her head the tiniest bit, Delilah muttered a gruff 'thanks' and then followed the man up the stairs.

5

Derek clutched the desk and tried to relax, as his guts went into another writhing spasm. There couldn't be anything left, surely. Beads of sweat broke out on his forehead and he gave in, snatching up his bunch of keys before dashing to the toilet at the end of the corridor outside. He'd slammed the door behind him to activate the lock and prayed the noise hadn't woken any of the kids upstairs. He wasn't ready to deal with them yet. Josh was always bad-tempered, but more so in the mornings, Blink was intense and there was the new girl to meet.

He sat on the bowl, with his elbows on his knees and his head in his hands, trying to recall the details discussed at the team meeting. She was young - only just 14 - and had an interesting name. Delilah. She could be defiant, abusive and had run away from another care setting. Her mother was potentially violent and not to be contacted, or allowed contact with Delilah, until various issues with the social worker and police had been sorted out. Fairly standard stuff. He knew the essentials and would read her file later, but Derek liked to get to know the young people on present merit before studying a detailed history of their misdemeanours.

Groaning, he limped his way back to the office. What a day for Gareth to have a flat tyre. Julie was managing nights this week and would normally have stayed to do a proper handover, but her daughter had some kind of medical appointment. They were already counting Sheila the cleaner as the 'third member of staff' because Lisa had booked a few hours off. He prayed the assumption that all the kids would stay in bed until Lisa did arrive would hold fast.

Dehydration would lead to a headache that he didn't need, so Derek poured a glass of tap water and eased himself into the chair. He drained half of it and grimaced at the tang of chlorine. Leaning back and closing his eyes, he tried to imagine healing water seeping slowly downwards through his body. A cool flush spread into his stomach, but it was not soothing. Instead, his mind formed an image of the stone being cast into the lake beside the Mines of Moria, its dark waters churning with increasing violence. Cramps spread both upwards and downwards and Derek suddenly feared full-on food poisoning. He should call Sheila, but he *had* to get to the toilet first.

As he hobbled down the corridor, clutching his stomach, Derek heard the office door bounce back off the lock behind him. Shit. There were not only reams of confidential information in there, but his wallet, car keys and cigarettes on the desk. He stopped, but a wave of nausea washed over him and he knew he wouldn't make it if he tried to retrace his steps. There was still no sound from upstairs. Sod it, he'd be as quick as possible.

~ ~ ~

The alarm on his phone launched into Motorhead's Ace of Spades at loud volume, but Jim didn't even twitch. He had been staring at the ceiling for at least an hour and counting down the minutes until he needed to rise. Still fully dressed from the previous night, he paused only to make a pint mug of coffee and pull on his boots, before taking Crank out for a quick walk around the block. The air tasted good and helped to dispel some of his night-time paranoia, if it was that.

Jim didn't think he was paranoid. There were plenty of people who would be pleased to see him dead, plenty more with very personal grudges and a significant number who would enjoy adding his hide to their trophy list. It was more than that though. There was a sinister vibe about at the moment and decent folk were being dealt dodgy hands. Decent folk usually were, he supposed, but he hadn't paid too much attention before.

Within half an hour he was on his way to the hospital, having changed his t-shirt and fed Crank. Shona was coming out first thing and was grateful for his offer to meet and escort her home. He felt a bit useless not being able to pick her up, but he'd never taken his car test and wasn't about to start lessons in his late fifties. Shona wouldn't appreciate having to climb onto his Harley though, or ram a helmet onto a badly bruised head. The bike was a bit conspicuous these days, but Jim couldn't think of an adequate replacement.

Shona was waiting in the reception area, looking rather grey and rumpled. A warm smile brought some life into her face when she spotted him walking towards her.

'Jim! It's so good of you to come again. I think I'm turning into a whittling old woman.'

'Balls. You were beaten up good and proper three days ago and I've seen supposed hard-men handle it worse. I can't wait to see how the fucker who did it handles it, when I return the favour.'

Shona stared at him in with such horror that Jim reached out in concern. She recoiled slightly, but then took his arm, steering them both in the direction of the sunlight outside.

'Don't be daft. With your record, they'd lock you up for so long that you'd never see the light of day again. It's my fault for getting mixed up with the wrong crowd. Just leave it, Jim.'

Jim said nothing, but kept revisiting that look of horror. There was more to it than concern for his future welfare. What was she hiding? He was distracted by Shona trying to walk across his path.

'What are you doing?'

'The bus stop's over there.'

'Yeah, but we're going to the taxi rank,' he kept a tight grip on her arm and altered their course to the right, 'and don't bloody argue, woman.'

He bundled her into the back and walked around to the other side. After telling the driver where to go, Jim lapsed into deep thought and silence fell on the car for rest of the fifteen minute journey. He had to rouse Shona from her own, unhappy-looking trance, when they pulled up outside her house.

'You're home,' he said, squeezing her arm.

She looked up and stared out through the window at her house for several seconds before moving.

'I suppose it'll still be quite a mess.'

'It's not too bad. I called in yesterday, I hope you don't mind.'

He'd put flowers on the kitchen table and set several sticks of Nag Champa burning. It might go some way towards countering any memories of her last few minutes in there.

'Thank you.'

Shona said it with feeling, but waved away his proffered hand and used the door to haul herself out of the car. She walked down the path slowly and seemed rather dazed, or as if she didn't quite want to reach her destination. Jim followed a few paces behind and was pleased when Shona opened the door and the heady scent of incense wafted out to greet them. She stepped inside without comment and he was about to follow when a harsh voice barked 'oi' from behind him.

He turned around and was confronted by a wreck of a woman, with tangled orangey-yellow hair that showed two inches of muddy grey at the roots. Staring at the ravaged face, Jim could see several clumps of caked mascara clinging to her eye-lashes and patches of darker colour on her cheeks, where whatever gunk it was had been applied with a shovel. The red slash of her mouth was wrinkled and pursed into an angry pout, reminding him of a dog's arsehole. Delilah's delightful mother. He shuddered.

'Will ya shout Shona for me? I wanna talk to her.'

Jim didn't want to talk to a pissed-up whore, but neither did he want her disturbing Shona.

'No. She's just back from hospital. Some fucker broke in and beat her up.' Kelly's expression didn't alter, so he added, 'She needs peace and quiet right now.'

'Yeah, well, Social Services have got my fucking daughter and she was picked up here. I wanna know what the fuck went off.'

She had her hands on her hips now and Jim felt a dangerous tickle in the palm of his hand.

'You weren't around. That's what happened.'

Kelly's piggy eyes narrowed further.

'That bitch social worker said something about a neighbour and a biker bloke. Are you him? Have you been fucking with my daughter?'

She had hold of the fence now and thrust her face towards him. Jim gritted his teeth.

'I gave her a cake when she turned up at Shona's, starving hungry. I walked her home from the war memorial, because she was sitting alone in the dark. We found Shona that same night and dealt with the police together. That's it.'

'So why did you let them take her?'

'You what? One minute you're accusing me of being a fucking paedo and the now you're asking why I didn't take Delilah home. I've had enough of you. Fuck off.'

He turned away and stepped into the kitchen. The yawping continued outside, but he ignored it. Shona had gone through to the living room and when she returned, her face was white and looked ten years older.

'Are you alright?' Jim asked, alarmed.

'No. Yes, I'm fine. It's just a bit of a shock, coming home.' She clutched the back of a chair by the table, but didn't even glance at the flowers. 'Look, thanks for fetching me Jim, but I think I need a bit of time on my own.'

'I'm not sure about leaving you. That fucking hag next door is on the warpath.'

'Oh, I'll just lock the door and ignore her. I really am fine, honestly.'

'How about I come back at lunchtime with some fresh bread and cheese? You haven't got much in.'

'Great. That sounds great.'

She had her eyes closed and her teeth clenched. She really did want him gone. He was a little disappointed, but under similar circumstances, he'd want leaving alone too. With reluctance, he took hold of the door handle.

'Alright. I'll see you in a couple of hours.'

He slipped outside and found Kelly, still waiting on the other side of the fence, glowering at him. Jim glowered back. He now noticed a half empty bottle of cheap vodka hanging from her left hand.

'You knock on this door and I'm going to come over there, pour that shit over your head and set fire to it.'

She continued to glare at him for a few more seconds and then, in a series of puppet jerks, lifted her arm and turned her head to examine the bottle. Jesus, it was only 8.45am and she was absolutely smashed. The head wobbled back to look at him and the red slash twisted into what might have been a smile, with a little more muscle control.

'That...would be a waste...of good booze,' Kelly said and with the same jerky movements, tottered off towards her own house.

Jim stood watching. When she covered the ten yards across the grass and kept going, he began to walk down Shona's path. He could hear Kelly chuntering, but ignored the noise until a few words caught his ear. He turned to look back. She was now wrestling with her own front door. Had she said 'fucking snake of a son'? Was she talking about Paulie? He thought about asking her exactly what she meant, but couldn't face it, and Kelly hadn't even been here when Shona was attacked. It bugged him all the way home, along with the comment about a 'waste of good booze', but he wasn't going to ponder on that too much. He wanted to agree with her, not feel sorry for the stupid cow.

~ ~ ~

The final check in his wardrobe convinced Shona that Paulie was gone for good. Her missing jewellery and the absent clock - her only family heirloom and most precious possession - were the first signs, but that could have been an opportunist burglar. The fact that Paulie's spare clothes and birth certificate were also missing proved a different scenario had played out here. The bastard. Just like his goddamned, bastard father, who he hadn't even seen since he was four. Shona knew which side of the nature/nurture debate she was on.

She sank down on the settee, but was too drained to find release in tears. She didn't have the energy to cry. There was no source of comfort, no small 'at least' to focus on. There was nothing left; no money, no blow, nothing of any value to pawn, no way of satisfying the dealers and loan sharks who would come knocking on her door over the next few days. It would be better if Paulie had killed her.

~ ~ ~

Sounds of violent retching now joined the amazing farts, so Delilah dared to creep out into the corridor. Whoever it was wouldn't be out of the bog for at least a few minutes and now she could see that the office door was open. There couldn't be anyone else around, or he wouldn't have slammed it last time. She crossed the corridor and crept along the wall until she could see into the room. There was no-one in her line of vision. She moved closer and pressed her ear to the gap, but it would be impossible to hear much over the noise from the toilet, which had just been flushed.

Without giving it any more thought, Delilah pushed through the door and scanned the room. It was empty. Her eyes lit on a slim black wallet that lay on the desk, next to two bunches of keys and a packet of fags. What a score. She snatched up the packet and finding it almost full, pulled out five fags and eased them into her pocket. The retching started again, so she inspected the wallet and found two ten pound notes and a fiver. With one of the tenners between her fingertips Delilah paused; she didn't actually need any money now she'd got some fags and McGrath's lecture popped into her head. He'd be well disappointed if she got done for stealing the very next day.

She shoved the note back into the wallet and made to close it, but a picture in the plastic-fronted slot caught her eye. It was of two little boys, leaning their heads together and grinning at the camera. They looked so happy that Delilah's own lips began to curl, but she felt a burst of sudden anger and wanted to rip the photo in two. She slung the wallet back on the desk and hurried back into the corridor, looking for the nearest exit. Walking into the lounge area she could hear noises from the other end of the building. They were kitchen noises, so hopefully that person would stay in there.

There were two patio doors on her left, with long curtains in front of them. She tried one of the handles and was both surprised and pleased to find it unlocked. She pushed it to behind her and took a few steps along the side of the building, thankful that it wasn't raining. Looking around the garden while she smoked, Delilah noticed a long punch bag hanging from a tree in the corner and a brick built barbeque on the slabs by the back door. It was nicer than the Assessment Centre.

A movement of the curtains in one of the upstairs windows caught her eye. Bollocks. She rushed the last few drags and tossed the nub end onto the grass, before slipping back through the door. The toilet was flushing again, so Delilah abandoned caution and sprinted lightly up the stairs, reaching her room without seeing anyone.

~ ~ ~

Derek crawled back to the office on his hands and knees. It took him almost ten minutes. In 37 years, he had never felt as bad as this and he didn't know whether to call his wife or an ambulance. Paramedics would be the most sympathetic choice - Talia would just say 'I told you so' for eating anything made by the mad old woman next door. The cake had been small though and looked more edible than previous samples of her home cooking. Innocent but deadly.

He reached the phone and dialled through to the kitchen, asking Sheila to come through immediately. She arrived in seconds and found him still on his knees by the desk.

'Good God! What's happened?'

She ran over to him, but Derek held up his hand to ward her off.

'Food poisoning. I need you to make a few calls Sheila, I can't wait for Gareth any longer, I need to go home.'

'He was just pulling on to the drive when I came through. Or at least, someone was.'

Oh please, let it be Gareth.

'Can you go and check? I don't want anyone else to see me in this state.'

Sheila vanished and Derek reached up to the desk again for his mobile. The movement prompted another spasm in his guts, but Talia said she would be with him in ten minutes. He heard the front door open and close, then Gareth's voice asking where he was. Derek sagged with relief.

'Wow, you look terrible,' Gareth said, appearing in the doorway.

'Thanks. I'm very glad to see you,' Derek paused to pant a few breaths. 'Talia's on her way and none of the kids are up yet.'

'Someone is - they've just been out for a smoke. I could smell it when I came through the lounge.

Derek felt a stir of unease. Blink didn't smoke, but Josh did and wouldn't have missed an opportunity to get into the office. It could have been the new girl. Greater stirrings suddenly overtook that thought process.

'Help me up. Got to get to the toilet,' he gasped.

Gareth bent down and hauled him to his feet, pulling one of Derek's arms around his neck. Derek managed a quick glance at the desk top before he was manoeuvred out of the door and was relieved to see his wallet, cigarettes and keys still there. A lucky escape.

He stayed in the toilet until Talia arrived. Gareth helped him out to the car and then passed him his work bag.

'I've put your wallet and keys in there. Give us a call later. I'll let everyone know the situation in the meantime and I've spoken to Lisa. She'll be here in forty minutes.'

'Thanks.'

Derek closed his eyes for a moment, but as Talia set off, the motion made his head spin. He snapped them open again.

'You're going to have to take it steady love.'

Talia just sighed. He looked at the bag on his lap and wondered which of the kids had got up, but when he checked his wallet, all of the notes were still there. Thank God his brief lapse had not been taken advantage of.

It wasn't until several hours later that the need for nicotine overtook his queasiness and he found a number of cigarettes missing. That got him thinking. It wouldn't be Blink and with his new passion for weed, Josh wouldn't have been able to resist the cash. So it was, more than likely, Delilah. What had stopped her taking anything else? Fear? Opportunity? Conscience? Was she smart enough to realise that he would be a lot less likely to report her theft if it was limited to cigarettes, given that he'd left the door open? He looked forward to finding out.

~ ~ ~

Jim found himself at the checkout with far more items than he'd intended to buy. His mental list read bread, cheese, milk, coffee, chocolate, but his trolley also contained fruit, vegetables, steak pies, a bottle of wine, several bottles of ale and a whole host of other edibles that he didn't remember picking up. It'd look well if he bumped into someone from the benefits office - there was a fortnight's money here. He'd have to top up his wallet from the stash in the garden.

It took Shona several minutes to answer the door and she looked awful. The invitation inside was unenthusiastic, but she took more interest upon seeing how many bags he was carrying.

'What on earth is all that?' she said, reaching to take the load from his left hand.

'Er, I went to get the bread and cheese for lunch, but I got a bit carried away.'

'A bit?' Shona let out a breath that was almost a laugh.

'Well the pies were on offer and I thought we could have dinner together. Your oven or mine, I'm not bothered. Just as mates like.'

Shona frowned a little and several more expressions flitted across her face before she replied.

'Alright. I don't feel like peeling spuds, but there should be some oven chips in the freezer. Pie, chips and wine might be just the right tonic. Thank you, Jim.'

She smiled at last and Jim turned to put the rest of the bags on the table to hide his pleasure. With dinner planned, he suggested coffee and cake instead of lunch and they took the mugs and plates through to the living room. Jim decided not to mention the attack unless Shona brought it up. He had a bad feeling about it and her head was clearly in a mess. They ate and drank in comfortable silence.

When the plates were empty, he pulled out a small bag of weed and rolled a spliff. He thought Shona must be ready for a smoke after two days in hospital, but when he passed it to her she looked at it for a long time before putting it to her lips. She exhaled, staring up at the swirling smoke with another frown.

'If you're clean out, you can have some of this,' Jim said.

Shona took another pull without answering and passed the spliff back. She leaned forward, rubbing her hands along her legs and then put her head in her hands.

'I'm more than clean out Jim. I get my weed laid on and pay when the next lot is delivered. It's not just the weed that's gone, but all the money I took last Saturday night.'

'Shit. When are they coming?'

'Tonight.' Shona burst into tears for the first time, but Jim resisted the urge to put his arm around her. 'It's just so bloody typical - they usually come on a Saturday, but I only had a few ounces left on Sunday, so I put a call in for some extra.'

'How much did you have?'

'A kilo.'

'Jesus, Shona.'

He thought, hard. That was 36 ounces and at that quantity, Shona was probably paying £120 an ounce for it. £4,320 was a big hole both ways round and without evidence of a bust there was no way the dealers would let her off.

'You owe them more than four grand then?'

'Five. I don't have the same purchasing power as you.'

Fucking hell fire.

71

'What time are they coming?'

'Around 9pm I think. You need to be gone by then Jim...you can't get involved in this.'

'We'll see about that, but thanks for the concern.'

'I mean it.'

'Yeah, well I want a favour from you too.'

'Ha. I'm no use to anyone.'

'Bullshit. But this is quite specific. That social worker texted me yesterday - they've found Delilah and she's in some care home on the other side of town. I want to go and see her.'

Shona raised her eyebrows.

'Why? You hardly know the girl.'

'Right, except I got the feeling I was one of her best friends. I don't know why, but we just clicked. Try explaining that though.'

'Hmmn,' Shona sounded dubious, but just shrugged. 'I'll come with you if you like. I wouldn't mind knowing she's ok, poor lamb.'

'Thanks.'

Jim pulled out his phone and sent a text to Becky, asking if he and Shona could visit Delilah. He received a reply within minutes.

'She says Delilah has a new phone and she'll give her my number in a day or two.'

'Who?'

'Becky.'

'Who's Becky?'

'The social worker.'

Shona's eyebrows shot up again, but she didn't comment, going through to the kitchen instead and putting the kettle on. Over the next hour, three cups of tea and several spliffs, Jim discovered that Shona also owed a loan company nearly £7,000 and was disgusted to learn that she'd only borrowed £3,000 initially and the rest was interest. She didn't dare go to the Citizen's Advice Bureau, as she'd have to explain that the money had gone on Paulie's drug debts. It was a very big hole.

He excused himself later in the afternoon on the pretext of walking Crank. For once he was pleased that it grew dark so early in December, as it allowed him to visit the purpose-built rockery in his garden without fear of being seen. Underneath three large

72

stones and a four inch layer of soil was a steel box, set in a deep bed of concrete. The double lid fastened in a way that allowed the padlock to sit in a dip, making it almost impossible to cut or smash off.

Jim lifted out a nylon bag and felt his way around the bundles of plastic-wrapped cash still inside the box. He couldn't use a torch this early in the day, but as each bundle represented £1,000 it wasn't difficult to take stock. There were twenty-four bundles left. It was a pitiful percentage of what he'd had stashed before being sent down, but at least he'd managed to recover some of it on his release. He took out five of the bundles, packed them into his jacket, started to put the nylon bag back inside the box and then hesitated. Shona played with the big boys now. The nylon bag followed the cash into his jacket before Jim locked the box back up. He replaced the soil and rocks with great care.

~ ~ ~

The presence of Jim was reassuring, but Shona didn't have any appetite for the pie and chips, though the wine was going down just fine. She glanced at the bottle, alarmed to see it less than half full. She'd need her wits about her later. Despite having explained to Jim that the people coming were not just dope dealers but heavy end criminals, he was working his way through an enormous plate of food without difficulty. The worms of fear in her belly continued to writhe, as she imagined the possible scenarios this evening could hold. They all ended in disaster. She abandoned her food and got up to make tea, needing to occupy her hands at least.

'Chill out woman, it'll be fine.'

'I don't see how, Jim. I know you're as tough as old boots, but these guys aren't the 'rough you up a bit' types. They'll pull out a gun. I'm going to ask them to give me some time, I'll think of something.'

'Better to get it over and done with.'

They'd been around this argument several times over the last few hours. Shona didn't want him paying off her debts while he was living on benefits and doing no work on the side. She didn't want him getting wrapped up in her problems when he was trying so hard to stay clean. Worst of all, she didn't think that whatever offer he made would sort the problem anyway, so his involvement would be for nothing. A tiny voice at the back of her mind was also urging her to leave her options open, in case selling more weed was the only ladder available.

She was washing up the dinner plates when the soft knock at the door came. Her stomach flipped. Jim stood up and pushed in his chair.

'Do you mind if I let them in?'

Shona nodded, still clutching a plate in both hands. She felt like some wild creature, facing certain death but paralysed and helpless. Jim opened the door.

'Alright? Come in,' she heard him say.

'What's this shit,' the familiar voice spat.

Shona pushed herself away from the sink and forced herself to turn around. She started to move towards the door, but Jim raised a warning finger and she stopped.

'It's ok Luke, he's cool,' she called.

Jim stepped back, opening the door wider. Luke came inside, moving slowly and - once he'd scanned the kitchen - not taking his eyes off Jim. He was followed by another man with a shaved head, who Shona didn't recognise. He was twitching and looked high on something. That was not good. Luke manoeuvred until he had Shona, Jim and the short passage through to the living room in view. The other one stayed by the door.

'Do you want a drink?' Shona asked, knowing she sounded nervous.

'No, I wanna get the fuck out of here.' Luke looked Jim up and down and then examined the bruises on Shona's face. 'What the fuck happened to you?'

She bit her lip and resisted the urge to look at Jim, who she knew was watching her.

'Someone broke in on Sunday night. Whacked me over the head and cleared me out.'

74

Concise and unpretentious. She'd been rehearsing it in her mind all evening. Luke's eyes narrowed.

'You saying you can't pay?'

'Whoever it was took all my money and the last of the weed.'

'So what are you planning to do about that?'

'I'd like a bit of time to work it out.'

'Well Tommy here has another kilo under that jacket. You could climb out of the seventies, stop spreading the love cheap and flog it for £200 an ounce like everyone else. You'd pay it back in no time...with a little interest.' He looked at Jim again. 'Is this why you invited your furry friend round?'

Shona's heart stopped beating for at least two seconds. Jim had put people in hospital for lesser insults. A flare of his nostrils and slight tightening of the lips were the only indicators of the self-control he was exerting.

'No,' she said quickly, 'he just came for dinner.'

'You've got no opinion at all about this difficult situation?' Luke said, still looking at Jim.

'I've got a much better idea than dumping a kilo of weed on a woman still due several visits from the police,' Jim said, staring Luke in the eyes.

Shona quailed. That was way more antagonistic than necessary. She didn't want a kilo of stinking weed, but if that's all it would take to get rid of Luke, then letting Jim stay was a disastrous error of judgement on her part. Jim might be 6'6" with a level of experience she didn't like to think about, but he was into his fifties and had several war wounds to slow him down. Neither of them was going to back down now. She glanced at 'Tommy' and saw his eyes glittering with excitement and his lips curling. He looked fit and well-muscled under his jacket. Shit.

'Really.' Luke's voice was low and strained. 'Well it'd better be a very fucking clever idea, old man.'

Jim swayed forward a little, but rocked backwards again. Shona's stomach clenched so hard, she feared she'd have to run for the bathroom. Jim took a very deep breath before speaking.

'I'm going to put my hand in my jacket and take out £3k in clean cash. I'm going to give it to you. You're going to leave and take the extra kilo with you.'

Luke let out a bark of laughter and Tommy's grin was sinister.

'And why the fuck would I take two grand less than I'm owed, never mind let your insult slide?'

'Because the weed's only worth £3k, because with the pigs sniffing around, the quicker this shit is sorted the better and because I actually think you're quite intelligent.'

Luke was only wrong-footed for a second.

'So, I'm a fool if I don't do as the big biker man says.'

He sneered and the knife appeared with such speed that Shona barely saw his arm move. Tommy inched forward, fists clenched. Jim smiled.

'Is that a no then?'

Tommy leapt forward just as Luke lunged with the knife and Shona clapped a hand over her mouth to cover a scream. There was a sickening crack and Tommy dropped to the floor, his knee destroyed by a vicious side-kick from Jim, who was now holding Luke close, the knife hand immobilised in an arm-lock. She could see the knife sticking out of Jim's jacketed arm and prayed it wasn't buried too deep. Luke struggled and then screamed as Jim tightened the lock. Jim's free hand went into his jacket and brought out...oh God...a gun.

'Jim!' It came out as a squeak. She swallowed hard, tried again. 'Jim, please don't kill him in my kitchen.'

Luke twisted his head to look at her. He must have seen her genuine fear and his eyes widened with understanding. The fight went out of him, but Jim kept the gun pressed to his head.

'Take a step back, but do it slowly,' he said, releasing the arm-lock. 'Any sudden moves and you're a dead man.'

Luke eased backwards and cast a quick glance at Tommy, who was still writhing on the floor.

'Alright man, take it easy,' he said and licked his lips.

'I haven't come *close* to losing my temper yet,' Jim said, shoving Luke's head sideways with the barrel of the gun.

He reached into his jacket again and pulled out three bundles of notes, stuffing them into the pocket of Luke's jacket. Shona watched in astonishment and Luke's face showed a fair degree of surprise.

'As I was saying, £3k is a fair price for a kilo of weed. Shona doesn't want any more for the time being, but she may be in touch in the future. I don't really give a shit what happens to you, but as you getting busted would have implications for Shona, you need to accept that the pigs really are interested in this place right now and stay away. Do we have an agreement?'

Luke started to nod, but stopped as the gun barrel caught his hair.

'Yeah man. That's a good deal.'

'I'm pleased too. Now get that prick out of here.'

Jim removed the gun from Luke's head and waved it towards Tommy. Luke bent down, took Tommy's arm and dragged him to the door.

'Get up man, you can fucking hop.'

He actually kicked Tommy up the backside and Shona wanted to laugh. It must be hysteria. Luke had now hauled Tommy to his feet and was manhandling him out of the door.

'Just remember lads, however high up the chain you get, there are always going to be bigger fish swimming around,' Jim said.

Luke shot him a last look before disappearing into the dark. Could there have been a slight nod? Surely not, although Jim could easily have sent them away empty-handed. He might have stripped their pride, but at least there would be no further reprisals. There couldn't be many plus sides to having had a gun to your head.

'Jim, you shouldn't have given them all that money. God knows when I'll be able to pay you back.'

He looked at her for several seconds, an expression of confusion on his face.

'I tell you what Shona, why don't you put the kettle on and we'll talk about the money later eh? I need to sit down for a minute.'

~ ~ ~

In the end, it was Blink who persuaded her to go downstairs for breakfast. He had droned on outside her door until she could stand it no longer. Delilah wondered how a 16 year old lad could sound like a boring old man and didn't say more than a few words to him, but Blink didn't seem to mind. He wasn't stupid, so how could he not notice that other people thought he was a total dickhead? Breakfast wasn't so bad though. She made her own toast, but the woman called Sheila - she was a kind of cleaner, except Blink called her 'The Housekeeper' - made her use a plate. The blackcurrant jam was disgusting, but she could have eaten the strawberry jam straight out of the jar.

Blink went off to school and she didn't see Josh until she went outside for another fag. He stuck his head out of an upstairs window and asked if she'd go twos. She had planned to save half the fag for later, but he might return the favour next time she couldn't get bacca. There was an awkward silence when he joined her under the tree, so she just gave him the fag and went back inside. She stayed in her room and played with the new phone until the other woman from last night, Lisa, turned up to take her shopping. Delilah would rather have been left alone, but she needed new clothes.

When Gareth, the beardy man, asked if he and Josh could hitch a lift into town, she just shrugged her shoulders. The fact that he didn't give her any shit made Josh alright, but they didn't speak on the journey. Only on the way back did she pluck up the courage to say she liked his new trainers. He went red, but asked what she'd got. They stopped for burgers and fries and Delilah shared another fag with Josh. He said more when Lisa and Gareth weren't around and made out he was a big weed smoker, although she didn't see how he could be when he didn't even have fags. She told him she smoked it when she got the chance and Josh said she could tag along with him that night - his mates always had weed.

So now she was in a flat, freezing cold, but too stoned for it to bother her much. It wasn't very comfortable, sitting on a bit of carpet, and it reminded her of home in an unpleasant way. There was a blanket up at the window and a mattress in the corner with a black stain down the centre. Apart from her and Josh, there were four other lads in there, all of them older. One had some horrible music blasting from his phone. It was so distorted, she couldn't even tell what kind of music it was and the lyrics were just someone shouting and angry. It didn't suit being stoned, but another tune came on that was slower and with less shouting. Delilah was pleased until the others started laughing and making sick comments.

'Do you do that Delilah?' the one called Gaz asked.

She didn't understand the question and just looked at him.

'Leave it out man, she's just a kid,' Josh said.

'She don't smoke like a kid. I bet she's been around. Well, do you?'

'What?' Delilah asked, though she knew he was taking the piss.

'Take it up the booty like eating tutti frutti.'

The others, except Josh, howled with laughter. She scowled at Gaz.

'Fuck off.'

He just grinned back at her.

'Heyyy, I aint hearin' no denial. You got a tight little booty too, innit.'

The way he talked was stupid and annoying, but Delilah was surprised he bothered to talk to her at all. He looked about twenty, was quite fit and wore a gold chain and massively expensive trainers. She wished he would stop staring at her though.

'Fuck off,' she said again, but with less force.

'She aint workin' it man,' one of the others said, shaking his head and laughing.

'Not yet she aint,' Gaz smiled, his eyes still fixed on her face, 'but I'm thinkin' she ready for some education.'

Josh shifted next to her and looked at his phone.

'We gotta go soon. Curfew aint chainin' me, but it's her first night out at Sunny innit.'

Delilah resisted the urge to look at Josh. Now he was talking like a gangsta too, but he didn't speak like that in the day. Gaz leaned forward and offered her a spliff.

'Take your time, baby.'

After a second's hesitation, Delilah took the spliff from him and inhaled deeply. She struggled not to cough - it was much stronger than the others that had been passed around. Her eyes stung, but she didn't want them to think she was just a kid. She took another drag, held it in for three seconds and then blew out a slow stream of smoke whilst staring back at Gaz, hoping her eyes said 'fuck you'. He just pursed his lips and nodded.

6

The email was waiting in her Inbox on Thursday morning, but Becky decided to make a coffee before opening it. She had heard nothing from Delilah, or Sunny Bank, since the moving in on Tuesday night. Neither had she been able to rouse Cleo, though she was at home for a change. Becky was working on the premise that no news was good news - the staff would have called if there had been any serious issues - and was reluctant to make any impression on that happy bubble by reading reality in black and white text.

Yesterday had been Delilah-free, but catching up on her other cases had made her realise how behind she now was. Sighing, Becky carried her coffee back to her desk. Maybe if Delilah did settle, it would be a good time to think about a career break; come off the pill and take full advantage of the maternity benefits available. Maybe…as long as Simon didn't wind her up to the point of leaving him in the meantime. The silent disapproval thing was beginning to needle her in a big way.

Stop, stop, stop - focus on the matter at hand. She clicked on the email, not realising how tense she was until her shoulders sagged with relief at the content.

Hi Becky

Just a quick update on Delilah, as requested.

No issues so far. She made and ate breakfast on Wednesday morning, went shopping for new clothes and

appears to be interacting positively with everyone. She also had dinner - no apparent eating disorders - and went out with Josh in the evening. They were late in, but only by an hour and to be honest, we were expecting worse as Josh is prone to bending the rules.

Only concerns at present are her smoking and education. Gareth asked her about going to school this morning and Delilah became withdrawn immediately. Gareth didn't press the point, but clearly this is something that needs addressing. Has any work been done with Delilah previously re smoking?

Regards,

Julie Montrose
Manager
Sunny Bank Children's Home

Becky typed a quick reply, stating that she had a meeting with Education Welfare later in the day and promising to send potential dates for the Personal Education Plan meeting. The PEP would take some setting up, but at least Delilah's school should take some responsibility for maintaining it...assuming they weren't planning to exclude her. She'd find out later, but needed to focus now on preparing for a Core Group meeting on another of her young people.

Everything had to go smoothly today. She'd promised to be home on time, as Simon's sister and her husband were coming for dinner. At least Simon was cooking and they'd bring a decent bottle of wine. They were pleasant enough company, but she'd rather order a takeaway and curl up on the settee to watch crap tv, just her and Simon. They needed to get over the polite wall that had risen between them before anyone came around, banging on about the lack of babies. Thinking of polite walls, she hadn't spoken to McGrath about Jim wanting contact. But the meeting agenda had to come first - she'd tackle the email later.

It was more than four hours before she returned to her desk. The Core Group meeting had begun well, with a first appearance by the girl's parents and a report of improved attendance from the school, but when the school nurse had raised the issue of the child's sexual activity, the father lost it. She understood his reluctance to accept that his little baby was no longer sweet and innocent, but not his refusal to allow the nurse to discuss and provide protection against pregnancy and STDs. It wouldn't stop those things being addressed - the nurse would see her away from the home - but the meeting had degenerated into a shouting match and in the end, the police had to be called to remove the irate father.

The necessary report would now take her over an hour to write and the meeting had lasted three times longer than scheduled. Damn the man. If he was so bloody protective, then why was his 13 year old daughter out every night with much older boys? But then his own history did not include a loving or stable family background, so how would he know how to create one? It was this relentless cycle that depressed her most about her job.

'Let go of your hair and wrap your fingers round this.'

'Oh!'

Becky had not seen Bill approach and started upright, embarrassed to be caught with her elbows on the desk and head in her hands. She took the mug from him.

'Bad day?' he asked.

'Yes, but nothing a cup of tea won't improve. Thanks.'

'You're welcome to dump on me for ten minutes.'

Becky snorted, but managed to cover with a gasp and a wave of her hand at the steam from her mug. How infantile. She was supposed to be a professional.

'I'd love to...to have a rant Bill, but I've got a horrendous amount to do and I need to leave on time.'

'Anything you can pass over?'

'Not really; a report, several logs and at least six emails. I do appreciate the offer though.'

'Ok, I'll leave you to it.'

He wandered off and Becky reflected that Bill was the thing that depressed her least about her job. If only Simon could be so supportive. She glanced at her watch and winced. The possibility of 'early' was now gone, 'on time' was looking less likely and 'late' loomed like bad weather on the horizon. She fired off a couple of emails and made four log entries that were so sparse, they would definitely cause comment in supervision if they were examined. She started on the report and after staring at the screen without action for eight precious minutes, chose to approach it like a rant to Bill and edit later.

It was alarming to find seventeen 'fuck's in two sides of A4 during the editing process. Becky also removed most of the 'and then's, replaced several bouts of wailing with 'visibly upset' and altered 'father is blinkered and ignorant' to read 'father has difficulty accepting his daughter's adolescence'. That would have to do. She sent if off to those parties concerned and checked the time display at the bottom of the screen: 17:37. She'd told Simon that she would definitely be home by 6 o'clock at the very, very latest and it was a thirty minute drive, so the Jim thing would have to wait.

But he'd texted yesterday. He was a completely unsuitable friend for Delilah. But he'd been instrumental in finding her. And she was now safely ensconced at Sunny Bank with her own peer group. But those young people got into the kinds of trouble that Jim would know more about than she did. Although the police had a handle on it and she was a social worker, not a detective cultivating an informant. But what if Jim turned up at Sunny Bank and the staff were unprepared? She brought up a fresh email and typed in McGrath's address.

Hello Andrew

Jim Travis - the large biker present at the scene of the assault - has asked me to pass his number on to Delilah in case she wants to contact him. I'm reluctant to encourage the friendship, but also familiar with how strong-willed Delilah is.

I am therefore eager to ensure that any meetings between them are conducted openly and with our full knowledge.

You mentioned that Jim has an extensive criminal record. Can you give me any more information about this so that I can make an informed decision? I would also value your personal opinion on the matter. My initial thoughts are that supervised contact, with one of Delilah's key-workers present, would be the most suitable approach.

Kind regards,
Becky

That would have to do. It was now 17:53 and Simon was going to be livid. Still, tomorrow was Friday.

~ ~ ~

He had been staring at the screen so long that the screen-saver kicked in. McGrath made no move to refresh it - he wouldn't forget the content of the email. The word conundrum sprang to mind, although he couldn't remember the last time he'd used it. There should be no question that Jim Travis was an unsuitable adult to have anything to do with minors, unless it was to deliver 'the reality of prison' lectures to young offenders. He had appalling form.

Most of Jim's convictions were for violent assaults. He'd been investigated in the cases of two unsolved murders - suspected gang hits - and there were clear links to a biker gang known to be involved in money laundering, drug running, prostitution and hired muscle. There were old drugs convictions for the possession of cannabis, amphetamine and cocaine, including one charge of dealing that had been dropped to possession because a key witness had withdrawn their statement. The man was a very unsavoury character on paper, but he was also Delilah's friend.

McGrath had to admit that his instinct - which had served him bloody well over the years - told him that Jim was alright. Had they met twenty years earlier, he was sure his feelings would have been different, but people did mellow with age and experience. None of that counted in terms of weighing up the facts. This was not a police decision however; the final call lay with the social worker. If he gave her all the relevant information, then his duty was done.

He hit reply and listed all of Jim's convictions including his links to the murder investigations and gang involvement. Although he was tempted to add that these ties appeared to have been severed since his most recent sentence, McGrath knew that it was impossible to withdraw from that scene without a change of identity. Jim would still be well connected, if you could call it that, but of more concern was the likelihood that rival gang members would still want him dead.

How Becky was going to justify any kind of contact between Jim and Delilah was beyond him, but at the end of the email, he wished her luck. He hoped she would pick up on his offer to discuss the matter further. There was no way he was going to commit his personal opinion to digital record, but he thought her approach was very wise. It would be far better to know exactly what Jim Travis was up to.

They were no closer to an arrest for the attack on Delilah's neighbour. In fact, the only lead was some intel from the drug squad, who suspected that cannabis was being sold from the property. She was operating under the radar, until an undercover operation on a big fish from Leeds, led to several smaller fish in Sheffield and then on to Shona's semi-detached council house. It corroborated what McGrath's nose had told him, but the drug squad weren't interested in an ageing hippy who still liked to get high with her ageing hippy friends.

McGrath thought there was more to it than that, but he didn't have the time or resources to pursue a case in which the victim was not just uncooperative, but, he suspected, feeding them misleading information. He had done a background check on Shona's son and found a series of convictions that escalated in severity, beginning with shop-lifting and ending in possession of a large quantity of amphetamine. Half way down the list was an aggravated assault and he thought that 'nasty little shit' was probably a fair assessment of Paulie. Her son's involvement would also explain Shona's vague account of the attack and insistence that the perpetrator was 'oldish' without providing any kind of description.

He shook his head and pushed the growing saga around Delilah to one side; his present workload did not allow for reprioritisation based on personal interest. If people chose to live outside the law, then they had to sort their own problems out. It was just a crying shame that so many kids got dragged into their parents' chaotic and criminal activities, without having the opportunity to choose otherwise.

~ ~ ~

He awoke on Friday feeling drained and exhausted, but Derek's conscience would not allow him to rest in peace. He was almost certain that the missing cigarettes were just that; missing cigarettes. Delilah could have taken the money and mobile phone if she wanted - his car keys for that matter - and would have had little inclination to explore confidential files about people she didn't know. But he couldn't be sure and he couldn't explore the matter further without dropping both Delilah and himself right in it. However much his rational mind tried to put it in perspective, the bored and frustrated part of his brain imagined fantastical scenarios with horrendous consequences, just for something to do. He needed to get back to work.

Talia returned from taking the kids to school as he was getting up. She said he was crazy, pointed out that she'd only managed to reclaim the bathroom the previous evening and stated that she would not run around after him if he had a relapse. She would never keep her word on that - Talia was a wonderful wife and mother; looking after her family, working part-time *and* studying for a degree in social work - but he knew that she struggled with many elements of his job and thought he gave too much.

Both his sets of grandparents were from Jamaica, but Derek's parents were from Birmingham and he had been born in Derby. He'd visited Jamaica several times and loved it, but he was British and this was his home. Talia, his beautiful African queen, had been born in Kenya, coming to the UK when she was seven years old. Her life had not been easy and she and her siblings had worked hard to integrate into an unfamiliar society. She could not believe the ingratitude of the children under his care, their flagrant disregard for the law, or that Derek was expected to take the verbal and sometimes physical abuse that he did, without being able to retaliate.

Since the start of her studies however, Talia's understanding of relativity was developing well. Gareth got more flak than he did anyway; the earnest young man was a staunch Catholic and had taken the sins of the church upon his own shoulders. When he first arrived at Sunny Bank, Derek feared he would be sucked dry within a few months, but Gareth was tougher than he looked, managing to radiate warmth in the most challenging of situations. The kids called him a pussy, but it was to him they turned when they were really in the shit.

He called Julie, who told him to take another day if he wasn't fully fit, but when he said he felt much better she groaned with relief.

'Thank you so much Derek, I'm on my second shift running and dog tired. Sheila's in this morning and Gareth's here, but Lisa's on training, Mark's mother has been rushed into hospital and none of the others could cover.'

'I'll be there in half an hour.'

Talia shook her head in disapproval, but kissed him goodbye and ran her finger down his face in that way that made his insides melt. For a moment, he regretted his decision to go back to work and trapped her hand against his chest. Talia laughed.

'I'm going to university this morning. We will be together again this evening.'

He stole one last kiss and then set off for the bus stop. His car was still at Sunny Bank.

It was almost lunchtime when Josh and Delilah came downstairs. Gareth said he'd tried to wake Josh up in time for his taxi to the Support Centre, but short of throwing a bucket of water over him, there was little that could coax him out of bed before 11 o'clock these days. He hadn't attended any education for at least a fortnight. Delilah was due to return to school next week, so her lie-in was legitimate. She looked startled to find Derek in the lounge area.

'Good morning...just. Did you two have a late one last night?'

He knew damn well they had. There was also a note in the diary to say that they both appeared to be under the influence of cannabis when they came in, two hours after the agreed time.

'Alright man,' Josh said, nodding at him.

Delilah said nothing, but she looked at him sideways from under a mop of black hair.

'Were you round at Drew's flat?'

'Uh, yeah.'

Josh disappeared into the kitchen and Delilah followed, sneaking a look back at him over her shoulder. Was she nervous about having stolen his cigarettes, or did she just not know any black people? He was amazed by how many of the kids that came through Sunny Bank didn't. Despite the size of the town it was still a rural area and for all their street talk, over half the kids he had worked with had never been to a city. Whenever an opportunity arose, Derek liked to divert outings via the rougher areas of Nottingham; it had reigned in quite a few young lads who thought they were cock of the roost.

He could hear low voices from the kitchen. It was good that these two were getting on - a clash of personalities was hell to manage long term - but Derek would be much happier if Delilah had hooked up with Blink. Not that that was very likely, but there were serious concerns about the people Josh was mixing with and Derek was quite sure that they had not been at Drew's flat. He suspected that Josh hadn't seen Drew for months. The local youth workers were great at feeding back information and Josh no longer visited any of the regular hang-outs that young people in the area used. When he was seen, it was with a bunch of older youths who were in their late teens or twenties.

Having given them ten minutes, Derek went through to the kitchen.

'No way! How do you make that many crumbs?' he said and laughed.

It was just a comment to ease his entrance, but then he noticed that Delilah was using a serrated knife to butter her toast. He took a butter knife out of the drawer and chucked it onto the worktop.

'You might want to try that on the next slice.' He turned around before she could react and went to lean on the table. 'Josh, I know you won't want to talk right now, but I could do with us having a chat before you disappear off anywhere.'

'Bout what?'

He sounded defensive and Derek realised that he might be in with a chance; maybe Josh would prefer to talk about school than be asked questions about his new friends.

'Quite a few things, but the most pressing is school.'

'Ah, don't start man, I fucking hate that place.'

'I know and you're voting with your feet. But I also want to know that you understand what will happen next.'

'Meetings. And more fucking meetings.'

Derek smiled and nodded, throwing a quick look at Delilah, who had her back to them but was obviously listening.

'I can't deny that you're right, but those meetings will have consequences. You might want to go through this in private, later.'

'Nah, she's alright and I'm not bothered anyway. So what'll happen?'

'Well apart from the lack of qualifications, you're on a Rehabilitation Order already and have further charges pending. If it's decided that a lack of education is partially to blame for your offending behaviour, then going to school can be made part of your next court order. You'll have to go.'

'Or what? They don't do nothing anyway, they just talk at me.'

'That's the point. If it's part of your order, then going to school is like an appointment with the Youth Offending Team - if you miss a few, then you can be taken back to court for breaching your order.'

'Breached? For not going to fucking school?'

'That's where you're heading. For the record, I don't think that crew you're hanging around will help you stay out of court.'

Josh scowled.

'What the fuck do you know?'

He spun around and punched the fridge. Derek was about to call for support when Delilah, unperturbed by the violent outburst, threw in a question.

'Which school is it?'

'It isn't - it's the fucking Support Centre. I got kicked out of school.'

'Can't be as bad as Woodlands.'

'Ha! Is that where you're at? What a shithole.'

'I know.'

Derek was stunned. It often took several hours for Josh to calm down once he was wound up, but now he was chatting to Delilah like the last five minutes hadn't happened.

'Can you smoke at the Support Centre?'

'At dinner, if you go off site.'

'Do you have to wear uniform?'

'Nah, fuck that.'

Delilah turned and looked him straight in the eye for the first time. Her eyes were very blue, her face still and her stare so direct that Derek found it disconcerting.

'Can I go to the Support Centre?'

~ ~ ~

Becky's heart was already low, after an awkward evening with Simon's sister and a silent breakfast this morning. It sank further as she read the list of convictions in McGrath's email. She would certainly look at Jim Travis in a different light when they next met. The last paragraph seemed straightforward, but she sensed that McGrath wanted to say more. Whether to warn her of unofficial suspicions or to approve her intentions, she wasn't sure, but he did wish her luck in determining the best way forward. He was covering his back well. It would be her tied to the whipping post if this went wrong.

She found his number and dialled, but was told that he would not be in until mid-afternoon. Bugger. It was action she needed, not contemplation of her to-do list, which just allowed her mind to wander to the weekend ahead. The beep of her phone was a welcome distraction, until she read the text. Its timing was so coincidental that she looked around the office for an unfamiliar face. With her new knowledge of Jim, she would not have been surprised to find a fake courier or electrician reading emails over her shoulder.

Hi Becky. If it makes things easier, my idea of seeing D is to meet up with her & Shona & take Crank for a walk via McD's. Jim

He seemed to understand the difficulty. Shona might not be what Becky would call a responsible adult, but was at least female and a neighbour. Crank, she assumed, was the dog. Jim was playing by the book and all of his actions so far had resulted in positive outcomes for Delilah. An over-reaction to an un-planned meeting between them would be less likely to have a positive outcome. She hit the dial button and he answered after one ring.

'Hello.'

'Hi Jim. Thanks for the text - you must have read my mind.'

'I just know you'll have looked me up.'

'And you also know, better than I do, how your history reads in the system, but for the record, I don't think you have any ill intentions towards Delilah.'

'Good, because I don't, but I don't mind the checks either. The care system used to be a sack of shit, this is an improvement.'

'I'm pleased you think so.'

But she wasn't. That was a very ominous take on things. If it was the care system that had turned Jim into what he was, then he could be one of the thousands who suffered abuse in past decades, which had all sorts of implications. She would have to explore further, but couldn't do a U-turn now.

'I like the idea of a walk with Crank. Is he your dog?'

'Yeah. He and Delilah are good friends.'

'Ah yes, I remember now. Well if you can guarantee that Shona will be with you and that you'll let me know about any arrangements you make, then I'll give Delilah your number.'

'Thanks.'

'It's quite a responsibility you know. Delilah is no angel and if she gets into any trouble while she's supposed to be with you, then a lot of questions will be asked.'

'I appreciate the warning. It might be a fuss about nowt anyway, it'd be better if she makes new friends over there and doesn't want to hang around with us oldies. I just don't want her to feel abandoned.'

Because he knew how that felt? He seemed to have more empathy than most of the parents she dealt with.

'I'm glad you understand that she might not contact you.'

'I know and that's fine. As long as it's her choice. I'll let you know either way.'

'Great, well, thank you and we'll probably speak again soon.'

'Alright. Bye.'

He hung up and Becky took the phone from her ear, looking at it for a moment. She would send an email describing the arrangement and the circumstances around it to the staff at Sunny Bank, and copy in McGrath, before sending Delilah the number. She would also have to try and contact Cleo again in case Delilah asked about her. So far, she had honoured her promise to wait for Becky to arrange contact between them, but if there was no mobile number soon, never mind a visit organised, Delilah would make her own way home.

Still, Delilah was seeing her other friend, Jono, tomorrow, so that would hopefully occupy her a little longer.

~ ~ ~

For the first time ever, Delilah felt some reluctance about visiting Jono. It wasn't that she didn't want to see him, but he would ask lots of questions and she didn't want to tell him about her last few evenings. She wasn't even sure what she would say if she did. It was nice to get out of Sunny Bank to a decent place, where you could sit and smoke. It was nice that Gaz and the other lads didn't treat her like a kid. It was nice to have a friend like Josh. But she didn't like it when they laughed about things that made no sense.

Sometimes she thought they were laughing at her without saying, but Gaz would just call her silly and paranoid. He had bought her cider on Thursday night, but she had refused it. When her mum drank cider, it made her red and stupid and Delilah didn't want to look like that. Last night he'd given her a whole pouch of tobacco and a packet of papers, even when she said she'd got no money. Her mum had only given her one Superking on her birthday.

Becky said she would post a letter giving her mum her new number, but she also said she was still drinking and might not call her straight away. Delilah knew by the way she said it that her mum was on a binge. She was horrible on a binge, so her not calling was a good thing. Becky also gave her Jim's number, but said she must tell the staff at Sunny Bank if she decided to meet up with him. That was a bit weird and she couldn't work out why Jim wanted her to call...unless it was really Shona and she just didn't have a mobile.

The end of Jono's drive came into view and Delilah stopped. She would sit on the wall and have a fag first. It wasn't that she fancied Gaz, well not much...she didn't think so anyway. And McGrath had made her and Jono swear they wouldn't do anything, so it wasn't cheating, even if Gaz giving her tobacco meant that she was with him or something. Josh said she might owe Gaz if she took stuff off him. But she didn't take the cider, just the tobacco and she wouldn't take anything else.

Jono was waiting in the doorway when she turned down the drive. It felt stupid, walking, while he sat watching. She didn't know where to put her feet. As she got closer, his big grin came into view and though she tried to frown, Delilah couldn't stop her lips curling.

'Hey Dee,' he called. 'Those look like new jeans to me, you must be making the most of the care system already.'

She shrugged, but then blurted out,

'I've got a new coat too and shoes and...some other things.'

She blushed, having almost told him about the underwear that Lisa had helped her choose, including three bras. She had never worn a bra before. But Jono was already spinning his chair around and didn't notice her glowing face. Delilah walked up the ramp and followed him into the house. He was taking a bottle of coke from the fridge and she could see two plates of sandwiches and a bowl of crisps on the worktop. It was a proper meal, not just snacks.

'So how come you're only here for lunch and not staying? Have you got a hot date tonight?'

She was glad he was pouring the coke and not looking at her.

'No, as if. I'm just going out.'

'Have you got some new mates? That's cool.'

'Just Josh - he lives in the home too - but he's got other mates.

She didn't want to talk about them.

'What about the other lad? I thought there were two at Sunny Bank.'

'Oh that's Blink. He's just...well, he's always at school.'

'So you're not?'

'No and I'm not going back to Shitlands.'

Jono raised his eyebrows at that, so she told him about the Support Centre that Josh went to and that Derek was going to bring it up at a meeting next week. She'd also sent Becky a text about it and was pleased when Jono said he was impressed. It was a good trick to learn - start talking about school and everyone got excited. Jono put the bowl of crisps in his lap and picked up the plate of sandwiches, wheeling himself one-handed over to the table.

'Are you going to bring the drinks over?'

She carried them across and sat down on the only chair. It was odd - she'd only ever sat on the settee before.

'Can't we just eat in front of the telly?'

'Right, so you kick up a stink about not being able to see me, but actually, you only want to come round here to watch films on the big screen. Isn't there a tv at Sunny Bank?'

'Yeah, but there're always people around, always someone wanting to talk to you. It does my head in.'

'It's certainly a bit more company than you're used to.'

'Loads more. They have, like, at least three staff on *all* the time and then Blink's always trying to tell me boring things, or get me to play some crap game. It was shit when Mum went out and there was no food, or the leccy had gone off, but most of the time I was glad when she went. I don't mind it on my own.'

Delilah stopped. She'd been talking for ages, so she ate a sandwich instead. Jono was watching her with a weird expression on his face, but he smiled when she looked up.

'Well this can be your safe haven then. You can come here once a week and just be quiet if you like, as long as we can have a half hour chat before we stop speaking.'

His smile changed back to the normal sly one and Delilah relaxed. It was beginning to feel the same as always. She told him about her room and showed him her phone. Jono talked about how his basketball team were going to thrash the other side at a match tomorrow and how there were a lot more people coming to watch now. She wouldn't want to watch, it must be sad to see all those men stuck in wheelchairs. They'd finished the sandwiches.

'There's a chocolate pudding in the fridge. Grab it if you want it and I'll find something decent on the movie channel.'

Delilah slid off the chair and went to the fridge. Jono bought great munch, even though he didn't eat much of it himself. She was glad they could just watch a film. Being around him without talking or doing much was even better than being alone.

The film seemed to last less than an hour, although it was 4:57 when she looked at her phone. It was nearly time to go and now she felt torn, like she had to go back to being someone else.

'Have you got to split?' Jono asked.

She nodded, not wanting to start talking again.

'Do you want to come back next week? Same time, same place?'

She nodded again and stood up. He spun his chair around and beat her to the hallway, turning to grin at her when he'd opened the door.

'Good to see you Dee and you look great. I think Sunny Bank suits you.'

She scowled at him, but remembered to mutter 'thanks' as she left. Just before she reached the end of the drive she turned to look and Jono was still in his doorway, watching her. He raised a hand and she waved back, feeling better but a little bit sad. She stopped around the corner to roll a fag and realised that she hadn't smoked the whole time she'd been at Jono's. No wonder she was gasping now.

Gareth was on duty when she got back and wanted to know all about her afternoon. He was proper wet for a bloke, but it was difficult to dis' him when he just kept smiling. He might even be a bit nuts. Delilah thought back to all the embarrassing shit that Becky and McGrath had gone on about and decided to head him off instead of ignoring him.

'It was good, we had sandwiches and watched a film. I didn't even smoke.'

His big smile broke into a soppy grin.

'That's wonderful! So will you make it a regular thing?'

'Yeah, I'm going again next week. Is Josh in?'

'He's in his room.'

Delilah headed for the stairs, but Blink appeared from the lounge.

'Delilah! I d..didn't know you were b..back.'

'My name's Dee.'

She tried to walk around him, but he put his arm out.

'H..hang on. G..gareth's on about t..taking us to the p..pictures. Will you c..come?'

'Nah, I watched a film this afternoon.'

'B..but he'll buy us s..sweets and a d..d..d..d...'

He got stuck on whatever the next word was and Delilah ducked under his arm, cringing with embarrassment. She hated talking to Blink when he went like that. She didn't know where to look and he was always ten times worse when he spoke to her than if he was talking to Gareth or Derek. She ran up the stairs and was on the landing when he got his voice back.

'Delilah!'

She ignored him and went to knock on Josh's door, but was struck by the fact that Blink never, ever stuttered when he said her name. Josh opened his door a crack.

'I just got out the shower. You comin' out tonight?'

'Yeah.'

'Well I'll wait half an hour if you want a shower too.'

'Uh, yeah, alright.'

The door shut again in front of her nose, so Delilah went to her own room. She'd had a shower yesterday and wouldn't have bothered, but she had noticed that Josh had at least one, if not two showers every day, so maybe she should. The shower gel that Lisa had bought for her smelled lush anyway and once she was under the water, she decided to wash her hair too.

Dressed and back downstairs, she found Gareth trying hard to persuade Josh to go to the cinema instead. Blink was lurking in a corner, looking sulky.

'Delilah, you'll come to the cinema won't you?' Gareth said, clapping his hands together. 'It'll be great fun.'

She raised her eyebrows and shook her head, glancing at Josh. His mouth flicked up at one side and then he pulled a face.

'Fuck that, it's for kids innit. We're out of this, man,' he said, looking at Delilah and jerking his head toward the door.

She followed him out without looking at either Gareth or Blink. They walked up the road without speaking and it was only an unfamiliar turn that roused Delilah from her thoughts.

'Where're we going?'

'Someone else's flat.'

'Who's flat?'

He didn't answer for a minute.

'Who's flat?' she asked again.

'Don't worry, Gaz will be there.'

'Eh?' Delilah frowned, angry at him. 'What did you say that for? I don't care, as long as we can have a smoke.'

Josh didn't answer her and she didn't bother talking to him again.

The flat turned out to be further away than Gaz's, above a shitty, second hand electrical shop, on a dead end street. The usual crew were there, plus a couple of other, even older lads, or men really. They didn't look pleased to see her.

'What the fuck you plannin' to do with the little girl...use her to distract the pigs?' one of them said to Gaz.

He sounded angry, but Gaz laughed it off and came over, putting his arm around her shoulders. She wanted to shrug it off, but it would be rude when he was defending her.

'Delilah's our lucky mascot, see?' he said, pulling her even closer to him. 'She just here to share a spliff and wish us good huntin' and then she going home to bed like a good little girl.'

The man grunted and began talking to his friend, but Gaz did not remove his arm. Delilah didn't like him calling her a 'good little girl' and she thought it was stupid to talk like gangsta rappers, when they were all white. Derek didn't talk like that and he was black, although he wasn't a gangsta.

'So let's go and have that lucky smoke, eh?'

He steered her towards a settee in the far corner of the room. Delilah looked for Josh, but he had his back to them. There was a funny atmosphere, everyone seemed a bit hyper and it put her on edge. And she didn't want to talk to Gaz on her own. What had he meant about 'good hunting'? They reached the settee and he somehow managed to swap arms and pull her down with him. It was low and deep. Her feet didn't touch the floor and the weight of the arm around her neck pressed her side into his chest.

Would Gaz be angry if she pulled away? What would the others do? No one was looking at them. It was her choice to be here after all and they had let her in, even though they didn't really want a kid around. She stayed very still, looking straight ahead, with his face about six inches away from hers. He was staring at her. It went on for so long that her body started to shake, no matter how hard she tried to stop it. Gaz laughed softly, right next to her ear, but he took his arm away and pulled a spliff out of his top pocket. Delilah moved a few inches down the settee while he lit it.

'So, how come you at Sunny Bank?' Delilah shrugged. She wasn't going to tell Gaz about her mum. 'Well, where was you before then?'

'The Assessment Centre, but I ran away.'

'Cool. Was it a great escape, or did you just stroll out of there?'

'I smashed my window and jumped out.'

'Whew!' He leaned back and squinted at her through the smoke. 'Did you fly through the hole like Tinkerbell?'

Delilah didn't know who Tinkerbell was, but it was an even worse name than Delilah. Gaz laughed and passed her the spliff. He was watching her smoke, so she tried to hold it in longer. The effect was immediate and she wondered if there was more than just weed in the spliff. She passed it back. Didn't he believe her about the window?

'I jumped through it and cut my arm.'

'No way! Was it bad?'

'It's still got a dressing on.'

'Let me see.'

He didn't believe her. Delilah thought about it; she was wearing her new bra which was embarrassing, but at least he would see that she wasn't a little girl. She shrugged off her coat and pulled off the two jumpers she was wearing, stripping down to her strap vest. It was cold. Gaz passed her the spliff again and touched her arm near the dressing, but he was looking at her bra. A few seconds passed and he was still looking at her bra. Delilah offered him the spliff back and reached for her jumper with the other hand, but he put his hand over hers.

'Lemme see the cut, you might be covering nothin'. Keep smokin' and the plaster won't hurt.'

Delilah just looked at him. He released her hand and took the edge of the large plaster between his finger tips, looking into her eyes as he peeled it back, very, very slowly. It pulled at her skin and was making the cut hurt, but she didn't flinch. The plaster was almost off and he still didn't look away. Bastard.

'Aren't you going to look at the cut?'

It was Gaz who wrenched his eyes away first, not her. He looked at the three inch ridge of scab for a few seconds and then gently pressed the plaster back into place. His hand moved up her shoulder and across to her neck, his palm pressing against the top of her chest. His fingers curled behind her neck and he started to pull her towards him. Delilah thought she was resisting, but her body still moved. Was he going to kiss her? She'd never kissed anyone before.

His face was just inches away, his eyes weird and spooky, when the main door opened again and several cheers greeted a new arrival. They both jumped and Delilah began to breathe again. Gaz looked back at her and was about to say something, when the man who had moaned about her being there shouted that they needed to get moving.

'What? It's still well early man,' Gaz said.

'We've got a drive tonight and we can't hang around waiting for you to get your dick wet. Come on.'

Delilah was surprised - Gaz was usually the boss. He looked angry.

'Sorry babe, you better go.'

He stood up and held a hand out to her, but she ignored it and got to her feet.

'Look, it's gonna be busy the next few days. Give me your number.'

He pulled his phone out and looked at her, so Delilah told him the number. The others were pushing their way through the door except the boss man, who was watching her and Gaz. She thought Gaz might try and kiss her again, but he just said 'see ya' and pushed his way into the group. She could see the back of Josh's head disappearing through the door ahead of him and hurried to follow, aware that the only person behind her was the horrible man. As the group moved down the narrow corridor, he got so close that his body started to press against her, even though she moved right up behind two of Gaz's mates.

Fear made her heart thump. What if he grabbed her? The outside door was only a few feet away, but they were moving quite slowly. She yanked on the coat of the lad to the left and he turned, lifting his arm. He swore when Delilah shoved her way through the gap and he pushed her in the back, but she didn't care, she was now outside. Josh was standing next to a dirty white van and she went over to him, but he had his hood up and didn't look at her. Why was he being so arsey?

'Are you coming then?'

He put his hands in his pockets and scuffed at the floor with his foot.

'Nah, I'm out with these. Tell Gareth I'm stoppin' at Drew's flat.'

'Alright,' Delilah said, but she was pissed off. 'Why did you bring me if you knew I had to stay behind?'

'Cos Gaz told me to ask you.'

'Oh.

Everyone else was now in the van and someone shouted at Josh to get in. He did, the door was pulled shut and van drove up the street. Delilah was left standing on the pavement and feeling stupid. It was only 8 o'clock, but she didn't know the area yet, or the people. Even if there was a park or something, there might be another gang like Doogie's and she was tired. The evening had been too weird already. She rolled a fag and set off, but soon realised she was on a street she hadn't seen before. Swearing, she turned around to re-trace her steps.

7

Derek yawned without bothering to cover his mouth. He was an hour off the end of his shift and still felt weak and dithery from the food poisoning. Julie was in the office and Gareth was out with Blink. God only knew where Josh and Delilah were. It was an hour before their 10 o'clock Saturday curfew, which Derek thought reasonable for Josh at 16, but a bit late for Delilah at just 14. He knew the issue was being brushed under the carpet because Delilah was integrating well and although they were both coming in late, Josh returned much earlier when he had Delilah in tow. Her presence was having a positive impact on Josh, but Derek was not so sure the effect would be reciprocated.

No one had yet got to the bottom of who he was hanging around with and Delilah was young and vulnerable. He had read through her file again this afternoon. The background information was circumstantial and there were no recent psychological or health assessments, but a report written by a school nurse five years ago expressed concern about Delilah's sexualised language and explicit knowledge on the subject. It wasn't surprising with a mother who was a sex worker, but sexually aware young girls and groups of older youths were not a good mix.

The front door opened and thumped closed again. Derek headed for the hall, hoping it was Lisa early for handover and surprised to find Delilah instead. She looked mad about something.

'Hi. No Josh with you...is everything ok?'

'Yeah. Except I got fucking lost.'

No Josh for some time then.

'Lost? Where did you go?'

'I don't fucking know, or I wouldn't have been fucking lost.'

It was a good point and he bit back a smile to avoid winding her up further. Maybe it was just anger at Josh for abandoning her, or maybe she had run away from something she didn't like. She wasn't just angry, but agitated. He wanted more information, but would get nothing if she went to her room. She was already heading for the stairs.

'Hey, you must be freezing if you've been walking about for ages. You've almost got the place to yourself, so why don't I go and make you a mug of the best hot chocolate you've ever had and you crash on the settee, stick the tv on and chill for a bit.'

She stopped, but still had her back to him, so Derek legged it to the kitchen before she could think herself out of it. He put the kettle on and then rang Julie, asking her not to send Lisa through when she came in. He would do a full handover after he had talked to Delilah...if she was still there.

Pleased to find a bag of mini marshmallows in the cupboard, he put two sachets in the mug to make the drink extra thick and then poured a good inch of the pink and white sweets onto the top. He took the mug and a spoon back to the lounge and was relieved to find Delilah perched on the edge of the settee. She looked ready to run, squinting with suspicion at the mug when he held it out.

'What's that?'

'Hot chocolate; the deluxe version, with marshmallows.' He put the mug on the coffee table and passed her the spoon. 'You can either drink it through the marshmallows, or stir them in.'

He stood and watched while Delilah poked at the marshmallows and then began stirring slowly. She seemed to like the pale swirls that the melting marshmallows created.

'Try it, it tastes even better than it looks,' he said, sitting down and picking up the remote control for the tv. 'Have you worked out how to use this yet? It took me a couple of weeks.'

Delilah shook her head, but didn't look up from the chocolate. Derek wondered if she even had a tv; the social worker said that there was nothing of any value in the house and Delilah had often been to neighbours for food. The most recent email had

104

mentioned walking a dog. If she was into animals in general, the Nature Channel would blow her mind. He flicked through, looking for lions or elephants, but found there was an underwater theme this evening.

'What's that?!' Delilah said from beside him.

Derek stopped his surfing.

'A sea horse. Pretty, isn't it.'

'What, like a horse that lives in the sea?' She sounded disbelieving. 'That's gotta be bollocks.'

'I don't think they're too much like horses, apart from the shape of the head and neck. They're quite tiny. There are loads of crazy things that live at the bottom of the ocean. Shall I leave this on for a bit?'

Delilah shrugged, but could not disguise her interest. Derek wondered what level of education she was at. She seemed bright enough, but was clearly missing some large chunks of experience. With any luck, the social worker would have set something up already, but he would talk to Julie and make sure that a visit was planned by the LAC Nurse. He wanted to ask about Josh - what had happened, where he was - but Delilah seemed edgy enough to leg it if she thought he was prying.

'This looks like a great programme. I'm going to make a coffee and see if Julie wants one.' Delilah ignored him, absorbed in the images on the screen. He got up and took a few steps, then stopped, as if just remembering something. 'Where is Josh by the way?'

Delilah's eyes moved half way towards him and she shrugged, frowning, but then her face changed a little.

'Oh yeah, he's gone to Drew's flat.'

Ha. Not bloody likely.

'Right. Have you met Drew yet?'

Delilah looked full at him, thinking about this for a moment. She must have reached the conclusion that she would not stand up to any further questioning.

'No. We were just out and he was going to Drew's and I didn't want to, so I came back here.'

'Ok, thanks.'

Derek walked away, considering the possibilities. 1) They had simply had an argument. 2) Josh had a girlfriend he was staying with. 3) Josh was doing something that Delilah didn't want to get involved in. 4) Josh was doing something that he didn't want Delilah involved in. 5) Josh's mates didn't want Delilah around. 6) Delilah didn't much like Josh's mates. The last conclusion was his favourite, but the least likely. This one had suffered a lack of attention for too long.

Julie never said no to coffee, so Derek made two mugs and took them through to the office. She looked surprised when he walked in and glanced at the clock.

'Thanks Derek,' she took the mug from him. 'You must be knackered, but I can't thank you enough for covering today.'

'No problem. I wanted to start getting to know Delilah anyway, although I think it's going to take some intense time and energy to win her trust. I almost wish I could stay a bit longer…she's in there watching tv at the moment, but I daren't say more than a few words at a time. I don't think Josh will be home tonight by the way.'

That grabbed Julie's full attention.

'Oh no! He's been so much better for the last few days. Where do we think he is?'

'Well, the message is that he's staying at Drew's flat, but I stopped believing that tale three weeks ago. Has there been no intel from the police?'

'No, not a thing. Either he's with a stay-at-home bunch, or they're more clever than I care to think about. He doesn't have the money for train fares does he?'

'No, but that doesn't stop one of them having car.'

'Ok. We'll give him until midnight and then report him missing.'

'Good luck with that,' Derek said. 'I'm going to go and sit with Delilah until Lisa arrives.'

He was just leaving the office when the front door opened again. Blink walked in, clutching a bag of sweets and a huge drinking cup.

'Hi Derek. The film was b..brilliant! You should have c..come.'

Gareth smiled at him over Blink's shoulder. At least they'd had a good evening. Blink started telling him about the film with just a light stutter and then registered the sound of the tv in the lounge.

'Are Josh and Delilah b..back?'

'Just Delilah. Why don't you go through?' Blink looked towards the lounge and hesitated. 'Shall I bring you a hot chocolate?'

'No thanks, I've s..still got some C..coke.'

Blink headed for the lounge and Derek turned to Gareth.

'I'm just going to loiter outside the lounge. Julie's in the office.'

He followed Blink at a cautious distance, stopping short of the doorway.

'Hi Delilah,' he heard Blink say.

'Alright.'

That was interesting - she normally protested at his use of her full name.

'You're b..back early.'

'Yeah.'

Pause.

'W..w..what are you w..watching?'

'Dunno. Something Derek put on.'

Long pause.

'I s..saved you some s..sw..sweets.'

There was another pause, and then a rustle of paper, and then movement on the settee. Had Blink sat down? Another short silence.

'Thanks,' Delilah said.

Derek smiled with satisfaction and crept back to the office. Perhaps it was not such a bad thing for Josh to be out for the night.

~ ~ ~

Shona woke on Sunday without the feeling of dread that had swamped her existence for a week. She hadn't reached cheerful, but was looking forward to getting up and making a cup of coffee. Another concern had morphed into a minor inconvenience overnight. Jim had given her a thousand pounds to pay off the loan man for a few months and she would even be able to go food shopping later.

Whatever Jim used to be, he was turning into a regular hero now. No-one had ever stepped in and sorted out her problems before - it was always she who everyone turned to when they wanted help. The only remaining source of fear was Paulie. Not just how far he would go next time, but what kind of trouble had driven him to these extremes and then, what would happen if Jim found out it was Paulie who had beaten and robbed her. She was quite sure her errant son would not show his face for a good few weeks however, so she pushed that last thought aside and got up.

The tidy up in the kitchen turned into a full deep clean of the house and by mid-morning, the place looked quite different. Shona went outside to empty the hoover bag and saw a man half running down Kelly's path, a look of disgust on his face. Kelly was standing in the doorway and Shona winced. His beer goggles must have been thick indeed - she looked more like a badly made-up corpse than a human being. Still bringing home punters while her daughter was in care. Shona shook her head, but felt a spurt of sympathy towards the woman. She almost called out, but Kelly's head lolled to one side, she staggered backwards and then the door closed.

~ ~ ~

The buzz of winning the basketball match carried Jono through the evening. Every time there was a flutter in his belly related to tomorrow, he relived his 11th hoop and heard the shouts and cheers from the audience. And there *had* been an audience, a crowd in fact, with a few lone watchers even sitting in the dead spot on the stand from where you couldn't see the scoreboard. He was fit and strong - he was man of the match. But still, he didn't want to face some clueless idiot from the benefits agency in the morning, telling him about ways in which he could make a 'positive contribution to society'.

He was almost ready. Six years might look a long time on paper, but he could still remember the freedom as if it were just a few months distant. On the flip side, another corner of his mind stored the virtual negatives of memory, stamped with every detail of every minute that had passed since the accident. For three years he had been in and out of hospital, undergoing operation after operation, each followed by intensive physiotherapy. When the doctors said there was nothing more they could do, he had poured every ounce of energy into adapting to his new life.

On good days, Jono considered himself lucky - he had achieved independence and was even rebuilding his social life, albeit with an entirely new set of people. On bad days he cursed God, cursed Fate, cursed the friend on belay who hadn't managed to prevent the fall, cursed the friend who'd got him into climbing in the first place, cursed the rest of the friends who had slipped away, one by one, cursed the paramedic who saved his life. The bad days were growing fewer and he had been thinking and planning for the future, but it needed to be in his own time.

Seeking distraction, he went online and logged in to one of the chat-rooms he had started frequenting. It was the easiest way of practising his social skills, something which he had not consciously thought of before. They'd slipped away without him noticing - he bought everything online and rarely received visitors. His parents didn't count. It was only when he joined the rest of the basketball team in the pub, after his first match, that he found most of the confident banter of his youth gone. His perspective on life had altered beyond recognition, but here, in the virtual world, he could be whoever he wanted to be.

There was a lot of buzz from the rest of the guys in the team under the hash tag 'champions' and someone had posted an amazing picture of his 11th hoop, the ball still two feet above its target. Jono threw in a few comments and left the page open, opening another profile in a different browser. The familiar thrill went through him; half fear, half excitement. He didn't know whether it was morally wrong or not to pretend he was someone else - he had no intention of meeting any of the people he talked to under the pseudonym 'Jonny Too Good'.

He wasn't even pretending he was someone else, just someone he used to be, on a site that was a bit sad and not likely to be visited by any of the old crowd. Jonny Too Good was a climber and mountaineer, fit and fearless, with big plans and a yearning to visit distant countries. He lived in a flat, not a bungalow and went to wild parties at weekends. The profile picture was real and his well-muscled chest attracted interest from quite a number of the site's other users, but he had cropped out all sign of the wasted legs below.

There were three new messages. The first was from a nerdy male climber he'd been having the crack with, asking if he'd climbed a particular face and suggesting they hook up one weekend. That would have to be ignored. The second was from a chatty girl who wore too much make-up, but who he'd enjoyed flirting with. He sent a brief but cheeky reply that would prompt a response and then looked at the third message.

The profile picture was of a group of young women leaping up for a netball, the most visible one at the centre stretching her lithe figure in a beautiful and dominant arc. Her shoulder length, blonde hair swung to one side and her mouth was open, perhaps gasping with exertion, leaving her with a sensual expression that stirred something in his belly. The message was definitely suggestive.

Hey, Too Good. You look like quite an adventurer. Do you have prowess in any other sporting fields? ;) Netty Netballer x

Jonny Too Good was a great all-rounder.

Hey Netty. I can hold my own in most fields, but ball games are a speciality. Do your skills go beyond the netball court? Jonny TG x

She was online and replied straight away.

Ball games...are we talking football, snooker, or pocket billiards? As for netball, that is the least of my talents...

Only after ninety-seven minutes did Jono realise the conversation was a mile from its starting point, the heavy-handed flirting having given way to chat about common interests and dreams. Netty was into botany and often walked the moors above Froggatt Edge, where he used to spend many a weekend climbing. They'd both been on wet, miserable holidays, hiking with the Scouts and Guides, both visited EuroDisney and hated it, both wanted to see Ayers Rock in Australia. Their taste in films was bizarrely similar and it was the desire to invite her over for an evening in front of his big screen that brought Jono back to reality.

There had been girlfriends since the accident - three, to be precise, plus a brief encounter. Two were genuine, but the first was highly irritating and only lasted a fortnight and the second left him after four months because she couldn't cope with his disability. The third he had met through a dubious website that a guy from basketball recommended. It was a fetish site that catered for a wide range of 'legal but alternative sexual interests', including those who had a penchant for the physically disabled.

Dominique - the name should have given him a clue - revealed herself as a leather-clad dominatrix within twenty minutes of knocking on his front door. He went along with it for the experience, but found little satisfaction. Clara - the brief encounter he met through the same site - he had asked to leave within an hour. She was just...weird. He had deleted his profile ten minutes later.

Last weekend, when Dee called round horribly early, was the first time a girl had stayed over since then. She was the sister of one of his basketball mates and they got on well, but he didn't think things would develop beyond friendship. She had slept on the settee after drinking too much vodka.

Have you gone to sleep?

The message popped up on the screen in front of him and Jono started, only half pleased to be drawn away from unpleasant memories and back into the conversation. However much he liked Netty, he was lying to her from the outset. Or misleading her at least. It couldn't go anywhere. He ought to leave it alone...or 'fess up.

Nah, call of nature. But I need to hit the sack soon - busy day tomorrow.

He half expected her to hit back with heavy innuendo, but then again, the spiky ladette of the first ten minutes had melted away and his more recent impression was of an outdoorsy, country-loving girl.

Oh yeah - Monday. What kind of hellish day job do you have to go to?

Shit. A *real* lie. Small, or big? It didn't really matter. He cast around for inspiration.

Computers. Boring, but sadly necessary. He didn't want her to ask any more questions, even if he now wanted to know what she did for a living. He should get back into the Two Good mind-set. **Look, I've gotta crash. Great talking to you - we should hook up again sometime. Night.**

He watched the screen, tense with anticipation. His reply was too terse - it wasn't a reasonable end to the conversation that had preceded it. She'd think he was an asshole.

Ok. Night.

Aw, he'd flattened her, but maybe not blown it. His fingers leapt to the keys, but her icon winked out before he could compose a message. He thought about sending one anyway. What wouldn't sound ridiculous after his abrupt farewell? It was 1am and he was tired, better to leave it alone.

Lying in bed, the vision of Netty's open mouth and her shirt pulled taught over high, jutting breasts kept Jono awake. His lower body might not function much, but those memories were still very alive and he took great delight in giving pleasure to others. In the end, he resorted to thinking about his interview tomorrow, but found he wasn't worried any more - the answer was clear. He wanted to work with computers.

~ ~ ~

Monday morning was peaceful in its emptiness, but with Josh still missing, Blink at school and her least favourite members of staff on duty, Delilah found the afternoon beginning to drag. It was too cold to go outside for anything other than for a swift fag and there was nowhere to go within walking distance. She could catch a bus to Jono's, or maybe Shona's, and she had Jim's number now, but that would have to be all 'official' and she couldn't be arsed to sort it out. She had come up to her room to escape interference, but was becoming bored of her own company.

Going downstairs, she found the lounge area empty and flicked the tv on. Blink had shown her how to use the remote control on

Saturday night and again yesterday. He was alright really, just a bit nerdy and annoying and even if she'd moaned at the time, the cooking on Sunday was fun. She had just found a film with Bruce Willis that looked interesting, when the blonde woman came through from the office. Sandra, or Samantha or something. She waffled on, asking stupid questions in a syrupy voice which Delilah ignored, hoping she would go away. The opening credits finished and the first scene brought the whole thing back - it was the one Jono had put on when she went round on Saturday. The one she had stared at without watching, because of all the shit filling her head. She jabbed the off button and threw the remote onto the table.

'What about doing some baking?' Sandra or Samantha said. Dee looked at the id badge around her neck - Sandra. 'I hear you and Blink cooked most of the Sunday dinner yesterday and that's no mean feat. We could try a cake today.'

Delilah frowned. That was actually quite a good idea. She loved cake and it would be amazing to make one whenever you felt like it.

'What...like a chocolate cake?'

'Yes, if we've got the right ingredients. We could go and buy some if not. Why don't we go to the kitchen and have a look.'

Why do you talk to me like I'm 6? But a chocolate cake would be a right result. Delilah stood up and stomped off to the kitchen, but realised she hadn't a clue what to look for. This might be more effort than it was worth. Sandra followed her in and went straight to a cupboard, taking out a large, thin book.

'We've got all sorts of recipe books in here. You can have a look at them, any time you like.' She held it out towards Delilah. 'Pick which cake you want to make and then we can go through the ingredients to see if we've got them.'

There was a chocolate cake on the front cover. It was coated in gooey icing and there was a slice missing, showing three more layers of chocolate inside. Delilah passed the book back.

'That one.'

Sandra looked at it and raised her eyebrows.

'That does look delicious, but also a bit complicated. We can try it another time, if you decide you like baking, but perhaps we should keep it simple for today. There will be an easier recipe for chocolate cake inside, if you have a look.'

And so it went on. Sandra made her do everything and turned it into some kind of lesson. It was almost as bad as being at school, except that when she got really pissed off, she could go outside for a fag. It was ok after they finished going through the stupid list of ingredients, with the stupid names she was supposed to read out, but didn't know. She remembered how to use the scales from yesterday and loved measuring out each thing and adding it the mix. It was cool that there were books telling you how to make anything you wanted, except she was crap at reading.

'Derek says you want to go to the Support Centre instead of school,' Sandra said.

'Yeah.'

Delilah was concentrating on spooning cocoa out of the tub without flicking it everywhere.

'Well if you do go there, you might be able to do a vocational subject as part of your timetable'. Delilah had no idea what that meant, so ignored it. 'You could ask to try a catering course and learn to cook *really* well, like a chef.'

'Honest?'

That would be proper interesting, and miles better than school.

'I think so. There's a meeting later this week to sort out your education, you'll be able to ask lots of questions and find out then.'

'I'm not going to any meeting.'

'Well, nobody will force you, but make sure that someone knows what you want to do. Derek's on tomorrow, you could talk to him about what you'd like to achieve in terms of education. Then he can pass on your thoughts at the meeting.'

'Yeah, alright.'

Apart from helping her with some of the instructions, Sandra didn't ask any more questions and let Delilah work in silence. She wasn't that bad really, apart from talking all posh and acting like a teacher. The cakes came out of the tins whole, even though they were sunken and sticky in the middle because she'd opened the oven door too early. Sandra said they had to cool down before they could be sandwiched together, so Delilah took notice this time and went outside for a fag. She was so excited by the thought of learning to cook that she texted Jono.

I just mayd a cake and I mite be abel to do cuking insted of scool

She'd only taken three more pulls on her fag before he texted back. This new phone showed all the messages in a conversation at once, instead of in separate texts like her old phone. Seeing his reply made something click in her brain. So that was why he sent weird texts, repeating everything - he was spelling it properly. Her face went red, but Delilah studied his message and then hers, and then his again.

Wow! You can make a pudding for Saturday then. You might be able to do cooking instead of school? That sounds good. I'm going back to school too - I signed up for a computer programming course this morning. We'll be able to moan to each other about how much homework we have ☺

Delilah wasn't sure what to say about that. She replied 'cool' and flicked back to her inbox. There was the text from Becky with Jim's number. She hadn't known what to say to him, but she did now.

I just made a cake like the won you gave me.

There'd been no text from Gaz and she was worried about Josh. He was the youngest out of all of those lads and the new blokes had been right shitty bastards. Where did they go? They couldn't really be out 'hunting', it was more likely robbing. So had they been nicked? But Gaz had said he wouldn't see her for a few days. Maybe Josh knew he wouldn't be back but just hadn't said anything.

She tossed her nub end onto the grass and returned to the kitchen to check the cakes. They were still warm, but Sandra said they could make the butter icing. Ten minutes later, Delilah was clutching a bowl full of sticky chocolate sauce to spread over the cake and couldn't help grinning at Sandra. She was re-covering the last thin patch on the side when they heard Blink come through the front door.

'That's good timing, don't you think? Sandra said. 'We could all have tea and cake.'

Delilah jerked upright and stared at her in horror.

'No way! This is MY cake!'

There was no time to discuss it, as Blink came into the kitchen.

'Hi Sandra, hi Delilah.'

Delilah glowered at him and his smile fell away. Sandra offered to make him a cup of tea and he nodded, coming over to the table. She felt a bit mean - he hadn't even asked for any cake, it was just stupid Sandra's idea.

'It s..smells amazing in here. Did you m..make that c..cake?' It's b..b..beautiful.'

Delilah nodded and fought off a smile. Beautiful. She hadn't thought of it as beautiful, but it was. She wanted to eat some, but didn't want to spoil the carefully layered icing now.

'Will I be able to make another cake?' she asked Sandra.

'Yes, but not tonight - maybe tomorrow, or the next day. And you might have to balance out cakes with learning to cook a few proper meals too.'

Delilah shrugged, it sounded like a fair deal. If she could make another one, then it didn't matter if Blink had some of this one. He might say that it tasted beautiful too.

'Do you want a bit?' she said and then giggled when Blink looked so surprised, that he stared at her without a flicker of his eyelids for at least five seconds.

~ ~ ~

The meeting went well and Becky was pleased that Delilah's wishes assimilated those of the several teachers present. The two key-workers were both enthusiastic about her eagerness to learn, but they seemed a little uneasy and she was not surprised when they asked to speak to her afterwards. Tuesday's emailed update had been so positive, surely nothing too drastic had gone wrong in the two days since then? Perhaps Cleo was now in touch, which would explain a turn in the positive tide. It was Derek who tackled the problem.

'It's nothing too serious Becky, in fact, it's more to do with another of our young people, Josh. He's had a difficult time and got in with the wrong crowd, ending up with a Youth Offending order. Last week Delilah went out with him for several evenings running, but over the weekend he went awol. Delilah didn't seem too bothered and a great relationship started to develop between her and our other young man, Robert. We were hoping this would stick, but since Josh came back on Tuesday night, Delilah has given us a few causes for concern.'

'Like what? And where had Josh been?'

'A police cell in Newcastle as it turns out. It sounds like some sort of industrial burglary gone wrong, with Josh and two others taking the rap for a larger gang. He wouldn't talk and the police had no idea he was only 16 when they picked him up. But in relation to Delilah, it's more an unknown contact we're bothered about. After Josh came home, they were closeted in his room for hours and since then, she's been receiving a lot of texts on her phone.'

'Well I know that she's been texting both Jim and Jono, they let me know, and I also gave Delilah's mother her number.'

'I have asked and I'm fairly sure it isn't any of those people. She was pretty rude to Robert when he asked her what was up and she went out with Josh again last night.'

'Surely he shouldn't be going out, straight after being returned by the police?'

Derek grimaced and half nodded.

'We can't physically stop him' he said, 'and as it's likely he'll be sent to a Young Offenders' Institution this time, he's hell bent on enjoying his freedom.'

'So what happened last night?'

'Well they came back in on time, although they wouldn't say where from. They smelled of cannabis and Delilah was noticeably impaired.'

Becky considered this. The cannabis was nothing new - Delilah had been smoking tobacco for years and she could still remember being shocked by the girl's knowledge of, and casual reference to, several types of drug, when she had first taken on the case. She suspected that Cleo used to give Delilah all sorts of things to keep her quiet in the evenings, but there were enough grounds for removing parental responsibility without pursuing the matter.

A group of older boys was a significant issue, but Becky did not have the power to choose Delilah's friends for her. She would try to consult the police, but knew it would go nowhere without a name.

'Do we at least know who Josh is hanging around with?'

Lisa answered this time.

'We've been trying to get names for weeks, but Josh has become very secretive recently. The local youth workers are onto it, but we have no information at all at the moment.'

'Alright, thanks for letting me know and I'll pass on anything I manage to find out.'

Becky made her farewells and headed back up the stairs to her office, relieved that Derek's parting comment related to an appointment he had made for Delilah with the LAC nurse. Any sex education provided by Cleo didn't bear thinking about. She dropped the files on her desk and looked up at the clock on the wall. It was after 5pm...technically, she could go home.

'How did that go?' Bill asked from behind the filing cabinet.

'Good...ish. We've got a plan in terms of Delilah's education, but she's making some unsavoury acquaintances.'

'I'd be more surprised if they were savoury.'

'I know, I know. She's just so vulnerable.'

'Aren't they all? Maybe she'll find a new crowd to hang out with once she's at the Support Centre.'

Maybe. Becky nodded and mustered a hopeful smile for Bill's benefit, but thought it more likely that Delilah would take what she wanted from education and raise a finger to the rest of it. Still, she was settled at Sunny Bank, there was a realistic plan for her future and there was now a host of other professionals to share responsibility for her well-being. Becky locked the files in her desk drawer and wrote a swift to-do list for the morning, before slipping out of the office.

She was home before 6pm and felt a flutter of anticipation in her chest as she pulled onto the drive. Simon would still be wreathed in a silent aura of neglect and injustice, but Becky felt thirty pounds lighter and ready to deal with it. She was back on top of her caseload, there was nothing planned for tonight, and a ceremonial binning of her contraceptive pills would go a long way towards repairing the rift between them. All energies could be directed towards relationship restoration.

Finding Simon sitting at the kitchen table, without even a paper, never mind a phone, tablet or lap-top for entertainment, her mild excitement morphed into moderate dread. He said 'hello' without raising his eyes from the wooden surface. At least there was no sarcastic comment about an early finish.

'Hello,' she said. 'Good day at the office?'

The kettle was half full so she flicked it on, still watching him from the corner of her eye. He didn't move.

'Not really. It's probably just my emotional weakness, but I couldn't concentrate on other people's business, whilst wondering exactly how low down I register on my wife's list of priorities. I'm sorry to be selfish, but this isn't working for me any more Becky.'

Boom. The rising nausea masked the wobble in her legs, until they failed altogether. She slid down the side of the worktop to sit on the floor. Simon's head turned an inch or two in her direction, but still he would not look at her.

'So what does that mean? Are you saying you're leaving me? It's over?'

There was a burning lump in her throat, but her eyes remained dry. This was too much, too sudden. Where were the warning shots? Why hadn't he said they were at crisis point?

'Well I don't see any point in carrying on like this. I never see you and when I do, half your mind is on something work-related. I want a family, Becky. I thought we'd bought a 3-bedroomed house for that very event, but it won't happen; not when you don't have time for me, never mind children. I don't believe we share the same dreams any more.'

'That's not true! It's just...'

'But that's it, there's always a 'just'; *just* until you've served enough time in the new team, *just* until you're on top of your caseload, *just* until you've got Delilah settled. I've tried to support you Becky, but we've been married for seven years now. If you remember, you wanted us to get married to provide the most stable background possible for our children, to avoid complications with names, to prove we were taking it seriously.'

'I do remember, and it might have sounded like a series of excuses to you, but all the focus on my career has been about financial stability, and ensuring I can take stress-free maternity leave.'

She wanted to scream with frustration. If he'd given her just one more day, she would have announced tonight that she was coming off the pill, but she didn't want to tell him this way, forced into it by an ultimatum. He still hadn't looked at her and now raised his hands in defeat.

'Yes, I know your reasons and they're all very logical, but I've gone beyond logic. I want a family. I want you to be a part of that family, but I don't believe it's going to happen. It'll take time to move on, so the sooner we end this, the better.'

He really meant it. Her face crumpled.

'I was going to tell you, tonight. I came home all excited and I thought it would be wonderful. I decided this afternoon; there's nothing more I can do for Delilah, so now's the time to come off the pill.'

He looked at her now, an undecipherable expression on his face. She shouldn't have mentioned Delilah. The decision should have been for *him* and not to do with work. Simon got up and stalked out of the room. Becky broke down at last, sobbing into her knees.

~ ~ ~

Derek knocked on Delilah's bedroom door.

'Hey Dee. Do you want to hear how things went at the meeting? You could come down and have a coffee or a chocolate with me in the kitchen,' he called through the wooden panel.

The length of pause before the muffled 'nah' that came back encouraged him to try again.

'It was all pretty positive. Don't you want to know what was said about school?'

'Yeah, but tomorrow or something. Bog off Derek, I'm getting dressed.'

Bog off. That was new and infinitely preferable to the usual expletives. He almost smiled, until the shower went on in the landing bathroom. Josh and Delilah were off out again then. But where to?

He went downstairs and found Blink rootling through the fridge.

'What are you after?' he said.

'Just s..seeing what we've got in. I've been looking up r..recipes that me and Delilah could c..cook'.

'I think she's going out.'

'Oh.'

Blink stopped pulling things out of the fridge.

'So what recipes have you found? Let me have a look.'

Blink spread a number of printed sheets out on the kitchen table, all of which required ingredients that were definitely not in the fridge. Derek leaned over them with feigned interest anyway. Minutes later, they heard Josh and Delilah coming down the stairs. Blink stood up and went out into the hallway.

'H...h...'

'Yeah, hi Blink,' Delilah said, scorn clear in her voice.

'Are you g..going out b..before tea? I got a r..r..recipe for s..spaghetti b..b..bolognaise. We could c..cook it ourselves.'

Derek winced, but had to admire Blink's perseverance.

'Spaghetti what? Why would I wanna cook something I can't even bloody say?'

Derek watched Blink's shoulders slump and then jerk a little when the front door slammed shut, half way through Julie's question about where the two of them were going. He hated cooking, but felt sorry for the poor lad.

'We're not going to have much of that in and I'm rubbish at cooking, but we could go shopping, get what we need and make a mess of it anyway.

He grinned, but Blink didn't even turn around.

'Delilah is a lot n..nicer when Josh isn't here,' he said.

Derek agreed more heartily than he could express to Blink.

'You find that with a lot of people, they act differently in different circumstances. Try not to take it personally.' Blink still didn't turn around. 'Are we going shopping then?'

'No thanks. I'm g..going up to my r..room. I'll have a s..sandwich later.'

Derek watched as Blink dragged himself up the stairs, his head hanging.

~ ~ ~

Walking next to a silent Josh, Delilah was no longer sure she wanted to be doing this. She thought the spaghetti thing was what she'd got covered in, hiding in Jono's wheelie bin. It would be interesting to try and cook it. Thinking about Jono made her remember that she hadn't replied to his last two texts, or the one from Jim. It was taking all her time to work out what Gaz meant in his texts, then what to say back, and how to spell it.

With her thoughts on Gaz, the sicky feeling in her stomach returned. He'd sent her some weird messages over the last few days. Some made her feel nervous and excited at the same time, one had grossed her out completely, several sounded like things she'd heard her mum's boyfriends shout through the bedroom wall, when she was supposed to be asleep. That seemed kind of wrong, but then Gaz couldn't think she was just a kid, which she liked.

Maybe they wouldn't see him at all. They hadn't last night, just met some kid even younger than her, who gave Josh a parcel and a message from Gaz. They'd gone to the park to open it and Delilah was impressed with the contents: a mobile phone, £50, a pouch of bacca and a bag of weed. There was also a pre-rolled joint and part of the message told Josh to share it with her. They'd sat under a tree and smoked the 'Gaz Special' as Josh called it, getting so smashed that they couldn't move for nearly two hours.

Josh said it was a sweetener for keeping his mouth shut and that his real share was a lot bigger. He sounded cool and pretty grown up, but Delilah remembered how pale and scared he looked when the police brought him home. Tonight they were supposed to walk up and down a particular street until Gaz called Josh with directions. She wouldn't mind if he didn't - she and Josh could go and get stoned in the park again without having to talk much.

They drew level with a shuttered shop frontage and Josh stopped, pulling her into the doorway by her elbow. Alarmed, Delilah looked back up the road to see if someone was following them.

'It's alright,' Josh said. 'I just want to talk to you for a minute.'

He stared at a spot on her arm and didn't say anything at all. Delilah hoped he wasn't going to go all weird as well. She liked having Josh as a friend.

'You don't have to come with me,' he said at last. 'I could say they wouldn't let you out.'

'But you asked me to come. You said Gaz told you to bring me.'

'Yeah, but if it's just for the bacca and weed, you can have mine.'

'I want to come.'

Josh shrugged, stepped out of the doorway and began walking up the road, faster than before. Delilah had to run to catch up, but before she could say anything, the phone in his pocket rang.

The garage was the only one in the row with a complete set of doors; the rest were missing, or just twisted pieces of metal lying half in and half out of the square black holes. Several had no roof, but this was dry and quite warm, thanks to a small gas fire that gave off a blue glow. For once, it was just Gaz – the usual crowd of hangers-on were missing. Delilah wasn't sure if that was a good thing or not. She noticed Josh was still frowning, even though they'd already had one spliff.

'Shit, I'm dry,' Gaz said, dragging himself up from a low chair. He pulled a £20 note out of his pocket and held it out towards Josh. 'There's a chippy just down the road. Go and grab a few cans of Coke will ya? I can't show my face around here too much.'

Josh took the note and shrugged, but looked at her. Delilah stood up to go with him.

'Nah, not you, Dee. Stay here and keep me company, I aint seen hardly anyone these last few days. Not scared, are ya?'

Dee sat back down on the beer crate, but felt a bit sick when Josh slipped out of the door and left her and Gaz alone. He didn't sit back down, but stood, watching her. She shifted uneasily.

'You don't look too comfy,' Gaz said, stepping forward and holding out his hand. 'Come and sit here, dere's plenty of room for two.'

Delilah didn't move, but neither did Gaz. It might have been a whole minute they stayed like that. She didn't know what to do, other than reach up and take his hand.

The seat was so low it felt more like lying down and she was pressed against Gaz, until he reached under her legs and lifted them up, so that she was sitting sideways across him. She wasn't so squashed, but now he could stare at her again. One of his arms was around her back and the other lay across her legs, his hand resting on her hip.

'I liked gettin' your texts,' he said. 'Did you like gettin' mine?'

Delilah dropped her eyes, but could still feel him staring at her. She shrugged, and then nodded. She did like it that Gaz bothered to text her. And she did like sitting on his knees, even if it was massively embarrassing.

'So you gonna be my girl then?'

Eh? Had he really just asked her that? She wasn't anyone else's girl, so what excuse could she use? Did she want to be his girl? Nob-heads like Doogie wouldn't dare mess with her, if she was with someone like Gaz. He was really nice to her.

'Well? You actin' like you like me.'

He stopped smiling and raised his eyebrows. Delilah became very aware of her position. How could she say 'no', when she was sitting on him, with his arms wrapped around her? She'd look like a right slag.

'Ok,' she said and blushed when it came out in a whisper. 'Yeah,' she said more loudly.

She was about to try smiling when his lips pressed against hers, hard. Their teeth knocked together and then his tongue probed inside her mouth. It was kind of gross, but other people seemed to like it, so she wiggled her tongue in return and Gaz pressed closer, gripping tighter.

The door banged and Delilah's heart almost burst with shock, but strong arms stopped her from leaping up. She twisted to look at Josh, but the small lamp and the gas-fire didn't light up his face at all and the dark outline of him just stood there, watching.

8

Lying in the dark, Jono found he wasn't anywhere near sleep. It was the second night in a row that he'd been in bed by midnight, but already the novelty was wearing off. His brain ached from the trials of the day, but that wasn't the same as being tired. What a shock to the system. The bloody woman at the benefits agency must be on some kind of bonus scheme to have pulled this off so quickly.

Last Monday being the 13th December, Jono was confident that nothing too life-changing would happen before Christmas, beyond his preliminary interview. The robotic cow had called him two days later, to inform him that, although he had missed most of the first semester, there was an ideal course at the local university and the tutor was prepared to let him enrol late, if he agreed to catch up on the units already covered. And oh, what luck, they didn't break up for Christmas until the 21st, so Jono could attend on Monday and Tuesday, get a feel for the course and collect his catch-up work before the holidays.

The over-efficient automaton even booked him a place on Special Needs Transport. Jono was tempted to take the easy ride for the first day and suss the place out, but was more confident knowing his car was there for a quick getaway, if he needed one. His course-mates were not very inspiring. They were polite, if reserved in their welcome, but Jono was grateful that no-one attempted any meaningful level of conversation with him; there was too much information to take on board in the first place.

The approach of the somewhat aspergic tutor was refreshing – in no way did he acknowledge Jono's disability. Even low-level eye contact was not an issue, as Professor Bateman did not look any of his students in the eye. The only time his face gained animation was in the reflection of a computer screen. He would be an ideal tutor.

The events of the day occupied his head until around 2am, when checking the time on his phone reminded him that Dee had still not replied to his last two texts. He'd heard little from her over the last week. Having bailed on their Saturday lunch date with a text saying 'not comin 2day not wel', she would only expand as far as 'bad guts'. Jono wasn't too worried. Their contact had ebbed and flowed throughout the three years he'd known her, the apparently random bursts of daily visits revealing themselves, once she trusted him, as times when her mother was on an alcohol binge.

He'd often considered contacting Social Services, but figured that Dee's school and neighbours were better placed for that kind of thing. Somewhere well buried, he was also aware of enjoying the fact that she needed him. Dee was a problem kid, he knew that - the first time they met, she was stealing a packet of biscuits from the local shop. Taking pity on the skinny, grubby little girl, he'd dropped a tenner outside, when he knew she was looking at him. His surprise had been huge when, two hundred yards down the road, she had tapped him on the shoulder and handed him the note. Dee had morals, but the wrong experiences in life.

So was she stuck into Christmas preparations at Sunny Bank, or out partying with her new friends? The former, he hoped. It was 3am now. Holding his phone in his hand, he thought of Netty. They hadn't exchanged any messages since that first conversation, but now he felt the urge to talk to her again and be more honest. A bit more honest. Surfing in the twilight zone was a bad idea, but he logged in as Johnny Too Good anyway.

Hey Netty. I wanted to ask what you do for a living last week, but have to come clean first. I don't work in computers – I'm on a computer programming course. It's too easy to exaggerate on here…

He didn't sign off with Jonny TG. He even wanted to add, as if it were an afterthought, 'oh, and I use a wheelchair', but he'd stick with one small truth at a time. He studied the profile picture for a few minutes, registering the two other people, just captured either side of Netty; a chubby, ginger-haired girl with glasses, who was pulling a gruesome face as Netty's leap pushed her aside and a brunette with a determined scowl and acne. Jono reverted his gaze back to the beautiful Netty, until he was sure he could retain the image in his mind.

It worked for a time, but when Jono fell asleep at last, he dreamed of Dee, not Netty. She was calling to him from the bottom of a deep hole, but he had no rope. All he could do was talk to her and tell her that help was coming, except he knew it wasn't.

~ ~ ~

Crawling slug-like from the depths of unconsciousness, it took some time to register the weight across her legs. When full realisation hit her, Dee swore. It was dark. Had Josh gone home? Was there still time to get back? Where the bloody hell was her phone? It was in her jeans pocket...but she wasn't wearing them. Stretching out an arm, she was relieved to feel a heap of clothes next to the mattress. Careful not to move too much, she poked about until she found the hard outline of her phone. Even this slight motion made her feel sick and brought on a headache. It was that second 'special' spliff Gaz had rolled, after she'd refused to stay over.

Wondering again what Gaz put in his 'special' spliffs, Dee brought the phone to her face and looked at the time. 3.30am. Shit. They would have reported her missing to the police by now. She turned on the torch app and flashed it around the room. There was no-one else there; just Gaz, who was snoring, but lying next to her and pinning her down with his leg. Very slowly, she wriggled sideways and got one leg free. Just as she was easing her other leg out, Gaz mumbled something. Dee froze, but then he grunted, rolled over and started snoring again.

Getting dressed was not that easy. Twice, she felt so dizzy that she had to kneel on the floor until her head cleared. When the door wouldn't open, Dee felt a moment of panic, but found it was a twisty lock you could do from the inside without a key. Outside was a dark hallway, with a dim light over the stairwell at the end. The stink of stale piss was even worse than when she'd arrived and Dee found a bloke in a big coat and woolly hat, slumped over the bottom step. The smell of alcohol joined the piss when she got close up, but the man never stirred as she jumped over him.

Only when she walked out into the freezing night did she realise that her coat was still in the flat. Bastard. It was at least a half hour walk back to Sunny Bank from here. She set off at a fast pace, wondering how she could get in without alerting the staff on duty. Josh might help. She slowed down a bit and sent him a text.

U stil up?

His reply came in seconds.

Yeh. Evry1s up cuz of u. U still at flat?

No. Comin back.

How could she avoid walking into a right load of hassle? Josh sent another text before she could think of anything.

Text wen ur near. Meet u in gardn.

That might work. Dee texted 'ok', then shoved the phone back in her pocket and her hands under her armpits. Her nose and ears were stinging with cold and it even hurt to breathe in. She increased her pace.

~ ~ ~

Derek looked across the desk at Julie. Her head was in her hands. It had been a very, very long night. At midnight, concern became worry. At 1am they reported both Josh and Delilah to the police as missing. At 1.30am Josh returned, claiming he and Delilah had split up earlier that evening and he had no idea where she was. He was angry and upset about something though, which wasn't reassuring. At 3.00am, the waning hope that Delilah might just be very late died, leaving only the questions of where she was spending the night and who with.

Josh muttered something about 'girly mates' but Derek gave that no credibility. Delilah responded much better to the male members of staff and didn't appear to have any female friends, other than the neighbour.

'I'm going to sit with Blink for a few minutes, he's still refusing to leave the settee,' he said.

Julie nodded without looking up. He picked up his coffee and walked through to the lounge. Blink was slumped sideways on the settee, but jerked awake as Derek sat down next to him.

'Is she b..back?'

'Fraid not. Are you going to go up to bed? You'll feel awful in the morning.'

'No, I couldn't s...sleep properly anyway.'

'Well, as a one-off, why don't you stay off school tomorrow? I can't remember the last time you missed a day and you won't function on no sleep. I can leave a note to make sure you get a lie in.

'R..really? That would be c..ool. I don't w..want to go anyway if Delilah d..doesn't come h..home.'

They sat in silence for several minutes, like-minded in their grim thoughts. Footsteps in the hall made them both turn around, only to see Josh walk through the doorway. He didn't look pleased to see them.

'Can't you sleep either?' Derek asked.

Josh shrugged

'I need a fag.'

He carried on to the sliding door, unlocked it and went out into the garden. The icy blast sucked in by his exit carried the twelve feet to the settee and made Derek shiver. Josh must be mad or desperate to go outside right now. One minute stretched into five. Mad, desperate, or have an ulterior motive.

'Do you th..think...' Blink started to say, just as Derek rose from the settee to follow Josh.

'Sshh,' Derek said, sure he'd heard Josh talking outside.

As he started over to the door, it opened again and Delilah stepped inside, her face a bluey shade of white. It looked like her plan was to dash across the lounge and head straight upstairs, but her movements were stiff and jerky, almost puppet-like.

'Delilah!' Blink cried.

She scowled and tried to move faster, but was overtaken by a huge shudder. Derek was horrified to see that she was wearing just a vest and a thin, long-sleeved top, that didn't even do up at the front.

'Good God Delilah, where's your coat?'

He shook himself and shouted 'Julie!' before heading Delilah off in the doorway.

'Fuck off Derek.' It was supposed to be a snarl, he knew, but it sounded more like a mewing kitten. 'I'm going to bed.'

'Not until I'm sure you're ok and we've got you warmed up. Bed won't help you in this state.'

Julie appeared and sagged with relief.

'Julie, Delilah needs a bath, but just warm to start with, she can add more hot water as she thaws out,' he turned to Delilah. 'I'll make you a hot chocolate to drink in the bath...get some heat inside and out.'

She looked at him in surprise, plainly expecting a bollocking.

'Oh don't be mistaken, I want to know where you've been and what you've been doing, but more than anything, we're glad you're safe.'

'W..w..we were r..really w..w..worried,' Blink chipped in.

Delilah dropped her eyes again.

'I fell asleep,' she said.

'You're alright then?' Derek asked.

She nodded, but he wasn't at all sure.

'Yeah, just cold.'

'Ok, well go on upstairs. You too,' he added, looking at the two lads, 'the excitement's over.'

Watching the little procession troop upstairs, Derek wondered how far they would be able to push Delilah for information.

'Ask Julie if she'll come and fetch your drink, eh Dee?'

He went through to the kitchen and put the kettle on, pleased when Julie joined him in less than a minute.

'Sorry for dragging you back down here, I'm not being idle,' he said, 'but I'm really bothered by Delilah's eyes. She's not one for looking at you at the best of times, but I caught her by surprise earlier and she doesn't look stoned. Her pupils are tiny, like she's been on something a lot heavier than weed.'

'No, you're fine Derek. I hadn't noticed, but I'll have closer look when I go back up with this. Can you ring the police and let them know she's back?'

'Sure.'

Having made the call, he sat ruminating in the office. Did Delilah know what she was taking, or had she been spiked? They'd struggle to get her to do a drugs test and if it was a Class A, all trace would be gone by tomorrow night. It was ridiculous how impotent they were, but then, it was hardly fair to lock Delilah up because she'd had a crap childhood. Maybe Julie would have a better plan. He bloody hoped so.

~ ~ ~

Hunger woke Dee at 11am. She was too warm and comfortable to move, but when her belly went from growling to painful, she leapt out of bed, dragged on some clothes and went in search of food. Finding Blink in the kitchen with Gareth threw her.

'What are you doing here?' she asked, stopping and staring at him.

'I'm w..wagging it off school!' Blink said, grinning at her. Then his face went all serious. 'Hey, are you o..o..ok? Shall I p..put some t..toast on for you?'

He was already fishing out two slices of bread, so Dee sat on a stool by the breakfast bar.

'Thanks.'

She ignored Gareth, who was way too cheerful in the morning. It was a miracle he wasn't already banging on about all the exciting-but-actually-boring things they could do today. She was even more surprised when he left the kitchen without saying a word. Still, one soppy bloke was better than two.

'Which jam?' Blink asked, holding out two jars.

He might not have stuttered, but he was grinning like an idiot. Dee frowned.

'Strawberry.'

It was sad to get so excited about making toast…but nice that he was doing it. Her phone buzzed in her pocket. A text. It was probably Gaz. She hadn't dared look at her phone yet, but perhaps she should.

The screen showed two missed calls and three new texts. Good job it was on silent. The calls were from Gaz and two of the texts were voicemail messages he'd left. They could wait til later. The most recent text was from a number not in her phone. Dee opened it.

Hi babe sorry 4 not calling Ive been ill but seen doctor. r u ok??? miss u. Mum xxxx

Dee gasped and read the text again, only looking up when a plate of toast appeared in front of her. It was cut into triangles and laid out in a line.

'It's my mum!'

Blink sat down next to her.

'That's n..nice. W..will you be able to s..see her?'

'Yeah. Becky said so. They can't stop me anyway.'

She started a text in reply, but had to stop to eat toast. It smelled awesome and she was starving. Blink was mumbling on, but Dee concentrated on shovelling food into her mouth, until she caught the word 'alcoholic'.

'Did you just say your mum's an alcoholic?'

Blink shook his head.

'She w..w…was. She's d..d..dd… Gone.'

'Oh. Sorry.'

Shit, she should have been listening. Blink started talking again. She wanted to pay attention this time, but a cold fear started to crawl down her back.

'Shut up a sec Blink.'

She picked up her phone again. There, it said in the text; her mum had been ill, ill enough to go to the doctor. Dee looked back at Blink, waving the phone at him.

'She's ill. My mum's ill and she's an alcoholic too. Do you think she's going to die?'

Blink shrugged.

'My M..mum was always i..ill, for y..years before... Is your D..dad around?'

Dee shook her head whilst punching in a reply.

I am ok. How ill r u? xxx

After staring at her phone for thirty seconds she turned her attention back to Blink.

'Do you see your Dad?'

Blink paused before answering. Dee could see the colour rising in his face and the hands clenched between his knees.

'N..no. H..he s..says a d..daft p..p..prat like m..me couldn't have c..c..come from his l..l..loins.'

Assuming loins was another word for cock, she couldn't help smiling. It was a pity he looked up and caught her.

'You're not a daft prat, you're a…a clever, nice prat.'

Blink's expression wavered and then he beamed.

'R..really?'

'Yeah.'

Dee found herself smiling back, but it fell off her face when Josh walked in, hood up and head down. Heat rushed up from her chest. She'd realised in the bath last night, or this morning really, that Josh knew exactly where she was and what she was doing. She couldn't even remember what had happened after the second Gaz Special, and hoped Josh and the others were gone before anything *did* happen. She didn't think it was much, she didn't feel any different…down there.

'I'm going to text my mum again,' she said to Blink, loud enough for Josh to hear, so he might not think she was avoiding him.

Upstairs in her room, Dee scrolled through her messages. Still no reply from her mum and she didn't want to listen to the voicemails from Gaz yet. The previous text was from Jim. It said he and Shona could meet her at McDonalds one day. Shona might have seen her mum.

hi jim can we meet soon

~ ~ ~

The call came through at 1am and all hope of sleep vanished with it. Jim smoked and drank whisky until the sky paled to grey, and was striding across the fields with Crank when the sun came up. He was angry. Angry that his number had been passed on. Angry that no-one believed he was out of it all. Angry that an easy question should have such a complicated answer. Why the *fuck* did it have to be Paulie? Anyone else, anyone in the world and it would have been a straight 'no', but when he realised it might be Shona's son, it was impossible not to ask for details. Given the option of 24 hours to think about it, he couldn't resist buying the time.

Now, he regretted it. Shona knew where Paulie was headed and Jim had more than a sneaking suspicion that it was he who had beaten and robbed her. He should have let things take their course and stayed well out of it.

'Ah damn it, Crank. I'm getting too old for this.'

The dog looked up at him and whined. Jim half smiled.

'I'm pretty sure that meant 'you and me both'. Perhaps we should piss off to the seaside for our retirement, eh? Morning walks on a nice flat beach.'

It wasn't such a bad idea. If they had his number, they'd soon know his address and although he had no direct fear of his former brothers in the bike club, he didn't know them all these days. If he deliberately screwed up a job, his personal information might get slipped to more interested parties. It was time to move on.

He crossed over a stile into another field. A big old oak had fallen from the hedgerow since his last visit and the icy wind made his eyes sting, as he stood looking at it. The branches of the canopy, the broad trunk and the curve of the partially exposed root ball formed a sort of 3-sided shelter. Jim walked over and hung his rucksack from a branch, feeling the difference in temperature immediately. He would have a coffee with the stricken giant, felled by the force that raised it.

After tossing a dried pig's ear to Crank, he filled his mug and leaned back against the trunk. This tree must be a few hundred years old and he could use some of that wisdom right now. Half of him wanted to talk the Paulie thing through with Shona, but the

136

other half of him knew she would be crazy with worry. There was also the potential issue that, although she wouldn't suggest it, Shona would want him to take the job to ensure that Paulie got off at the light end of a heavy beating. It was an option Jim considered, but only briefly. If he did half a job, Paulie would get another beating anyway and his own problems would quadruple.

The sun, pale and insipid all morning, now fought through a thinner patch of cloud, and bars of light burst through the branches of his tree-cave. Jim laughed. Prison would be the safest place for Paulie. Shona might even agree, as if he was right about her attacker, then it would be safer for both of them. He'd have to play it very, very carefully, but it could be a solution.

The slight lift in Jim's spirits waned again when his phone beeped. He'd agreed 24 hours, they shouldn't be hassling already. He needed to speak to Shona, if not to tell her what was happening, at least to try and gauge her thoughts on Paulie.

But it wasn't anything to do with Paulie. It was Delilah – the very last person he wanted to hear from right now.

~ ~ ~

Shona was loath to open the door and let the cold in, but something in the bin smelled awful. The whole kitchen was starting to stink. She hoisted the bag up and dashed outside in her slippers.

'Shona!'

Oh *shit*. She didn't want to get frostbite or talk to Kelly, but she damn well wasn't inviting her in either. Turning around with a prepared look of mild disapproval, Shona's mouth fell open at the sight of her.

'Jesus Kelly…you're yellow!' A ridiculous thing to say really, but a statement of fact. It was incredible that the woman was on her feet. 'What the hell is wrong with you?'

'Jaundice. Apparently my liver's fucked.'

Shona noticed there was no bottle in her hand, but she could smell alcohol from across the fence.

'Have you seen Delilah?'

At least the woman cared enough to blush.

'No, I...I didn't want her seein' me like this. I was going to ask you the same thing.'

That brought out Shona's blunt side.

'If you don't stop drinking Kelly, you aren't going to look any better than this before you're dead. Perhaps now is a good time to see Delilah.'

She expected a mouthful of abuse in return, but Kelly's face crumpled, revealing brown teeth.

'She's p'raps better off without me.'

Shona felt some sympathy rising, but it didn't overcome her revulsion.

'Perhaps, but she certainly doesn't think so. She wants her mum.'

Kelly's face creased in misery and Shona was so cold that she was on the verge of offering to put the kettle on. The appearance of a mythical creature at the bottom of the garden path saved her.

'Fuckin' 'ell,' Kelly muttered and staggered off.

Did she really think that The Green Man was visiting on the Solstice, or had Kelly and Jim already met? The vision wasn't any less realistic up close. Ivy trailed over both of Jim's shoulders and sprigs of holly and berries stuck up from his jacket pockets, casting a green tinge on his beard.

'Wow!' Shona laughed. 'Have you been forced to walk the streets with him looking like that, Crank?'

'Just spreading a bit of festive cheer, thought you could stick this lot up around the house. Are you making a brew?'

They went inside and Jim off-loaded his pickings while Shona filled the kettle. He draped one length of ivy over the top of the dresser and reached up to wind another around the curtain pole. It did look beautiful. Shona smiled, but it faded as she remembered the times she and Paulie had done this together.

'Heard anything from Paulie?' Jim asked, startling her.

'No, no I haven't. Not that I'm expecting to really. I sometimes wish he'd get locked up - I'd know where he was, and he might actually learn something useful inside. Knowing Paulie though, he'd probably come out as a master pick-pocket or lock-breaker.'

'It can go either way,' Jim admitted. 'I was pretty illiterate until the last stretch. My pad-mate was a lifer and always had his nose in a book. I took the piss at first, but I suppose I was jealous - it's amazing how many hours a half decent read can eat up. I went to a few English classes and things got a lot easier.'

'I won't give up hope then,' Shona said, but was glad she could turn her back and make tea.

Paulie was not a comfortable topic of conversation with Jim, but he seemed happy to drop it on this occasion, asking after Kelly instead.

'She wanted to know if I'd seen Delilah. Apparently she's been too ill, although I have to admit, she looks bloody awful. I won't be surprised if she ends up in hospital.'

'Crap for the kid though,' Jim said, frowning. 'She's sent me a text about meeting up. Are you still ok to come with me?'

'Yes, of course.'

Shona was surprised to realise it was the truth. She missed Delilah's impromptu and often awkward visits. It would be good to see her scrubbed up and wearing decent clothes.

'Well if you're not busy, I'll suggest later this afternoon. I'm probably going to head off to the coast tomorrow…see some old mates over Christmas.'

'Oh, ok.'

There had been no conversation about Christmas, but with Jim being so involved recently, Shona assumed he would come to her for Christmas dinner. Now it seemed she was in for a lonely one. Maybe it was time to get a cat.

~ ~ ~

Jim waited until he got home to make the necessary phone calls. The first was to Becky and he was perturbed when a man answered, but he knew all about the arrangement and okayed a walk to McDonald's and back, via the park. He would let the staff at the care home know. Becky was off sick and he promised to pass on Jim's regards, if he got the opportunity.

'I'm glad you understand what we're trying to do here,' Bill said. 'Becky really stuck her neck out in approving this contact.'

'I know. You'd be even more impressed with her bravery if you met me.'

Jim hung up and rolled a cigarette, uncomfortable with the imminent switch of character and role. He wasn't sure if Becky was brave or just naïve, but then he'd never believed in goodies and baddies. He lit the fag and picked up his phone again.

'Yeah, it's me. I'll take the job. I'll come to the clubhouse tonight to sort the details.'

Done. There was no turning back now. Switch and switch again. Jim texted Delilah and then fetched the box of ten, large, duty-free pouches of tobacco he'd bought the week before. He wrapped two up in a carrier bag with no sting of conscience. He remembered only too well the things he'd done to get tobacco while he was in care and didn't want to contemplate the further options open to a girl. Delilah's lungs would recover sooner than her head if she was forced to explore them.

9

The throbbing in her head was awful. When she tried to get out of bed, Dee was overcome by dizziness and flopped back onto the mattress, shivering and sweating. That didn't make sense. You couldn't be cold and hot at the same time. It was so annoying that the urge to smoke doubled, but her throat was already on fire. It was bloody sick, when she had the best stash of tobacco ever.

Jim had bought her tons of food from McDonald's yesterday, then slipped her a parcel on the way back. It was a Christmas present, but he said she could open it straight away. It was nice to see him and Shona, but everyone stared at them. She was glad when they'd taken the food to the park, instead of eating in.

She didn't know whether to be more or less worried about her mum. Shona said she was still at home and seeing a doctor, but it didn't sound like flu and she didn't know people could go yellow. Blink might know what it meant. She'd ask him later, but not now...her throat was *killing*. There was a knock on her door.

'Delilah? A..are you aw..w..wake?'

She couldn't answer, it was like swallowing knives.

'Delilah? It's n..nearly lunch-t..time.'

'Feel shit' she croaked.

'What? Are you o..ok?'

Idiot. She'd just said she felt shit.

'Delilah, c..c..can I c..come in?'

She groaned, pulled the duvet over her bare legs and gave an affirmative 'mmm'. It hurt less. The door opened slowly and Blink peered around it. His expression confirmed that she looked as bad as she felt.

'Are you s..sick? Shall I g..g..get someone?'

Dee shook her head, but managed to say 'drink'. Blink disappeared. She imagined him going back down the stairs, past the long trails of tinsel they had wrapped around the bannisters yesterday. He'd droned on and on about putting the Christmas decorations up, until it was easier to give in, but Dee had been secretly delighted with the plastic tree and two cardboard boxes full of tinsel and baubles he dragged out.

Her mum didn't have any decorations and Shona and Jono didn't bother much. The only other house she had been in at Christmas was Chelsea's. They had loads of stuff, but it was all flashing plastic lights and toys, which got on your tits after a bit. These were much nicer – everything sparkled in silence. Josh was well mardy about it, but the staff were extra nice to him.

There was a thump on the landing and Blink reappeared with a tray, which he put on her bedside cabinet. There were two mugs, a glass of water and a glass of orange juice.

'I d..didn't know w..what you w..wanted, so I b..b..brought everything.'

Dee was quite stunned. Blink stood there, hopping from one foot to the other, looking all eager. She pulled her knees up and gestured towards the end of the bed, waiting for him to sit down before she picked up the orange juice. It was cold and delicious, but agony to swallow. Grimacing, she drained the glass.

'D..does your throat h..hurt?' Blink asked. His face was pink. 'I could f..fetch you some i..ice cream.'

Dee raised her eyebrows. They wouldn't let her have ice cream for breakfast. She shrugged, but whispered,

'It's ripping.'

'You've d..definitely got a t..temperature too. They'll w..want you to see the d..doctor.'

She scowled and shook her head.

'A..alright, I'll s..see what I can do.'

Blink left again and Dee flopped back against her pillow, moaning as her stomach gave a sinister gurgle at the arrival of the juice. God she felt shit. But at least she would be able to reply to

142

Gaz. In fact, she could do it now and he might stop messaging her.

soz 4 not txting lm ill in bed x

She chucked the phone back onto the duvet and closed her eyes, hoping that Blink wouldn't reappear too soon. It was nice that he was sorting everything out for her, but he was still annoying. Dee began to wonder how Gaz would be if he met Blink and drifted into unpleasant, semi-conscious imaginings. She pulled the duvet tight around her shivering body, though her temples were slick with sweat.

~ ~ ~

By the third ring, Becky knew it was a mistake, but could not now hang up and leave a missed call. What if Bill rang back when Simon was around? Damn it. He answered on the seventh ring.

'How nice of you to call to wish me a Happy Christmas,' he said, without bothering to greet her, 'as I know you wouldn't threaten my professional integrity by asking any questions about work.'

'Hi Bill, Happy Christmas,' she said, 'although, while I'm on...'

'Not a chance, Becky. You're off with stress for God's sake, I'm not allowed to talk to you about work. You've been in this game long enough to know that case updates aren't usually a reassurance.'

'Oh hell, what's she done now?'

'Who?'

'Delilah.'

'Nothing unexpected.'

'Oh no, she's not run away again has she?'

Bill sighed in a very deliberate manner down the phone. Becky crossed her fingers, arms and legs in silence.

'No. She stayed out a couple of nights ago and was reported missing, but turned up, frozen stiff, in the early hours of the morning. Since then she's stayed at home, but is now suffering from a heavy cold or flu. She's refusing to see a doctor and is being waited on hand and foot by one of the other kids. Apparently it's a positive relationship, but some unknown person has also sent an expensive bunch of flowers. Delilah refused to say who it was, but her reaction suggested it wasn't her mother, who now has severe jaundice as a result of alcohol abuse and Hepatitis C.

'In other news, Conner got arrested again for selling cannabis and legal highs, but is cooperating with the Youth Offending Team this time and voluntarily attending drugs awareness sessions. The Case Conference for Paige went well, she's been moved back down from Child Protection to Child in Need, as you recommended. She almost sent her best wishes.'

'Ha. I bet,' Becky said, pleased nonetheless.

'Ah, but that reminds me, someone did send their best wishes; Jim, the biker dude. He called to arrange a visit with Delilah and the neighbour. Seems to have gone ok.'

'That's good, I think.'

'Yes, well is that it? Are you happy now? Oh…er, sorry.'

Wow. Bill was never embarrassed by anything.

'Much happier, thanks Bill. I do appreciate it. Have a good Christmas.'

'You too, now bugger off. It's the 23rd of December and I need to get a lot finished today. Don't even think about work, chill out properly and I'll see you in the new year.'

The line went dead before Becky removed the phone from her ear. Bless him. It was Bill who had persuaded her to go off with stress in an attempt to save her marriage. It wasn't too far a stretch – work pressures were a lot to do with the giant chasm between her and Simon, although she would manage them fine if she didn't have to worry about him. But then, as Bill had also pointed out, she would probably end up working seventy hour weeks as a singleton. With ten days holiday booked over Christmas, it would only mar her sickness record with a week off. Sod it.

So, back to the kitchen and into her new role as domestic goddess. Simon had gone out to do some present shopping and Becky was having a cooking day. Not that she enjoyed cooking, or was gifted with any natural culinary talent, but she was determined to develop her skills as a wife and potential mother. There were some benefits – the Christmas cake and trifle currently in progress required brandy and sherry, and the risotto she planned for later would demand the opening of a bottle of white wine.

Recent reflection made her realise that a lot of the household chores – including cleaning, shopping and cooking – had been falling heavily on Simon. Voicing this had brought him back from the spare room, but things were still delicate. The secret diary of her working hours that he'd kept over the last six months was a shocker. Once over the initial fury, she understood his reasoning. It wasn't a schedule that left any time for mothering and little for being a wife, or even friend.

~ ~ ~

Shona was prepared, but still recoiled in horror when Kelly opened the door. Her face was gaunt, the skin yellow and leathery, even the whites of her eyes were tinged yellow. The bottom half of her hair was still dyed black, but there were five inches of grey above it and another inch of white hair through which a yellow scalp was visible. The house smelled vile and she hadn't even stepped inside yet.

'Jesus Kelly, shouldn't you be in hospital?'

'They can't make me, not yet. Can't smoke or drink in there, I'd go fuckin' mad.'

Shona shook her head, but pursued her mission.

'I thought I'd pop a Christmas card up to Delilah for you. I've put a tenner inside, all you need to do is write in it,' she took the card from the envelope, removed the tenner and passed it to Kelly. 'I saw her, she's worried about you.'

Kelly stared at the card and then at Shona. She wobbled a bit and then seemed to wake up.

'Come in, I'll find something to drink.'

'No, thanks, I need to get off. It's Christmas Eve. Here,' she passed Kelly a pen, 'just wish her a Happy Christmas and tell her that you love her.'

Kelly's hand shook, but she took the pen and leaned against the wall to write inside the card. The script was as shaky as her hand

and Shona wondered if it wouldn't make Delilah worry more, although it didn't look like Kelly was much more literate than her daughter. It would be better than nothing.

Taking the card back she saw a tear drop from beneath Kelly's bent head and her heart warmed a little.

'I'll call in and see you tomorrow, eh?' she said.

'Thanks Shona.'

The door was shut before she turned away and Shona heard a dry sob from behind it. Poor, sad woman. How had she come to this?

She tucked the card into her handbag and set off down the path, but her conscience grew heavier with each step. It was impossible not to feel selfish, getting all depressed at the prospect of spending Christmas Day alone, when the woman next door – the ex-friend next door – was also alone, quite possibly on the verge of death and without creature comforts.

Shona remained cross at finding herself in this situation all the way to the bus stop, but became resigned to the fact that there was no real choice during the journey into town. By the time she'd bought a few things and posted Delilah's card through the letterbox of Sunny Bank, she was focussed on the personal satisfaction that would come from following her moral duty, and planning a hot bath and hair-dying session for Kelly, as well as dinner.

It might make their first meeting in weeks less of a shock for Delilah, but there was nothing she could do about the colour of Kelly's skin. Only Kelly could make a change there, but Shona wasn't hopeful. It would be a miracle if Kelly made it through the festive season and into the New Year.

~ ~ ~

It was one of the most pleasant Christmas Eves that Derek had experienced on shift at Sunny Bank, in terms of general harmony. Josh had torn down all the decorations that Blink attempted to put up last year, even dragging the real Christmas tree outside and setting fire to it in the garden. He must care for Delilah a lot, to be tolerating the vibrant display in every room of the house. Not that he spent any time there, other than in bed.

His behaviour was understandable, having lost his father to a heroin overdose aged 7 and found his mother gone the same way with sleeping pills, on Christmas Day, aged 12, but it was hard on the other kids. Blink would be more sympathetic if he knew the details, but it was confidential information and Josh would never talk to him on that level. So Josh was out somewhere and Blink was teaching Delilah how to play battleships in her bedroom.

Blink had spent as much of the past three days as she allowed, by Delilah's side. It was incredible that he hadn't caught whatever was ailing her, although he was buzzing with more energy than Derek had ever seen him possess...until the anonymous parcel arrived this morning. That it would all come crashing down around Blink's ears when Delilah was better was always fairly inevitable, but now Derek was sure of it.

Blink was excited about the gift at first, thinking it was from her mother, but within minutes of taking it up, he was back downstairs, Delilah having asked him to leave her alone. It was a necklace, he said, a gold necklace with a 'D' hanging from it, with little jewels on. There was a card in there too, but Delilah wouldn't say who it was from. Derek called the guy covering for Delilah's social worker, but knew there was nothing anyone could do.

Blink was allowed back upstairs, to convey a card delivered by hand, a few hours later. It looked like a child had written 'Delilah' on the front of the envelope, but this time Blink was positive it was from her mother. Derek supposed it wasn't just a detective or doctor who would recognise the shake of an alcoholic hand. Right or not, he had been ensconced up there ever since. Perhaps tomorrow would also be relatively tranquil.

Despite having booked Christmas day off last January, Derek now felt guilty, as only he and one other, part-time member of staff, were not on shift at any point. He had promised Talia though and his children deserved a happy Christmas too.

~ ~ ~

For once, there were better ways in which Jim could be spending Christmas Day. If it wasn't for the stupid little twat slouching up the street in front of him, he could be warm and comfortable at Shona's, with a bottle of whisky and a decent dinner to come. In retrospect, he could at least have left Crank with Shona, instead of home alone – there was no need for all three of them to be miserable.

Paulie dropped something from his pocket and stopped, scrabbling about on the floor, trying to pick it up. Jim slid into a doorway and began rolling a fag, but kept an eye on his target from under the peak of the cap he was wearing. It was a carton of bicarb. The idiotic prick was walking down the street, with a carton of bicarb in his pocket. Someone must have laid on more gear, that he was now going to cut the shit out of and sell on, to pay back his other debts. Judging by the look of Paulie, most of it was going up his nose, or even into his arm.

Jim followed him back to a small, terraced house, with a taped up panel in the battered front door. There was a sheet or blanket fixed over the window on the inside that billowed when Paulie slammed the door behind him. The wooden window sill was rotting away, decay encouraged by a damp patch from a dripping overflow pipe, further up the wall. It was grim, even by Jim's very modest standards.

Returning to the deep and shaded entrance of a closed carpet shop up the street, he was glad of the flask of coffee. There really wasn't a worse day of the year to be doing this – cold, wet, no passing traffic, nobody about. There were fewer potential witnesses perhaps, but also nothing to draw unwanted attention from a big, lurking biker. On the plus side, the cops would be busy dealing with violent, drunken domestics all over the county. A decade ago, he would have been glad of that fact, but now he found it depressing.

Thirty minutes or so passed before a slow trickle of people appeared, all heading for Paulie's door. The first was a young lad, 17 or 18, furtive but healthy-looking, decent clothes, but not over-stated. On the gear a few months maybe, still spending his savings, or not yet caught selling his Dad's power-tools. The second was a girl, similar age, but less well-groomed, a little more desperate. The third was an emaciated man who could be his own age, or a younger man who just looked like shit.

The dozen or so people who followed were of a similar ilk. Paulie was more together than he looked, with a client base from which he could target the inexperienced, the vulnerable, those who couldn't or wouldn't protest when he sold them crap. Bastard. Jim had seen enough and took the opportunity of a lull in the human traffic to slip away.

His bike was in a car park more than a mile off. It wasn't a subtle form of transport, but the ride home would cheer him up. It had been too long since he felt this freedom and the route from Manchester back to Derbyshire allowed for plenty of glorious diversions, but Jim abandoned the last one when ice began to form in his beard. Crank would be ready for his dinner anyway.

It was almost 8pm by the time he'd put his bike away and got into the house. It wasn't much warmer than outside. He lit the gas fire, fed Crank and then made himself a hot toddy. Happy bloody Christmas. Returning to the front room and the fire, he made the call he favoured least. It rang and rang before a pissed off voice answered.

'What's up? It's Christmas for fuck's sake. I've got kids you know, they've been screaming the fucking house down all day.'

'Sorry, I thought I'd better get straight with you asap. I've been up to check out that prick today. He's flogging over-cut shit to kids from the front door, one of which looked a damn sight more like an undercover pig than a druggie. I can't get near without witnesses and if the pigs are hooked in on Christmas Day, then he's well covered.'

There was a taut silence. Jim knew what he was thinking; that made Paulie harder to get at in every way, they would be even less likely to get the money owed, therefore there was a greater need for a lesson to be taught and observed by others.

'So what are you saying? You need more time?'

'It's too hot for me. The cocky twat's about to get busted and I don't want dragging into that.'

'We had a deal. You're backing out of that deal?'

149

'Circumstances make the job impossible. I can't do it.'

There was another pause.

'I hear you, but it isn't just about me these days. I need to talk to other people. I'll call you in a day or two.'

Click. No better or worse than he'd hoped for. No option but to wait. If the cops weren't on to Paulie already, they certainly would be after the call Jim had made from a layby just outside Glossop. The phone was a cheap pay-as-you-go, used once and now residing in a ditch behind the layby. It could not be traced back to him.

~ ~ ~

Boxing Day was always a bit of an anti-climax, but this year Jono felt downright wretched. He couldn't bear to spend another whole day with his parents, but now questioned his decision to spend it alone. Yesterday had been filled with the same family traditions; his sister, her husband and two kids – still shy of him, but getting over it – providing the festive cheer, his brother sending the usual, sunny video-message from California, his mother cooking a vast dinner.

The big difference was so small, that the only other person who noticed was his mother. Twice, Jono's father seemed to have forgotten about the accident, forgotten that his youngest son could no longer walk. The first was when he admired Jono's biceps, asking why there wasn't a young lady he could bring to dinner. Jono's sister joined in with complete innocence, talking about his new fame as a basketball star, without realising that their father's normal opinion was that no independent young woman would willingly tie herself to a cripple. It was intended as a practical, rather than cruel observation, but no less painful for it.

The second was when the kids went out into the garden, up the stone steps to the top lawn, to try out their new swing-ball set.

'Why don't you go and show them how it's done?' his father said.

'Because you never did take the steps out and put a ramp in,' his sister answered for him with a fond chuckle, then went outside to join her family.

She missed the puzzled frown before his father focussed on the wheelchair, and the shaking hand he put over his face. His mother tried to dismiss the awkward moment.

'He'd forget his head if it wasn't fastened to his neck.'

But Jono knew from the shape of her mouth that she was trying not to cry. What was it, Alzheimer's? Early dementia? His father was only 64. He should talk to his sister about it...or maybe his mother...but not yet.

It was no good reliving every minute of it, there would no doubt be similar experiences and worse to come. Jono wondered if Delilah's Christmas Day had been any more pleasant than his. For the last two years she had spent hours and hours watching films with him over the Christmas holidays. He only bought all the chocolate for her and now found himself with a cupboard full of it. Dee hadn't visited again since the first Saturday she was in care.

It was good. She needed to make friends of her own age, go out and have fun. As long as it was just fun and not trouble. He didn't text her yesterday...she still hadn't replied to his last few messages and he was quite prepared to let her slip away without fuss. As long as she was ok. He picked up his phone.

Hey Dee. Hope you're having a good Christmas. I've got lots of munch in, if you want to pop round. No probs if not ☺

Hitting send, Jono realised how much he hoped she would reply. It wasn't healthy. With any luck, Delilah was about to break out and find herself and he wasn't likely to be a feature in that. He ditched the phone and went over to his main computer. There was still a mountain of work to catch up on from his uni course, although he'd made a significant start. He logged on to the university site and drifted around for a while, but was uninspired.

Netty popped into his mind. They'd exchanged quite a few more messages, but the tone was more reserved. Interesting that they were both persevering with the disjointed conversation anyway. He hadn't wished her a Happy Christmas either. When he logged into the chat room, he found she'd beaten him to it.

Hey TooGood. Hope you're having a cosy Christmas. x

Cosy? He hoped she was out partying and having a wild time. Sort of.

Hey Netty. It's definitely a steady one for me. Hope you're having a good one too. Have you had lots of nice presents? x

A little fanfare erupted from the phone on the breakfast bar. Jono went over and found a reply from Dee, who would be arriving in about an hour. He spent most of it washing up, making his bed and wrapping the tablet he'd bought for her.   It wasn't an expensive one, but would allow her to play games and access the net with Wi-Fi; albeit in a limited way, thanks to the programmes he had installed.

It was only when he knocked the mouse and the computer screen lit up, that he noticed the reply from Netty, sent within seconds of his message being received.

A rose pink onesie from my mother. It's absolutely gross and I had to wear it for most of yesterday afternoon. Just me and the cat now…bliss. Did you get anything awful? x

Damn. Damn, damn, damn.

Sorry – unexpected guests. Love the thought of the onesie. I really, honestly, got soap-on-a-rope…didn't think they still made that crap! Gotta dash, but talk later. Enjoy chilling with the cat. X

Dee was knocking on the door. He ditched the messaging page, spun around to the entrance hall and threw it open, surprised again by how different she looked with clean hair and nice clothes. And by how much better she smelled.

'Hey Dee! Great to see you, come in.'

Jono turned around and went back to the kitchen without waiting for a reply, but he didn't miss the grin that spread across her face.

'Coke?'

'Yeah, please.'

He pulled two cans from the fridge and two glasses from the cupboard. Delilah sat on the stool by the breakfast bar.

'So, are you all better now? I have to say, you look better than I've ever seen you. Crap timing to be ill though.'

'It's been alright really, I only got up yesterday afternoon. Blink brought me loads of smoothies. It got a bit boring, but he showed me how to play loads of games too, like Battle-Ships and Cluedo.'

'Yeah? I've got a game for the X-box that's a bit like Battle-Ships. I'll show you in a bit.' He hadn't bothered before, as co-ordinates were way beyond Dee's level of maths. This Blink lad sounded ok. 'Are you ready for some junk food then? I got a toastie-maker for Christmas and there's nothing better than a cheese n' bean toastie. There's a mountain of munch in the cupboard, too.'

'Sounds cool.'

Jono set about preparing the food, but when he pulled out the machine and Dee realised there was something similar in the Sunny Bank kitchen, she came to stand beside him and see how it was done.

'Ah, didn't you say you might be doing a catering course?'

'Dunno yet. I've got to go to the Support Centre next week and sort it out.'

'I start back at uni next week too. I'll warn you, it's knackering to start with.'

Delilah's usual mode of conversation was to assault you with a barrage of questions or remain silent, sometimes for hours. Today, they shared a two-way conversation throughout the making of the first two toasties and then Dee asked if she could take over for the second pair. Two hours later they were still talking at the breakfast bar, drinking coffee now, with a half-eaten box of chocolates between them.

'Hey, I said I'd show you that game. Do you want to take a look?

Dee frowned and pulled out her phone to check the time.

'I've gotta go...I'm going out tonight.'

'Anywhere nice?'

She blushed and turned her head away.

'Just out...with some mates.'

'Is Blink going?'

'No! I told you, he's a nerd, he doesn't smoke or drink, or even listen to music. He's boring.'

'He must be half alright, if he's feeding you up and keeping you company while you're all snotty and ill.'

...and managed to teach you more in a few days than you've learned in the last year. Dee's expression was half angry, half sulky, so he changed the subject.

'Have a good night, anyway. You'll have to come back and tell me all about your new school and courses. In fact, when you're a few weeks in and know how to avoid giving me food poisoning, you can come and cook dinner here.'

She half smiled at that.

'Alright.'

He saw her to the door and waved her away, but couldn't help laughing on his return to the kitchen. If Dee wrought this kind of destruction whilst making toasties, then it would take him a week to clean up if she ever cooked a full dinner. Deciding to leave the mess until tomorrow, Jono went back to his conversation with Netty. There was no reply, but then he'd made it clear he was logging off.

You still there? he typed.

More often than you think was the immediate response.

What was that supposed to mean? And what the hell should he put in reply? It was the kind of thing a stalker might say and he was pleased that it was such an implausible idea.

Sorry. My dark sense of humour comes rocking out when I've had too much wine. I opened a bottle earlier, but the cat wasn't interested. Have your visitors gone?

Phew.

Yup. I've got a kitchen full of dirty dishes now, but they can wait. So what was your best present?

~ ~ ~

It was a relief that Jim had texted and not just turned up. Shona wasn't vain, but it would be embarrassing to get caught still in her pyjamas in the afternoon. It was time to pull herself together anyway, there was only so long she could allow the hangover to hold sway. By God, it was one almighty hangover though. She

154

had no comprehension of how Kelly could drink that volume on a daily basis…and she was taking it steady at that.

A shower would wake her up and force her to get dressed. She climbed the stairs slowly and fetched clean clothes from the bedroom, but upon pulling back the shower curtain, found the bath and tiles around it splashed with black stains. Oh hell. The hair-dying session. Shona didn't remember it going quite that badly and neither could she recall which substances – if any – would now remove the ugly mess.

Bending down was not an option, so she squirted some cream cleaner at the worst stains, tossed a sponge in and did the best she could manage with her feet whilst in the shower. It wasn't a vast improvement, but the water felt so good, she didn't care all that much. There was a temptation to linger, but she didn't want to be dashing about when Jim arrived. There wasn't a dash in her.

She was making tea when he knocked on the door, before letting himself in. He eyed her pale face with concern.

'Have you had a peaceful couple of days? No visitors?'

'I know I look awful, but the fault is my own. I invited Kelly round yesterday and we got absolutely plastered.'

'Delilah's mum?'

'Yes. I felt sorry for her, but it was ok in the end. I remember now why we were friends…before she let alcohol take over her life.'

'So what about Delilah?'

'I got Kelly to write a card for her and took it over to Sunny Bank.' Shona paused, the conversation stirring up other, alcohol-clouded memories. 'And I think I might have agreed to help her clear up the house so Delilah can visit.'

'Jesus. I hope you've got a rubber suit.'

~ ~ ~

It felt weird walking next to Josh again. She'd barely seen him for days and not spoken to him since the night she'd passed out with Gaz. Not that he was talking now. Having been prepared to go and find Gaz on her own, she was still more glad than annoyed when Josh knocked on her bedroom door, saying he'd been asked to take her over.

Blink and Gareth tried to say she wasn't better yet and should have an early night, but she really did feel good. Apart from being a bit nervous about seeing Gaz. And wondering what was wrong with Josh. Blink said something bad had happened to make him hate Christmas, but no-one would say what it was. He had flipped out yesterday afternoon, when Sandra tried to get him to stay in and have Christmas dinner.

Their destination turned out to be the same flat as before, at the top of the pissy stairwell. The music was loud and including Gaz, there were six lads already there, plus three girls Dee had never seen before. One eyed her with suspicion, the other two whispered to each other and laughed. Everyone looked wrecked and there were bottles and cans strewn around the floor.

'My Princess has arrived!' Gaz shouted, throwing his arms out.

Dee didn't move from the doorway. There was no way she was going to kiss him in front of those bitches. Josh left her and dropped into a space on the settee, Gaz let his arms fall and staggered over to her.

'Aw, don't be shy babe, these are all sound.' He waved an arm at the room in general and the girls laughed again. 'Did you like your present?'

He threw the other arm around her and pulled her close. He stank of beer.

'Yeah, it's gorgeous.'

'So have you brought my present?'

Dee blushed. She didn't have any money, she'd told him that in a text.

'No. I said...'

'I know what you said babe, I know dat. I aint thinkin' of the kind of present that needs wrappin'...'

The girls laughed, one lad whooped and another said she should tie a bow around her booty. Dee wanted to leave, but Gaz was pulling her over to a beanbag in the corner.

'C'mon, I'm just messin' with ya. You owe me a kiss though, you gotta own that.'

156

She supposed that was fair. He must have spent a lot of money on the necklace, or taken a big risk nicking it. The girls were talking now and the lads were passing round a bong, so no one was watching. Gaz collapsed onto the beanbag and pulled her down on top of him.

10

Derek was surprised by how little Delilah protested at being woken up at 7am. Josh told him to fuck off three times before Delilah banged on his door and begged him to go with her, after which he got up, with much grumbling. It was fortunate that Blink was also tired after a fortnight of lie-ins and ate his breakfast in sleepy silence, not launching into his usual morning monologue.

He decided to turn a blind eye to the four roll-ups Delilah smoked before the taxi arrived and hoped she would make it to lunchtime before the next one. She'd probably lose her place on the course if she got excluded on her first day for lighting up in the loo. The change in her over Christmas gave him reason to hope, but the steep backward slide over the last week was ominous.

Blink was the last to leave and the house had only been quiet for ten minutes when the phone rang. It was Delilah's social worker, back at work and wanting to come over for an update. They arranged the meeting for mid-afternoon so that Becky could also see Delilah when she arrived home. Derek would rather have let her come in and just chill after her first day, but he also wanted to share concerns over Delilah's mystery boyfriend.

The call at lunchtime was not unexpected. Josh had not returned for the afternoon register. The Support Centre would report him missing if he did not show up there, or back at Sunny Bank, within the next twenty minutes. It was doubtful that Josh would show up anywhere before midnight, but Derek went through the process and logged the call. He wasn't worried about Josh – he had done this dozens of times – but he was disappointed that he'd left Delilah. At least she hadn't followed him out.

When the door alarm went off fifteen minutes later, Derek thought it was Becky arriving early and was amazed to find Josh in the hall.

'Hey! I didn't think we'd see you til later.'

'I just couldn't stand it man, they do my fuckin' head in and the other kids are complete dicks.'

'You managed half a day though, that's a definite step forward. So how's Delilah doing?'

'Alright. Dee's palled up with Carla and she's promised to look after her this afternoon.'

Derek was torn. This was the longest conversation he'd had with Josh in weeks, but he needed to call the Support Centre.

'Look, I've got to call and let them know you're back...you know the story with reporting you missing. Do you want some food? Delilah's resurrected the toastie-maker.'

Josh shrugged, but he didn't otherwise move.

'I'll be two seconds.'

Derek ran to the office and punched in the number.

'Hi, it's Sunny Bank, Josh has turned up here. Yes, no problem, bye.'

Josh was half way up the stairs when he got back to the hall, but not moving fast.

'Do you want a toastie then?' Derek said. 'I can do cheese, or beans, or cheese and beans. There might even be some mushrooms and peppers in the fridge.'

'I'm alright,' Josh said after a pause.

'Better than eating crap later and I'm having one too. I haven't seen much of you for the last couple of weeks, it'd be good to catch up for half an hour.' Josh was rigid and silent on the stairs. 'I'm going to go and make mine, anyway.'

Derek went into the kitchen and began taking things out of the fridge. The toastie-maker was warming and the kettle nearly boiled when Josh slid through the door.

'Good timing. Do you want beans, or just cheese?'

'Whatever.'

Josh sat down at the table with his back towards Derek. It was a good sign, he talked best that way. Without asking any more questions, he made Josh a coffee and put it on the table, surprised to receive a mumbled 'thanks' in return. He went back to the worktop and started slicing cheese, slowly.

'You've impressed me over the last few weeks Josh. It must have been hard, with Blink and Delilah going crazy over the decorations. On the whole, you've handled it well. Definitely more man than boy.'

There was another long silence before Josh spoke.

'Don't feel like a man. I'm shit scared of going inside.'

'Hey, most people are scared of that, whatever their age. What takes guts is to admit it.'

'Doesn't help though, does it.'

It didn't, not really. He was going down this time, the only question was how long for.

'It could, a bit. You know the score. If you can prove you're taking it seriously this time - engaging in education, keeping to curfews, staying out of trouble - you'll get a much shorter sentence. You've made a start on that today and you can try again tomorrow. Every effort you make will have its reward now.'

'Nah, it's all fucked. I won't get a job with that on my record. What's the point in trying?'

'That's not true. You'll still have lots of opportunities and you're a bright lad. You have to attend education on the inside too you know. Why not take the opportunity to get some qualifications and prove what you're worth? Why not start now? Go in again tomorrow, Delilah could use your support.'

Josh shuffled in his seat and Derek wished he could see his face.

'She don't need me.'

'I think she does, she's a vulnerable young girl.'

Josh didn't reply and the toasties were ready. Derek put them on plates and carried them over to the table, sitting down next to Josh, but passing in front of him first and clocking the deep frown on his face. They ate in silence for a minute, but Derek couldn't let the opportunity pass.

161

'She was in a bit of a mess when you came back on New Year's Eve.' He left another pause. 'Looked like a bad combination of alcohol and weed to me.'

Josh shrugged.

'It was a party. She don't stick with me all night.'

'No, and I'm not suggesting you've given her drugs.' Derek waited until Josh had eaten several more mouthfuls of his toastie. 'I was more bothered about the love bites all over her neck actually. Has she got a boyfriend?'

Josh dropped the last bit of his toastie onto the plate.

'I know what you're tryin' to do man and I'm not rattin'.'

'I know you know, you're not naive, but Delilah is only 14 Josh.'

He scowled and shoved his chair away from the table.

'I need a fag.'

'Can I come with you?'

Josh shrugged, so Derek followed him out into the garden.

~ ~ ~

Becky regretted having arranged to visit Delilah. She was late already and knew the schedule for her first day back at work was way too ambitious. So much for all those resolutions. Perhaps she would see Delilah another day and just catch up with her key workers for now. Simon had kissed her goodbye this morning. She wanted a kiss hello when she walked in too.

There was a strange atmosphere when she arrived at Sunny Bank. Gareth took her into the office and made her tea, saying that Derek was with one of the other young people and would be with her shortly. Becky was glad of the opportunity to check her emails and settled in a corner with her lap-top. When Derek came in twenty minutes later, she told him to take his time and grab a drink if he wanted.

'No, I think we need to talk as a matter of urgency,' he said, his face grim. 'I have some more information about Delilah's new friends...not that enlightening I'm afraid, but very worrying.'

Becky closed her lap-top and tried to relax her stomach, stop the bile rising up her throat.

'Are we talking exploitation?'

'I think so. Josh still won't give any names and reckons the ones he does know are nick-names and won't help. From what I can gather, Delilah is now the girlfriend of a local 'gangsta' in his twenties. He's fairly small fry from the sound of it, but has some nasty acquaintances.'

'If Josh is worried, why won't he say more?'

'He's more scared of them than the police and it's not the boyfriend as such, or at least that's what Josh thinks. It's some older men, the ones who set up the industrial break-in that Josh was the scape-goat for. He overheard them talking to the boyfriend, but didn't think much of it at the time. The phrase only stuck in his head because it was funny and didn't make sense, but now he's worked it out.'

'Oh God, what was it?'

'Softly, softly, catchee monkey.'

Becky went cold.

'He's sure they were talking about Delilah?'

'Yes, and there's something else. They said 'don't spoil the goods'. He assumed they were talking about the stolen goods at the time, but now he's not so sure.'

'Christ Almighty.'

Gareth, still sitting behind the desk, winced and turned away. Was it her language or the topic? Either way, this was a disaster waiting to happen.

'So we know the danger she's in, but do we have anything to take to the police?'

'All Josh would say was 'tell them to fix the cameras', which would explain why there's been no intel up to now.'

'Has Delilah said anything at all?'

'No. She was ill over Christmas and holed up in her room with our other lad, Blink. He would tell us straight away if she let anything slip, but Delilah also knows that. The boyfriend sent her a gold necklace, but we only found out through Blink…she wouldn't talk about it. As soon as she was better, she was back out with Josh.'

'Ok. I need to get back to the office and pass all this to the police. Is there anything else I should know?'

'Only suspicions. You're already aware that Delilah smokes cannabis, given the opportunity, but she was also drunk on New Year's Eve and maybe under the influence of something else. On quite a few occasions, her pupils have been tiny when she's come in. I did ask Josh, but he says he's never seen Class A's around, just some super-strong cannabis resin.'

'Right.'

Becky added 'super-strong hash?' to her notes and then shoved the pad and computer back in her bag.

'I won't stay now, but I'll be back to see Delilah as soon as possible. Please say hello to her from me and I'd really appreciate an email about how she got on today.'

'Of course.'

Derek saw her to the door and Becky dashed to her car, but when she got inside, she closed her eyes and gripped the steering wheel for a moment, trying to still her spinning mind. There was a lot to do, but she must take a calm and rational approach...and not ram her car into a tree on the way to the office.

Still only semi-composed when she passed a Co-op, Becky pulled in and bought ten cigarettes, abandoning yet another resolution in the process. She hadn't smoked for a fortnight, damn it. Bill wrinkled his nose at her when she walked into the office.

'Oh dear. One of those days then?'

'Worse. Is Clare in?'

'Our conscientious manager was on call over most of Christmas and New Year and will be back tomorrow. Have you got big trouble?'

'Potential sexual exploitation...of Delilah.'

'You'll have to go above her.'

'I can't afford to spend an hour filling someone in, who isn't familiar with the case. Delilah's at school at the moment, but will probably be back out tonight. This could kick off at any time. I'll do the necessaries with the police and report it up later.'

'It's 2 o'clock.'

'I know.'

164

'I'll make tea then.'

Bill got up and Becky switched on her desktop, gnashing her teeth at its slowness. Having made the necessary referral to the Child Sexual Exploitation Investigation Unit, logged her actions on the multi-agency system and emailed Josh's social worker to suggest he read her notes, it still didn't feel like she'd done enough. She sent a brief, 'are you at work?' email to McGrath and then called the local multi-agency team manager, to give her the heads up about the possible activity in the area. McGrath replied before the end of the call.

In, but have meeting in 10 mins. Email me and I'll respond asap.

Becky briefly outlined this morning's revelations and where they had come from, then bullet-pointed her main questions.

- **Josh said 'tell the police to fix the cameras'. Who do I contact to check where the CCTV is down and how soon it can be repaired?**

- **Is there any legal pressure we can put on Josh to force him to give us more information?**

- **Staff at the care home suspect that Delilah has taken Class A drugs on a number of occasions. Josh insists she's only smoked cannabis, but that some of this was 'super-strong resin'. Could you possibly speak to someone (or give me a contact number) in the drugs squad and find out what that might be and if it narrows down the possible list of those involved?**

I'm sorry to drag you into this and bombard you with questions. I have informed the CSE Unit, but don't have another contact in the police to lean on. Don't get emotive, stay professional. She changed 'lean on' to 'speak to'. **I understand that it might not be appropriate for you to follow this up, but would appreciate any help or advice you can offer. Kind regards, Becky Stocks.**

~ ~ ~

Two hours passed before McGrath sat down to reply to Becky, but he had not been idle. There were two sets of CCTV cameras currently not in operation; one was an electrical problem and the other had been damaged a fortnight ago, the incident logged as a fluke success by young kids, chucking stones and launching steel bearings with a catapult. Now that footage was being re-examined. Budget restrictions and workload over Christmas had pushed the repair down the priority list, but now it was right back at the top.

The only delay was coordination between departments; the CSE Unit didn't want any repairs alerting the occupants of the nearby block of flats, before a surveillance team was in place. A surveillance team would not be available until late tomorrow, due to other, more pressing demands on their services. He informed Becky of this, gave her a contact number for her query regarding drugs and suggested keeping Josh on side and watching him for now. There were a number of charges that could be brought against him, but in McGrath's opinion, it wouldn't be that helpful at present and was not his call anyway.

He'd sent the email some time ago, but was still sitting, staring at the screen when Becky's reply popped up. What were his thoughts on informing the three adults already involved with Delilah that she was at risk; namely Jim, Shona and Jono? Was there any possibility that Jim could be involved? She shouldn't be asking him. The CSE Investigation Unit were running this now and bypassing them was both inappropriate and liable to cause serious ructions.

Despite his annoyance, McGrath considered the questions at length. Jono he actively liked and admired, in spite of his collusion with Delilah when she ran away. Even consciously applying the cynicism so necessary to his job, it was hard to see Jono in an exploitative role. Making a link to Jim was reasonable, given his background, but his extensive record included nothing involving children, or women for that matter. He also seemed genuine in his concern for Delilah, though there was no denying that he would have the contacts.

Jim had been on McGrath's mind recently. During the initial stages of the investigation into the assault against Shona, the whereabouts of her son Paulie were unknown and McGrath had revisited his file several times. Between Christmas and New Year, Paulie was picked up in Manchester during a drugs bust, following an anonymous tip off. McGrath asked that the assault on Shona be mentioned during interview. The report back was that Paulie denied all knowledge, but in the opinion of the interviewing officer, was lying through his teeth.

It could be coincidence, but if Jim knew more than they did about the incident – which was highly likely – would that not be a suitable retribution? For the son of a friend, who was sticking by that son? McGrath suspected that, twenty years ago, Paulie would be in hospital and not a warm, safe police cell. But what would be suitable retribution for the abuse of a child? Jim would have greater resources in terms of underworld intelligence than the police did and what action might he take, if he thought Delilah was in danger?

Hi Becky.

As I'm sure you're aware, you can't discuss the details of this with anyone at present. However, as Delilah is so uncommunicative, it makes sense to approach those she is close to for information. Stick to concerns about her current friendship group and ask them to pass on any names and unusual comments or behaviour. I have no suspicion that Jim Travis is involved, but be very careful what you say to him – he may decide to take his own measures to protect Delilah, if he realises the nature of the danger she is in.

Regards, Andrew McGrath.

~ ~ ~

Trying to keep a lid on her anger and disappointment, Dee decided she would reward herself with a Gaz Special, if she managed to escape without putting Stacey's head through the window. It hadn't occurred to her that any of Doogie's lot would also be at the Support Centre. At least they were inside the building before Stacey spotted her and the staff jumped on it straight away. Josh reckoned Stacey was the biggest gob there and caused loads of trouble. Even though most of the others respected or were scared of Josh, nothing he said could shut her up.

Up to now, they'd been in different classrooms, but Delilah knew it wouldn't take Stacey long to turn everyone against her. Lunchtime would be hell. Yesterday was almost decent, but even if Stacey was only there on Tuesdays, everything was ruined now. It was fifteen minutes before the end of the last morning lesson. Dee went to the teaching assistant, who was softer than the teacher.

'I'm going to the bog.'

The woman looked up at the clock on the wall.

'It's nearly lunchtime, can't you wait?'

'No.'

Dee turned and walked to the door, praying. Nothing more was said and she slipped out without issue. She waited in the toilets for twelve minutes and sent Gaz a text asking if she could come over. The Support Centre wasn't that far from the flat, it'd only take her half an hour to walk. He'd stopped moving around now and been in the same place for nearly two weeks. Josh didn't have to be with her every time.

When the lunch bell rang, she raced outside and out of the gate, not stopping until she reached the park. There was a sheltered space under the bushes behind the caretaker's hut and she hid there, smoking a fag and reading the reply from Gaz. It was fine to go and see him. She peered around the wall of the hut, but nobody appeared to be looking for her, so she set off again at a quick walk.

There was a truck opposite the entrance to the flats and two blokes in overalls, one in a little crane thing on top of the truck, the other on the ground, looking at a lap-top in his hands. Neither of them paid her any attention as she walked past, so she looked closer at what they were doing. The one in the crane was fiddling with something just under the roof of the pub. It looked like a camera, but surely Gaz wouldn't hide out smack opposite somewhere with CCTV. Perhaps it was just for the pub.

She buzzed the flat, gave her name to whoever answered and the door popped open. Climbing the pissy stairs, she tried to work out what was different and realised there was no music booming out from the top landing. Apart from a baby crying in one of the ground floor flats, there was no noise at all. Damo let her in. He must have answered the buzzer, but despite him always being with Gaz, except that night at the garage, she'd never heard him speak.

He was massive, with muscle not fat, very quiet and a bit weird. Several times she'd caught him staring at her, but he always looked away. He didn't speak now, just turned around and walked back into the flat. Dee followed him in and saw Gaz on the settee, talking to someone in a chair with his back to her. Gaz looked up and grinned.

'Alright babe? I'll be five minutes. Sort her some gear out Damo.'

Damo grunted, picked up a pouch of bacca, a bag of weed, papers and a lighter from the settee and took them through to the kitchen, jerking his head at her as he dropped them on the worktop. Bloody cave-man. Dee began rolling a spliff, but stopped to check her phone when it buzzed in her pocket. It was a text from Josh.

They call the pigs if ur not back 20 mins after lunch. Call Sunny Bank.

Shit. Gaz wouldn't like that. She couldn't call from here though. Looking through her contacts she found the office mobile number that Becky made her put in. She'd try texting first.

Its D scool shit 2day gon 2 parc bak l8r

The phone started buzzing again within seconds, but thankfully it was still on silent. It was the office phone calling her. She killed the call and sent another text.

Wot

The reply took long enough for her to finish rolling and she lit up before looking at it.

Thanks for texting, but we need to see you to know you are safe. Why not come home and we can do some cooking. Sandra

No wonder it took her ages, stupid old cow. She probably didn't even have a phone. She was alright at cooking though.

In a bit

Delilah shoved the phone back in her pocket just as Gaz called through from the living room.

'Hey, Dee. You gonna bring dat thru here?'

She walked out of the kitchen, but stopped dead when she saw the other man, facing her now; the same man who was there the night they all went off robbing. He was looking her up and down with a nasty smile.

'Hello Delilah. How are you?' he said.

She ignored him and went to pass Gaz the spliff. He pulled her down next to him on the settee, but that left her opposite the other man and now she wanted to leave.

'You can talk to dis guy, he's ok,' Gaz said.

'I've gotta go, I only called in.'

'Woah, baby. You can't run out on me now, you only just got here. Smoke some more.'

He passed her the spliff back and his comment reminded her of the truck outside.

'Is there CCTV out there?' she asked.

Gaz laughed.

'There was, but we fixed it for a bit. Why you askin'?'

'Cos there're two blokes outside, with a truck and crane, messing about with something.'

The smile fell off his face and he jerked upright. The other man stood up.

'Are you saying there are pigs out there?'

'They don't look like pigs,' Dee said, alarmed by how angry he was, 'just two blokes and a truck.'

'I'm leaving,' he said to Gaz. 'You should get the hell out too.'

'Where the fuck to?'

'I don't know. You're a big boy, sort yourself out.'

He left in a hurry. Gaz jumped up, pulled a rucksack from behind the settee and started throwing things into it.

'Damo, check I've left nothin', grab what you want and get out, but stay covered up.' He threw a large, black hoodie at Dee. 'Put this on.'

She caught it and pulled it over her head, but didn't see why it was so important.

'I'm not on the run, I could just leave,' she said.

Gaz spun around and grabbed her arm, hard.

'No you can't!' he relaxed his grip and tried to smile. 'We'll go out together and then split.'

She shrugged and let him pull the drawstrings tight, so the hood squeezed in around her face. He kissed her lightly and then let go.

'I might not see you for a few days, so take dis.' He took a small lump of resin from his pocket and passed it to her. 'It should see you right. Go easy though, it's good shit.'

She stashed the lump and waited, while Gaz collected a few more things and issued a final order to Damo.

'Wipe everything man. I'll catch up with you later.'

Gaz took her hand and led her from the flat, turning right down the corridor instead of left. She stayed mute.

'Good girl,' he whispered, 'just be cool and follow me'.

They pushed through a fire door and paused at the top of the steel fire escape while Gaz scanned the parking area. It seemed clear, so they hurried down the stairs as fast as they could, without too much noise. Crossing the tarmac, Gaz headed for a section of wall with a bush or tree growing over from the other side. Two bricks had been smashed in, providing foot holds and an easy route over. He must have planned this.

'You first, but wait for me on the other side,' he said.

Dee put her foot in the lower hole and reached up, ready to grab the top course of bricks. She was an experienced wall-climber and already gaining momentum, when Gaz gave her an extra shove upwards. Missing her grip and shooting over the top, she tried to grab a branch, but caught nothing more than a handful of leaves.

Her body landed first, on something soft, but as her legs slammed down, there was a burst of pain, just above her foot.

171

Dee smothered a cry with her fist, but agony bloomed outwards from her ankle bone and several tears squeezed between her eyelids.

11

Becky could not believe the texts on her phone on Wednesday morning. It was a bloody good job that the one resolution she *had* stuck to, was turning her phone off at 6pm and back on at 7.30am the next day. There were three from Sunny Bank, one from Jono, one from Jim. There were also several missed calls, including two from her manager. She prayed that they too related to Delilah and there was only one child in crisis. It was 7.45am...not a promising start to the day.

The general theme was that Delilah had fractured her ankle bone in several places, falling off a wall. Jim and Jono wanted to know if the accident was related to Becky's understated warnings of the day before, the messages from Sunny Bank suggested it might be. Sighing, Becky flicked off the toaster, chucked the lukewarm bread in the bin, threw her coffee down the sink and picked up her car keys.

She pulled into the car park behind Bill and when he spotted her trying to balance a take-out coffee, a bacon wrap and two work-bags, he came over to help.

'Breakfast on the run, eh? I'm glad you're settling back in slowly.'

'Ha, fat chance with Delilah on my case-load, although on the drive here, I realised that what I thought was a disaster, may turn out to be a blessing in disguise. She ought to be safe from any kind of exploitation whilst immobile in bed.'

'She spent the week before last in bed! What's wrong with her now?'

'A smashed up ankle, from what I can gather. I'll know more when I get to my computer. I don't want to make any calls before getting as clear a picture as possible. So far, I've received three very different, very sketchy versions of the same story and I smell a rat.'

Climbing the two flights of stairs up to their office discouraged any further conversation. The emailed report from Sunny Bank said that Delilah left the Support Centre at lunchtime, texting to say she was at a park and would be back later. She refused to answer her phone. Josh - who was still at the Support Centre - received a text from Delilah to say she was hurt and went to help her. On finding her unable to walk, he called a taxi, which staff paid for when they arrived back at Sunny Bank.

It wasn't obvious how badly Delilah was hurt at first, as she didn't appear to be in too much pain. She was however, under the influence of something. Two members of staff talked to her and she claimed to have fallen off a wall, messing about, garden-hopping. As she managed to talk coherently, refused medical help and had no other visible injuries, she was allowed to go to bed. At 2am, staff heard sounds of distress and went into Delilah's bedroom. She was still asleep, but awoke screaming when they called her name. Her ankle was massively swollen.

This time, she agreed to go to hospital and the x-ray showed several fractures to the ankle bone. Delilah's leg was put in an adjustable cast and she was instructed to keep all weight off it for at least a week, probably two. Strong pain-killers had been prescribed, but were locked in the medicine cabinet at Sunny Bank, with a dispensing chart.

There was also an update from the CSE Unit, which didn't mention the ankle. The damaged CCTV camera had been repaired, with a surveillance team in place. Delilah arrived at the flats opposite the camera at lunchtime, clearly taking notice of the repair team. A man already known to the police and observed entering the flats earlier, left shortly after Delilah's arrival. Another man and a young girl, presumed to be Delilah, left from a fire exit minutes later, both wearing hoodies to conceal their faces. They climbed over a wall at the rear of the flats, but there was no further information, as the surveillance team were not authorised to pursue. When officers called Sunny Bank, they were told Delilah had returned home with a twisted ankle and was now in bed.

So the bastard, who was probably the boyfriend, left her lying behind the wall with a shattered ankle. Nice. Becky hoped that Delilah saw some fault in this, but suspected not. The notion of being cared for was so unfamiliar, she wouldn't expect it in the first place. It was dog-eat-dog in her world.

By 8.30am she felt informed, if not prepared. Time to go and give Clare all the details. She was fortunate to have a manager like Clare, who would share responsibility in a case of this nature. Her last boss would have left her adrift and then bollocked her for any poor decisions. The only downside was Clare being a tad too efficient - she might invite Josh's social worker to share the briefing, and he was a dick.

Becky read the texts from Jono and Jim again on her way to Clare's office and did some mental maths. If Delilah hadn't gone to the hospital until 2am, she must have texted them between then and 7.30am, when Becky switched her phone on. No wonder they were worried. She checked the times on their messages. Jono was politely concerned at 6.30am. Jim was a little more direct and a little less patient, at the almost-reasonable time of 5.59. She imagined him, sitting in a chair, watching the progress of the hands on an old clock, which was a minute fast.

Hi. Had txt from D. Says she has broken ankle. Linked to new friends you talked about? Is one a boyfriend? No 14 yr old lad would take D on. Any more you can tell me? Thanks, Jim.

Damn. McGrath was right and she would have to warn him that Jim was not far off the mark already. She would talk this through with Clare too...the reply would have to be worded with care. Too much information and he could blow things with Delilah or take the law into his own hands, too little information and he might stop co-operating *and* take the law into his own hands.

~ ~ ~

It was no use pressing Dee. He'd asked once and she hadn't answered, asking again would only put her guard up. Teenagers were notorious for only taking advice from their peers, but Dee didn't have any friends her own age. And she was a girl. Jim had never understood women and knew even less about girls. He knew all about kids in care though.

The social worker was being cagey, but at least admitted it. There were serious concerns, she said, but the police and staff at Sunny Bank were on to it. Unfortunately, due to the confidential nature of the investigation, she couldn't tell him anything more and hoped he would help, by not getting involved at present. She would still be grateful for any insights he had and appreciated his concern.

Shona had mentioned helping Kelly clean up the house so that Dee could visit. That would be the easiest way of bumping into her for a casual chat, or at least it would have been. He was keeping his distance from Shona for the time being, as Paulie got busted sooner than he expected. Having not actually seen any sign of undercover cops on his trip to Manchester, Jim thought it would take them a few days to verify his anonymous call. Instead, they arrested Paulie that same evening.

It was too soon. He knew, the moment the voice on the line gave him the information. They were suspicious; he went up to suss out the job, tried to pull it and then the target got busted. Too convenient by far. He was 'invited' to the clubhouse to talk through events, but had no intention of going. The next invitation would be less cordial and if they were watching in the meantime, visiting Shona would pretty much confirm their suspicions. There were those who would remember her from the old days, when they all partied in the same pubs, and put two and two together.

The flip side was that if he continued to avoid Shona, she would also work out his involvement, when she discovered Paulie was in prison. And he wanted to talk to her.

'Come on Crank,' he said. 'I need some fresh air to get my brain working.'

They took a circular route in a different direction to their usual walks, following country lanes through the old, outlying villages, rather than muddy footpaths across fields. There was so much to look at that Jim stopped thinking for a while and the ache in his head eased. They swung back west towards town and were about two miles from the estate when an A-board on the verge caught Jim's eye.

2 for 1 Afternoon Tea. A selection of sandwiches, cakes and a hot drink. £3.99.

It was a café in a plant nursery, set behind the high walls of an old farmyard. A wisp of smoke rose invitingly from a low chimney and Jim could murder a mug of tea. It was also the kind of place that none of the heavy mob would think of visiting. He carried on for another two hundred yards and found a junction with the main road, just beyond the tight bend, as he expected. There was a bus-stop to the left. He examined the timetable and then called Shona.

'Do you fancy afternoon tea?' he said, instead of hello. 'There's a new café opened at that old plant nursery up the road and it's 2 for 1.'

'Er...I'm in my scruffs and...afternoon tea? Is that really your kind of thing?'

'I've been out with Crank for two hours...any kind of tea is my kind of thing right now. It's quiet and they've got a log-burner. The 92 bus comes past the end of your road in twelve minutes and arrives here in twenty-two.'

'Oh sod it, alright then. You know you're getting old, when afternoon tea feels like an adventure. See you soon.'

She hung up and Jim slipped the phone back into his pocket. It was an adventure really, but as there wasn't much risk to Shona, she didn't need to know that. However unpleasant the circles he moved in, they weren't going to hurt her to get at Paulie. He walked back to the café, bought a mug of tea and ordered the 2 for 1 with half an hour's notice. The young girl at the counter gave him a curious look but he didn't care, she was way too up-market to know anyone who knew him.

Jim drained the tea, explained that he would be back shortly and went outside to where Crank waited.

'I'm afraid there'll be a bit more of this mate,' he said, 'but we can go and meet Shona now and I'll save you a sandwich.'

Before Shona stepped off the bus it was obvious the game was up. She was a floaty kind of woman, with long, flowing hair, which still looked good grey, long, flowing skirts and long, flowing cardi-things. Today was the first time in thirty years he had seen her wearing trousers, along with boots, a thick coat and a hat. Her hair must be tied up, as he couldn't see any at all. Both her eyebrows were raised and her lips pursed as she looked him straight in the eye. Maybe it wasn't that subtle an idea after all.

She took the hand he offered as she climbed down, but let go the moment she was level again.

'Hello Jim,' she said and bent to pat Crank 'and hello to you, Crank.'

'You've certainly dressed for the weather,' he said, unable to think of anything else to say.

'I've dressed with practicalities in mind. How far is this café?'

'Just a few hundred yards.'

'Far enough if we walk slowly then, but let's not beat about the bush, eh? Jim, I'm not a daft old woman yet and though I always tried to stay on the periphery of the bike scene, I'm well aware of what went on and still does. You've never cared a rat's fart about Paulie - you had no reason to - but you've asked after him six times in the last month.'

Jim did not interrupt, rolling a fag instead. They might as well have it out.

'I thought you suspected him of beating me up.' Shona continued. 'As a matter of fact, you were almost right...he did hit me and I cracked my head on the table or chairs on the way down. He'd come for money, he was in a lot of trouble, but I wouldn't give him anything. He didn't deserve what I thought you would do if you found out.'

He bloody well did, but that was irrelevant now. Shona was using the past tense though, surely she hadn't sussed out the whole thing?

'So when I got a letter from him yesterday, from prison, I remembered our last conversation about Paulie; when I said he might be better off inside and you got all enthusiastic on the subject, verging on cheerful. Then you went off somewhere on the bike. Since then you've been avoiding me, or so I thought until today, but perhaps it's just been public avoidance.'

Yup, she was there. They would have to slow down a little more. Not a conversation for a tea room.

'You got him locked up didn't you? Was it because of what he did to me? Was it to save him from something worse? Where did you go, Jim?'

He struggled to focus, a large part of his mind wondering why on earth he wasn't married to this woman. It was pointless to lie or fabricate, so he told her everything, though not quite how low Paulie had stooped. She was calmer than he expected, but he still reiterated the lack of options.

'He was in too deep Shona, on a scale way beyond our lack of resources. It's the best way out.'

'I know.'

She put a hand on his arm, but they were by the gate to the nursery now and Jim could see the waitress watching them from the window of the café.

'Let's get inside,' he said. 'Our tea will be getting cold.'

They sat by the stove, cosy in its warmth, although Jim feared that the small wooden chair, supporting only two thirds of his backside, would not hold out much longer.

'How's the clear up at Kelly's going?' he asked.

'Slow to start with and now at a halt. She's in hospital.'

~ ~ ~

The last stretch in bed was a new experience; Delilah had stayed there by choice and quite enjoyed being looked after. This was very different. Her ankle hurt like hell, but the rest of her was bored and frustrated. Blink was at school, so she couldn't even learn new games, although he did promise to help her with the work sent by the Support Centre. Woopy-fucking-do. Even Josh had gone to his mechanics course.

179

Yesterday, Derek had started teaching her chess. It was proper complicated, but she liked it. It was like having a mini war with your own tiny gang and it would be good to surprise Blink. He made her feel like an idiot, even though he never said anything like that. Today sucked. Big time. Becky had been to see her this morning, banging on about all sorts. She was vulnerable, she should be careful who she chose for friends, did she have a boyfriend, would she see the school nurse, was she taking drugs.

The only good thing about Becky's visit was the box of Maltesers she brought with her. It saved Dee from eating the disgusting soup that Sandra gave her at lunch. Sandra, who kept trying to read to her. Sandra, who wanted to teach her how to knit and crochet. Sandra, who Dee had told to fuck off about an hour ago and was now cross with her. Derek wouldn't be on until tonight, when Blink and Josh would be around anyway.

She'd texted Jono and her mum and even Jim, but not Gaz, as she didn't have his new number yet. She played games on her tablet until the battery ran out and the socket wasn't close enough to use it plugged in. Now she was bored. So bored, that the only thing she could focus on was the throb in her ankle. It didn't hurt at all after the painkillers kicked in, but the last hour before she was allowed any more was a nightmare. This hour.

Dee thought about the lump of hash in her bedside cabinet. Gaz had made her eat half of it after she fell off the wall and it did sort out the pain, kind of. It was still there, but not hurting, almost funny. She was going to save the rest for a few spliffs, but that wasn't happening anytime soon. She could just eat a bit. A little ball of it wouldn't even need chewing, she could just swallow it.

She extracted the lump from the back corner of the top drawer and sliced a piece off with her thumbnail. Good job it was squidgy. Washing it down with a sip of water, Dee wondered what to do while she waited for it kick in. She eyed the book that Sandra had left on top of the cabinet. Alice in Wonderland. What a stupid title. It sounded like a book for babies. But there was nothing else to do.

~ ~ ~

Blink arrived home, breathless, at 3.45pm. He must have run all the way. Anything to get home before Josh, who wouldn't disturb Blink and Delilah, but wouldn't let Blink inside the room if he got there first. Derek often wondered whether to warn Blink in more clear terms that he was heading for heartbreak, but the lad needed to learn about his feelings and how to deal with them. It was best done with people around to support him. He was also an enormously good influence on Delilah.

He shot straight up to see her, but was back downstairs within ten minutes, making coffee. Derek walked through to the kitchen.

'What are you up to tonight then...is Delilah going to do her homework?'

'Not yet, she w..wants me to explain a l..list of words out of her b..book first.'

'What book? What's the list?'

'A l..list Delilah has made...of w..words she doesn't know in the b..book she's reading, Alice in W..wonderland. It's q..quite a long list.'

It would be. According to the last education report, she was barely literate.

'We got some pizza bases in for tea, do you want to come and make them?'

'N..not really. H..has Delilah just had her p..painkillers?'

'Not long ago, why?'

'She's a bit s..spaced out, but they are s..strong.'

'They are, but she's only on those for a week.' The coffee was made and Blink was visibly itching to get back upstairs. 'I'll give you a shout when the pizzas are ready.'

Sandra liked cooking and was on shift for another two hours. With any luck, she would volunteer to make the pizzas. He went back to the office, where she was working at the desk.

'I hate to say it, but being confined to bed does Delilah the power of good. Blink says she's reading a book!'

Sandra's eyes narrowed.

'Which book?'

'Alice in Wonderland. She's written out a list of words that she doesn't understand.'

'The little minx. She told me to fuck off with that book earlier.' The frown fell away and a satisfied smile spread over Sandra's face. 'I love it when a plan comes together.'

'Blink isn't bothered about making pizza tonight, surprise, surprise.'

'Well, neither am I. Delilah said my soup was disgusting at lunchtime, so she'd probably throw my pizza out of the window.'

'No problem, it's got to be my turn anyway,' Derek said, smiling as his heart sank.

Thank God it was only pizza. Having spread tomato puree over two bases and added slices of pepperoni and cheese to one, Derek realised he had no idea what Delilah would want on hers. There weren't many options and he started to duplicate the first one, until it occurred to him that it would be a good opportunity to check out Blink's earlier observation.

At the top of the stairs he could hear Blink talking about a kind of jam made with oranges. Marmalade was on the list then.

'I'll n..need to fetch my g..globe for the next t..two,' he said and pulled the bedroom door open, just as Derek was about to knock.

'I've just come to see what Dee wants on her pizza,' Derek said.

'Have p..p..pepperoni, it's l..lush,' Blink called, going into his bedroom.

Derek stuck his head through the open doorway.

'Hi Dee. Can I come in?'

'Course.' She was lying on her bed, propped up on one elbow. 'What's pepperoni?'

She rolled her head a little, as if trying to focus on him and then smiled. It was a slow and beautiful smile...disturbing in how alien it appeared on Delilah's face.

'It's sliced up spicy sausage. How are you feeling?'

'Cool, 'cept the smashed up ankle. S'ok with the tablets though.'

There was a drawl to her speech that wasn't there yesterday and that odd smile still lingered. He would double-check with Sandra how many tablets she was taking and read the whole pamphlet too. Maybe the effects built up over a few days. Blink returned bearing a globe and squeezed past Derek in the doorway.

'So what word do you need that for?' Derek asked.

'T..two words.'

Blink picked up a sheet of paper from the bed and held it up. 'Remarkable', 'presently' and 'marmalade' were crossed out, 'latitude' and 'longitude' were next.

'Ah, some good discussion points there,' he glanced back at Delilah, who was watching Blink set up the globe and looking rather mournful now. 'So, do you fancy pepperoni?'

Delilah's eyes moved back to him, slowly, her eyebrows rising without her eyelids following.

'Sausage, no. What else is there?'

'Just cheese, or tuna and sweetcorn.'

'Tuna and sweetcorn, I think.'

'Ok. Blink, are you going to come and fetch them in ten minutes?'

'Y..yeah,' he said, still trying to level the globe at the foot of the bed.

Derek went to the office before the kitchen. Sandra was still writing her report.

'How did Delilah seem to you today,' he asked, 'was she spaced out after taking her painkillers?'

'No, not really. She was a little less grumpy, but there were no unusual behaviours or mannerisms. Why?'

'Cos I would say she's pretty spaced out now. Super-stoned, but languid, rather than lethargic. It makes it difficult to judge when the person is lying down and on legal meds to start with. She gave me this lovely smile...'

'Delilah?'

'Exactly. It seems harsh to single that out as strange, but it was strange and it wasn't just the smile. She's slurring her words too, well not slurring, but talking with a lazy drawl. Blink noticed it when he first went up. I'll ask Delilah, but I'll ask Blink to keep an eye out too.'

'Good idea. I'll log it for you, while I'm on the computer anyway.'

'Thanks.'

He went back to the kitchen, threw the topping on Delilah's pizza and put both of them in the oven, brooding. If she was high, then whatever it was must be stashed in her room, very close to the bed. He would talk to the LAC nurse. They could hardly search her or lift the mattress in this situation and a drugs test would be pointless at present.

Blink interrupted his thoughts and saved the pizzas from burning. Derek pulled out two trays and some paper napkins and topped up an almost empty bottle of squash with water, while Blink sliced up the pizzas.

'I think you were right earlier, when you said Delilah was a bit spaced out. Just keep an eye out for her taking anything, won't you,' Derek said, trying to sound casual.

'S..sure. There's q..quite a lot Delilah d..doesn't know, even i..if she knows about other…th..th..things.'

Blink's cheeks turned a pale red.

'Very true, although that's true of most people. That's why it's good to talk and fill in the gaps. Like you know way more than me about astronomy and speaking French, but I know things that you can't know yet, because I've got a wife and kids. You can always ask anything you want though and I hope you would feel ok to do that.'

'Y..yeah, I know. We'd b..best get these ups..stairs.'

'You take yours then and I'll bring Delilah's.'

Derek followed Blink, wondering what on earth Delilah had been telling him. She was lying on her back when they went in, gazing at the ceiling, her arms spread out either side like an angel. She made no effort to move.

'Dee, you've got to sit up to eat,' Derek said. Not a flicker. 'Dee, are you ok?'

Derek and Blink both tried to put their trays down at the same time and resulting clash snapped Delilah out of her trance.

'What're you doing?' she said.

'Being rubbish waiters. Are you ok? You look a bit out of it. Have you taken anything other than your tablets from the hospital?'

She laughed at that.

'Yeah, I floated out of the window and flew across town to score.'

'Well just promise me that you'll remember you can't fly, eh? Those painkillers you're on are strong and taking anything else on top could have a bad effect, you know?'

'Yeah. S'not gonna happen stuck in here though, is it.'

'It had better not, young lady. Enjoy your pizzas.'

He left them to it and went downstairs, wondering where Josh was. He would be the likely courier, if Delilah did have any drugs, but how were they going to manage that? Although they might not have to for much longer, as his court date was only eleven days away.

It was going to be very hard on the lad to lose his liberty, but it might just be the making of Delilah. Derek wouldn't voice it out loud, but the broken ankle could not have been better timed. If they could keep her on board until Josh got locked up, the positive influence of Blink might sway things.

~ ~ ~

Although everyone was around at the weekend, Dee felt utterly miserable by Sunday afternoon. She had taken the last tiny blim of resin the night before and was now realising how much it helped with the pain in her ankle. Not only that, but she was on different painkillers as of yesterday, which didn't seem to touch it. She was wide awake, not even a little stoned and in a foul mood.

Even Blink gave in at lunchtime. But she didn't want to think about what a bitch she'd been to him…it wouldn't make her feel any better. When was bloody Josh going to wake up and reply to her text? She wasn't even sure he was in his room – he hadn't come back before 1.30am, the last time she checked her phone before falling asleep.

The smell from the half-eaten omelette on a plate by her bed was rancid and making her stomach curl, but no-one would dare come up to see her before tea-time, unless she shouted. That wasn't going to happen. She sucked on the white plastic thing that the LAC nurse had given her on Friday. It was supposed to

185

contain nicotine, but it did fuck all. She wondered if her mum had one in hospital. She would text and ask...later.

Her one attempt at smoking, with the aid of Blink and a fan, went well in terms of no-one noticing, but the agony of getting back from the window just wasn't worth it. Dee threw the plastic fag back on the cabinet and glared at the omelette, beads of fat glistening on the top. Gross. But potentially useful as an ash tray. Fuck it.

She took her tobacco from the top drawer and rolled a fag, then stashed the pouch in her pillow case. Pausing before she lit up, Dee wondered what the consequences would be. What could they do, really...ground her? Ban her tv time? Stop her spending money? She couldn't get to the tv or the shops anyway. The nicotine hit was strong, after not smoking for four or five days, and Dee revelled in it. She was taking her third drag when the door burst open.

'What the fuck ya doin'?'

Dee buried the fag in the omelette before she realised it was Josh. Bollocks.

'What does it look like? Smoking. I'm pissed off.'

Josh pulled the door shut behind him and went to open the window.

'I can smell that from my room. Can't believe no-one's come up yet.'

'I'm not bothered if they do,' she said, shoving the stinky plate away from her. 'Hey, what are you doing with my coat?'

'Trying to stop any more smoke going out onto the landing.'

Josh pressed the coat into the gap beneath the door with his foot and then dragged the fan over, pointing it towards the window and flicking it onto the highest setting.

'It's bloody freezing now,' Dee grumbled, knowing she was being mardy.

'Don't get a face on with me. So what's up anyway? You asked me to come and see you.'

She didn't want to ask him any more. But she was desperate.

'You haven't got any weed have you? I've been eating some hash that Gaz gave me, but I've run out. My ankle's killing and I'm bored out my brain.'

Josh sat on the floor with his back against the door. Dee didn't look at him.

'I saw Gaz last night. Got a new phone number for you.'

He didn't sound very pleased about it and Dee would rather Gaz sent more resin than a phone number. She wasn't missing him that much.

'Oh. The pigs haven't been on to him then.'

'Dunno. He's clammed up cos I'm in court a week tomorrow.'

'Oh.'

That wasn't far away, if he was going down this time. Maybe that was why he was quiet and miserable. She didn't want to ask about the weed again, although she'd go mad if he didn't sort something out.

'Are you scared? Of being sent down?'

Josh shrugged and said nothing.

'I'd be scared. It's bad enough here, but at least you can go out, when you don't have a broken ankle.'

'Yeah, ok, I'm trying not to think about it.' Josh got up and stuck his hand in his pocket. 'Gaz sent something else for you.'

He handed her a piece of resin, bigger than the last one, and a slip of paper with a phone number on. Dee pinched a piece off the lump and swallowed it before putting the paper and resin in her top drawer. She looked up and was startled to find Josh watching her. She'd never really looked straight at his face before. He was quite alright-looking.

'I'm not sure about that shit,' he said. 'Did you want it bad?'

Dee was about to say it was stronger and more weird than anything she'd had before. But she wanted it and didn't want to work out what he was saying.

'Only cos I'm bored and my ankle hurts. It's doing my head in.'

'I don't think it's just hash. I asked Gaz, but he just laughed and said it would sort you out.'

'Well it does. I'd go mental without something. I can't even fucking smoke.'

'That's not what he meant.'

'I don't care. It didn't come with a crack pipe or a pack of sharps did it, so it can't be that bad.'

'Just be careful, eh? I won't be around much longer and it's different for girls with that crowd.'

'I can look after myself.'

'Not always…'

Dee blushed, knowing he was talking about that night she passed out. She still couldn't remember getting into bed with Gaz.

'Aw, fuck off Josh, I don't need a lecture.'

'Whatever. I'm going to get some food.'

He pulled the door shut behind him and the ensuing silence was heavy. A combination of rancid fat, egg and fag ash wafted up from the plate by her side and Dee gagged. The bin was against the far wall and there wasn't a bag or anything to chuck it in, so she put the plate on the floor and shoved it under the bed. It fixed the smell but now she was in an even worse mood than before. The stuff wasn't kicking in yet, or maybe she hadn't eaten enough.

She took the lump of resin from the drawer and examined it. It looked and smelled like nice squidgy black. Not that she'd ever had much before. That would be it – she was just used to smoking weed and this was a different kind of hit. She pinched another piece off and washed it down with the dregs of the orange juice.

12

Reading the text again, Jim shook his head. He might not be so worried if it was late on a Friday or Saturday night, but it was Wednesday morning. Scrolling back through the previous messages from Delilah, the point at which they altered was clear. Before the ankle incident, her texts were brief and bland, with bad spelling. Those since the accident grew longer and more bizarre each day, although the spelling was better. It could be someone else using her phone, but he thought not.

She would be on strong painkillers, but surely not morphine or anything crazy? And certainly not now, a week after the event. He shouldn't get involved. There was no point, not if he was going to have to flit, which he was and pretty damn soon. The two phone calls since his no-show at the clubhouse were not friendly and three Harleys had ridden, or rather crawled by his house, at 1am.

His gear was packed, including the contents of the container under the rockery. The furniture could stay – none of it was worth anything and with the rent paid for another fortnight, it would be useful to leave the house looking occupied for a while. He'd paid the deposit on a static caravan on the east coast using his debit card, aware that if he turned up on spec, no-one would rent him anything. At least he'd be able to settle the rest in cash.

The bike trailer with the kennel conversion he wasn't so sure about, but it was the best he could do. Despite having driven plenty, Jim did not have a driving license so hiring a van wasn't an option. He could stop every few miles and check on Crank though, who had suffered worse experiences in his early years.

Although the timing was bad in some respects, he'd seen his Probation Officer yesterday and wouldn't have to report again for nearly a month. Released early on parole, Jim's licence was in place until the middle of next year and he should inform them before moving. His half reasonable, if wet, Probation Officer understood the difficulties in escaping gang culture however, and Jim was confident he could talk his way out of it. If he made it to that point.

Shona knew of the plan, if not the details. She was blaming herself and, if Jim was honest, she was the source of his most recent grief, but the unexpected pleasure of being someone's rock, of having the ability to dig someone else out of the shit, more than compensated. Then there was Delilah, a kid he barely knew, yet who struck his conscience, and perhaps heart, in a way he'd never experienced. There were so many similarities between them, however inconspicuous to anyone else. She was eager to learn, fiercely independent but, like him, too ready to take the easiest and quickest route to her goals.

Not that he could be her saviour, but he would have preferred to be around, be able to offer advice and support if she wanted it. He could not leave without saying goodbye, or without checking why she was off her head on a Wednesday morning. Maybe Becky would agree to him visiting the home, but it would have to be this afternoon – he planned to leave as soon as it was dark.

~ ~ ~

Derek looked out of the office window for the tenth time in as many minutes, but on this occasion, was rewarded with a swooping sensation in his gut.

'Bloody hell fire,' he said.

Gareth got up and joined him at the window.

'Ah. Right. I see what the social worker was on about now.'

Glancing down at the death grip Gareth had on the window sill and translating the small, throat-clearing noises he was making as significant fear, Derek decided to handle the visit himself. The guy walking down the drive was a serious dude, who might not

190

appreciate Gareth simpering and fluttering out of nervousness, although his steps slowed as he approached the house and he looked a little less confident.

'I'll sign him in and take him through to the lounge. At least Delilah isn't still in bed...that would have been too awkward. Are you alright to make drinks?'

Gareth nodded, still gazing out of the window.

'Good. Get a grip then.'

Derek went out into the hall, latched a smile onto his face and opened the door.

'Hi. You must be Jim. I'm Derek, one of Delilah's key-workers.'

He held out his hand, which was engulfed, and received a shake that sent ripples through his shoulder.

'Can I just ask you to sign in? It's a standard thing, even the social workers have to.'

'Sure.'

He sounded as much like a bear as he looked, but Derek noticed his handwriting was an elegant script and tried not to be too surprised.

'You've timed your visit well, it's the first day Delilah has made it downstairs. She's in the lounge, watching television. Shall we go through?'

He led the way without waiting for an answer, relieved that both Josh and Blink were still at school. Delilah was stretched out on the settee, watching the door. The grin that appeared as they walked in was reassuring, though it slipped a little as they rounded the settee.

'Didn't you bring Crank?' she asked.

'Nah. I didn't know if dogs were allowed, but he says hello.'

Her grin kinked at one side.

'Say hello back.'

Jim sat down and filled one of the armchairs, Derek perched on the edge of the other, unable to imagine how this was going to work, but determined to give it his best.

'Do you guys want a tea or coffee? Hot chocolate, Dee?'

She nodded and Jim asked for a coffee, just as Gareth made his appearance. He gave an unfortunate little wave from the doorway, at which Jim raised an eyebrow and Delilah snorted.

'That's Gareth,' she said to Jim. 'He's a...'

'He's the nice man who's offered to make you and your friend a drink,' Derek interrupted, 'so be polite, please.'

Gareth scuttled off to the kitchen and Delilah pouted.

'I was only going to say he's a drip, but he's ok really.'

'That's still not very kind.'

'I tell you what, girl,' Jim said, 'I'd have been happy with a few more like him when I was in care. There weren't any 'ok drips' around then, just big bullies with hard sticks and no-one watching.'

Delilah stared at him for several seconds, her mouth slightly open. Derek knew this, because he was looking at her in an effort not to stare at Jim too. This could be more interesting than he thought...and twice as heavy. No wonder Jim looked uncomfortable. He must be what, mid to late fifties? That would put him in care in the 60s and 70s, a time about which more horror stories were revealed in the press every month.

'I didn't know you were in care too,' Delilah said.

'Not many people do. I don't talk about it because I don't like to remember. It was terrible, worse than you can imagine.' He rubbed the side of his beard, staring at a spot on the floor between him and Delilah. 'This is going to sound patronizing and I'm sorry for that, but you really don't know how lucky you are. It doesn't feel that way, I'm sure, but it's good to remember there are always folk worse off than you.'

She said nothing to that and was saved the need to by Gareth returning with the drinks. He put them on the coffee table, smiled round at everyone and left again. There was an awkward silence, but it wasn't Derek's place to fill it. He picked up his coffee and shuffled back a bit in the seat, trying to relax. Delilah looked at him, frowning.

'You're not going to stay in here are you?' she said.

'Fraid so. That's the condition of Jim's visit.'

'But he's my friend. How can we talk with you sitting there?'

'I know it's awkward.'

192

How to explain without offending Jim? A little more notice of the visit would have been helpful, as right now, his mind was a blank. The man himself came to the rescue.

'This is just what I'm trying to say, Dee. You've got to accept that at 14, you don't know it all - you can't, you haven't been around long enough. You think I'm a decent bloke, that friend of Shona's who gives you cake and has a nice dog, who saved you from getting beaten up by the estate gang. But you know what? I've spent more years in prison than you've been alive.'

Judging by the look on her face, Delilah was unaware of that, although she didn't seem too perturbed.

'Yeah, but I bet it was for fighting, or weed or something. Not like, horrible stuff.'

Jim shook his head, what might have been a sad smile just visible beneath the whiskers.

'This man,' he pointed at Derek, 'could tell you different and if he doesn't know the details, your social worker definitely does, because I've talked to her about it.'

'Eh? You've talked to Becky? Why? What's she got to do with you?'

'Nothing, but she has everything to do with you and she's got balls that most men would be proud of. She shouldn't have let you stay in contact with me, never mind go on trips to McDonald's. I've beaten people to within an inch of their life Dee, and not because they offended or threatened me, but because I got paid to do it.'

Holy Mother of God. Becky might have balls the size of an elephant, but Derek could feel his own shrinking rapidly and would be having words after this. What the hell was she playing at? This man should never have been allowed through the door and now he wondered whether to ask Gareth to head off Josh and Blink. Except that Jim was looking at him intently, a half smile lifting one side of his moustache.

'Sorry for dropping that on you pal, but I can assure you I'm a reformed character.'

Like that was a comfort and like there was anything at all he could do if it wasn't true. Even Delilah looked dubious.

'So...you don't do shit like that any more then?' she said.

193

'No, but I'm 57 and my last stretch inside was 11 years. What I'm saying, is that sometimes other people know more about your friends than you do and if they try to stop you seeing them, it's because there's a reason and not because they like giving you a hard time.'

Delilah's eyes narrowed. Jim seemed to clock it too, picking up his coffee and looking round the room as he took a sip.

'It's really quite smart here,' he said. Delilah remained silent. 'Alright, no bullshit. I never wanted to give you a lecture Dee, and even trying makes me a hypocrite, but I thought I would be able to keep an eye out for you. Now I can't...I've got to go away and I don't want to leave without saying a few things I've got on my mind.

'You see, you can't escape your past...it'll always catch up with you sometime or other. Mine has caught up with me, again. You don't have a past yet, you're making your history now and I want you to understand that. I think you're in with a dodgy crowd and from the texts you've sent, you're not just sticking to the weed. Be careful Dee. There are guys out there who seem nice, but are just out to get you hooked on something, so you end up doing what they want, anything at all, just to get your fix.'

Derek didn't dare breathe, but sent a silent apology to Becky in his head. Delilah looked like she might cry.

'I'm not stupid...I wouldn't touch any Class A's. Where are you going?' she said.

'Only Crank knows that, but I'll stay in touch and let you know if I get a new phone. You can always call me if you're really up Shit Creek.'

Jim took an envelope from inside his jacket and passed it to her.

'There's a card in there with Shona's new number. It's worth having, now I've bought her a phone that actually works. She's been to see your mum and says she's looking a lot better. I reckon she'll be out soon and you'll be able to go and see her too.'

'Really?'

'Yep, as long as you look after that ankle.'

Clever man. Delilah was almost smiling again as Jim stood up and she took the hand he held out. It was a very gentle shake.

Derek slipped out to the hall first to give Delilah a few seconds of privacy, but stayed by the open door. Jim did not linger.

'There's just Shona's number and £20 in that card,' he said in a low voice as Derek saw him out. 'She's got a bad nicotine habit you know.'

'I know, and I appreciate what you said in there. She won't take that kind of thing from us.'

Their handshake was of the same, ligament-tearing intensity, although Jim's grip was mild and his eyes warm-ish.

'You take care,' Derek said.

'I'll try. You take care of Delilah.'

'I'll try.'

~ ~ ~

The alarm burst on his ears in an unpleasant way, having gone through the soft, gentle sounds of the first few seconds without impact and being now at the NUUURRR NUUURRR NUUURRR stage. Jono yanked the duvet over his head with one hand, stretching out the other to silence his phone. He was almost used to the long days and physical exertion required in getting around campus, but had really, really been looking forward to a lie-in today. Until Dee decided she would come for lunch after all, as one of the staff would give her a lift over. At 11 o'clock.

Sitting under a hot jet of water in the shower, he imagined Netty rubbing soap over his chest and shoulders. They were talking online every night now, sometimes teasing and intimate, but often just...talking. Jono couldn't say about what exactly, but it was never boring. It could never be boring anyway, not when there was always the possibility that she would suggest meeting up. He still didn't know how he would respond if she did.

Unhappy with that line of thought, he focussed instead on the match tomorrow. There had only been one practice since Christmas and everyone was slow and lethargic, but they'd need to raise their usual standard to beat the Tameside Owls. Or even give them a decent game. There hadn't been much time for shooting hoops since he started uni and that was something else he wanted to do today.   Still, it would be good to see Dee, especially after the weird texts she was sending him.

She was fifteen minutes late, which suited Jono fine, and the care worker didn't come in, which suited him even better.

'You're looking pretty good with those sticks,' he said, as Dee swung her way down the hall.'

'They're alright, but they wreck my arms.'

'I bet.   That plastic cast thing looks like it weighs more than you do.   Go and get your leg up on the settee and I'll make us a drink.'

She didn't put the tv on as she usually would, probably overdosing on it at home now.

'Has it been boring as hell then?' he called, over the hiss of the kettle.

'Yeah, deadly, but I've read a book and I'm reading another one.'

'Yeah?   Which ones?'

'Alice in Wonderland and now I'm reading The Hobbit.'

That could not be possible, not in that space of time.   A month ago, she was pretty much illiterate, but then he only knew that from her texts, which were markedly different now.   Maybe that sharp little mind was just waiting for some nourishment and would prove dazzling in its brilliance.

'So what's happened about school?   You only did a day and a half.'

'They've sent work to me, but it's shit and I'm not going back.'

Or maybe it would flower briefly and then wither, from lack of care.

'What about the catering course?'

'I'm still going to try that, but there's probably a load of bitches there too.'

'Ah.'

Jono put the mugs down on the coffee table.

'Are you still doing your computer course?' Dee asked.

'Yeah.   It's hard work, but it makes me do things I wouldn't do otherwise and meet new people.   And it would be good to get a job and earn my own money.'

196

She took her time digesting that and Jono went to put the pizzas in the oven. They were, apparently, Dee's new, favourite food.

'Hey, don't forget you were going to cook dinner. Just because you've broken your leg doesn't mean you can't start planning. You could bring that Blink lad as well if you want.'

'What? No way!'

'Alright, just a suggestion. What's the other guy like?'

'Josh is cool, but he's gonna get banged up on Monday.'

'Ok. What for?'

The story was long and complex, with Dee missing bits out, then trying to fill in retrospectively when she realised it made no sense, but without names. Jono was confused about the detail and unhappy with the general gist. This was exactly the kind of thing Becky was asking about, but now he felt like an under-cover cop, with an opportunity to wheedle information from an unsuspecting conspirator. Except Dee was the potential victim.

'Am I right in thinking that these are the same bunch of guys you've been hanging out with? They don't sound like great company to me.'

'They're alright, mostly, and they always have bacca and weed, but don't you start banging on about it too. Everyone's been getting on my back.'

'Ok, ok.'

Instead, he told her about the dweebs on his course, who never said anything that wasn't about computers, and the guy who was a top class hacker. It was only when Dee asked what botany was that he realised he was now talking about Netty.

'Er, botany? It's about plants.'

'And you met her online?'

'Did I say that?'

'Yeah.'

'Er…yes, I did. That's the only way I've met her so far.'

'Does she know you use a chair?'

Ouch.

'No, not yet, not ever probably, it's just talking, online chat, you know.'

Dee raised both her eyebrows, looking very scathing and at least 20 years old.

'Yeah right, you've been going on about her for half an hour. Show me her profile pic.'

Jono hesitated, but didn't see the harm. He could hide the chat stream.

'Go and get the pizzas out while I log on then. If you leave them on the side, I'll bring them through.'

He was impressed to find the food on plates and cut into slices. Dee had not understood the purpose of plates when they first met and maintained a distrust of cutlery for some time after that. She sat down on the settee, chewing slowly and staring at the picture of Netty for a good minute before pronouncing her judgement.

'She looks like a bitch.'

'Most girls look like bitches to you.'

'Yeah, but she properly does. Quite pretty I s'pose.'

'I think so.'

'That's a crap reason to fancy her though, if she's a bitch.'

'She might not be, and fancying someone because they're pretty, isn't as bad as hanging out with someone because they've got weed and bacca.'

She frowned at him over a second slice of pizza, but didn't reply. Yes, chew on that, Dee. They ate the rest of their food in a moody silence, but his curiosity about her reading The Hobbit returned and it would be a pleasant change of direction.

'So how come you're reading Tolkien...isn't it a bit heavy going?'

'It's harder than Alice, but I like the story better. Blink explains the bits I don't understand. It's his book, he borrowed it me.'

'He lent it to you, you borrowed it. Tolkien and chess. Are you sure you won't bring him round?'

'No! He'd think it was a date or something. Yuk. Come to Sunny Bank if you want to meet him so much. You could get in through the patio doors at the back.'

'I might do that. He sounds too interesting not to meet.'

'Huh.'

It was late afternoon before Dee's lift returned and too cold and dark to take the basketball outside. Unable to face staring at a screen, Jono put some music on, but the thumping dance tunes just gave him more energy. He did some chair-lifts and then went over to his pull-up bar, but that didn't occupy much time or use much energy, as he didn't want to risk straining anything before tomorrow.

Watching the Tameside Owls on YouTube seemed like a good idea...spot the demon players and suss out their strategy. After five minutes he gave it up as too depressing. They were going to get nailed tomorrow. He flicked up the chat site and sent Netty a message.

Argh! Visitors. Very pleasant to have company, but they don't half mess up your plans. Have you had a nice day?

He'd always thought the 'nice day' thing was a bit of a cliché and only ever asked from a sense of duty, but he genuinely did want to know if Netty's day had been good and what she'd been up to. That had to be significant. Though significance was irrelevant when the relationship was thus far based on a lie. His lie.

You seem to have a lot of visitors. Should I be jealous? Is it a party house?

Ha! Yeah, a rave a minute.

Nah, not really. In fact, it was the same visitor today as on Boxing Day. A curious kid I know, who doesn't have many friends.

It occurred to Jono that beyond the police and the social worker, he had never talked to anyone about Delilah. His parents wouldn't approve of their friendship and perhaps Netty wouldn't. It wasn't a wise line of conversation anyway; he was typing as Jono and not TooGood. A mistake.

Is he curious as in, an interesting character, or curious as in, a kid with a lot of curiosity?

Uh-oh. A big mistake, but he wasn't going to start a whole new set of lies.

He's a she – Delilah – and she's curious in every way possible, bless her. Crap home, weird upbringing and now

she's in care. **She ran away at first and came here, with the police and Social Services hot on her heels, but it's all cool now.**

Too much information, but the questions were inevitable. That seemed to summarise the answers to most of them...except the one about how they met. He'd deal with that if it came. It was a full minute before Netty replied, by which time Jono felt sick.

Have you talked to her about me?

Not at all what he was expecting.

Yes. She wanted to see your profile picture this afternoon.

Oops. How far to take the honesty?

And what did she say?

All the way.

Bearing in mind that Dee is pretty much a street kid, 14 years old and with a stinking attitude towards other girls as a result of bullying, she thinks you look like a bitch.

Was this really an exercise in improving his charm and banter?

I like Dee already. Your friend might be wiser than you think...don't say you haven't been warned.

Interesting. That was one of the things he liked about talking to Netty – he could never guess how she was going to respond. Dee wasn't that wise though, as Netty clearly wasn't a bitch.

~ ~ ~

Josh was already out when Dee got back from Jono's, but Blink was in the kitchen, cooking tea. She needed a drink, but having talked all afternoon, she wanted to go and chill in the lounge, not have him yabbering at her. Neither could she make a drink without offering him one and she couldn't be arsed. Sandra, who had driven her back, followed her into the lounge.

'Aren't you going to say hello to Blink? He thought you might like to help cook tea.'

'No, I just want to watch tv for a bit.'

'Alright, I'll leave you to it.'

Cow. She could have fetched a drink, although Dee would have said no if she'd offered. Flicking through the channels, there was nothing that looked any good. She picked up her phone and scrolled through the texts. Her mum hadn't replied for a couple of days. If nothing came tomorrow, she might have to call bloody Becky and ask her to check at the hospital. She still owed Gaz a message, but that was too risky outside of her room.

Not the slightest bit hungry, the smell of frying mince wafting in from the kitchen made Dee want to puke. She gave up on the lounge and made her slow and laborious way upstairs, each step pissing her off a little bit more. Her ankle was throbbing by the time she got to the top, but her bed and the lump of resin were only a few feet away.

Leaning out of the window with a fag, the curtains closed behind her, she wondered why she always forgot to smoke when she was at Jono's. It was good though, cos the hit was loads better if you hadn't smoked for a few hours. The hash she'd just swallowed would kick in soon too and she might be able to chill out. Dee flicked the nub towards the hedge and pulled the window to, but not shut, squirting a bit of deodorant in the air as an extra precaution.

'Delilah! D..dinner's nearly r..r..ready!'

It sounded like Blink was at the bottom of the stairs.

'I'm not hungry!' she yelled back.

She waited for his second try, but it didn't come. He must have gone back to the kitchen, probably dragged away by stupid Sandra, who said yesterday that Blink was too nice to her. What was that supposed to mean? She flopped onto the bed and let the crutches slide to the floor. The list of words from reading last night was still on top of The Hobbit. She'd meant to take them to Blink when she got back from Jono's and there were several bits she didn't get at all.

Sighing, she hoisted her bad leg onto the bed and lay back on her mega-comfy pillows. Jim was right...there were worse places to be and now the swirly numbness from the hash was tickling her head. Once you were used to it, the feeling was lush and she could try putting some in a joint now she could get outside, see if the feeling was the same.

It wouldn't be the same as smoking a 'special' with Gaz though, not the same as lying on her own bed, on her own, with no other people watching and saying shit. Was he in another garage, or a flat, or someone's shed, or...in a cave in a wood somewhere? A hobbit hole would be a nice place to hide out, if it didn't have a hobbit in it, or a talking rabbit.

Dee giggled. She would like to talk to a rabbit though, it would be more interesting than talking to people, unless they just talked about grass and dogs chasing them and people shooting at them. But if Gaz lived in a cave in the woods, he might have to kill rabbits to eat them and it would be horrible if he killed one she'd been talking to. He must be lonely. She should text him.

R u in a cave?

She wanted to say something else, but couldn't remember what it was, so pressed 'send' anyway. Letting her head fall back into the soft squishiness, Dee drifted off until the phone buzzed in her hand.

Ur crazy babe u bin munchin that stuff again? U high?

So he wasn't in a cave. That was boring.

Not high, lying down but its nise.

Nice, nice, white mice. If mice talked, they would probably have annoying, squeaky voices.

Lying down and tinkin of me yeh? I like it. give ur tittys a stroke 4 me

She did, but it was just...normal. She tried it underneath her t-shirt like Gaz did, sliding a hand inside her bra and squeezing a bit. That was nice. She put her other hand up and pushed the bra off completely. That was really nice. She let go with her right hand to text him.

2 hands is nise + no brah

She carried on until he texted again.

Ohhh babe ur hot. Wen can u cum c me?

It would be nice to see him, he said nice things and gave her nice things and did nice things, mostly, and some things that were weird but not too weird. Everyone was so totally freaked out that she was having sex, but he was nice, they didn't even do that, just lots of other stuff. And this lump of hash wouldn't last for ever and

202

especially not now she was having bigger pieces, now she was used to it and it was just, nice.

~ ~ ~

Shona was appalled by how much she was missing Jim. He'd only been gone four days, but it was more the knowing he was no longer just across the estate. It was ridiculous, when they were never close in their youth and she hadn't seen him at all for more than a decade, but over the past year they'd become friends and during the past few months, he'd been her rock. She was a great believer in cycles however and this felt like a new turn of the wheel.

With no debt to the dealers and the rest of the gift from Jim feeding the shark for a while, she was getting her finances in order. Paulie had replied to her letter, but was not at liberty to rob her blind. He even mentioned sending her a visitor's order. The greatest relief was having passed, or rather not passed, the fitness for work tests. The fear of losing her benefits had been over-hanging Shona for months, but her doctor had written a strong supporting letter, detailing the damage to her hip from the bike accident and confirming that she could not remain in any one position for long, without suffering severe discomfort.

Intent on passing on some of this positive karma and with a nod to her Catholic upbringing in being kind to others on a Sunday, she decided to go and see Kelly in hospital this afternoon. She had also promised Jim that she would get in touch with Delilah and it would be good to have some news for her, assuming Kelly was better and not worse.

There was a bus from town straight to the hospital, but Shona had to ask directions from three different people to find the ward. It was quiet and depressing, with the white, sterile background and complete lack of make-up doing Kelly no favours. She looked about 75, but was at least pasty grey, as opposed to yellow. The grin when she saw Shona did not improve her visage.

'Bloody hell. Fancy coming to see me. It's good to see ya girl.'
'You too.'

WHAT a lie, but a very pale one. It was quite terrifying to see her like this. There but for the grace of God go I.

'Didn't slip a couple of miniatures in your bag did you?'

'I'm afraid not. Just one would probably kill you, Kelly. Are you not going to think about knocking the drink on the head?'

Kelly shuddered.

'First thing I'll do when I get out of here is buy a bottle of vodka. I can't hack it Shona, reality fucking stinks, what do I want to hang on to it for? Might as well go out with a bang.'

'That'll be nice for Delilah.'

'She's better off without me. She's got clothes and food and money now, somewhere nice to live, new friends, folks taking care of her. I haven't even got any credit to text her.'

'That doesn't mean she doesn't love you and need you. My mother used to beat our arses bloody with a cane, but I still missed her when she was gone.'

'I raised a glass when I heard my mother had croaked it. She fucked off and left us with me Dad, an' he only saw one use in girls. I haven't done much better for Dee.'

That explained an awful lot and Shona felt the surge of sympathy she'd been praying for.

'And there was me, thinking we were having a nice time clearing up your house, making it ready for Dee visiting. Anybody would be depressed, Kelly, stuck in here. Just give life one more go when you get out, eh? I'll be there to help.'

'Yeah? I can't do it on my own Shona.'

'You won't have to. Hey, remember that stitch and bitch group we went to for a bit? I found a huge bag of wool under my stairs last week. You could be sitting here, making gorgeous new blankets and cushions for when you go home. So could I, for that matter.'

'Hmmn,' Kelly said, but there was a spark of interest in her eyes. 'You still getting grief off your lad?'

Shona sighed.

'Not grief exactly and I won't for a while now. Paulie's been locked up.'

'What, for beating you up? Was it him? I can't remember.'

Was it a slip of the tongue, a product of Kelly's warped mind or was it just that obvious? Shona still felt sick at the mention of it, but there was no panic or fear now. Another debt she owed Jim.

'No, for drug dealing. I didn't do a very good job of bringing him up either. He wants me to go and see him though.'

'In the nick?! You'll get sniffed out before you get through the first door.'

'No I won't, I've packed up with that lark. I'm trying to get my life back on track too, that's why I think we should make some changes together, while we still can.'

'Ha. We're nearly old aren't we Sho? Soon we'll be like those old crones we used to laugh at when they tutted at us in the street.'

'I don't think either of us will ever be the crown-of-white-curls sort, but I wouldn't mind an evening at Bingo, if you fancy it?'

Kelly laughed, but it turned into a hacking cough. She was an old woman already, but there might be a few half decent years left in her yet, if she stayed off the booze.

13

The twelve month sentence Josh received cast an atmosphere over Sunny Bank for days. Delilah freaked out when told the news, shouting, swearing and whacking things with her crutches for over an hour. If she was any more mobile, they might have been forced to call the police. The memory of his white face being led from the dock haunted Derek. Josh was expecting six months, relying on halving that to retain any hope of survival. Where his head was at now didn't bear thinking about.

Even Blink was subdued, but that could be more to do with Delilah's utterly unreasonable treatment of him. She would let him fetch and carry for her, keep him closeted in her room for hours playing chess, or translating endless lists of words and phrases, then refuse to see or speak to him, if the mood took her. On occasion, she would throw him out with a mouthful of abuse, if he said something she didn't like. Of course it was frustrating, being stuck in bed and then inside, for weeks on end, but Derek thought there was more to it than that.

A pattern was starting to emerge; Delilah's mornings were slow and quiet, she would be bright and talkative by lunchtime and then cook, play a game, or watch tv in the early afternoon. Whatever she did would end up irritating her and she'd go back to her room for an hour or two. When Blink came home, he would go straight up to Delilah and either remain with her, or sulk elsewhere, for the rest of the evening. It wasn't a healthy routine for anyone.

On top of that, Becky had been on to the drug squad and discovered that there was a type of cannabis resin that contained opium. Not common and not in evidence locally, but out there and the most plausible answer to their suspicions about Delilah. When she refused a blood test, her room had been searched, but nothing was found. It didn't sound like something difficult to hide however.

The weekend was almost here again and Derek was planning to shake things up a bit. He was taking Delilah and Blink to the hologram museum in Matlock Bath tomorrow morning, then they were going to the cinema in the afternoon and, Delilah-willing, would stay out for pizza in the evening. There was also a visitor coming today, another friend of Delilah's - the woman who lived next door to her mum, whose number Jim had given to her. She should be interesting, if she was a friend of his.

The woman, Shona, turned up just after 11 o'clock, while Delilah was still nursing a coffee in the kitchen. She looked like the good witch in a children's story and a lot less scary than Jim. Derek had half expected a hard-faced, leather-clad, biker chick and was pleased with the alternative.

'Delilah's not been up long,' he warned her as they went through to the kitchen.

'That's no bother. Near the kettle is the best place to be in January,' Shona said.

Delilah looked up as they entered and Shona was awarded a rare smile.

'Wow, haven't you gone up in the world? I've always wanted a breakfast bar.'

'I like your table better,' Delilah said.

Shona smiled and dumped her bags on a chair. It looked like she was carrying half her life around with her.

'Would you like a tea or a coffee?' Derek asked her.

'Ooh, a tea please.'

Delilah frowned at him.

'You don't have to hang around like you did with Jim...Shona isn't going to beat me up or kidnap me.'

'No, I'm just going to make her a drink and then I'll leave you to it.'

She was too smart, this one. He'd leave them to it alright, but he wasn't going very far beyond the kitchen door. Derek took his time making the tea and listened to their inconsequential chatter.

Delilah seemed relaxed and obviously knew Shona better than Jim.

'What's all that shit in your bag?' Delilah said.

'Well, you know I went to see your mum? Before she went into hospital, we'd made a start on tidying up the house a bit. The social worker said you should be able to go and visit, but you know it was in a bit of a state. Your mum's a lot better, but almost bored to death, so I suggested we start making some new blankets and covers for the furniture, to cheer the place up. I thought you might like to help, or at least choose a few colours.'

Delilah was poking about in one of the bags with a sour expression when Derek put Shona's tea on the table.

'It's wool! I'm not fucking knitting, that's for old women and saddos.'

Shona just laughed.

'I won't argue that point with you, but it's not knitting, we're going to be crocheting. There is a difference. Me and your mum learned together, at an evening class. It was a good laugh.'

She pulled some works-in-progress out and laid them on the table. They were quite bright and funky; even Delilah had a look, whilst feigning disgust. Derek picked up the other two drinks he'd made.

'I'll leave you to it, ladies.'

He went back to the office and found Sandra eating her lunch.

'Have you just left them in the kitchen?' she asked.

'I don't have much choice – this is the woman who was a kind of chaperone when Delilah met up with that biker bloke and Delilah knows it. I'm going to find something to do in the hall, but I'm not too worried. She wants to teach Delilah how to crochet.'

Sandra choked on the mouthful she was chewing and a small piece of lettuce shot out onto the desk.

'Oh God, sorry,' she put a hand over her mouth and swallowed the rest. 'Crocheting? I tried that with her once, but not with much hope and without any success. It's not going to happen and if by some miracle it does, I think we should employ her immediately.'

'We'll see. I've given up trying to best-guess Delilah's friends. I'll go and loiter for a while.'

He found Shona and Dee heading for the lounge. Shona smiled at him.

'We're decamping to the settee...my bum wasn't made for stools,' she said.

Derek clenched his teeth, managed a slow nod and changed course to the kitchen. Delilah always created double the volume of crumbs than the toast she consumed and Derek wiped down the work-top, trying to suppress the laughter rising up his throat. No wonder she had enjoyed Alice in Wonderland - the characters surrounding her in real life were almost as random and bizarre as those in the book.

There was as much curiosity as concern behind his desire to overhear their conversation and enough moral justification to warrant it. If Delilah was comfortable and relaxed, she might just let something slip about the boyfriend. Derek sat on the bottom step of the stairs and listened to Shona's casual attempts to get Delilah interested in the wool, Delilah's impolite refusals, her questions about her mother and Jim, her further questions about whatever it was Shona was making.

He was about to go and offer Sandra good odds on Delilah picking up a crochet hook, when the conversation moved into a different, darker zone. Delilah was asking about the woman's son and there was a definite reluctance on Shona's part to answer. When she did speak, her voice was quieter and Derek strained to hear. Money...prison...drugs...he moved closer to the open door, on tiptoe.

'...stop you thinking straight, Dee. Nothing else matters but getting a fix. You think you're in control, but it slips away without you realising. With Paulie, it was 'just a bit of phet' to start with, then a lot of phet, then coke, then God-knows-what. The only way to pay for it is stealing or selling, either way you're going to get caught. It's worse for us girls of course, cos we have other things to sell.'

Derek was beginning to suspect a level of coordination behind Delilah's visitors and their non-conformist approach to drugs education. Whether Becky was the organiser or mere facilitator, he saluted her bravery once again.

'Shona, have you ever tried hash with opium in it?'

Yes. Yes, yes, YES.

'Once or twice, but it's rare and too heavy for me. I prefer a lighter buzz.' For God's sake shut up woman and remember where you are. 'Is that what your friends smoke?'

'Sometimes. I think he mostly keeps it for me though, my boyfriend.'

'As a treat, eh? It sounds like someone's out to make a puppet of you, Dee.'

A thoughtful silence followed and a shiver of un-spent energy ran through Derek's upper body, but he remained still, waiting for Delilah's response.

'I can handle it.'

'I've heard a lot of people say that, just before they went down the pan. I have to say you're looking good though and you know where I am if you want to talk. Just make sure you don't get pregnant, eh?'

'Eugh! No way.'

'Haha, I'm pleased to hear that, but don't get into having that hash every day either or you'll end up in a mess.'

'Mmmn.'

It was a scarily non-committal murmur of assent.

~ ~ ~

It took all of Becky's will-power not to laugh when she walked into the lounge of Sunny Bank. She was proud of her effort, but Delilah still gave her a suspicious glare, from underneath a pile of crocheted squares of various, earthy colours.

'Hi Dee, hi Blink. What are you up to?'

Delilah looked away, scowling, but Blink grinned up at her from the other end of the settee.

'W..we've got to s..stitch all these t..t..together to make a b..blanket.'

'Wow. That looks like a lot of work. Have you made all these?'

'I only m..made three, Delilah did the r..r..rest.'

'Gosh. I'm impressed.' She really was, although gob-smacked would be closer to the truth. 'Well I'm not stopping long, Dee, I just called in to see how you got on today. Did you enjoy it?'

'It was alright.'

Well, it must be a catering course from heaven to get that much of a response.

'You managed without your crutches ok then. Are you going to go again tomorrow?'

'Yeah.'

'Excellent.' Two responses to two direct questions. She would risk sitting down. 'Well that's Thursdays and Fridays sorted. Now I've spoken to the head teacher at the Support Centre and they're going to keep your place open...'

'I'm not fucking going.'

'Yes, I know, please let me finish. They're going to keep your place open in case you change your mind, but we're also looking at home tuition. Would you work with a teacher here?'

'What, just me and a teacher? That sounds shit.'

Becky took a deep breath and let it out slowly.

'It probably would be quite intense, but I think you'd make a lot of progress and it's an alternative to attending school.'

'Still sounds shit.'

'W..what about f..f..functional skills?' Blink said. 'You can do m..maths and English o..o..online from anywhere. Y..you get your own p..p..profile that you l..log into.'

'Er...right. I don't know anything about that, but I'll look into it, thanks,' Becky said, not sure if she wanted to kiss or strangle Blink.

'So I could do that here, on a computer, on my own like,' Delilah asked him.

'Yeah and I'd h..help you.'

Delilah looked up at her and then away again.

'Can you sort that out?'

'I'll certainly ask, but as I said, I know nothing about it. Derek said there was something else you wanted to talk to me about?'

'Delilah's m..mum is out of h..h..hospital. That's who w..we're m..making the b..blanket for.'

'Yeah and I want to go and see her this weekend.'

Becky had spoken to Kelly – who had dropped the 'Cleo' thing at last – several times over the previous week. Real conversations, which were very encouraging, despite the obvious coaching from the neighbour, Shona. Pre-planned statements were less of a worry, if it meant that Kelly was going to have some support at last. One exchange even contained an off-hand apology for the attempted wrecking of her car.

'Ok. I'd rather someone from here went with you the first time, though. It's been two months since you've seen your mum.'

'So fucking what?! She's my mum, you can't stop me seeing her.'

'I'm not trying to Delilah.' It was harder to keep her cool, knowing that Delilah understood exactly what she was saying and was being awkward and offensive for the sake of it. 'I'm just saying that it's been a long time. It might be good to have someone with you for a bit of support...and so you can leave whenever you need to.'

'Shona's gonna be there. You didn't mind me going out with her and Jim and my mum's not more dangerous than him. I don't want some twat hanging over my shoulder, it's not fucking fair.'

It would be such a shame if Delilah let her un-tapped intelligence go to waste. Under different circumstances, who knows what she might achieve? Although she wouldn't have got this far without the input from Blink. The issue with her mother was neglect and not abuse, so there wasn't any real barrier to contact.

'Let me speak to my manager and your mum and Shona tomorrow. I'll call you before the end of the day and confirm the arrangements. When do you want to go?'

'Saturday night and I AM going.'

'Have you spoken to anyone here about getting a lift over?'

'No. I can make my own way.'

'I know you can, but a lift would be easier.'

Becky stood up to leave. The level of conversation would not improve while Delilah was this cross and sulky, but in fairness, it was one of their more productive meetings.

'Well I'm glad you enjoyed today and I hope tomorrow goes well too. I'll look into those Functional Skills and speak to you when you get home about Saturday. Nice to see you Blink. Good luck with the blanket.'

'Thanks. B..bye Becky,' Blink said.

Delilah didn't speak, but Becky wasn't expecting her to. She was still furious about her room being searched and laid all the blame firmly on Becky as the one who'd instigated it. She went through to see Gareth and Derek in the office.

'I hope you're going to nominate Blink for cloning when it arrives, he's a bloody saint.'

Gareth gave her a pained smile, but Derek laughed.

'He is. A houseful of Blinks and our job would be a doddle. How did you get on with Dee?'

'Oh, full of charm as usual, but she's positive about the catering course, for now. Blink mentioned some sort of online system for doing maths and English that Delilah seems fairly set on. Is that something you could facilitate here, if I look into it?'

'Yes, I don't see why not,' Derek said. 'What's happening about her seeing her mum?'

'She wants to go on Saturday, unsupervised. I need to run it past my manager, but I'll let you know tomorrow.'

'Ok, thanks. As you know, the neighbour, Shona, has visited several times over the last few weeks. Not the most ideal role model, but she's had a positive impact and offers good advice, which Dee seems to take heed of. I confess to eavesdropping on a regular basis, but nothing major has come to light since the question about the laced resin.'

'Do you think she's still taking it?'

'Not sure. She's still moody, but then Dee is moody.'

'She's a lot brighter in the mornings,' Gareth put in, 'and according to Sandra, was up and ready without any prompting today.'

'Good. Well, we'll see what happens, now she's back on her feet. I'm hoping that contact with her mum will take priority over hooking up with whoever she was hanging out with before.'

'Fingers crossed,' Derek said.

214

Becky noticed Gareth's palms clasped together in a prayer-like position. She had more faith in the crossing of fingers, but made a mental note to ease off on the blaspheming.

'Alright, thanks guys and I'll speak to you tomorrow.'

She signed out and got in the car. 5.22pm. She'd be home just after half past and earn yet more brownie-points. Delilah's broken ankle had gone a long way towards further restoring her relationship with Simon, her immobility having significantly reduced Becky's stress levels. The CSE Unit had informed her that the older man, seen leaving the flat Delilah visited, had been arrested on other charges. The younger lads were local small fry - still a risk, but not on the same scale. Progress with Kelly was beyond expectations.

Of her other two major-input cases, one was in a secure unit for the next year and the other had clicked with his most recent foster carers and was settling into a routine. It was a temporary calm, but she appreciated it nonetheless. The six weeks of using alternative contraception, after coming off the pill, were at an end and excitement at the prospect of becoming pregnant almost outweighed her terror.

Almost. It was one thing identifying where parents were going wrong, assessing the impact on the family and trying to manage the results of poor parenting, it was quite another facing the application of those principles herself.

~ ~ ~

The second day at the catering course was not so good. They tried to make her write up what she'd done the day before and Dee thought she was going to get kicked out after telling the tutor where to stick her pen, but they got another tutor to write for her instead. The dish they cooked was some kind of disgusting, spicy rice, but Dee was so surprised about the writing that she didn't complain too much. They would be making cakes next week.

She was on her own in the taxi on the way home, so put her leg up on the back seat. Her ankle was wrecking and she hardly had any hash left. She was rationing it and only having a tiny bit at night, instead of in the morning too, but she didn't dare say anything about the pain, in case they stopped her going out. She could see Gaz tonight and her mum tomorrow.

There was a message from Becky when she got in. Dee was cool to get dropped off at her mum's, as long as whoever gave her a lift saw Shona before leaving. A teacher was going to come and talk to her about the Functional Skills thing sometime next week, but she wasn't that interested. Blink might nag her into it, but he wasn't home yet and she could forget to tell him. She decided to have a bath.

Tonight would be the first time she'd seen Gaz since she broke her ankle, just over a month ago. She was excited, but as much about being able to chill out and smoke, as seeing him. He wasn't very bothered about Josh when she texted about his sentence, just said it would toughen him up. Dee wondered if Gaz had ever been inside...she'd ask him later.

When she came up for air after rinsing out the shampoo, she could hear Blink's voice downstairs. He always wanted to do things on a Friday night and she hadn't told anyone she was going out yet. The less notice she gave, the less argument there would be, but she felt a bit bad. He was telling Sandra what films were on at the cinema, but she wouldn't be able to go tonight or tomorrow...and he'd helped her loads with the blanket, even though he didn't like doing it much. But he'd get over it.

Dee dressed with care, stashing her bacca and the remaining tenner from the £20 Jim had given her, inside her jacket. She also had some change for the bus, as she didn't fancy walking very far. If they gave her grief downstairs, she could just leg it without having to fetch anything. She abandoned the plastic cast. It'd look proper stupid without crutches, although her ankle felt weak and exposed without it.

When she walked into the kitchen, Sandra put her hands on her hips and raised an eyebrow, but Blink grinned.

'Hi! You're r..r..ready already. Are we g..going to M..mackies on the way?'

Dee shrugged, but cow-face was still staring at her.

'Are you planning on coming to the cinema, Dee?'

216

'No, I'm going out.'

'What? W..w..where?'

'None of your business,' Dee said.

Blink looked gutted, but it was Sandra that was making her narkey. Not that she would tell Blink either. She went and got some sliced cheese from the fridge and started making a sandwich.

'You c..can't go out w..without your c..cast though, w..what if you kn..knock your ankle?'

'It'll be fine and I'm going to my mum's tomorrow, so just, go to the cinema will you? Save me some sweets.'

'B..but I thought you w..wanted to go.'

'Yeah, just not this weekend.'

'Dee, I don't think it's a good idea, not without your cast or your crutches. You might end up back in bed,' Sandra said.

'I'll end up in a fucking loony bin if I don't get out of here soon.'

She'd need a drink with the sandwich and Sandra was now on her way to the office. Dee found a carton of juice in the cupboard and stuck it in her pocket, wishing Blink would stop staring at her. It was making her feel shit, but she should be able to go out. This wasn't supposed to be a prison.

'I'll see you later, or tomorrow,' she said and headed for the patio doors in the lounge.

He let her go, which was nice. He'd stopped being so clingy and it made him easier to be around.

'Delilah!'

It was Gareth this time, coming into the lounge behind her. The patio doors were locked, but there was just one key to turn.

'I'll be back by ten,' she called.

'But we can give you a lift, or...'

His words were cut off as she shut the door behind her. She wanted to run, more from exhilaration than anything, but didn't trust the ankle. Using an exaggerated limp for the sake of speed, Dee went around the side of the house and up the street to a driveway bordered by two high hedges. She walked down it a few yards and once out of general view and the main gusts of drizzly wind, she stopped to text Gaz.

He replied in less than a minute, saying Damo would meet her at the bus stop near the Tesco, on the other side of town. Great. Damo the creepy freak. She actually knew which bus to catch, thanks to Sandra insisting they go shopping that way to 'improve her independent travel skills'. Dee made a conscious effort not to add it her mental list of crappy tricks that Sandra pulled, which did in fact work. Cow.

It was a house this time, a boarded up semi. Damo led the way around the back, at the end of a ten minute walk of agonising speed. When she asked him to slow down, he didn't respond at all, but then he never did. Dee wasn't sure he even understood. It was so dark, she didn't see the pile of bin bags until she caught it with her foot.

'Fuck!'

She stopped, panting in her effort to fight back another yell. Something hard had bashed her ankle and now she couldn't put her foot down. A dark shape loomed in front of her. Damo.

'I can't walk,' she gasped.

He moved closer, leaned towards her and without even a grunt on his part, she was whipped off her feet and being carried like a baby. Dee shut her eyes tight, rather than accept the closeness of his face. He shoved the back door open with his foot and eased her through the gap, squeezing her legs in, so her ankle wouldn't knock against the frame. She warmed towards him a little and said 'thanks' when he lowered her into a half-collapsed armchair, in the dingy room beyond the wrecked kitchen.

Both rooms were empty, but the seat was still warm. Gaz must have been sitting there and the sound of a toilet flushing upstairs relieved her alarm at the prospect of being alone with Damo in a dark house. Footsteps clattered on the stairs and Gaz appeared. Maybe it was the candlelight, but he looked kind of greasy.

'Babe. You ok? Is your foot still bad?'

He bent down and kissed her forehead, just as Damo returned from closing the back door.

'Are you gonna fuck off home for a bit Damo? I'll buzz you in an hour or so.'

Damo nodded and turned around again. Dee was almost sorry to see him go. She was knackered and her ankle hurt like hell. She would rather have a few of the lads about, so she could just sit and smoke. There wasn't even a spliff on the go. The back door slammed shut and Gaz squatted down in front of her.

'You int sitting comfy there and there int no other chair anyway, so how about we move over to the bed.'

He didn't wait for a response and scooped her up, with a lot more straining than Damo had done, half dropping her on top of a sleeping bag, laid over some cushions in the corner. She wasn't in the mood for getting off with him. At all.

'You got any weed?' she said. 'I smashed my ankle on something outside. It's fucking killing.'

'Course babe, course. In fact, I got somethin' new to try, a legal high, it help us to fly.'

Quit the rapping bollocks and just roll something. Anything.

'Whatever. What is it?'

'Mamba.'

She didn't know what that was, but didn't bother asking any more questions. It might slow him down even more. At least she was lying flat now and her foot wasn't throbbing so much. Getting home was going to be a problem, but she'd worry about that in a bit.

The spliff, when Gaz finally passed it to her, tasted weird and the hit wasn't much like weed. It slowed things down though, so she hung onto it. He was lying next to her now, one arm around her shoulders.

'You still got some of that kickin' hash?

She shook her head and then realised he wouldn't see, with only two candles lighting the room.

'Nah. I ran out yesterday. It's opium innit…in the hash.'

'Clever girl. Tint like the real hard stuff tho, just a little bit special. So how you figure that out?'

She took one more drag and passed the spliff back, a dizziness creeping up on her.

'Just talked to some people. I know dealers too.'

'That so? Anyone I know?'

'No way, she's ancient.'

'She? Ah, that's alright then. Well you in luck baby, cos I bin shoppin' today.'

He held up a piece of black hash in front of her face. It was four times the size of the last lump he'd given her.

'Awesome. Roll one with that then.'

'Ooh, easy baby…and what you gonna do for me if I do that for you?'

He turned his face towards her, smiling, running a finger down her cheek. He smelled quite bad, now he was close. There probably wasn't any hot water here. Maybe she'd feel like getting off with him if he rolled a spliff with the opium hash. She wanted one anyway.

'Roll one and find out.'

14

A rare day of mid-February sunshine enticed Jono outside with his lunch, although it was still cold. Apart from a few clumps of snowdrops, the campus was bleak and wintery, but the bare-stemmed trees and bushes looked promising for a summer display. Even noticing that surprised him, but then he'd been talking botany with Netty until the early hours. Well, there was an element of botany within the conversation.

She'd been collecting plant samples at Chee Dale yesterday, which was one of his favourite climbing spots before the fall. There was no hope of him visiting there again. The gorge was not accessible to wheelchairs and he wouldn't want it to be made so, or the novelty of stepping stones and pushing through undergrowth would be lost. He could visualise everything that Netty described though, almost smell the wet greenness and hear the river's chatter flowing by.

The much louder and more raucous chatter of students flowed by him now, a whole crowd of them spilling down the steps to his left and flooding the path below. A girl coming the opposite way stepped aside, admiring a cluster of snowdrops while she waited. Two thick, fox-coloured plaits swung out from beneath a multi-coloured crochet hat as she bent to look at them.

The hat brought a smile to his face, reminding him of Dee's most recent texts, which hinted at a mild obsession with crocheting. It was favourable over other potential pastimes, although he had threatened her with death, or at least an end to their friendship, if she dared to make him a lap blanket. This hat looked quite funky though.

Watching the girl as she resumed her walk towards him, he wondered if she was the, 'cool uni image but actually a stay-at-home straight' kind of hippy, or the 'alternative lifestyle, festival-going, adventurous' kind of hippy. She was plump, in a healthy way, with very rosy cheeks. The stripy leggings didn't quite go with the patchwork coat, but big black boots drew the eye away from that.

He watched her all the way to the bottom of the steps, where she disappeared from view in the cutting. When she reappeared, head first, at his floor level, she was staring straight at him. Jono jumped, but couldn't help returning her huge grin. And it was a big, big smile, but all her teeth were white and even and it was an infectious sight.

'Hi!' she said.

'Hi,' he said back.

'Admiring the view?'

'Not much to see really.'

Aww, that was rude and a lie, when he'd been so interested in watching her.

'Oh, but there will be and the snowdrops are beautiful.'

'Yeah, I was thinking that and I watched you admiring them.'

'You have to take advantage of an opportunity. They're here and gone so fast and they're so pretty and small and brave, when everything is so bleak and wintery. I always see them as the first sign of spring.'

Bleak and wintery. They were the very words he had been thinking. That was really, a bit odd.

'Sorry, I'm gabbling on,' her rosy cheeks turned a shade darker, 'and I'm already late for a meeting with my tutor. I don't normally come in on Wednesdays. Lovely talking to you. Bye!'

She trotted off, her cheeks almost steaming. Jono became conscious of how cold his felt by comparison and turned to go back inside too. From this angle, he could not fail to notice the girl's large, but round and firm buttocks, bouncing up and down in her leggings as she hurried towards the main doors. They made him smile.

The image of them kept making him smile throughout the rather tedious afternoon, to the point of drawing a sarcastic comment from Professor Bateman. Once home though, his thoughts returned to Netty. He looked forward to 'talking' to her each evening and was conscious of his reliance on their conversation. He should broach the subject of his disability, before either of them was sucked any further into a virtual relationship based on deception. But not tonight.

He made a toastie and took it over to the computer. There was a message waiting for him already.

Was your coding flowing well today?

Huh. His coding wasn't working at all today.

Nah, couldn't concentrate. Think there's a whiff of spring in the air. How was yours?

He took a bite of toastie and waited. Most of her replies were made from her mobile, so she was usually online.

Interesting. All my samples from yesterday remained intact and the photos are fab. I'll send you some over.

Now that *would* be interesting.

Any with you in?

Nope. I took them all and I'm not into selfies. There's a stunner of an Oyster Catcher though.

He flicked up Chrome and discovered it was a long-beaked bird.

Cool.

The toastie collapsed and boiling bean juice ran down his arm, so he hit return and dashed to the sink. The reply waiting for him was peculiarly out of context.

I can't believe you're not going out on loads of hot dates, now you're at uni. You must get chatted up all the time. Any attractive girls on your course?

Was she just fishing? Or was becoming 'matey' her way of cooling things off? He didn't want that. He really didn't want that.

Nah. I'm not really into the social scene and there are NO fit girls on my course. But that sounded a bit sad. He could stretch out the encounter with the bouncy-bottomed girl today without lying. **I thought I was gonna get stalked by a Ginger Hippy today though.**

A Ginger Hippy? Do tell.

Jono wondered what Netty, with her sleek dark hair and her smooth bronze arms, would make of that crazy mish-mash of styles. Not much probably.

Well she looked like she'd gone and blown all her cash in a vintage shop whilst very drunk. The crochet hat sealed it, especially with orange pig-tails sticking out underneath. She just came over, gabbled away for five minutes, went bright red and then ran off. I couldn't have got a word in edgeways if I'd wanted to.

The reply was some time coming. Maybe she really was easing back, or just in the shower, or eating her tea too.

Sounds like a nightmare.

The girl's beaming face popped into his mind and he couldn't tarnish the memory further.

Nah, not really, she was funny.

Bless. Gotta sign off now. Catch ya later TooGood.

Why did she need to sign off? He wouldn't ask what she was doing.

K. Have a good one.

Maybe he should have chatted up the Ginger Hippy earlier. She wasn't even ginger; her hair was a dark red and he had liked the hat. And the bottom still made him smile. God, he was crap at this, even when he tried. Perhaps he ought to give up and get a dog.

~ ~ ~

The sea air seemed to suit both of them. Crank chased sticks on the beach like a puppy and Jim was sleeping for two and three hours at a time during the night. Most of the mobile homes around them were occupied by older people, but Jim liked it, it was quiet and anonymous. After six weeks, a few were even starting to nod and smile at him. Crank had made the most friends amongst the old folk though, having split up a near fatal fight between a Jack Russell and a Pekinese two days ago.

The local car boot sale was a boon. Once you knew the stalls, you could buy anything from black market tobacco to locally grown veg, with a few cheap, second-hand mobiles and pre-paid SIMs in between. Jim allotted each of his three 'new' phones a different set of contacts, before throwing his old phone over a cliff. Today he was carrying the 'home' phone, with the intention of calling Shona. It was also the number he had given Delilah and she might appreciate a text about Crank's heroism.

He climbed the steps by the pier and crossed the road to the pub, leaving Crank outside whilst he ordered a pint and a hot beef cob. Stepping back out into the beer garden, Jim caught the eye of a man walking along the far pavement. They both nodded, their gazes remaining locked for a second or two longer, before the other man turned his head towards the sea. His hair was a biker cut, short on top and long at the back, but the plain leather jacket and camo trousers gave no clues.

There were a number of ageing bikers and long-hairs around here. They were pretty harmless; either addled by booze and drugs, or seeking anonymity like him. This one he hadn't seen before though, at least not recently and not here. And he was a little young to be called ageing. Nothing he could do about it though, other than stay on the ball. He took a sip from his pint and dialled Shona's number.

'Hello?'

'Shona, it's Jim.'

'Hey! How are you?'

'Good, thanks. All settled and ticking along nicely. Crank's loving it.'

'Aw, that's good. You've not had any more grief then?'

'No,' he wrapped his fingers around the arm of the wooden bench seat and glanced up the road, but the man was gone. 'How about you?'

'Oh, I'm fine. Busy helping Kelly get the house sorted and teaching Delilah how to crochet. She's not a very patient student.'

'I bet, but I'm impressed that she's bothering at all. Does she seem ok?'

'Yes, although I've not seen her for the last week or two. Why?'

'I made some enquiries through an old girlfriend up in Sheffield. There was a bit of opium hash about, but you can't buy it for love nor money now. Some cold fish takes the lot for top dollar, moves in a different scene, with rich pickings...plump, barely ripe pickings, some say. He isn't liked and I don't like the sound of it.'

'No.' Shona went quiet, thinking for a few seconds. 'She was suspicious though, or she wouldn't have asked me about it. Hopefully she's canny enough to steer clear of anything too dodgy, but her idea of normal behaviour can't be that of your average 14 year old, with her upbringing.'

'Try and see her again will you? Just keep an eye out for her, if you can. I really feel for that kid,' Jim said.

'I will, and it won't be just me; there's a young fella in that home with her, who thinks the sun shines out of her backside. He's a tad unfortunate, but has a heart of gold. Not that she sees that.'

'Ha. I'm sure she doesn't. What about your lad, heard anything more from him?

Shona let out a long breath.

'I've been to see him, inside, a couple of days ago.'

'You're bloody soft, you.'

'I know, but he's my son and he didn't have the best of upbringings either, Jim. He's all I've got and I'm all he's got.'

'Does he see it that way now too?'

'Only in the sense that he's still trying to get me to bail him out, but don't worry, I said no.'

'Good. I don't mean to lay it on, Shona, but I don't want all that trouble to have been for nothing. You've got to stand your ground with him or he'll never respect you.'

'I think he might have a lesson coming to him anyway...the guy at the next table went berserk when Paulie started mouthing off at me. They both got dragged away by the guards.' He could hear imminent tears in her voice. 'It was horrible.'

'I can imagine.'

'Oh I'm sorry Jim, of course you can and I'm sorry to moan when you've called for a chat. I can't tell you what you've done for me, I feel like a different woman and the New Year really was a new start for once. It's just too easy to lean on a big bear like you, but I do appreciate it.'

'Don't give me too much credit; it's not like I've spent a lifetime helping others and right now, I'm sitting watching the sea, with a pint in my hand, waiting for someone else to cook my lunch. Moan away, I'm quite happy. How's it been with Kelly then?'

He rolled a fag and leaned back on the bench, content to listen to her chatter until his hot beef cob arrived. Once the conversation ended however, the face of the man from earlier returned to bother him. It was familiar, but the context escaped him. Not prison, he would remember that, but there were a vast number of potential settings that preceded his last stretch. Without an indication of which club he was associated to, it would be difficult to narrow it down.

Jim passed the last mouthful of cob to Crank and drained his pint. It was a worth a wander up the road. If the guy was still around there might be a bike parked up somewhere, with more information to offer. He crossed over and from the far pavement could see about half a mile ahead. There was nobody whose figure matched the one he sought. Having familiarised himself with the broader village within a week of arriving, he decided to criss-cross his way through the built up streets parallel with the road, just a few hundred yards in, just to be sure. It was roughly the right direction for home anyway.

There wasn't the same distinction between weekdays and weekends here, with a greater percentage of the community being retired or incapable of work, but mid-afternoon on a Wednesday was never a busy time. Jim saw nothing of interest for ten or fifteen minutes, until he hung a left to take him past the tiny park where the drunks gathered in the evenings. Only one man was sitting on the benches and he wasn't a drunk. It was the one Jim thought of as The Indian.

The guy was white, but wore his grey hair very, very long, with a centre parting and no beard. He looked to be in his sixties and his mannerisms suggested one mushroom too many, or that he was still eating them. Jim saw him often on his walks with Crank and had twice received uninvited pagan blessings on the beach. He was a pleasant and harmless fruit-loop, who talked to himself and prayed to the sky, but today The Indian was agitated, almost frightened.

'Are you alright fella?' Jim said, stopping a few feet away.

The Indian raised wide, hopeful eyes towards him, but upon recognition, let out a thin wail and put his hands over his head.

'I don't know anything! I'm not of your world, I cannot…please, let me be.'

'Woah…steady on, friend, I don't want anything from you.'

Jim backed away, troubled, watching The Indian peer at him through his fingers and rock back and forth. He started to walk on, giving The Indian a wide berth, but a hundred yards further up the street he stopped when the man cried out again.

'We are haunted by the past, but not all are ghosts!'

That was too fucking relevant to ignore. Jim turned to go back and question him, just as a loud roar burst out in the next street along. He ran ahead, reaching the turn in time to see a fat Harley take off in the opposite direction. The bloke from outside the pub was riding it and the bike's colours told Jim everything he needed to know. Dicko, one of the ex-bikers, stood on the pavement watching him leave, pulling his hand from his jacket like he'd just tucked something away. This many coincidences added up to a certainty that he'd been found.

Dicko fell squarely into the 'drunk' category, which was a positive. Jim was torn; he could go and give him a bang on the head that would make him forget his recent encounter, he could offer more money than Dicko had been paid to spy on him, or he could wait for a quieter time and a darker street. Retreating back around the corner, before the dickhead could turn and see him, Jim decided that buying him a crate of whisky would probably solve the problem with the least mess.

Any action would only be a short term solution though. This wasn't the recent business; it was an old score, a very bitter and deadly score, in which the pissed up idiot would only ever be an insignificant pawn. It wasn't even worth moving on again, if they'd managed to follow him here. The only question remaining was when it would happen.

~ ~ ~

Dee examined the text from Shona. She hadn't bothered reading it yesterday, but her mind felt clearer this morning, even though she hadn't slept much, having run out of resin. That shit-bag was only giving her little bits now. He wouldn't sell her any weed either. 'My girl don't pay for weed', Gaz kept saying, but then only let her have enough for a couple of spliffs.

It was nice that he wanted to see her all the time, but it would also be nice to stay in and just chill. She hadn't played chess with Blink for ages and he might beat her again, if she stopped practising. She'd also missed two days at catering, through being too hung-over and knackered to get up. That pissed her off, enough to stay in last night so that she could get up this morning, even if she'd been too pissed off to actually do much or talk to anyone.

Maybe Shona would be able to get her some weed. She read the text a third time and realised that she hadn't seen her mum for nearly a fortnight. Where did all that time go? Right, she would see Gaz tonight and go and see her mum tomorrow. If he wouldn't give her any weed, she'd try and skank a bit. He couldn't have total control, she would have a night off if she wanted to.

'Do you want some breakfast, Dee?'

It was Derek, at the bottom of the stairs. He must have heard her alarm go off. That was a result...he wouldn't talk at her like Sandra did over breakfast.

'Yeah, toast and strawberry jam,' she yelled.

'Please Derek?'

'Yeah, whatever. Please, please, please.'

Maybe he was going to be a pain in the arse after all. She pulled some clothes on and went downstairs. He'd made her coffee too.

'Thanks,' she said.

'It's a pleasure. I'm impressed that you're up in time for the taxi.'

He took a bowl and a box of cereal from the cupboard and put them on the table. She'd forgotten about Blink. He came bouncing in thirty seconds later.

'Delilah! I d..didn't think you'd g..go today.'

'Yeah, well I am.'

'C..c..cool.'

Not really, but she'd let him off.

'Do you want a game of chess on Saturday?'

'Y..yeah, that'd be c..cool.'

Urrrrr, he was doing her head in already. She picked up her second slice of toast and the coffee.

'I'm going to finish getting ready.'

The day was a disaster. She couldn't concentrate and got into loads of shit for walking off and smoking, but the fags only worked while she was sucking on them and the minute she went back inside, she wanted another one. When the taxi dropped her off at Sunny Bank, Dee ran straight up to the shower and managed to get out again without talking to anyone.

Her ankle still ached, but she was a lot more careful after that first night out, when Damo had carried her to a park bench and then watched from the shadows until Sandra came to pick her up. Unable to escape from the bollocking that followed, she had learnt her lesson and was going to wear the cast for another week yet. Sod how stupid it looked, it was better to be able to leave when you wanted.

Gaz had tidied up the house a bit and there were more chairs and more visitors now. The lads next door were mates, so it didn't matter if he played music and made a noise, but only Damo and one other person were there when Dee arrived. It was the second of the older men who'd been there the night of the robbery. Not the creepy one who was pissed off about the cctv cameras and she was glad of that. This one was quiet and even though he didn't smile, he wasn't as scary.

Damo passed her a bag of weed to skin up with and she took the opportunity to drop a small bud into her tobacco pouch. Gaz and the man were talking in low voices in the kitchen, so she loaded the spliff and sat back in the chair, blowing a long plume of smoke into the air. Her eyes wandered around the room, taking in the new sofa-bed, the new stereo with a hand-held video thing perched on top, the electric lamp that was on. Maybe there was hot water now too.

She became aware that Damo was watching her from under his cap and held out the spliff, but he shook his head. Shrugging, she took another long drag and closed her eyes so that he would disappear. Then she opened them again. There was a large, leafy plant in a pot by the bed. It wasn't a weed plant. What the fuck did Gaz want with that? Damo was still watching her, so she shut her eyes and forgot about the plant.

Her pleasant doze was disturbed by a cold draft and the bang of the back door. Gaz came through from the kitchen.

'Sorry babe, just sortin' a bit of business.' He bent down to kiss her and took the spliff. 'Giz a whack on that. Stick some sounds on, Damo.'

'Where's all the new gear from?'

'I bin getting' sorted here too. Lads next door know the landlord, he int bothered as long as he gets the rent, so I'm stayin' for a bit.'

'Why are you still hiding anyway? I thought Josh took the rap for the robbery.'

'Yeah, but I got more business than that, babe. That other geezer - the one who was here when you did your ankle - he got lifted and we thought it was all up. I just heard he's gone down and kept quiet though, so we runnin' free again. Time to celebrate.'

He passed the spliff to Damo, flopped down on the chair opposite and started rolling one with the black hash. He looked at her while he licked the rizzlas and blew her a kiss.

'Do you wanna drink? I got some cider and beers in.'

Damo went to the kitchen and came back with an armful of bottles. Gaz selected a fruit cider and flipped the top off before passing it to her. She took a small sip and then a bigger one, it was lush and tasted more like cherryade than cider. Gaz brought the 'special' spliff to her and then went over to some boxes in the corner. Dee took another swig of cider and a long pull on the spliff. She felt sooo much better.

The stuff Gaz was pulling out of the boxes was totally random. A white fur that he threw on the bed, sparkly eye masks, like you'd wear at a fancy dress party, a load of posh scarves. She half wanted to ask but couldn't be arsed, so she drank more cider instead. Drinking made her want to smoke and smoking dried her mouth out, so she drank again. She realised that she'd hogged more than half the special spliff when Gaz asked for it back.

Oops. It was still early though...there'd be plenty of time to straighten out later and she didn't have to get up tomorrow. Good job, cos she was feeling pretty smashed already. Gaz must have loaded that spliff. She was also very hot and it was normally freezing in here. Leaning forward, Dee opened her eyes with reluctance and pulled her jacket off. There was a nice glow in the room now.

'Why don't you come and try out the sofa-bed,' Gaz said.

It did look well comfy, with that soft, white fur spread over it. He was sitting on the end of the bed and plugged in another lamp, with a red bulb that looked really cool. She drained the last of the cider and stood up, feeling a bit dizzy, like a whitey was coming on. The bed was a good idea. She went over and flopped on it, face first.

'This is lush,' she said, turning her head so she could breathe.

Gaz laughed and lifted her legs onto it, so she was lying lengthways. There was a clink of glass and a hiss.

'Another drink, m' lady,' he said and put another bottle of cider on the floor next to her. 'You gotta sit up to have dis though, y'aint burnin' a hole in my new bed.'

She squirmed around and took the spliff off him, watching Damo load a short, stubby pipe, while Gaz went over to the stereo. He changed the music and turned it up a bit, it was more mellow, still a strong beat but slower, like a pulse. It was good, it suited her mood. She tipped her head back and took another swig of cider and when she went to put the bottle back down Gaz was sitting on the floor, very close to her. He held out the pipe.

'Try it, babe. It's just the black hash, but it's a better hit like dis.'

Why not. She was lying down. Dee took the pipe and sucked while Gaz held a lighter to the bowl. It was hot, bursting on her lungs and still hot when she coughed it out.

'Easy, babe, it's a pipe, not a hoover. Here,' he passed her the cider.

It was cool and soothing on her throat. The pipe worked. Her head felt heavy and her vision was blurring, but not too bad. She tried it again, with Gaz holding it and then lay back to appreciate the effects.

Interesting. She felt like she was melting into the sofa and the music was in her head, in her whole body. There was a pleasant tickling too, running up from her ankles, but she wasn't sure if it was inside or outside. It ran right up her shins, over her knee-caps, up her thighs, over her hips, circled her stomach. She lifted a hand to touch it and found Gaz's hand, it was his fingers tickling. He hadn't touched her like that before and it was nice. She wanted him to carry on doing that, just that. He offered her the pipe instead.

'I'll hold it, you jus' breathe, baby.'

She let him push it between her lips and inhaled. He withdrew it a little, then put it back when she'd breathed out. She took another drag. It was like being a queen, lying on furs and not even having to hold your own pipe. Her head was spinning again, so she lay back and drifted off with the music, smiling when the tickling began again at her fingertips.

Time blurred into feelings, intense feelings. They put masks on, for fun he said, but it was weird, like kissing a stranger. She couldn't remember taking her clothes off, but realised at some point, that all she had on was a scarf around her throat. It didn't matter though, because it was warm and the fur was soft. It occurred to her at another time that she didn't know if Damo was still there or not. She couldn't see him, but she couldn't see much except for the red glow.

Her body felt different too, all over. Gaz was slow and gentle, but went a little further than normal, with everything. It wasn't scary; he didn't hurt her and her wrists weren't tied, just looped with scarves to the bed. The scarf around her neck he used to

233

bring her close, not strangle. He kept moving her, turning her, rolling her over. She felt floppy, like a doll, but it wasn't uncomfortable and some of it felt good.

A cry burst from her lips and she was slow to understand the source of it, the pain and strange sensation, taking long seconds to realise he was now inside her, thrusting hard. The bubble of outrage billowing in her chest deflated again. It didn't hurt any more, in fact it felt ok and he was definitely enjoying it. It went on and on, moving into different positions like before. Every so often a pipe would appear and send her back into the dream zone.

It was only the pressure on her bladder that made her refuse the next pipe. She really, really needed a wee and didn't know if she could walk upstairs.

'Need a piss,' she mumbled to Gaz.

'Right now?'

'Yeah.'

She pushed him away and struggled off the bed, but her legs wouldn't work at all. He laughed and picked her up, carrying her up the stairs and plonking her on the bog.

'We got paper, hot water and everything now,' he said. 'Take your time.'

She did. She sat there for ages, until her head stopped spinning. She opened her eyes and tried to focus. The first thing she noticed was that she was naked. Looking around the bathroom, she spotted a towel over the edge of the bath. She had a quick wash over the sink, dried herself on the towel and then wrapped it around her chest. Her legs were wobbling like mad and she was sore down there now. God knows what time it was, but she needed to go home, whatever.

She went back downstairs and found Gaz and Damo sitting side by side on the bed, watching a video on the hand-held camera. So Damo *was* still there. Her face flooding with heat, Dee went straight for her clothes and pulled them on behind the chair, strapping the cast on over her jeans. Gaz offered her a spliff, but she shook her head and checked her phone instead. It was 10.30pm. Half an hour over curfew already and half an hour to get home, but she wouldn't get into too much shit if she left right now.

'Aw, you not goin' already babe?' Gaz said, although he didn't get up off the bed.

'Yeah.'

'You comin' back tomorrow?'

'Nah, I'm going to see my mum.'

'So Saturday then.'

She would quite like to stay at Sunny Bank on Saturday, maybe even go to the pictures with Blink, but she couldn't tell Gaz that.

'Yeah, probably. Can I have some weed? I don't mind paying for it.'

'Why don't you have some of dis instead.'

He picked up the lump of black hash and held out his hand to Damo, who took a knife from his pocket. Gaz cut the lump in two and passed the small piece to her.

'I'd rather have a bit of normal weed,' she said.

'Dis aint so smelly, you don't wanna get sniffed out at home. You can smoke weed here.'

It was better than nothing, so she took it. Looking at them, both sitting on the bed that not long ago, she and Gaz were having sex on, made her sick with embarrassment. She backed towards the door.

'Hey, no kiss goodbye?'

Gaz jumped up and came towards her. She ducked her head and he laughed.

'Don't go pretendin' you shy, babe. That hot li'l booty was on fire an hour ago. You wasn't shy then.'

'I've got to go.'

She let him kiss her and then hobbled through the kitchen as quickly as she could. Her legs still weren't working right and when she got outside the cold air made her head spin. She leaned against the wall for a few minutes, taking deep breaths, but she didn't want Damo coming out and carrying her off to the park again. She walked around the side of the house and started up the road, wishing she had her crutches with her. It wasn't just the ache in her ankle; her thighs ached, her hips ached, her belly ached and her fanny was stinging like a bastard.

Her heart sank even further when she realised there wouldn't be a bus at this time. If she called Sunny Bank someone might come and fetch her, but she didn't feel like being stuck in a car with any of the staff right now. Bed, that was all she wanted, her own bed, but it was a couple of miles away and she was struggling already.

Swiping angrily at the tears that trickled down her cheeks, she lurched on at a more determined pace, until the appearance of a cop car, slowing down on the opposite side of the road, knocked the remaining fight out of her. She had no idea what the one driving was saying out of the window; she couldn't hear him over the roaring in her ears as she collapsed onto the pavement.

15

There were four messages waiting when Becky turned on her work phone on Monday morning. Although the second one from Sunny Bank was worrying, the third concerned her most. It was from Jim, on a new number, saying that Shona had seen Delilah on Friday night and was concerned by several things, could she call him back please. Yes she could...when she was in the office with the emailed report from Sunny Bank in front of her.

She made herself sit down for breakfast with Simon first. Her period was a week late and he would notice the delay soon. When that happened, Becky wanted it to be in a warm atmosphere of mutual love and consideration, not the middle of an emotive debate over her working too many hours. There was no way she could let the chaos that surrounded Delilah damage her marriage again, not if this really was it. But she did have to make a conscious effort to stop her leg jiggling under the table.

Having kissed Simon goodbye and driven sedately around the corner, Becky put her foot down. It seemed the crocheting craze was not a sign of things to come, but a temporary means of alleviating boredom. Delilah was straight back into trouble as soon as she was mobile. She knocked ten minutes off the usual journey time, but didn't attempt to run up the stairs. Until a pregnancy test confirmed things either way, she was going to be careful.

No-one else was in the office yet, which was a relief. She flicked the computer on and went to make a coffee while it booted up. Taking the lid off the milk made her feel nauseous, so she added a sugar instead and had it black. Back at her desk, she logged on and opened her Inbox, sagging a little at the number of little yellow envelopes that popped up. One training day on Friday and now there were forty-seven emails to catch up on.

A quick scan told her that the first one from Julie at Sunny Bank – sent at 1.03am on Thursday night/Friday morning - was still the priority. Delilah had been brought home by the police just before midnight, under the influence of alcohol and at least one other drug, quite upset about something. She was found staggering along a residential street on the other side of town, but wouldn't talk about what had happened. Julie and one of Delilah's key workers had both noticed that she appeared stiff and delicate, over and above the effects of the slow-healing ankle.

The second email from Julie informed her that Delilah was visiting her mum on Friday night and a member of staff would drop her off, ensuring that Shona was present before leaving. It also noted that Delilah appeared even more stiff on Friday, but refused any medical attention or to speak about the previous evening. So Shona would have phoned Jim after seeing Delilah, either with her own concerns or because Delilah let something slip.

Scrolling through the log on her phone, she found the un-named mobile number and hit 'call'.

'Hello?'

'Jim it's Becky, returning your call.'

'Ah right, thanks. Yeah, Shona called me on Saturday, after seeing Delilah round at Kelly's on Friday night. She said Dee seemed very subdued and less happy…no sparkle is how she put it. Dee wouldn't say what was wrong, but Shona thought she might be in a bit of pain, sore down there, if you know what I mean. And, it was hard to tell because she's still limping, but she was walking like, as if, er…she'd had a…heavy evening, the night before.'

'A lot of sex you mean.'

'Yes. And Shona's pretty sure Dee was still a virgin the last time she saw her, because she actually asked her, casual like, and Dee said her boyfriend was nice and didn't hassle her to do that.'

'Ok, that's great. I mean, not great, but very useful information. It matches up with the report I had from the home and fills in a few blanks. Thanks Jim.'

'So what's going to happen now?'

She wasn't sure. The CSE Unit were still investigating, but the arrest of the older man had not been the breakthrough they were hoping for. They were no closer to shutting down the wider operation, if there was one. Maybe Delilah was still at risk of commercial exploitation, or maybe there was no value in not 'spoiling the goods' now and Delilah was at the mercy of the boyfriend/potential pimp.

'I don't know Jim and I probably wouldn't be able to tell you if I did. I will report all of this to the police unit already monitoring the situation, but if it is just the boyfriend, who is very, very careful about his identity, I don't know how much we can do. We can't lock Delilah up for her own safety, when she hasn't done anything wrong.'

Becky listened to the deep intake of breath, followed by a long sigh, at the other end of the line, wondering if it was an anger management technique learned in prison.

'Alright, thanks for being honest. I guess you are a bit stuck,' he said, sounding more resigned than angry. 'If there is anything more you can tell me at any time, I'd appreciate a call.'

'Sure.'

They said their goodbyes and Becky hung up, not very sure at all. It could be nothing, but she felt an odd sense of role reversal. The conversation ended with him awaiting information from her, not promising to be in touch with more, as usual. Had she said anything she shouldn't? Taking a sip of coffee, she replayed the conversation in her head and the hot fluid came to a gurgling halt, half way down her throat.

'…if it is just the boyfriend…' she had said, and then implied that there was little they could do to protect her anyway. Shit. She'd better warn McGrath.

~ ~ ~

During the week after Delilah's return by the police, Derek found himself worrying about her at home, as well as at work. She agreed to go to the cinema with Blink on Saturday night, but barely

239

spoke all evening and ignored a lot of Blink's comments, although she didn't bitch at him either. On Sunday she stayed in her room all day, went out in the evening, but returned within an hour in a foul mood.

She attended the catering course on Monday, but Sunny Bank received a call mid-morning, asking someone to fetch her, as there was no point her being there if she was going to stand outside smoking. Becky came to see her in the afternoon, but Delilah told her to leave in very unpleasant terms. By Tuesday she was shivering and refused to eat, saying she had flu. The notes in the evening log described her rebuffing Blink's attempts to talk to her with a vile torrent of abuse.

On Wednesday, Derek was on shift when Delilah went out in the afternoon, looking ill. She wouldn't accept a lift or say where she was going, but was home by tea-time and seemed a little more upbeat, all flu symptoms having vanished. She even played chess with Blink and went to bed early. On Thursday however, she was still in bed when he arrived at lunchtime, having refused to get up for the catering course.

Checking the log, Derek found that Julie had emailed both the social worker and the CSE liaison officer, with their suspicions that there were signs of substance withdrawal. He was still in the office when Delilah surfaced at around 3pm and he found her in the kitchen, bleary-eyed and starving.

'Shall I make you a coffee?' he asked.

She pulled a face.

'Urgh, no, tea...please.'

'You always have coffee when you get up.'

Delilah was too busy ramming bread into the toaster to reply and he figured it was afternoon now and not morning.

'You could have a proper dinner instead of just toast, it is 3 o'clock.'

'I will, after the toast.'

'In fact, you could make enough for Blink too, to compensate for not attending catering today.'

She gave him a look, but it was a reassuringly Delilah-esque look.

'Maybe if Sandra was here, but you wouldn't be much help.'

'I could try, and Blink's not too fussy.'

'He might be a nob, but I don't want to poison him.'

That was quite a confession. Perhaps she was feeling guilty about her horrible behaviour. Keeping up the chit-chat, Derek manoeuvred into a position from which he could see her face. She was pale, but it was only March and she was always pale. Her eyes were hooded, but then she was not long out of bed. This was as talkative as Delilah got and her conversation was not impaired in any way.

They were making toasties when Blink returned from school and came bursting into the kitchen.

'Delilah!'

She screwed up her forehead in the frown that meant she was trying not to smile. Derek hoped that Blink had sussed that one out too.

'Do you want a toastie?' she said.

'Er...y..yeah, that'd be aw..aw..awesome, thanks.'

'What do you want in it?'

'Cheese and b..beans, p..please.'

'Alright, but you can make your own drink.'

Blink grinned and Derek marvelled at his capacity for forgiveness.

He wasn't on shift again until Saturday evening and was disappointed to read in the log, that Dee had gone out on Friday night and returned in a mess. This time she was not drunk or stoned, but furious, with scratch marks across her cheek and a swollen hand. She was already at her mum's when he arrived at Sunny Bank and Sandra was tasked with fetching her later, but he made sure that all the ingredients for a super deluxe hot chocolate were in the kitchen cupboard, before taking Blink out to play pool.

It was a recent discovery in terms of hidden talent. Blink was not a natural sportsman, but a maths question concerning angles that used a pool shot as an example, seemed to have inspired him. He proved to be rather good and Derek would much rather be playing pool, than stuck in a chair watching dross at the cinema.

Keeping an eye on Blink as he ordered two cokes from the bar, Derek remembered that he would turn seventeen in a fortnight. Most lads were trying to get served beer at that age, but Blink wasn't interested and wouldn't stand a chance if he was. With his chunky glasses, too-short clothes and loose grin, he looked like a very tall 12 year old. Blink put the cokes on the table and picked up his cue.

'Is it m..my turn?'

'Yeah, but I was just thinking, it's your birthday soon. Any idea what you might like as a present?'

Blink shrugged and bent over the table, examining the new layout of balls. He took the shot and potted his target, turning around to grin at Derek.

'Maybe a decent p..pool cue?'

'Doesn't look like you need one,' Derek said, watching him pot a second ball. 'So what is it you're saving your clothing allowance for?'

Blink ignored him while taking his third shot, which left Derek with three nigh impossible options. He looked very smug, but didn't jeer.

'A r..really good suit,' he said. 'I want to get a g..good job when I leave s..school next year, even if I go to u..university too.'

'Wow. Well I like your thinking, but you do know you can buy a half decent suit for £80 these days? And a real smart one for £150? Once you're earning, you can spend what you want, but to be honest Blink, I think you'd be better spending some of it now. I mean, you look ok, but your sleeves and trousers are a bit short.'

Blink looked down at himself and his smile faded.

'I d..don't know what to b..buy though. I don't really l..like jeans and I think w..wearing tracksuits to w..walk around in looks stupid.'

'Well why don't you and me go shopping next weekend, on Saturday. Honestly, you could get new trousers and a top for £50. If you're not bothered about labels, you'll get half a new wardrobe for £100 and I happen to know you've got £175 of clothing allowance saved up.'

Blink looked up at him and a slow smile spread across his face. 'Alright, that'd be c..cool.'

~ ~ ~

Kelly's offer to clear the pots involved taking her own plate into the kitchen and disappearing upstairs for a crafty swig of vodka. Shona didn't mind; Kelly consumed a lot less alcohol on crafty swigs, than she did when attached to a bottle, and she wanted five minutes alone with Delilah anyway.

'That's a good scratch on your cheek,' she said. 'Have you been messing with somebody's cat?'

'Nah, it was that bitch Stacey, Doogie's girlfriend...except she's seeing someone else now.'

'Oh? Where did you bump into her?'

'She turned up with this lad at...where I hang out.'

Delilah wised up pretty fast, but seemed quite eager to talk about it. She rolled a fag and Shona waited.

'She had a go as soon as she walked in, so I had a go back. There were a few lads there too and they were shouting 'bitch-fight' and that. I didn't want to fight her, but she hit me first, did this with her ring.'

She pointed at the scratch and Shona noticed that the eye above it was bruised too.

'Did no-one try to split it up?'

'No. Like I said, they wanted us to fight. She went to hit me again, so I hit her in the face and it made her nose bleed, then I kicked her knee in, to stop her trying again.'

'And then what? Did the police come?'

'No, her boyfriend took her away and the others were all excited and...well, they thought it was cool and I thought I'd like smashing her face in, cos she's done it to me before, but I didn't.'

'Well that's a good thing. Don't feel bad for feeling bad, for goodness' sake.'

Delilah gave an amused huff, but her expression didn't lift. This lot sounded a right bunch of shites.

243

'And was that boyfriend of yours there? Is he still nice and undemanding?'

The glowering face turned a dark shade of red. Obviously not then, the bastard.

'I don't want to talk about him. Where's Mum?'

'Upstairs. Why don't I go fetch her down while you put the kettle on and make another coffee.'

Kelly was flaked out on the bed, her hand around a bottle that was sticking up from the drawer of a bedside cabinet. Shona loosened her grip, laid the bottle flat and closed the drawer.

'Kelly? Are you awake?'

There was no response, but Kelly's chest was moving in a steady rhythm, so Shona pulled the duvet over her and went back downstairs. It was 9 o'clock though, she'd done well to last this long. Dee was still in the kitchen.

'Your mum's asleep I'm afraid, but don't take it personally love, she's not one for late nights these days.'

The thin shoulders rose and fell.

'She's better than she was.'

'That's right and getting better all the time. Now are we having that coffee?'

'I don't fancy one. I might go home, I'm knackered.'

'Ok. Have you phoned for your lift?

'Not yet,' Delilah paused. 'Shona, have you got any weed? I can only get hash and...I don't like it.'

'I'm sorry Dee, but no. I haven't bothered since all that trouble.'

She was sorry, but also relieved to be telling the truth. That would have been an awful dilemma.

'What, not at all?'

'No, and there's another reason I perhaps should have told you about. Paulie's been sent to prison and I've been to see him, I'm going again next week. You can't go near the stuff if you've got to get past sniffer dogs.'

'Oh, sorry, that's shit. Say hi from me.'

Delilah looked so dejected that Shona was tempted to say she'd make a few calls, but she'd better not get involved, it would only lead to trouble for everyone. She put a hand out to squeeze the girl's arm and Delilah jumped at the touch, making out that she was just reaching for her phone.

'I'll call Sunny Bank,' she said and turned away.

Shona frowned. The signs were small, but added together, they were beginning to create an unpleasant picture. It was a good ten minutes before the car arrived and Delilah said little in that time, smoking two roll-ups back to back.

'I'll lock up, I've got a key now,' Shona said.

'Alright and thanks for the bacca.'

'Come back soon and call if you need me in the meantime.'

Delilah nodded and walked off down the path. Shona went back inside and took a glass of water upstairs for Kelly, making sure she was well covered and still breathing. She checked the kitchen, turned the lights off and locked up, glad to be heading for her own settee.

Once settled with a cup of coffee, she checked the time. 9.45. Not too late to call Jim. He answered in two rings.

'Shona, you ok?'

'Yes, fine, sorry it's so late. Delilah's just gone, so I thought I'd call you with an update.'

'I was going to call you in the morning. I've been doing some digging and the shit coming up stinks. I'm seriously worried.'

'That makes two of us.'

~ ~ ~

It was just this kind of thing that had made McGrath steer clear of the Vice Squad, throughout his twenty-seven year career. It made his skin crawl and awoke the vicious streak buried deep within him. He took notes that scored into the pad on which he wrote, while he listened to Becky.

'It would be easier to put this in an email,' he said.

'Easier, but less anonymous.'

'Have you not discussed this with your link in the CSE Unit?'

'Yes, but she seemed to think I was grasping at hearsay and rumours. She said she'd make a note of it, but you know how well-informed the source is.'

He did, but that made it even more inappropriate to collude in the 'anonymous' line and put him in a compromising position. There was a contact he could approach however and if anything did come of it, then he could pass the information to the relevant person. He wasn't going to interfere in someone else's case.

'Alright. Leave it with me.' He wanted to point out that this bordered on an abuse of their acquaintance, but decided her Monday morning was difficult enough. 'I'll be in touch if I learn anything.'

'Thank you and I know I'm a cow for asking,' she said.

'Yes, well, it's for the right reasons I suppose.'

He hung up and called her something worse than a cow, but fired off the email before he did anything else. Delilah's thin, wary face floated into his mind, the way her eyes lit up when he was telling her about the Scottish Clans and the way she smiled at Jono. It was a sick world. He got up with the intention of going to see his Detective Sergeant, but stalled when his desk phone rang.

'McGrath,' he said, brusque with frustration.

'Hey, this is the quickest response you've ever had to an email, don't bark at me.'

'Sorry Mike, and thank you for calling back. Please tell me I'm a fantasist who shouldn't listen to gossip.'

'Fraid not, you're bang on the nail. A real upper class market, if you can call it that. Buy yourself a virgin for the night...and you can imagine the price for such a rare commodity, especially with the advance grooming.'

McGrath sat back down in his chair.

'How the hell is that happening if we know about it?'

'Cos they box clever, cut down on the laws broken. The girls are of age, just, and consenting, kind of, cos they're so desperate for a hit. These are smart, well-connected bastards.'

McGrath let out a breath that he wasn't aware he was holding. Delilah was nowhere near of age.

'And what about the other stuff, the 'franchise porn', is that happening too?'

'Ah, we know less about that; it's a new head Medusa has sprouted. You knock out one spawning ground of filth and another

246

one pops up somewhere else, with slightly different methods. What you mentioned about one buyer for all the opium hash backs that theory, although there are plenty of other, much more subtle and suitable drugs available. It's probably part of the targeting. Horses for courses as they say. Where did you say the info came from?'

'I didn't, but he doesn't know anything more. If he did, you'd probably have all hell breaking loose over there.'

'Right, well we do have an insider now, so we're getting access to a lot of material. Similar theme, but a broader catchment area and a 2nd class ticket. Instead of doing it yourself, you get to see the movie of the virgin being broken in, with a distasteful amount of detail. We think they're using a web of local small fry, giving them the means to groom and purchasing the final product to then distribute. Problem is, the operation's so fragmented, it's hard to pin down the players.'

'So what happens to the virgins after they're deflowered?' McGrath asked.

He cursed himself for doing so. He already knew the answer and didn't want to hear the cynical response of someone hardened to it.

'Depends on the small fry operation. They could be kept on the hook and just used or pimped, or let off the hook to fall back onto a dry riverbed. I don't know. So what's your interest anyway?'

He hadn't had time to form a plausible answer to that before the phone call.

'A local girl, who may be involved. I was on the scene when she was first taken into care. Her social worker has hung on to my number as a police contact and she phoned me this morning with the information.'

'Right. Well send me her file over, any identifying marks et cetera and we'll see if there are any matches.'

'If you don't mind me passing your details over to the CSE Unit who are already involved, that would be more straightforward.'

'Fine, whatever works best.'

'Thanks Mike.'

'No problem. You never know, depending on where this goes you might be giving me a lead too.'

McGrath shuddered.

'No offence, but I sincerely hope not.'

He cradled the handset and picked up his mobile to call Becky back, relieved when the answerphone kicked in. A brief affirmation of the potential risks, an instruction to pass Mike's email and phone number to her CSE Unit link, a careful recounting of those details and he could hang up and push it from his mind.

He hung up, but his mind clung obstinately to those unwanted images, which then turned vengeful. Vengeful and bearded. He picked up the phone again and redialled Becky's number. It went straight to answerphone this time, so she was probably listening to his message. He left another one.

'It would be good if you can avoid speaking to Jim. If you can't, please tell him that we are dealing with it, that the information has been passed to the unit right at the heart of these things and beg him not to get involved.'

~ ~ ~

Dee managed to scrape through Monday at catering. She was forcing herself to use only tiny crumbs of the black hash, although she wanted more, not less. The bits of bud she had managed to pocket from Gaz's were helping, but didn't go far. He was messing her about. After moaning that she wasn't going round every day, he kept cancelling on her now, at the last minute. She'd only seen him twice last week and Friday's visit was horrible.

Stacey arrived before she'd even sat down and after the fight, Gaz was quite weird. He had a massive boner and pulled her upstairs, into one of the damp, scabby bedrooms with no furniture. It was just a shag - no kissing or nice things - but at least it was quick and didn't hurt. The good bit was that several little baggies of weed fell out of his pocket while they were doing it and she managed to put her foot on one. He went back downstairs without noticing.

There were five lads apart from Gaz in the lounge. They were being alright and calling her ninja, but she couldn't help wondering if they also had boners and felt so uneasy that she left early. Not before she'd managed to pocket two half-smoked spliffs though. Gaz said he'd see her Sunday, but sent her a text in the afternoon saying he was busy. They were still on for tonight, for now.

The atmosphere at Sunny Bank was strange when she got home. There were voices in the office and Gareth met her at the door, even more soppy than normal, trying to get her to go to the kitchen for a drink.

'I don't want a drink, I'm going for a shower,' she said.

'Just for five minutes. Becky's here and she needs to talk to you.'

'Well I don't want to talk to her.'

Dee squeezed around him and shot up the stairs. She grabbed some clothes and locked herself in the bathroom. They weren't going to follow her in here. She was still washing her hair when there was a soft knock on the door. What the fuck?

'Piss off, whoever it is, I'm in the shower.'

'Bad luck, Dee.' Shit, it was Becky. 'I'm not trying to get in, but I know you're going to run off the minute you're out and there are some things you need to know, if you don't already.'

'Aw, just fuck off, will ya?'

'What I'd really like to do, is lock you in there until you're off whatever it is you're on. As I can't do that, I want to make sure you're as safe as possible, by knowing the risks that you're taking.'

Like Becky knew anything about anything. Dee ignored her.

'I think you're smoking or eating, maybe both, some black hash that's unusually strong. I can't prove it, we haven't found anything, but I've been doing some research anyway.'

There was a squeezing sensation around Dee's heart and she stood still under the running water. That had to be Shona or Josh, but she couldn't imagine either of them grassing. Someone had though.

'It's rare, Dee, there isn't much of it about around here. The only people who have access to it are nasty characters. They're not just drug dealers, they're into sexual exploitation and porn. You know what that is, we've talked about it before.'

She still didn't reply, but turned the shower off so that she could hear better.

'Look, if it makes any difference, your friend, Jim – the big, hard biker who isn't scared of anyone – he's scared about you, Delilah and he's very angry with me for not protecting you.'

Tears joined the drops of water running down from her wet hair. How could he? He said he'd be there for her, she thought she could trust him. But he didn't like the police or Social Services either. He wouldn't talk to them, Becky must be lying.

'You're a lying bitch!' she shouted, yanking the shower curtain aside and snatching the towel off the rail.

There were more voices from downstairs and doors banging. Someone was calling to Becky, but the stuck-up fucking slag just got louder.

'You believe what you like, Dee, but hear me out before you make your mind up. These people get young girls hooked on drugs and then sell them for sex. They also film the girls when they're having sex and sell the videos for money. I don't want you to be one of those girls and I don't think you do either. Please, just think about it, think about what you're doing and for your own sake be careful.'

Julie was outside the door now too. She sounded angry, but with Becky, not her. Their footsteps went off down the landing and Dee had a last scrub with the towel before pulling her clothes on. She still had a few quid left from her pocket money, so she could just get out now and buy some chips for tea. Becky was a horrible, lying, fucking bitch. She wasn't a fucking prostitute, she'd only shagged Gaz and he was her boyfriend, so that didn't even make her a slag.

Confident that there was no-one else upstairs now, she ran across to her room and shoved bacca, money and her phone into her pockets. Front door or patio doors? They couldn't stop her. Fuck all of them. She ran down the stairs and straight for the main door. No-one even stood in her way, but Blink shouted her name from the lounge. He must have come home while she was in the shower.

She paused and looked through the doorway.

'Delilah! Don't go!' he shouted again and she was shocked to see he was bawling his head off, his mouth all screwed up, tears pouring from under his glasses. What the fuck was up with him? She wanted to know, but needed to get out. She tore her eyes away and ran to the door. Weird that he hadn't stuttered. She'd talk to him when she got back.

It was starting to rain, so she bought chips from the kebab shop near the park and took them to the bandstand. There was no-one else about, no distraction from Becky's rant. Gaz wasn't selling her for sex and she wouldn't do it with anyone else, even if he did try to make her. She might talk to the LAC nurse though. Derek said she wasn't allowed to tell other people what they talked about. Gaz reckoned he was on the male pill, so he didn't need to use jonnies and Dee wanted to check that was true.

She'd almost finished her chips, when a memory of Gaz and Damo looking at a video camera surfaced, that first time she had proper sex. It was hard to picture it clearly, she'd been so smashed at the time. There was the potted plant, which was now brown and droopy on the back yard, and a white fur. New stuff everywhere, a stereo, a camera, that they were looking at when she came down from the bathroom. Oh FUCK...what if Damo filmed the whole thing?

The last chip she swallowed stuck at the bottom of her throat and she threw the rest onto the floor of the bandstand. The bastard. She'd ask him, but would he admit it? The sooner she got there, the more chance there was of catching him alone, or at least just with Damo. She jogged the rest of the way to the bus-stop, pleased that her ankle stood it fine.

The back door of the house wasn't quite shut, so she knocked and pushed it open. There was no-one in the kitchen or lounge, although there was a smell of perfume. Footsteps thudded above her and then started down the stairs.

'Who is it?' Gaz shouted.

'It's me,' Dee said.

She wondered if she should have waited outside, but he looked pleased to see her.

'You're early, babe. That's not always a good idea, but today, your timing is perfect. I been revvin' up, thinkin of you.'

He pulled her close, kissing her hard and she could already feel the bulge in his jeans. The perfume smelled even stronger on him.

'Why does it stink of perfume? You stink of it too,' she said, pulling away.

'My sister's been round, she gave me a hug.'

'Where's Damo?'

'Helping her home, she got a lot of shoppin' to carry.'

Dee scowled, not quite ready to believe that, but more bothered about the video.

'Did you film me, us, shagging? That first time, with all the weird masks and scarves and shit?'

'Jesus babe, you need to chill out and stop bitchin'.'

He let her go and went over to the fireplace, picking up a ready-rolled spliff from the top. Lighting it, he took a couple of pulls and then passed it to her. She wanted to refuse it, but she was gagging for something, anything.

'Sit down and smoke it hot…this one's really special, a treat, cos you my beautiful girl.'

He collapsed onto the settee and pulled her down beside him. She let him put his arm around her but wasn't going to let the video thing drop.

'You haven't answered. I remember the new camera and you and Damo watching it afterwards. Did you film it?'

'Listen babe, it was your first time so it had to be special and I wanted to record it, make it last forever. It aint on the net or nuthin. You look like a fairy queen in that mask, it's beautiful, you wanna see it?'

Dee shook her head and got slip-streams. This spliff was crazy. Thinking about the masks eased the knot in her stomach though, as even if Gaz was lying and he had posted or sold the video, nobody would recognise her. She couldn't be bothered to argue now anyway, she was too stoned, or something. He was feeling her up, but she still felt a bit sick about the video.

252

'I'm not in the mood yet,' she said.

He slid off the settee and knelt between her knees, gripping her thighs with his hands.

'You need to get in the mood babe. I got an urge that needs satisfyin' and you my girl, or do I need to find me another girl?'

Dee shook her head.

'Good. You jus' keep smokin' dat and we'll both get into the groove.'

16

It was years since he'd pulled a sickie and Jono was pleased that it still felt naughty. There was a match tonight and he wanted to be fresh, not knackered from a day at uni. He lay in bed for most of the morning, enjoyed a big brunch and went through a steady work-out in the afternoon to warm his muscles slowly. Only once did he allow himself to log on and check his chat stream with Netty.

It was almost three weeks since she'd backed right off and she hadn't even read his last two messages. It was ridiculous to miss a person he'd never met to this degree, but he was gutted, devastated even. The logical side of his brain was beginning to take over now though, bringing relief that it had happened before she found out about the chair. Only himself to blame.

The banter at the match cheered him up, as did his team's win. The only disappointment was the small crowd, which was unusual these days. Even the person who sat behind the scoreboard was missing. Jono realised that he wasn't sure whether it was a man or a woman - he'd only ever registered the presence as a bundle of clothes. When a couple of the lads suggested going to the pub, he jumped at it; anything to take up more of the evening, when the urge to bombard Netty with begging messages was worst.

It was around midnight when he arrived home and Jono managed to go to bed and switch the light off without logging on, but the presence of his tablet on the bedside cabinet wormed its way into his head. A thirty second check was preferable to lying awake for ages trying to resist, so he pulled the light cord and picked up the tablet. There were no new messages and no indication that Netty had been online.

Clicking on the profile picture to enlarge it, Jono gazed at Netty's fine cheekbones and pouting lips. How could Dee say she looked like a bitch, when she was so glorious? The other two girls did look less than chuffed though. Maybe the sour-faced brunette was scowling because Netty had just kicked her in the shin. The ginger one's screwed up face suggested pain and she was definitely being shoved aside.

A cold trickle ran down the back of Jono's neck. Without bothering to get dressed, he hauled himself out of bed and into his chair, went through to the desktop in the living room and logged back on. He saved Netty's profile picture to his drive and opened it again, chopping out Netty and the brunette and blowing it up as big as he could. It was a very unflattering picture of the ginger girl, but with darker hair in winter, different glasses, her cheeks not bunched up and her mouth relaxed...oh shit, shit, fuck, shit, shit...no...NO!

He went to the messaging screen, scrolling back through the chat, cringing over those with the Ginger Hippy theme, but making sense of many more. The fact that he had noticed her use the words 'bleak and wintery' when they met, that he had even thought it strange...why did it not nudge him harder? She probably thought it would, after they had virtually constructed a poem on the theme the night before.

Further back, to Christmas, when he told her about Delilah. She didn't question why a 28 year old man was friends with a 14 year old girl, who visited him for lunch. She warned him that Delilah was wiser than he thought. Even further up the stream was the message that had freaked him out a bit: **You still there?** he had asked. **More often than you think** was her reply.

Jono stopped scrolling and read it again, his stomach performing another roll. Other than that one occasion, he couldn't recall seeing Netty/the Ginger Hippy around at uni. She may have seen him of course, but there could be another explanation. He brought up a different browser and found the basketball team Facebook page, flicking through the photos of the previous matches until he found one that included the scoreboard and the figure behind it.

After giving the photo the same treatment as the profile pic, Jono groaned. The shapeless, androgynous clothes were a patchwork jacket and a crochet hat. There was even the suggestion of a plait hanging over one shoulder.

~ ~ ~

The bus journey was over an hour long and Shona was fidgeting ten minutes into it. Paulie had apologised in his letter, asking her forgiveness and begging her to see him again, but it couldn't dispel the horror of the last visit. Perhaps Jim was right and she should let him stew in his own juices for a while. There was the hook though, clever little shite that he was, the 'really important thing' that he could only tell her to her face.

It had better be important, or she would take Jim's advice and try to forget she had a son, until he came to find her and make amends. But there at least was something she could do to take her mind off it. Delilah was over visiting Kelly last night and she had promised to let Jim know how she was doing. She began the text with DON'T CALL BACK I'M ON A BUS. There were two women in front of her who would hear every word.

She told him Delilah seemed well enough, though still quiet. When Kelly went to bed she'd asked a lot of questions about her mother, including whether she was a 'proper' prostitute and how it came about. Dee was still smoking a lot, but didn't ask for anything else. Shona's thumb was aching by the end of it and she wished she was familiar with predictive text, especially when Jim fired back a load more questions. She promised to call him later.

Paulie was waiting at a table when she finally made it through all the checks and gates and even managed to smile at her. He stood up as she worked her way across the hall.

'Hi Mum.'

'Hello you. How have you been keeping?'

'Alright thanks, yeah. The food might be crap, but I wasn't exactly eating three square meals a day before I landed up in here. I've even started going to the gym.'

'Good God,' she said, sitting down. 'You've not 'seen the light' or anything, have you?'

He laughed and Shona pressed a hand to her mouth. It wasn't a sound she recognised and she realised she hadn't heard him laugh, not in a genuine, amused way, since he became an adult.

'Nah, but I am clean. It's been hard the last few weeks, but I'm getting to enjoy being straight. I can think again and it isn't as frightening as I thought it would be.'

'Paulie, that's fantastic, I'm so proud of you.'

She reached out for his hand and he took it in both of his.

'I don't know how you can say that,' he whispered.

'I can say it because it's true,' she said fiercely, her eyes hot but her cheeks dry. 'You might have been a real bastard over the past few years, but you haven't had an easy time of it either and you're still my son. I love you Paulie and if there's a chance you can leave all that behind you and make something of your life, then I'll be with you every step of the way.'

He said nothing for a minute, gripping her hands tight, a muscle flexing in his jaw, then his arms relaxed and he smiled again.

'I'll get a finger up my arse after all this hand-holding, so I hope you're gonna give me a hug before you go.'

'Oh no! Oh God, I'm sorry, I didn't think.'

He shook his head.

'Don't worry, it's worth it. So what have you been up to anyway, did you manage to sort...things out? I must have made it all worse.'

'Well I can't say it wasn't difficult and quite terrifying at one point, but I had a bit of help and we sorted out the problem. No more hassle from that quarter, no more involvement at all in fact.'

'That's so good to hear. I've been doing some sums and getting a bit bothered.'

'Don't go wasting your time thinking about that, you get yourself fit and healthy again. Have you had any more grief off that fella? The one who attacked you last time?'

Paulie gave a wry laugh.

'That was Blake, my pad-mate. It's him who got me off the gear and made me sort my head out. He's the best friend I've ever had. Sometimes you need to have the sense beaten into you and I think I was overdue a good kicking.'

'Well...'

Shona didn't want to agree or disagree with that, but the pause lengthening in the middle of her sentence was growing uncomfortable.

'Anyway, this thing I wanted to talk to you about,' Paulie said.

So the 'really important thing' wasn't him straightening out. Oh please, let that not have been ground preparation for the next request for money. She couldn't bear it.

'Like I said, I've been doing a lot of thinking and... I'm not laying this on you, ok? You don't have to do anything, but I kept thinking you might want to know, that it might be important to you. And if it isn't, that's fine. I wasn't very interested before I came in here, but...'

'Paulie please, just spit it out.'

'Alright. When I was in Manchester there was this girl, hanging around. I mean, there were a few, but this one mostly stayed at my place. The week before I got busted, she found out she was pregnant. I wasn't very nice, well...I was a complete wanker, to be honest. I said it was nothing to do with me, that it probably wasn't even mine and she should get rid of it. Except, I think it is mine.'

Shona's hands flew back to her mouth. That was dreadful...and weeks ago.

'Who is she? How old is she? Is she on drugs? Have you heard from her?'

'Her name's Laura, I don't know her surname. She's 18 and has a quite a coke habit, but she's bright too. I think she'll be at her mum's, cos my house got pretty smashed up during the raid and she won't be able to pay the rent.'

'But where is your house? Where does her mum live? Paulie, this is awful. What if she's already done as you asked?'

'She might have, but I don't think so. She wasn't happy about being pregnant, but Laura's got loads of little brothers and sisters and loves kids. She was gutted after what I said to her.'

'I should think so. But what shall I do…go and see her? I don't suppose you have a phone number.'

'No, but I've written out what I can remember about Laura and both the addresses here.' He passed her a sheet of paper that had been lying face down on the table. 'I've had it approved, so you can take it home, if you want. You don't have to do this though.'

'I don't have to check on the welfare of a grandchild you've disowned before it's even been born? Well that's kind of you, but I think I just might.' She shook her head. 'You are a bag of shite, Paulie, but I'm glad you told me.'

There was a general shuffling around them as visiting time came to an end. Shona stood up and put her hands on her hips, shaking her head again.

'You still up for that hug? Paulie asked.

'Just, and only just my lad.'

He smiled and came around the table, giving her a tentative hug at first, but his arms tightening around her when the bell went off.

'Thank you,' he said. 'Not just for this, but for still being here.'

'I'll let you know if I find Laura,' she said and reaching up, stroked his cheek. 'You take care now.'

~ ~ ~

Although Derek offered to take Blink to play pool, cook with him, get the chess-board out, or set up the X-box, he was still moping in the lounge, flicking through the tv channels every few minutes. Dee was out, again. Thanks to Blink, they were at least now fairly confident that she wasn't sleeping with multiple, unknown men. It was just the one, immoral scum-bag by the sound of it.

Even Dee's hard little heart had softened, when she found him in a sodden heap on her return, the night of Becky's 'inappropriate tirade' as Julie put it. Privately, Derek thought it was an entirely appropriate challenge of Dee by Becky and a good thing that Blink knew the details of what she was up to. They lived in the same house, she was more likely to disclose things to him than any member of staff and he had a crush on her the size of a mountain.

Apart from all that, Blink was almost a man. The new clothes and glasses he'd consented to for his birthday made a drastic difference to his appearance and the recent enlightenment had sobered him. It was as if, on the stroke of turning 17, he had left childhood behind. Positive in one sense and sad in another.

The relationship between him and Delilah had changed too. There was trust between them, after opening up to each other that night, and Derek suspected that a large part of Blink's sadness was the burden of detail he *hadn't* passed on. Plus the fact that Dee was still going out three or four times a week, still getting wrecked on something and still unhappy.

Deciding to give it one more go with Blink before leaving him alone, Derek went through to the lounge.

'Hey, do you want a drink or anything?'

'Nah,' Blink said, not even looking up.

Derek sat down in the nearest armchair.

'I'm not going to hassle you all night mate, I promise, but it's doing my head in, seeing you like this. It won't change anything you know. The best thing you can do for Dee is be there to lean on when she needs you.

'I kn..kn..know and I w..will be. I can't help w..worrying though.'

'It is hard, but you'll be no use to Dee or yourself if you drive yourself crazy in the meantime.'

'I c..can't just f..f..forget.'

'No, but you can focus. My brother had a massive problem with anger management when he was younger, but once he got into martial arts, he never got into any more trouble. It was the discipline of training he reckoned, the ability to focus your whole mind on the present moment and have a complete awareness of your body and what it's doing.'

'I'm not g..going to take up k..karate while Delilah is out d..d..doing whatever.'

Blink sounded cross and Derek smothered a smile at the thought of it.

'No, but it sounds like a kind of meditation to me. Now I'm not suggesting you sit in your room staring at candles either, but I brought in a body-weight training dvd a few days ago, I thought you might be interested. It's about improving strength and balance without using weights or going to a gym. It'd take the same kind of focus I reckon. Do you fancy a look?'

Blink shrugged.

'Can't be any m..more boring than the t..tv.

Derek fetched the dvd from the office and sat down with Blink to watch it. It was a Christmas present from one of his cousins and he hadn't seen it himself yet. The dvd started with a display of amazing physical feats; the guy went from a flat press-up to a handstand press-up with slow and graceful moves, balancing on one hand and then the other. He walked up imaginary stairs whilst doing a pull-up, held himself horizontal, lifted and rolled with incredible control.

'It's awesome, b..but a bit b..b..beyond me,' Blink said.

'Me too,' Derek admitted.

The routine finished and the guy walked up to the camera.

'Think that was cool but totally beyond you?' he said, in an American accent.

Derek and Blink both laughed. Apparently, they were only weeks away from noticing a significant difference in their bodies and being several steps closer to ultimate physical control. Rah. By contrast, the first week's routine they were supposed to follow was quite bland, consisting of a reasonable number of press-ups, sit-ups, pull-ups and squats.

'You know, I think I could manage that,' Derek said.

'R..really?'

'Yeah.'

He got down on the floor and knocked out five press-ups. Pushing back onto his knees, he said,

'See? No bother.'

Blink stared at him.

'But you're p..panting and you're s..supposed to do twenty.'

'Yeah, well, it's late and I wasn't concentrating. Think you could do it?'

Blink looked at him for a moment longer and then climbed off the settee. His arms were so long, Derek had to shove the coffee table aside to make room. He managed seven slow, regulated press-ups and then collapsed onto his face.

'Crap,' he said.

'Not at all, they were bloody good press-ups. I reckon you could do two sets of ten, if you were prepared for it. I'm on a sleepover tonight. Shall we try it together, tomorrow morning? Get a bit of a competition going? I need to tighten this up anyway,' Derek said, slapping his stomach.

Blink rolled over.

'Alright then, but we haven't got a bar.'

'It's Saturday tomorrow. If we do the rest of the exercises and decide we're going to do it again, I'll see if Gareth can take you into town to buy one. I don't think they cost that much.'

They shook hands on the deal and Blink went up to bed. It was a step forward, even though Derek knew just how much he was going to hate himself at 7am.

As predicted, he was cursing before even switching the alarm off and Derek had to force himself to go and knock on Blink's door. They drank a morose coffee together in the kitchen and went through to the lounge with extreme reluctance. Seeing the lithe figure leaping about in tight shorts wasn't any more inspiring, but he wasn't going to back out on Blink, who seemed to feel the same way.

They moved the coffee table out altogether and began with the press-ups, having to pause the dvd so they could rest between sets of ten. They managed various other exercises and only had to pause again during the sit-ups. The squats were last and by then, Derek was feeling quite energised.

'You know what? I think we're gonna feel great after a shower,' he said.

Blink grinned.

'Yeah and I'm g..going to keep d..doing this.'

'You're on. Every day for seven days and then we move onto week two.'

'Alright. I'm g..going for a shower.'

'Have a good day. I'll see you tomorrow.'

Blink started up the stairs just as Delilah shot out of her bedroom and across to the bathroom, still wearing her nightie. The sound of retching followed. It must have been an alcohol night; although it wasn't her drug of choice, she would resort to it if there was nothing else.

'Delilah, are you o..ok? Are you i..i..ill again?' Blink called through the bathroom door.

'It could just be a hangover Blink,' Derek said, still standing in the hall.

'N..not really. She was l..like this y..yesterday t..too.'

Oh please, no.

~ ~ ~

Dee sloshed water over her face and then dried it with the towel. She still felt sick, but the sterile smell of the bathroom made it worse. She had to get out. Why were Blink and Derek up at this stupid time anyway? She went onto the landing and leaned on the bannister rail.

'You're very p..pale,' Blink said. 'H..how do you f..feel?'

'Sick.'

Wasn't that obvious? She looked down at Derek, who was still standing in the hall. He wasn't grinning like he usually was, his arms were hanging by his sides and he looked sad.

'Morning Dee,' he said. 'So you were sick yesterday too?'

She nodded.

'And what about the day before?'

She thought about that. She had got up to go to catering, but felt sick, so went back to bed.

'A bit,' she said.

Derek dropped his eyes and Dee saw Julie walk through from the kitchen.

'Gosh, you're all up early. What's the great debate?' she said, smiling up at her and Blink.

Nobody answered. Dee didn't understand what was going on and heard Derek ask Julie for a word in the office. Blink was giving her a weird look.

'H..hang on,' he said. Derek and Julie stopped moving below. 'Is it m..m..m..morning sickness?'

What the fuck was that? Some kind of disease?

'It could be…any number of things,' Derek said. 'Dee, you know Debbie, the LAC nurse, the woman you talked to before? I'd like to call her, see if she can pop over to see you. You need to get this sickness checked out.'

'Alright, but what *is* morning sickness?'

Blink had gone all pasty and wasn't looking at her any more. She directed the question as much to Derek as to him, but it was Blink who answered, still without looking at her.

'You m..might be p..pregnant,' he said, quietly, his head hanging.

PREGNANT?

'I can't be! He says he's on the pill! No *WAY!!*'

She clung to the bannisters, feeling ten times more sick. Blink was crying now, the stupid, fucking dickhead. It wasn't him with a…*thing*…growing inside him. Derek was coming up the stairs and Julie was on her mobile already. This could not be happening. Another wave of nausea swept over her and Delilah lurched towards the bathroom, her legs weak and uncooperative. She made it through the door, but puked into the sink before she could get to the toilet.

Once the retching started Dee found she couldn't stop, her stomach heaving and heaving, until she was just spitting out horrible-tasting goo. She wanted to lie down, but daren't move. Keeping her grip on the sink, she squatted down, misery at last starting to outweigh sickness. Why did all this have to happen? If only she could go back to a normal Saturday, with toast round at Jono's in the morning and tobacco to skank from Shona later.

She was supposed to be seeing Shona tomorrow…and her mum. What if they guessed? Shona wasn't even smoking any more and if her mum hadn't let her be taken into care, she wouldn't have met Gaz. What would *he* say? The spasms in Dee's stomach had calmed down and now it gave a hollow growl, although her need for a fag was even stronger than the need for food. Maybe she wasn't pregnant - being really hungry always made her feel sick too. A mug of coffee and a fag would probably sort everything.

Pushing open the bathroom door with a fresh sense of purpose, Dee was surprised to find Derek and Blink sitting on the landing. She'd forgotten about them.

'Better?' Derek asked.

'Yeah. I'm going to get a coffee, have a fag and then make some toast.'

'B..but...'

Blink started to say something, but Derek slapped a hand over his mouth.

'It's a plan and having a plan is a good start. Why don't you get dressed and I'll go and put the kettle on.' He turned to Blink. 'Sorry chap, but I don't think Dee wants any advice right now. Have a shower and then we'll all have some breakfast. You need to eat, after training like that this morning.'

Blink nodded, but looked proper mardy. Why was he crying anyway? It was her that should be upset, not him. She went back to her room before he could say anything else and pulled off her nightie. Examining her naked body in the mirror, she could see no difference; her stomach was still flat and her tits still looked like two, small, fried eggs. The pregnancy thing was a load of bollocks, she was just sick.

It was like a miserable party in the kitchen when she went downstairs. Derek was making coffee and toast, Blink was at one end of the table, talking to Gareth. Julie and Sandra were at the other end, writing some sort of list. There were too many people for her present mood and Dee started to reverse back out of the door.

'Hey! Don't disappear, your coffee's here and I've just opened a new jar of strawberry jam,' Derek said.

Julie looked up at her. Dee could see the huge, fake smile on her face, even from the corner of her eye. Sandra said 'good morning Dee', but she ignored them both and turned her head away so that she wouldn't have to see Blink and Gareth at all. She walked around the table with her face to the cupboards and picked up the mug Derek slid towards her.

'Thanks,' she said. 'I'm going for a fag.'

She heard at least two of the twats mutter something about smoking as she left the kitchen. This was going to be a nightmare until she could see the nurse and prove she wasn't pregnant. The very thought of giving up smoking made her light a second fag straight after finishing the first and Dee resolved to get hammered that night. It was Saturday...and it wasn't like she *knew* she was pregnant.

~ ~ ~

Jim told himself that there could be an element of paranoia to his present concern. Keeping your own company for years on end allowed a lot of time for self-examination, if you were so inclined. It was a long and painful experience, but also useful at times like this. He was already on edge, with Dicko the drunk doing an abysmal job of keeping an eye on him and two further visits to the village by Harley-riding hard men. Thinking about Delilah was not a good diversion and he might just be shifting the threat of imminent danger onto her situation.

But then, Jim thought of the expression his old friend used to use. Ed always claimed he was not paranoid, but 'acutely aware', which made sense when, in the instances of crossover between the parallel worlds of organised crime and everyday people, the opposite of paranoia was ignorance. With greater insight into just how vulnerable Delilah was, Jim decided he was not paranoid, but well informed. He'd also heard little from Shona since the revelation that she might be a grandmother, which was a second excuse to call her for an update. He dialled her number.

'Oh Jim, you're just too bloody intuitive sometimes,' she said, by way of greeting.

'Meaning what?'

'Meaning I was just sitting here, wondering whether to call you or not.'

'So why do you sound pissed off?'

'Because I hadn't made my mind up.'

'Right. So does the bad news relate to Paulie, or to Delilah?'

There was a pause. Jim clenched his teeth, but didn't push her.

'I found the house alright, from your directions,' she said at last. 'It was empty, like Paulie thought it would be, but the neighbours told me where to find his girlfriend.'

'You've seen there then?'

'No, I just met her vile mother, who wouldn't even let me through the gate. She went on a right rant about people poking their noses in and Social Services being on her case. When I managed to explain who I was, it got worse. She called Paulie a lot of names and then me a lot of names for giving birth to him, but she did calm down a bit when I agreed with most of it.'

'So where's the girlfriend?'

'She wouldn't say. Inside the house I expect, but all I can hope is that she passes on the card with my contact details. She almost tore it up, until I promised that Paulie was locked up for a good while. I feel so bloody helpless Jim, but I don't know what else to do.'

'You could try contacting Social Services up there. They won't tell you anything, but if they're on the girl's case before the kid's even born, then they might be interested to know it has a friendly, close relative, who isn't on drugs. They might even encourage the girl to contact you herself.'

Jim rolled a fag and poured another shot of whisky into his glass, listening to Shona ramble on about how to find the right contact number, working out an easier way to travel up there, whether she should tell Paulie of her progress. The longer she stalled, the more the heat rose in his chest, a physical manifestation of mounting anger, which he had learned not to ignore. He opened the caravan door and walked out into the night, lifting his face to the cool drizzle of rain.

'Time's up,' he said, interrupting a line of conversation so inconsequential, he hadn't even bothered to follow it. 'If you didn't want to tell me, you should have hung up ten minutes ago. What's happening with Delilah?'

There was another pause.

'Don't hold out on me, Shona.'

'Alright, don't growl like that. I just...look, don't go mad, will you? It was inevitable really, but admittedly, a bit...sooner than anyone would like.'

'*What*, for God's sake woman?'

'She's pregnant.

Jim let his breath out in a long hiss, fists clenched, awash with rage. Fat lot of fucking 'care' Delilah was getting, although she was no safer with her mother. How could people believe in a God, if he left innocent children with no options? There wasn't anybody watching over this one. He put the phone back to his ear.

'I'm sorry Shona, I didn't hear anything beyond 'pregnant'. Look, can me and Crank crash at yours for a couple of days? I won't be in your way much.'

'Er...yes, I suppose so, but...is it really a good idea? At least wait until tomorrow. I was just saying that Delilah is seeing a nurse in the morning. She was supposed to be doing a pregnancy test then, but she came round here this afternoon, absolutely smashed, freaking out at Kelly and demanding the money to go and buy one. At least she came back here to do it, but she still flipped when it came out positive. The woman from the care home was livid when she came to pick her up.'

'Call me as soon as you hear from her, but I'm still coming over.'

'Oh, alright then. There's no need to bring anything, you can have Paulie's room.'

'Thanks. I'll see you tomorrow, early afternoon.'

He could hear her still talking as he hit the red button, but didn't trust himself to say anything more. Some sleazy, low-life, mother-fucking, bag of *shit* was going to pay for this.

17

There was no longer any surprise when the world fell in on a Monday morning, or sulkiness at the unfair timing, it was just the nature of her case-load. Since Delilah was taken into care, Becky had stuck to her weekday working hours, leaving her charges two whole days and three nights to get into trouble, while she remained in somewhat less than blissful ignorance until communication resumed. This Monday however, the old thump to the stomach made a return, with its crippling mix of disappointment, pity and despair.

It was a double-whammy. Bethany – a fairly new ward, who Becky was still trying to build a relationship with – had been taken to hospital following an overdose, while a blunt message from Sunny Bank suggested that Delilah was pregnant. Becky threw the phone on the table, pushed her coffee away and burst into tears. She jumped when a hand touched her shoulder, but Simon just massaged gently and said nothing.

It was a full ten minutes before she managed to pull herself together and she felt washed out, without having even left the house. If she was this over-emotional at nine weeks pregnant, how was she going to make it to maternity leave?

'You're going to have to tell them at work you know,' Simon said, when her hiccoughs subsided. 'Sod the twelve week thing. They'll understand...and you only have to tell your manager...and maybe Bill.'

'It'll feel like tempting fate,' her chest heaved with a fresh sob, 'and if anything *does* go wrong, it'll be my fault, or at least my job's fault.'

'Should that happen, you'll be one of the many women who miscarry through no fault of their own.' He pulled out a chair and sat down beside her, taking her hand in both of his. 'You've made massive changes to your routine already and now you just need a bit of extra support. It won't be like this the whole time, but your hormones must be going crazy at the moment.'

He was being so nice, it made her want to cry again, but the 8 o'clock news on the radio jerked her awake. She couldn't be late on top of everything else. Simon's grip tightened.

'Get going, but please, speak to your manager before dealing with whatever horrors are on your answerphone.'

'Alright, I will. Thank you.'

Becky meant it, and kissed him to reinforce the statement. On the rare occasions that Simon dared to venture into hormonal waters, things did not always end well. She went to the bathroom and attempted to repair her face, but almost melted again when she came out to find a banana, toast wrapped in kitchen foil and a travel mug of coffee on the table. Simon was trying hard not to look smug.

'I do love you,' she said, resting her head on his chest.

'And I love you. Just think, you'll have a whole year without Monday morning traumas.'

'Mmmn,' she murmured into his jumper, thinking that every morning would be traumatic, trying to get herself into a functioning state and deal with a screaming baby on minimal sleep.

She pushed the thought aside, or rather, cushioned it with counter arguments; it would be *her* baby, which she would love with all her heart; Simon would be there to support her; there would be just one child demanding her attention; it wouldn't tell her to fuck off for trying to help...at least not for a good few years yet. She found a wry smile on her lips and relinquished her hold on Simon. Time to face the day.

Greeted with a 'God, you look tired' from Bill when she walked in, Becky almost gave him the news first, but decided to follow some sort of formal procedure. Clare was alone in her office, so there were no excuses. She wondered why she would have

272

wanted an excuse, when Clare thanked her for being honest, agreed it was a good idea to tell Bill and said she was pleased that Becky was 'aware of potential influences on professional judgement'. Upon hearing the morning's other news, Clare actually put a hand over hers.

'I'll call the hospital for an update on Bethany. She's on a full care order, isn't she?'

'Yes,' Becky felt her shoulders dropping another inch. 'Thank you. I'll catch up on Delilah and come back in twenty minutes, shall I?'

'Perfect, we can swap information and you'd have to share it with me anyway. Do make yourself a cup of tea on the way back though; you can't talk, never mind think properly, with a dry mouth.'

Becky smiled and got up, thinking that she should take Simon's advice more often. Bill was on the phone when she returned to their office, so she logged in and scanned her emails. There was one from the duty social worker who Bethany's foster carers had spoken to, but it contained no more detail than the message they left on her phone. The first email from Sunny Bank said that Delilah appeared to be suffering from morning sickness, but they couldn't be sure until the nurse visited on Monday morning. The second pretty much confirmed it – Delilah had gone to her mum's and taken a pregnancy test there.

No one had seen the physical proof, but Delilah's reaction suggested the result was positive. She was still spitting and swearing when brought back to Sunny Bank and went out again within minutes. Returning an hour before curfew, under the influence of something, she was still coherent and not 'wasted' - a more frequent occurrence of late. It was not as terrifying a consequence as Becky would have expected with forewarning, although this was just Day 1.

The nurse was visiting at 9.30am, so would still be there now. Becky called Sunny Bank and the news was good, in relative terms. After some rather abusive resistance, Delilah was now closeted in the kitchen with her, having done a second test. Late lunch would be the best time for Becky to visit, which was perfect in terms of what she needed to do first. She got up and made two cups of tea, leaving one next to Bill, whose phone was still glued to his head, and taking her own through to Clare's office.

Clare was the chamomile tea kind of social worker and Becky didn't have the first idea what to do with herbal sachets. Happily, there was already a steaming mug on her desk. The news on Bethany was encouraging – she would be kept in for observation until tomorrow, but arrived at hospital fast enough for her stomach to be pumped before any lasting damage was done. Physical damage, that was. The number of paracetomol taken constituted a serious attempt. Clare appeared almost as worried by Becky's update.

'Is Delilah likely to want a termination?'

Becky considered this and realised she had no idea at all about what Delilah would be thinking.

'She doesn't sound pleased about it and she is very young, but I can't honestly say which way she'll turn. I wouldn't even like to hazard a guess. What are the chances of finding a place at a mother and baby unit, within a fifty mile radius?'

'Zero.' Clare sighed and leaned back in her chair. 'Less than zero, there's a long waiting list. You could triple your radius and the answer would be the same.'

~ ~ ~

Watching Jim fasten up a stab vest, Shona felt a lurch of real fear in her stomach. He hadn't bothered with anything like that when facing down her dealers, and they were tooled up to the nines. What in God's name was he expecting to find? But she didn't want to know the answer.

'Are you coming back?' she asked.

'If all is quiet, and if that's ok, but I'll take my stuff with me and disappear if anything goes down. I've got to get back to Crank anyway, I left him at home in the end.'

'Oh Jim, can't you leave this to the police? What if they're watching and think you're mixed up in it?'

'Not been any use so far, have they? I'll be careful. Don't worry and try to stay off the phone...I might need to call. I've got a bad feeling about this, Shona.'

'She's been seeing the guy for months. What's going to be any different tonight?'

'Well at the very least, Delilah's in for a nasty surprise. Whoever the fucking sicko is, he's not going to be very impressed with a 14 year old girl bearing evidence which could put him inside. I'll just follow her if she leaves Sunny Bank, make sure help is close by.'

It wasn't an angle she'd considered, but then Jim came at most things from a different perspective. God, there was such a vile underbelly to the human race and so many folk staggering along its surface, trying to drag their feet free of the sucking ooze. Prison was proving to be a life raft for Paulie, but what of Laura? What of her child, his child...would they be pulled under too?

Jim threw his rucksack over his shoulder and touched her arm.

'It's been good to see you, if only for a couple of hours,' he said.

'Snap, but I'm hoping you'll be back later.'

'Me too. I wish I could invite you to the seaside for a day or two, but it's not...well...we'll talk about it some other time. I hope you hear from Paulie's girl soon. Take care, Shona.'

She did not get up to see him out and he left without looking back. The bleak feeling persisted and Shona sat at the kitchen table for over an hour, lost in a series of maudlin memories, until the beep of her phone brought her back to the present. She snatched it up, praying that Jim wasn't in trouble already, but the text was from an unfamiliar number.

Hi Shona. My name is Liv and I'm Laura's social worker. I understand you tried to contact Laura about a possible relationship between her and your son. She's having a difficult time right now, but asked me to call you. Please let me know when that would be convenient. Thanks.

Shona read the message twice, got up, made a cup of tea, sat down and read the text again. Her thumb hovered over the dial button and then she remembered Jim's request to leave her phone free and put it back on the table with a shaking hand. Laura wanted to get in touch. Surely she wouldn't bother, if she'd already got rid of the baby. Her grandchild must still be alive.

The reply took an age to write, as Shona made more changes than there were words in the first place, but at last, she was satisfied that it would give the right impression.

Hi Liv. Wonderful to hear from you. I guess you know my son, Paulie, is in prison. He told me Laura is pregnant with his child and I'd like to offer my support, though I'm not well off financially. I'm busy this afternoon, but free all day tomorrow. I look forward to talking to you. Shona

The very second she hit send, Shona kicked herself. She should have just made the call - now she would now be on tenterhooks for the next 24 hours...or at least until Liv rang her. Delilah was probably having a bath and an early night anyway. She prayed that *was* the case, as Jim was quite capable of starting World War 3, and getting caught up in the fall-out would not strengthen her chances of establishing contact with Laura.

~ ~ ~

The argument on the landing sounded like it was escalating. Derek opened the office door so he could make a more informed assessment, just as Delilah started shrieking again.

'Look, you've been cool today, alright? I wanted you there, but now I need a break from people sticking their noses in and I *don't* want to talk about *fucking* babies any more. If you don't move, I'm going to shove you down the stairs.'

'B..but you n..n..need to stay s..safe, even m..m..more now. I..it's...'

'Blink!' Derek shouted. 'Don't lecture Dee about staying safe, when you're standing at the top of the stairs, arguing with a pregnant woman. You are involved in a very high-risk activity yourself, believe me.'

'B..but....'

'Blink! You need to leave it. Right or wrong isn't relevant...you can't stop Dee going out.'

Derek hoped this appeal to Blink's intelligence would pierce his emotional outrage. He agreed 300% that Delilah should not go out, not alone and not in her current state of mind, but they couldn't stop her. All they could do was create a home she would want to return to.

He went out into the hall as Delilah stomped down the last few steps, her scowl making it clear that she too had understood his comment. She paused in front of him, her small chin stuck out in a definite challenge, which he did not rise to.

'Have a good evening,' he said and smiled at her. 'If you're back early enough, we can do super-deluxe hot chocolate. I stocked up on marshmallows *and* chocolate sprinkles yesterday.'

Her scowl deepened but she shrugged, so he risked a last assurance.

'And no baby talk, I promise. Just believe that no-one here will judge you, whatever you decide, and let the shock pass before you think too hard about what to do, or you'll drive yourself mad.'

Derek thought that the mini-lecture would have her running, but still she hovered. Blink was hovering too, sitting on the stairs, remaining silent with a surprising display of tact and self-control. If only she would stay at home tonight...but he daren't even suggest it, for fear of her feeling pressured and spinning away. She wanted to, he could see her indecision, but Delilah wanted other things more.

She left without saying a word, although Derek sensed there were a thousand things she wanted to ask. Worst of all, it was fortunate that she wasn't asking too many questions yet, as the social worker was clear that there were no specialist places available. There were not many options for Dee to consider at present.

'So w...what are her o..options?' Blink said, from three inches behind him.

'You're getting a little too good at moving around quietly.' And hearing more than you should, Derek thought. 'I don't actually know yet, but whatever they are will be Dee's business really.'

'B..but if there aren't any mother and b..baby places, then w...won't she be staying here?'

He was either a mind reader, or had pressed his ear to the office door earlier.

'Look, nobody knows what will happen yet, but I'm sure Dee will discuss it with you. You two seem to be talking a lot more these days.'

'W..we are, b..but she still d..does whatever she w..wants.'

'But isn't that everybody's right? To do what they want, as long as it's within the law?'

'B..b..b..but it's n..not within the l..l..law, is it! Taking d..d..drugs and having s..s..sex b..before she's s..s..sixteen. Delilah doesn't c..c..care what's r..right or wr..wrong.'

He had a point. Derek remembered the incident with the open office, on Dee's first day there. It was possible that she might have worried about getting into trouble, but he thought not. Her need for cigarettes was desperate, but she stopped short of taking money or his phone.

'I don't think that's entirely true...I think Dee does care, but her version of right and wrong is a little different from mine and yours. That line - the one you won't cross, which might sit beyond the law in places - its path is unique to every person. You'd steal food, if you were hungry enough, wouldn't you?'

Blink thought about that and right on cue, his belly gave a hollow rumble. Derek laughed.

'Let's go and stick a pizza on and finish this discussion in the kitchen. It'll be comfier than standing in the hall anyway.'

He headed that way without worrying whether Blink would follow. An evening of intense conversation loomed ahead and the next question hit the back of his head before they were through the door.

'B..but why does she n..need to hang out with i..idiots when she's g..got us and that J..jono as f..friends already?'

'Maybe they have something that she needs, or wants very badly. Maybe they don't seem like idiots to her. I don't know a massive amount about Dee's life, but she's had a rough time or she wouldn't be here. If you're brought up around drugs, sex, alcohol, animal cruelty, in filthy living conditions, whatever it is, if it's all you've ever known then that's normal to you and anything better is going to seem ok.'

That kept him quiet long enough for Derek to pull out a couple of frozen pizzas and stick them in the oven. His dietary conscience was relieved by the discovery of a bag of salad in the fridge, but the subject matter caused him no guilt. Blink was a mature 17 year old, he could leave Sunny Bank if he wanted and start a family of his own. It was important to know and understand these things, especially if he was going to fall in love with complex and very needy women.

'W..why can't Delilah just s..stay here?' Blink said, perhaps too uncomfortable with the previous line of conversation, which was as relevant to him as it was to Dee.

'We're not set up for babies and it wouldn't be fair on you, being woken at all hours.'

'B..but I wouldn't m..mind! I'd r..rather Delilah d..didn't have to m..move out.'

That was quite obvious and Derek winced at the thought of Blink's fragile heart, hanging from his sleeve, exposed to every barb directed its way.

'Dee won't snap out of this behaviour, you know,' he said. 'She might gain wisdom with experience and mellow out a bit, but she is who she is. You won't have an easy life, if you set your heart on her.'

Blink's cheeks flushed with heat, but he managed to look Derek in the eye.

'L..love isn't about ch..choice though, is it.'

Damn bloody 'A' level English literature, feeding him tragic romances. But then, the statement could have been as much about his parents as Delilah and was, in essence, true.

'I suppose not.'

~ ~ ~

There was a bench around the corner and Dee sat on it to roll a fag. The idea of Gaz's flat, busy and loud, was not that appealing right now. Her head was spinning and she needed to think, but she didn't want to think, or believe that she really was in this fucking mess. An image of Gaz saying 'chill babe, I take the male pill, innit' kept popping into her head, making her want to smash his face in. She'd swallowed the lie, like a stupid kid.

What she really wanted was to get shit-faced and blank it all out for a bit. It was still the favourite plan, but now she couldn't ditch the nagging fear of what would happen...*if* she stayed pregnant. The nurse said there was a good chance she would miscarry and she could also choose to get rid of it. No more problem. A miscarriage would be easiest and getting hammered might make that happen, but if it *didn't*...and she *kept* it...Blink said it would hurt the baby.

Twat. He was acting like it was his or something and telling her what to do all the time. It was kind of nice that he was still her friend and hadn't dumped her though. Sometimes she thought he fancied her, which was gross, but he hadn't gone nuts about her being pregnant. Jono. How could she tell him? It would be...way past embarrassing. He'd be gutted, and think she'd been making it up, about fancying him. Maybe he'd be glad about that.

Pushing the thought of Jono away, Dee rolled another fag, but it did nothing to sort her head out. Fuck it. Gaz had texted, told her to go round, said he had some new stuff in. She needed a spliff and the lump of black resin in her bedroom was scarily small now. It was also cold, just sitting and smoking, so she got up and started walking, fast, focussing on the street ahead and not thinking about anything.

The music was so loud that Dee could hear it outside and expected to find loads of people in the kitchen. Her heavy knocking was answered by a muffled shout and she was surprised to open the door and find the kitchen empty. Gaz and five others were sprawled in the front room, all wasted and not even trying to talk over the painful volume of the stereo. Dee winced and put a hand to her ear.

'Come a' sit down babe,' Gaz said, lifting a hand towards her.

His words were slurred and his eyelids didn't lift high enough for him to look at her. The wavering arm made slow and jerky progress towards the stereo and Dee watched, as he made several attempts to turn the volume down. None of the others seemed to have noticed her. She looked around; two she knew as mates of Gaz, two she didn't know, one with a pile of sick next to his head and Damo in the corner. She realised, with a lurch of shock, that Damo was staring back at her, his dark eyes fixed on her face.

Tearing her eyes away from his, she stepped over one of the bodies and hunkered down next to Gaz. He slung an arm over her legs and threw a sickly smile in her general direction.

'Th' new shit's awesome,' he said and patted his hand around the carpet next to him. 'Rolled one f'ya ready.'

Dee frowned at the short spliff he held up. It was only 6 o'clock and a Monday, not even the weekend. She didn't want to get as wasted as them and there'd be no end of grief at Sunny Bank if she did.

'Int there any normal weed?

'Wassup? My shit not good enough for Princess Dee no more?'

He laughed, a slow and guttural noise. There was a splutter from one of the bodies on the floor and Dee wanted to cry and kick him at the same time. Fucking arseholes.

'Tell you what, you can smoke it, or piss off. We aint got no use for kids round here,' Gaz said, tossing the joint into her lap.

She wasn't a bloody kid. In fact, wasn't she like, technically, a *mother* right now? The thought made her shudder. She wouldn't call herself a woman yet, never mind a mother. But didn't that make her responsible for the thing, even if it wasn't staying, even if she wasn't ready?

'What's in it anyway?' she asked.

'A cool line of H, baby. Makes your dreams come true.'

Huh. Her dreams were all nightmares at the moment and she still didn't know what it was.

'What?'

'Aw, don't spin out. I aint tryin' to stick a needle in your arm or nothin' babe, just get it down ya.'

She could just have a couple of toots. Her mum had been pissed for as long as she could remember and more besides, so whatever Blink said, it couldn't do that much harm. She would put it out and save the rest for later anyway...long before she got into the same state as this lot. Dee pulled a lighter from her pocket and sparked up. There was a harsh taste and it burned hot, but it wasn't horrible, in fact, by the second pull, a pleasant wave began to wash over her. She took another drag, and another.

The wave was bright and sparkling, but there was darkness underneath. If she stopped smoking, Dee knew she would slide into that darkness and it was sooo nice to be lifted above everything, leaving all the shit down there. Gaz was moving about now, but she didn't want to open her eyes and risk reality sucking her back down. Someone put a drink into her hand...and then another spliff. Perhaps she was a princess after all.

She must be a princess. Strong arms were lifting her onto the settee, propping her head up on a cushion, gentle hands stroked her face. It was blissful...until the hands started to travel away from her face. That wasn't what princes did. Dee opened her eyes a crack. Gaz. *He* wasn't a prince. But he was her boyfriend, so it was probably ok, they did do that kind of thing. His hands were squeezing harder now though and she wasn't in the mood.

The wave was making her feel sick too, or maybe the baby, swimming around inside her. She should tell Gaz, it was his baby too.

'I've got your baby inside me,' she said, or tried to say, except her lips felt weird.

The hands stopped moving, gripping tight on her thigh and left tit.

'Pregnant, eh?' There was a pause. It might have been short, or long. She wasn't sure. 'Don't know it's mine though, do I? And they won't let you keep it anyway. Damo!'

What? The nurse said they would help her keep it, if she wanted. The hands were at it again, rougher now, but she was too busy thinking to bother about it. Why would Gaz say it might not be his? She'd never had sex with anyone else, he must know that. Her throat was parched, but someone was looking at her thoughts and put a straw between her lips. It was like Gaz said about dreams coming true. It tasted mostly of orange, so she drew on the straw until she was sucking up air, only the aftertaste making her wonder what else was in it.

Her head began to spin, slowly at first and then faster. Dee concentrated on not feeling sick and ignored Gaz, who was on top of her now. He pulled down her jeans, but she was too far away to stop him, or even say anything. It didn't last very long, which was fine, until she realised he was just rolling her over and pulling her legs over the side of the settee. It started again, harder this time, so hard it hurt. The pain was something to focus on. It made her angry and that cleared her head.

It wasn't the wave getting rough, but Gaz, jerking her about, his fingers digging into her hips and his thing smashing her insides up. Right where the baby was. Dee cried out, but that seemed to make it worse. A surge of rage flooded through her and brought strength to her limbs. She reached behind, catching at his arm, scratching with her nails, twisting, shoving, until she could pull free and scramble up onto the settee. There were hairs under nails where she had scraped at his skin.

Immobilised with horror, Dee stared at the bleeding arm of Damo, the whole room caught in a freeze frame for several seconds. Gaz was crashed out on the floor several feet away, the others were lined up on the opposite side of the room, watching, faces flushed with excitement. Damo caught hold of her ankle, just as Dee turned aside to puke over the settee. She spat and then launched a vicious kick at his face with her other foot.

The kick connected with a satisfying crunch. She was still wearing her trainers and blood burst from Damo's nose as he reeled backwards. Yanking up her jeans, Dee saw Gaz rising up from the floor and coming towards her. Her pockets were empty, but she could see her phone and bacca at the other end of the settee. She reached out towards them just as Gaz swung an open-handed slap at her, so the blow glanced off the back of her head.

Another surge of adrenalin cleared the last of her dizziness and as Dee shoved her phone into her pocket, she realised that Gaz was between her and the door. Without hesitation, she threw herself off the settee and straight at him, bringing up both elbows in the hope of smashing his nose too. It didn't work. He ducked a little, caught her around the waist and spun her upside down, so that all she could do was beat at his legs, as the blood flowed fast into her head.

She was on the point of passing out, when another set of arms lifted her by the shoulders. What would they do to her now? There was shouting, muffled by the pounding in her head, but it sounded like Gaz. He dropped her legs and she opened her eyes in time to see his palm, inches from her face, before the blow struck. Tears blurred her vision, but one of the hands still holding her shoulders let go and she heard a grunt from Gaz, before she was lifted, upright this time, and walked into the kitchen.

One arm still held her while the other reached out to open the back door and Dee felt a lurch of fear when she saw the thick, dark hair and knew it was Damo. With his arms keeping hers tight against her body and lifting her feet off the floor, he walked outside and around the side of the house, where he put her down. His arms were still wrapped around her and Dee hardly dared to breathe, but he muttered a low 'sorry', let go of her and ran back into the house.

Dee stood, just breathing, the energy draining away now she was free. All she could think, was that Damo had said something. In all those months, she'd never heard him speak. And he had hit Gaz to protect her. Damo. She was sick again and felt better for it, except her mouth tasted like shit. She had to get home, but when she started walking, her legs turned to jelly. Taking hold of the neighbour's fence, she dragged herself along until she could slump down, out of sight of the house.

The memory of what they'd done made her stomach heave again and now she understood what Gaz had said about the baby. What if it had happened before and not just with Damo? What if those other lads were just...waiting their turn? Crying now and retching, over and over, Dee didn't register that her phone was ringing, until it stopped and started again. Probably that bastard, calling to laugh at her. But it was Shona.

18

What began as mild dread grew into a sickening certainty, with each new piece of information that came in. The latest report brought a clammy sheen of sweat to McGrath's forehead and left him with little doubt. It also left him with no choice. The request to escort an ambulance - called to assist 'a bunch of paedophiles with head injuries' – had caused his eyes to narrow. The surveillance intel from the Child Sexual Exploitation Unit, identifying the victims, gave duty a weight he'd been trying to ignore, but the sighting of an 'enormous biker-type in the back garden' by a neighbour at the scene, forced his hand.

'Pull up details for Jim Travis, late '50's, right now,' he barked at Robson, his Detective Sergeant. 'He's on license after a long stretch, plenty of form for violence and links to a girl wrapped up in the CSE operation. He's been helpful up to now, but it's possible he got tired of waiting for us to nail these guys the legal way.'

Robson stared back at him for a second, unusual for a man who tended to act like an army subordinate towards his superiors.

'So the hospital cases are suspected paedophiles and this Travis guy will go back inside, even if we're just interested?' he asked.

McGrath frowned, masking relief that his own reluctance to pull Jim in was not personal.

''Suspected' means not convicted and, innocent or not, these men are victims of a serious assault, which we're investigating. I will contact Travis's Probation Officer, who will want to arrange a Risk Strategy meeting before making any decision about a recall. Now we need to get someone round there, asap.'

'I'll go,' Kath, the new Detective Constable said. 'I know where he lives. I've been there before and he was fine with me.'

'Ok, go with her Robson, but don't hesitate to call for back up and take it easy for now. We just need to establish his whereabouts and see if there's any physical evidence that he was involved. There are six victims, so it's likely that their attacker or attackers were also injured, but there's so much blood at the scene, it'll take a while for Forensics to process it.'

'Yes Sir,' they said in unison and turned to leave.

'Hang on, where's the girl, Delilah?'

'The CSE report said she was at the house of her mother's neighbour,' Robson said. 'She was visibly impaired and upset when she left the scene and then took a call on her mobile. The surveillance team decided to split and follow her and they think it was during that brief discussion that the attacker slipped into the house. The remaining guy had no idea that anything was going on inside, until we turned up. He heard a bit of shouting and a smash like glass breaking, but it was nothing out of the ordinary.'

McGrath shook his head. The situation bordered on ridiculous, but the flood of information was beginning to slide into place. There were too many coincidences for them to be linked by chance alone.

'That neighbour is a good friend of Travis, it's where I first met him. Was it her who called Delilah? At that precise moment? There's every chance she knows something about this,' he said. 'I'll go around there with Jones. The two houses are on the same estate, so back up will be close by, but Travis was in at the heavy end of organised crime and he'll have access to weapons. Don't take any chances, none at all. If it feels wrong, get the hell out of there. Do you understand?'

'Yes sir,' Robson said again, while Kath just nodded.

McGrath hoped her confidence was well-founded. He should be sending an armed response unit really, or at least be running it through the Dangerous Persons lot. The attacker must know he'd gone too far, or he wouldn't have called an ambulance. But if that attacker *was* Jim, he would be very reluctant to go back into prison. He trusted Robson and Kath to be both cautious and open-minded, a faith he did not have in all of his officers, but he was aware that this was a high wager on gut instinct.

~ ~ ~

The mile and a half walk from the lock-up where Jim kept his bike almost finished him off. The adrenalin was long gone. His arm hurt like hell and was heavy with the weight of blood, soaked into his jacket. Several pot-holes and a sharp stop during the eighty minute ride had made him shout with pain, and his head was throbbing, but the lack of visible injury was one thing that had gone well. The shop was a diversion he now wanted to skip, but it would reinforce his alibi and he needed some medical supplies anyway.

He draped the folded dust sheet from the garage over his left shoulder, hoping to mask the warm, metallic smell of blood and hide any damp patches on his jacket. Beyond whisky and a first aid kit, he gave little thought to the other items he threw into the basket and was in and out within a few minutes. Leaving the cover over his arm, Jim carried the two shopping bags in his other hand with an ostentatious swing, as he walked through the caravan site. It was still only 9.40pm and he was hoping that someone would at least notice him, if not stop him for a chat. His own van was in sight before anyone obliged.

'Aha! Bit of moonlight shopping, is it? I wondered where you'd disappeared to, without Crank in tow. Promised the lad I'd bust him out if you weren't back soon. Thought he was going to break the door down himself, when I knocked on it earlier.'

Shit. How much earlier?

'Sorry Bob. I ran dry of whisky, and while Crank still thinks he's a pup, his arthritis is playing up again and he needs to chill out a bit on the walks.'

'I know the feeling.' Bob sighed and shook his head. 'He should accept old age gracefully, like we do.'

Jim snorted.

'Disgracefully, more like. What were you after...a game of whist?'

287

'I'm in more of a poker mood tonight, especially if you've just stocked up on whisky. The missis is wrapped up in old soap re-runs, it's driving me nuts.'

'Sounds good. Give me twenty minutes to get the shopping away and sort Crank out, then come on over.'

Bob grinned before disappearing back inside and Jim hurried to his van. Twenty minutes was not long, if his arm needed a stitch or two. Crank's frantic wagging soon stopped and he gave an agitated whine as the smell of blood hit him. Jim paused to ruffle the thick fur on the back of his neck.

'It's alright lad, nothing a wash and a plaster won't fix. No walk tonight though, so you'll have to nip outside.'

Crank nuzzled his hand in return and then shot through the still-open door. There was no mess inside, despite having a long day on his own, which Jim would reward him in a princely fashion for. He eased off his jacket and lobbed it into the shower tray, alarmed to see the whole sleeve of his sweater was soaked a dark red. After ditching the stab vest, freeing his other arm and pulling the sweater over his head, he peeled the sleeve down. The deep and open gash ran along the outside of his bicep, from just below his shoulder, almost down to his elbow. That would need several stitches, but he didn't have time now, not if he had to clear the mess up too.

He rinsed off his arm in the sink and poured antiseptic wash, straight from the bottle, along the gaping cut. Growling through gritted teeth, he wound surgical tape around and around his arm, bringing the raw edges closer together. He stuck two pads on top, holding them in place with more tape, and then wound a bandage around the lot, as tight as he dared. The sound of Bob's door slamming urged him to greater haste.

Pulling two clean sweaters from a drawer and yanking them over his head, Jim prayed the bandage would stem the bleeding a little, at least for an hour or two, until he could stitch it up. The bloodied sweater, vest and jacket, he shoved in a bin bag and onto his bed, returning to the kitchen area just as Bob stuck his head through the open door.

'Ready for a fleecing?' he asked, rubbing his hands together.

'Ready to give you one,' Jim said, smiling with genuine pleasure, as the alcohol fumes riding on Bob's breath reached him. 'Can I tempt you to a dark malt?'

'Always.'

Even better. Bob would be too pissed to notice anything was wrong or unusual. All in all, it had been a successful evening, so long as that dark-haired lad didn't die. As the one who had man-handled Delilah out of the house and then been the first to tackle him when Jim burst through the back door, that one had taken the worst of it. Even if he did survive, he probably wouldn't see again and the sly fucker who had stabbed him would need some serious plastic surgery too. The others hadn't put up much of a fight.

They'd all be in hospital now though. He'd only dared wait twenty minutes before calling 999, spoiling the alibi a little, but not too much. The police investigation would just be kicking off and here he was, over sixty miles away, playing poker, after a walk to the shop. He hoped Dee wouldn't be too upset, but thought not, after seeing the state she was in. Jim felt no other qualms over his actions. They were scum and needed stopping.

The police might come knocking in the morning, but tomorrow was another day. The mobile phone and the fucker's knife were safely in the sea.

'You can deal,' he said to Bob.

~ ~ ~

Blink was, at last, settled in the lounge, with two movies lined up and a pile of chocolate. The several hours of pouring out his soul had left both him and Derek drained, but Derek now needed to write it all up. He went into the office and found Sandra, ten minutes early for handover, thank God. He was exhausted and wanted to go home to Talia, although he was disappointed that Dee hadn't come back in time for that hot chocolate.

Gareth was on the phone and his grim expression did not suggest good news. Sandra took his arm, whispering so as not to distract Gareth.

'It's the Child Exploitation Liaison Officer. Sounds like Delilah's in a mess.'

Derek sank into a chair to await the news. Gareth took a deep breath after hanging up.

'Apparently Delilah came out of a house the CSE unit have under surveillance, looking traumatized and under the influence of something. She was so distraught, the team split and one followed her to Shona's house.'

'Ah shit. I've spent half the evening trying to persuade Blink that this wouldn't happen,' Derek said. 'Chuck us the mobile, Gareth.'

He called Dee's mobile, but there was no answer. He sent her a text.

Hey Dee. Everything ok? I can come and get you if you need a lift back. I'll call again in 5 mins. Derek

'I don't think we should leave it to Delilah, Derek. Can't we just fetch her?' Sandra said.

'Of course, but it's worth giving it half an hour to see if Dee can make it her own choice. You wouldn't go and check on Blink, would you Gareth? He's taken to listening behind doors.'

'Sure.'

Gareth left the room and Sandra suggested starting their handover. Derek smiled without humour.

'I'll tell you how today has gone, but I doubt I'll be going anywhere just yet. This doesn't feel good, Sandra.'

'No. I assume the nurse confirmed the pregnancy this morning?'

'Yes. I'm just going to call Dee before I go into it though, I said I'd ring in five minutes.'

He was about to hit the dial button when the land line rang again. Sandra jumped up to answer it and her face paled as she listened.

'Yes...yes...I understand...we're just sorting that out now...ok, thank you.' She replaced the handset and looked at him. 'That was the police, but CID this time. There's been a serious, violent incident at the house Delilah was visiting this evening. They don't know if Delilah is involved or not, but they want us to get her back here as soon as possible.'

'Ok. Give me one minute.'

He hit dial, each ring seeming to last an age. Dee picked up on the fifth.

'Hello.'

Her voice was dull, subdued...and she never said 'hello'.

'Dee it's Derek. Are you alright?' He could hear her breathing, but she didn't answer. 'Look, it's late and I'm supposed to be going off shift in a minute, but I'd like to know you're back here and safe before I go home. Where are you?'

'Shona's.'

'Ok. Well I'm going to nip over now then, with Sandra.'

'No, I'm fine. Don't come, I want to stay here.'

'I'd like you to come!' a woman's voice called from the background.

It must be Shona, who was pleasant enough, but obviously anti-establishment and who still wanted them in her house.

'Alright then, but don't bring that cow,' Dee said.

Derek breathed out. That was a more normal Dee response.

'I'm sure she won't mind waiting in the car.'

He was sure she would, but Sandra had gone to apprise Lisa, just arrived to take Gareth off, of the little they knew about the current situation.

'Huh,' Dee said and cut him off.

It didn't look like he or Gareth would be going home anytime soon. Derek dialled Julie's number, but there was no answer. He didn't bother leaving a message; he couldn't explain the unknown and she would call back. Dropping a quick text to Talia, he hoped it wouldn't turn into an all-nighter.

'Blink's fast asleep on the settee,' Gareth said, coming back in, followed by the two women. 'So what's happening now?'

Derek described the second call and his conversation with Dee.

'Are you alright to stay on for another hour or two?'

'Of course,' Gareth said.

'Right, we'll go and fetch Dee and either you or Lisa needs to stay by the phone. We don't know what we're going to find, Julie will call back and I suspect the police will be in touch again...at least I hope they'll call and not just turn up here. We'll be as quick as possible.'

Hovering between the kitchen and the front room while Shona made tea, Derek watched Dee, white faced, chain-smoking roll-ups on the settee, with her knees pulled up to her chest. She hadn't responded to him at all yet and he wondered if Shona was any wiser. The only communication had been a pair of raised eyebrows on her way to put the kettle on.

'Look, if you're not ready to come home just yet, that's ok, but can Sandra come into the kitchen, if she doesn't try to talk to you? It's pretty cold out there.'

A shrug. At least she was listening.

'Thanks, I'll just go and tell her.'

He went through to Shona.

'Is it ok if my colleague comes in and sits in your kitchen? She isn't Dee's favourite member of staff, but I don't like to leave her outside in the car.'

'No problem at all.' Shona lowered her voice. 'Something terrible has happened this evening, but I've no idea what...Dee has barely said a word since she arrived, but she did ask me what 'H' is.'

'H?' A cold shiver went down his neck. 'Did you tell her it's probably heroin?'

'Yes. She got angry, and then upset again. I know she shouldn't be smoking, but I thought she was going to tear herself to pieces, it was just awful. She's a lot calmer now.'

'Well I'm sorry you're having to deal with this. I'll just go and fetch Sandra,' he said, wondering why Shona hadn't called Sunny Bank herself.

He was walking down the path when a silent police car rounded the corner and pulled up behind Sandra. Shit. This would really stir things up. No-one knew what Dee had been through tonight and the more people and pressure applied, the less likely she was to talk. Doors slammed. Sandra was first out, looking quite prepared to block the way of the middle-aged man and younger woman who got out of the police car.

292

'Sandra!' he shouted. 'I was just coming to fetch you. Dee isn't going to move for a while, so you might as well come and sit in the kitchen,' he said, ignoring the police for the moment.

The male officer changed course and strode towards him, looking affable, if not actually smiling.

'So Delilah is still here then?' he said, holding out a hand. 'I'm DI McGrath, CID. This is DC Jones. You two must be from Sunny Bank.'

Derek relaxed a little, introducing himself and Sandra.

'I don't mean to be rude, but having just seen Delilah, I don't think she's in any state to be questioned this evening,' he said. 'I thought that police matters were to go through her CSE Liaison Officer anyway?'

McGrath held up a hand.

'We're not here to see Delilah, although it would both please me and help a separate investigation, to confirm that she's physically unharmed. Your protectiveness is reassuring though.'

'It shouldn't be...I have no idea what's going on,' Derek said, struggling to hide his resentment.

~ ~ ~

Peering around the curtains in the front room, Shona swore.

'What?' Delilah said from behind her.

Shona feared her reaction, but Dee would find out, soon enough.

'Er...it looks like the police are here too.'

'The pigs? What do they want?'

'I don't rightly know.'

Shona realised with some relief that she didn't. They were supposed to be gathering evidence against the toe-rag that got Dee pregnant, weren't they? Perhaps it was to do with that. But then, whatever Jim had planned was also to do with that. She moved away from the window, trying to stay calm. At least she didn't have to run around, stashing ashtrays and sweeping bits of weed off the surfaces. Having nothing to hide was comforting in itself.

Dee's knees were pulled even tighter into her chest and she was shivering, poor lamb. Shona would have liked another hour alone with her, convinced the girl would talk when she relaxed a bit. There had been a spark of interest when she told Dee about Laura and Paulie's baby and she wanted to know what the Social Services lot were advising Dee to do about her own pregnancy. A loud knock on the back door made them both jump.

'Right then, we'll see what they're after, eh?'

She wasn't expecting a response, so went to let them in. The two from the care home were back, plus two police. They filled the kitchen, but Shona gave a polite smile. The male cop was the same one who'd investigated her assault and she hoped there weren't any new leads on that, not when Paulie was just getting himself together.

'Gosh, this is turning into quite a party! I'm not sure Dee's in the right space for it though.' She turned to Derek. 'Your tea is on the side there. Anyone else want a cup?'

The other three declined the offer. McGrath seemed impatient and was trying to see through to the front room.

'Is Dee in there?' he asked.

'Yes, but...'

'It's alright, I'm not going to go barging in.' He took another step out of the kitchen. 'Dee? It's McGrath, the Scottish cop that bored you half to death the last time we met. Can I come and say hello?'

There was a faint 'yeah', but Shona was pleased when Derek grabbed the cop's arm.

'Look, you may have met Delilah before, but I doubt you're fully up to date with her present circumstances,' he said in a low voice, 'the nurse only confirmed that she's pregnant this morning'.

This McGrath chap was a cool one. His expression didn't change and his eyes held Derek's, but Shona could see a muscle flexing at the corner of his jaw. The rigid arm, that Derek still held, relaxed and McGrath inclined his head a little.

'Thank you for your restraint,' he said. 'Delilah and I got on quite well and I am being both over-eager and incautious as a result.'

Shona felt an appreciative smile warming her lips, but in the next instant, was impaled by a gaze that was shocking in its cold intensity.

'Does Jim know?'

McGrath's voice was quiet and dangerous. There was too much control being exerted.

Shona shook her head lamely for a few seconds, until she managed a pathetic 'what?'

'Does your friend, Jim, know that Delilah, is pregnant?'

His words were slow, deliberate, and his eyes still ground into hers. Oh God, what had Jim done?

'Well, I might have mentioned it, on the phone. There was quite a scene on Saturday. Dee did a test here first you see, with her mum, and Jim called me yesterday, just to catch up, you know, he's moved away, so...'

'What?'

McGrath's eyes narrowed, but did not release her. Shona swallowed and wound the end of her shawl around her fingers, realising that this was the perfect course to take.

'Yes, he went off to Lincolnshire a couple of months back, trying to get out of the way. He wants to keep his head down and stay out of trouble - he's an old man now and wants a peaceful life - but there are those who just won't let things lie, so, he had to flit.'

It was a true story and a portrait of a tired retiree, not a violent thug. Shona was pleased with the response and unprepared for the next shot.

'Why did you call Delilah earlier?'

Her lower teeth turned to lead and her jaw flapped, until again, half a truth came to the rescue.

'I was worried, especially after Saturday...she's hanging out with a bad crowd and her mum's poorly again. I've promised to keep a close eye on her.'

Hang on a minute, how would he know she'd called Dee? A twitch of his lips suggested he was guessing. Shit. But then, why shouldn't she call Dee, like she just told him.

'I'd like a look at your phone,' McGrath said.

'I'd like to warn you, sir, that my colleague is on the phone, to the CSE unit, explaining why we haven't yet collected Delilah and taken her home, as we were instructed to do well over an hour ago.' Derek looked angrier than McGrath, though he kept his voice low. 'I have no idea what this is about, but I do know that there's a traumatized and possibly injured girl in there, who we are all ignoring. I ask that you at least move aside, so that I can go to her.'

Surprise and shame both flashed over McGrath's face and he was clumsy in his haste to get out of the way. Shona gasped, as the absence of his bulk revealed Delilah, standing just a few feet behind him.

'What's going on? Why are you here?' she said to McGrath, ignoring everyone else.

'First things first Dee, are you ok?' he said.

She frowned and then shrugged.

'Why are you asking about Jim? What's happened?'

'Well, those friends you've been to see tonight...'

'Those shit-head wankers are *not* my friends, not any more,' Dee spat, and then her chin came up. 'How do you know where I've been? Are you spying on me?!'

'Look, this should not be happening, please stop,' Derek said.

The other one, the woman Derek had fetched, came back in.

'The CSE link is on her way,' she looked straight at McGrath. 'She's not happy.'

'I'M not happy!' Dee shouted. 'What the FUCK is going on?'

I'm not happy either, Shona thought, and there are even more of them coming. The female cop retreated behind the table and started taking notes, everyone else seemed stuck, unsure what to say or do. Dee came right into the kitchen and spoke to Derek.

'I'm not talking to that stupid CSE bitch, she treats me like a baby. I'll tell McGrath and he can tell whoever else.'

'Tell me what?' McGrath said.

'It doesn't work like that,' Derek said, at the same time.

'Here,' Dee pulled a half-smoked, rather squashed joint from her pocket and held it out to McGrath. 'It's got heroin or some shit in it.

296

That fucker Gaz, who's supposed to be my boyfriend, gave it to me, and then gave me more, even after I said I was pregnant.'

They all stared at it for a second, then McGrath asked the other cop to fetch an evidence bag.

'And call Robson,' he added, as she went out through the door.

'I'm going to put the kettle on,' Shona said, to no-one in particular.

The tension was unbearable and she was glad to turn her back on them all. Hurrah for Dee though – there would be saliva on that spliff and the more focus there was on the evil bastard who gave a pregnant child heroin, the less there would be on Jim.

'Now it's your turn,' Dee broke the silence behind her and it was McGrath who answered.

'Dee, I'm here because Gaz and several of his friends were beaten up tonight, very badly.'

Shona turned around in time to see the look of perfect shock on Delilah's face.

'Eh? I only left there a bit back,' Dee said and looked at the clock on the wall, 'not even two hours ago.'

'How many people were there, in the house?' McGrath said.

'Six lads.'

'Did you see anyone else?'

'No. I left, then Shona rang and I came here. Probably didn't pay their dealer or something.'

The female cop came back in, wearing gloves and holding a plastic bag. She took the spliff-end from Dee and murmured something to McGrath. Shona only caught the words 'weeks ago', but McGrath looked pleased with the communication. Dee, who was closer, scowled at him.

'Is that why you're asking about Jim? He can't have done it, he doesn't even know them and he moved away. I haven't seen him for ages.'

'Good, that's good. We just want to rule him out, that's all,' he looked across at Shona.

She stopped breathing again, wishing she'd stamped on her phone like Jim told her to. The call from him would be there, in the log, just at the time Dee had left the boyfriend's house. A car pulled up outside and several doors slammed. McGrath held her eyes for a few seconds longer, pursed his lips a little and then turned back to Dee.

'Well, I'm going to be the one in trouble now, but it would be a good idea to tell these people everything you know, Dee. It might stop other girls from getting mixed up with Gaz and his mates. I'm sure they won't mind waiting until tomorrow though.'

'But I'd rather tell you,' she said.

'Not all of it, surely, and they're experts about this kind of thing...I'm not.' Her head drooped and McGrath reached out, took her shoulder. 'Have you seen much of Jono?'

Dee's hanging head moved from side to side.

'He won't mind you know, about the baby. He'd make a good god-father, don't you think?'

The head moved upwards again and Shona's heart warmed to see the half smile on the girl's lips.

'Yeah, he'd be awesome.'

Without warning, Dee threw herself at McGrath, wrapping her skinny arms around his and burying her head in his chest. His hard eyes went shiny. The look on Derek's face was almost comical, but the look on the face of the woman who marched through the back door at that very moment, without so much as a knock, was not.

19

Dee took a sip of hot chocolate, looking at Becky over the edge of the wide mug. Becky looked back at her, smiling a bit, but not saying much at all. It was ok. For the first time ever, she wasn't bothered by Becky being there; maybe because she wasn't telling her what to do right now, or maybe because she had to admit that Becky had been right, about Gaz and them anyway. She came yesterday too, but Dee was not in the mood then, not after three hours with the CSE woman.

It was a nightmare. The whole thing was a nightmare, starting at midnight, when she was still in the middle of a physical examination that made her want to die of shame. The evil bitch that kicked off at Shona's got a bit nicer, but Dee would have told her to fuck off if McGrath hadn't asked, begged her, to do whatever she said. At least they didn't try to talk to her as well. Not then.

They came back the next morning. It was Shona she thought of, during the hours of questioning. Shona, who seemed to know what had happened, even though Dee hadn't talked to her.

'Tell em everything Dee,' she'd said. 'All the gory, horrible detail that you wouldn't even dare write in your diary. They've heard it all before, and worse. They won't think badly of you, whoever you've had sex with and whatever other things you did. The only bad outcome will be if these lads don't pay for it, and do the same thing again, to someone else.'

They've heard it all before, and worse. They've heard it all before, and worse. She repeated it in her head and kept her eyes closed the whole time, but told the woman with the tape recorder everything. Every last thing. She identified mug shots of Gaz,

Damo and one of the other lads, and a photo of the quiet, older bloke, but all she could say about him was that she'd seen him twice. At the end, the woman smiled and said she was proud of her. Proud...after telling her all that shit!

It was a shame that Becky was waiting when she came out. All she wanted was a fag and to be on her own. Seeing Becky was a reminder that it wasn't just the woman in the room who knew everything she'd done, not for long anyway. Dee told Becky to fuck off and called her every foul name she could think of. But here she was, the very next day, not pissed off and acting as if she'd never said all those things.

'So does it feel better or worse, now you've shared it with someone else?' Becky asked.

It was both. It felt good, knowing that Gaz was going to get it in the neck. The CSE woman had told her a few more things about him, which did add up, and made her hate him with a violence that left her shaking when she thought about it. But that was the bad thing. All she felt now was anger; the tiny bits of magic were gone, the parts that were nice were now dirty, she felt stupid, taken in by his lies, by all of those lads, who must have been laughing at her the whole time. So Dee shrugged in reply.

'Do you think you might still go to your catering course this week? Sometimes, the best way to move on is to get back into a routine, go out and mix with other people.'

Dee dropped her head, frowning. She wanted to go, but what if they could tell she was pregnant? Becky would tell the staff anyway and she still didn't know what to do about the...thing. Was Gaz even the father? Or Damo? It might be one of the other lads. It would be better if it was Damo's. She didn't feel as angry at him now, even though he'd...but he didn't fight back when she kicked him in the face and then he stopped Gaz beating her up. He was weird, weird in the head, but maybe that's why he did whatever Gaz said, like a slave.

'Are they all in hospital then?' she asked Becky. 'The lads that got beat up with Gaz, on Monday night?'

'I think so, but even if they're not, they aren't allowed to come anywhere near you. You'll be totally safe.'

300

Dee raised an eyebrow.

'I'm not scared of them, and I wouldn't talk to them, not now I know they're shit-heads. I just wondered how bad they were beat up.'

'I don't honestly know, Dee. It's a separate investigation, so they don't have to tell me anything.'

'But they don't think it was Jim any more?'

'I don't know that either. Why don't you ask your CSE link? She might be able to tell you.'

'I'd rather talk to McGrath.'

'Hmm…I'm not sure he'll be allowed to talk to you for a while.'

'But I like him.'

'Tell your CSE link that too.'

She would, in a day or two, but she'd talked to her enough for now.

'Will you tell the tutors at catering that I'm pregnant?'

'Yes, I'll have to. There are a whole load of health and safety reasons why, but they won't talk to you about it, or tell the other students.'

'But what if I get rid of it?'

'Then I'll tell them you're not pregnant any more. I won't go into the how and why of things.'

Dee nodded. Maybe it would be ok, for a bit.

'You won't be the first pregnant, 14 year old, who's attended that course you know,' Becky said. 'Ask anyone who was there last year. And I don't think you'll find them turning against you. From what I've seen, they'll all become mother hens, some might even envy you.'

'Eh?'

That couldn't be true. They'd all call her a slag, she knew they would.

'Remember, this isn't school. Go in and talk to the other girls, judge for yourself. You don't have to tell them anything, you're bright enough to think of a way to bring up the subject generally.'

She might, but the thought of it made her want a fag. She stood up.

'I'm going outside now.'

'Ok. Well thanks for talking to me and I have to say, Dee, I think you're amazing, for doing what you did yesterday.'

Dee scowled. There was nothing amazing about talking. It was a stupid thing to say, but stupid the same way Blink was. He felt sorry for Becky because he'd seen her crying in her car. She gritted her teeth and put one hand on the door.

'I didn't mean that shit I said to you yesterday, I was just angry.'

Done. Dee legged it outside and rolled a quick fag, hoping that Becky would bugger off. She wasn't looking forward to the rest of the day; Sandra had made Blink go to school as he'd wagged it yesterday, so now there was her, Julie and Lisa. Derek wasn't on until tomorrow and even Gareth wouldn't be around until later. The lack of interesting company made her think of Josh. It was only about a month since he'd been sent down, but she could hardly remember what he looked like.

Maybe she should write to him, see if he was ok and tell him about Gaz. There were about five texts from Jono she should reply to as well, but she didn't feel like it. The only thing she wanted to do was get out of her face and forget everything, but there was no-one to score from now and she'd rather die than go and find Doogie. Thinking of him made her think of Stacey, but not for long. She didn't care what happened to that bitch.

Dee didn't feel like going to catering the next morning, or going shopping with Derek and Julie. The one thing she could get into was playing chess with Blink, but only when he promised not to talk to her.

She didn't feel like going to catering the week after either and the week after that, there didn't seem much point.

~ ~ ~

Three weeks into the investigation there was a bit of pressure mounting, but nothing too severe. The press weren't going to howl for justice on behalf of a bunch of petty criminals and public sympathy would be behind the vigilante, if any details did come to light. McGrath was following up several lines of enquiry relating to the assaults on 'Gaz' Gascoine and Co., the main theory being that it was inter-gang violence. The lack of forensic evidence was not helping and suggested a professional hit...or at least an experienced perpetrator.

The lack of outcry was interesting in itself. By now, one or two family members at least should be squalling for justice for their 'innocent boy' in the local papers. But it was still quiet, both publicly and in terms of general activity. McGrath almost wished he had some inner-city experience – perhaps he'd know what it meant when the bad guys got scared. Perhaps he should be more worried.

Jim's alibi was strong, though not, in McGrath's eyes, cast iron. Lincolnshire was a fair distance and the timescale would have been tight, but not impossible. Not with a bit of foresight....and experience. The rest of his team seemed satisfied and this particular doubt was not one he wanted to dwell on, but they were still waiting for a couple of key witness statements and if any fresh evidence pointed to Jim, connexions would be made and questions asked.

The four victims who were fit for interview all said the same thing; it was some big, terrifying, biker bastard, who none of them had seen before. The use of knuckle-dusters and hob-nailed boots was seriously old school. The 999 call was made from a mobile, no longer active, triangulated to an area roughly seven miles to the north. It was pretty inconclusive, but his Sergeant thought it pointed to Sheffield. McGrath had studied his own O.S. map at home and found several quiet routes to Lincolnshire, avoiding main roads, but allowing a fast run on a motorbike.

'Biker' was a very generic description and there were plenty of them, but he would go and see Jim again. First though, he would interview Gascoine. The doctor was still dubious, saying his speech was limited and his morphine dose high, but McGrath didn't care - his key witness was also the sick bastard who had defiled Delilah. The CSE unit had passed on enough information for his unwilling imagination to fill in the rest. He wanted to lay eyes on the piece of filth who had led Dee to believe he was her first boyfriend.

Calling to Robson to follow him, McGrath snatched up his keys and walked out, suddenly desperate for air and a brief respite from walls around him. When Robson caught up, he was leaning against the bonnet, talking deep, rain-laden breaths. After the bollocking from his opposite in the CSE unit, now was not the time to show any emotion.

'Do we get to interview Gascoine?' Robson asked. 'Have you spoken to the doctor?'

'Apparently he isn't up to saying much, but we'll give it a try.'

McGrath said little else on the way to the hospital, worried by the prospect of an imminent breakthrough and very bothered by that sentiment. Roll on retirement, although Robson seemed to be struggling with this case too. He was young and fresh, still riding the upsurge of his career and hadn't even met Delilah. This would be a difficult interview in every way imaginable.

A rather harassed doctor took them into a small office when they arrived.

'Look, we're extremely busy today, so can I give you a brief summary of both patients and leave you to it?'

'Fine,' McGrath said.

Robson got out his notebook.

'Ok, apologies if some of this is already familiar. Gascoine has undergone a series of operations to repair damage to his face. We had to rebuild his nose and one eye socket, pin his jaw and re-shape his mouth. He also suffered a dislocated shoulder, several broken ribs and a dislocated knee-joint, with multiple fractures to the surrounding area. Further surgery may be required in the future, but we've done our best for now. He is conscious, but on a morphine drip and talking for extended periods will still be uncomfortable for him. I'm afraid some of your colleagues have already been in and interviewed him on a separate matter, so please keep this as brief as possible. He may even be sleeping now.'

McGrath nodded. Someone from CSE must have been camped outside Gascoine's room, but he didn't begrudge them first dibs.

Not in the least. Hopefully the little shit was even more uncomfortable now. The doctor paused, waiting for Robson's scribbling to stop.

'The news on Smith is less positive. The top half of his face was basically pulped, by repeated blows with a knuckleduster. We weren't able to save either eye, although we have rebuilt his nose to a functioning form. He has broken ribs, a shattered elbow and damage to his genitals caused by an extreme impact, which I assume was a hard kick with a heavy boot. He hasn't yet regained consciousness and we don't know if there's any brain damage. Your colleagues did inform us that he may have learning difficulties and hardly spoke before the assault. He's in the room next to Gascoine if you need to see his injuries for any reason and on the off-chance he should regain consciousness, he answers to the name 'Damo'.

'Thank you,' McGrath said. 'If you could just show us where Gascoine is, we won't take up any more of your time.'

The doctor inclined his head and left the room, so he and Robson followed, taking a series of turns along anonymous corridors, until the doctor indicated a door to their left. McGrath pushed through it, a spasm of shock hampering his next in-breath. Gascoine looked like Frankenstein's Monster, his face a patchwork of stitches and part-healed scars, one leg encased in plaster, the tube running from the back of his hand reminding McGrath of a marionette's string.

The ravaged face turned towards them and exhaled a long breath with a hiss.

'Got nuthin' more to say, leave me alone,' Gascoine said, through swollen, crooked lips.

McGrath stared at him, speechless for several seconds. Gaz the Pretty Boy would not be returning to this carcass and his days of smarming up to young girls were definitely over. The injuries were horrific and McGrath was struggling to reconcile viewing such damage without feeling the smallest grain of pity. The thought over-riding all others, was how effective this solution was in limiting the risk this turd presented to society, rather than several years in jail.

305

It was a dangerous line of thinking and he banished it, clearing his throat and taking a step closer to the bed.

'We're from a different unit. I'm Detective Inspector McGrath and this is Detective Sergeant Robson. We're looking into the assault upon you and your friends, although I have to say, we don't have any strong leads at the moment. We're hoping that you can tell us a little more about what happened, or who might be responsible.'

'No fucking idea who he was…just some massive, wanker of a biker. An old bastard, dark hair, but going grey.'

'So you don't know who might have sent him? No scores to settle?'

'I got no beef with anyone. He's probably some 'care in the community' fucking psycho, let out of a mental ward. This is bullshit anyway, you must have DNA from the house.'

'Only that of you and your friends. There was no physical evidence of another person present.'

Watching Gascoine's features contort further was painful, but still inspired no sympathy.

'Bollocks! I stabbed the fucker! Ripped his fucking arm open! There's gotta be blood on the knife at least.'

'We didn't find a knife,' Robson said. 'Your attacker must have taken it with him.'

The eye without massive scarring narrowed.

'Yeah right, or maybe you lost it.'

'We wouldn't lose an important piece of evidence like that,' Robson said, sounding as cold as McGrath felt.

'Not unless you wanted to.'

'And why would we want to?'

Robson's tone now carried a distinct note of spite and McGrath decided to take back the lead.

'Well that brings us back to the bit about you having 'no beef' with anyone,' he said. 'Is it not possible that one of the girls you have groomed and abused has a father, an uncle, a brother or a friend, who might be angry enough to do this?'

Gascoine hissed again and McGrath wanted to rip out the stitches in his lips with a fork.

'Fuck that. It int abuse when they're beggin' for it, and they aint them kind of girls anyway, with family and shit. No-one cares about them 'cept me.'

Robson started to say something, but McGrath took his arm. Limits reached. He took a card from his pocket and put it on the bedside table.

'Well if you do think of anything else, give me a call,' he said, 'because from where I'm standing, it looks like you pissed somebody off good and proper. Let's go, Sergeant.'

~ ~ ~

His parents were now concerned that he was sinking into depression and Jono knew he should do something about it, before other people started poking their noses in...again. That would be much worse. His life, however miserable, was at least his own right now. There were no issues with his course – most of the other students were so bloody insular and inexpressive, they hadn't noticed his low mood. The few lively, gregarious ones weren't interested enough in him to be aware of any change.

The time he attended uni was the easiest really. There was no chance of bumping into Trudy – the fictitious 'Netty' – on his usual days. The mortifying encounters were of his own making and the memory still made him wince. He had gone every day for a while, watching until he sussed out when and where Trudy's lectures were. The fact that this constituted stalking hadn't occurred to him, until one of her friends pointed it out, loudly, along with the statement that 'being in a wheelchair didn't make him nice, he was just the same kind of dickhead as every other bloke and only interested in a girl's appearance.'

If only Trudy would give him the opportunity to explain, to convince her that she was the loveliest and most interesting girl he'd ever met, before or since the accident. The dozens of messages he'd written to that effect remained unread and on top of the whole Trudy mess, was his uncertainty over Delilah. She hadn't replied to his texts for over a month now and although he was worried, he was also anxious not to impose himself on her. If

307

she was moving on with friends of her own age, then great. But there was also the possibility she was in trouble at a new level and too afraid, or embarrassed, to tell him.

The social worker was being cagey, suggesting Dee would contact him in her own time, but also hinting that she would need her friends. He was left hanging. If he was completely honest with himself, he also wanted Dee's advice, or rather, he wanted her pragmatic thinking applied to his situation. She had known there was something fishy about the Netty thing from the start and would see the answer in black and white. He could always call Sunny Bank.

The woman who answered was cool and wary to start with, seemed about to issue a brusque dismissal, but then asked him to hold for a second. The next voice was male.

'Jono? My name's Derek and I'm one of Delilah's key-workers. I've been hoping you'd call.'

'Oh...' Jono said, taken aback.

'Yes. Have you been in touch with Delilah's social worker at all?'

'I have, but she won't...sorry, I know that's a 'can't', tell me anything. I know you can't either, but I just wanted to check that Dee's ok. I haven't heard from her for almost six weeks.'

'She's been through a lot, but it's for her to tell you, if she ever wants to. I can say she's safe now, but there are difficult times ahead and I also have a message from someone else who was hoping you'd call. Has Dee mentioned a lad called Blink?'

'Yes, a few times. From what I can gather, he's done more for her education in six months than anyone else managed in six years. Blink is an unsung hero in my book.'

There was a warm chuckle at the other end of the line.

'I like you already, Jono. Well, Blink says if you want to visit him, here at Sunny Bank, then he'd love to meet you.'

That was interesting. He didn't want to form a habit of befriending waifs and strays, but perhaps this was a plea on Delilah's behalf.

'And do you think that's a good idea?' he said.

'Probably. Blink knows Delilah better than any of us and everything he does is with her in mind. You're welcome here anyway.'

'I use a wheelchair. Will I be able to get in alright?'

'Sure. We've got a ramp for the front or patio doors at the back. When are you thinking of coming? Blink's at school for most of the week.'

'How about Saturday afternoon, around 4pm?'

'That'd be great and I'll be on shift again. I'll let Blink know and I look forward to meeting you. Thanks for calling.'

'No problem. See you on Saturday.'

Jono hung up, wondering if it would be great. Dee might flip, if she really didn't want to see him, but he got the impression that Derek had already thought it through.

Derek and Blink were waiting for him at the front door, although Dee apparently thought they were winding her up about him coming to Sunny Bank. She made an appearance on the landing, having heard his voice in the hall and Jono was disappointed to see her hair as greasy as it used to be. The look of shock on her face lasted several seconds, before turning to fury. She swore at Blink about stealing her friends and then shot back into her room, slamming the door behind her.

The situation felt awkward, but didn't appear to have moved Blink at all.

'A..as you can s..s..see, Delilah is t..t..technically ok, but p..pretty m..mad at the world,' he said. 'She r..really wants to s..see you, b..but she's t..too angry to be n..n..normal with anyone. Would you l..like a cup of t..tea?'

'Er, yeah, thanks.'

Jono followed Blink into the kitchen, wondering why he had agreed to this. He wasn't capable of sorting out his own life and emotions, never mind someone else's. And it was only going to frustrate him, trying to talk about Dee, with two strangers, who could tell him nothing about what had happened. Something major clearly had. Not that anyone *was* talking. Derek was filling the kettle, Blink was pulling mugs from a cupboard.   Perhaps he should make an effort.

'So, it's you who taught Dee how to play battleships then?' Jono said, towards Blink's back.

The lad turned, grinning and blinking in fast little sets.

'Yeah! And p..proper chess, though Derek g..got her s..started. Do you p..play?'

'Never very well and I'd be pretty rusty now. I don't mind you giving me a thrashing though, if Dee's going to be anti-social.'

'Cool!' Blink said, moving to a jar of tea-bags.

Very cool.   Once they were all sitting at eye-level, Blink and Derek would forget he was in a wheelchair and stop hopping around, looking uncomfortable with the use of their legs. As if he caught the thought in the air between them, Derek leaned back against the worktop with folded arms, giving Jono an appraising look, that was softened by the broad smile beneath.

'You know, a few of Delilah's friends have visited here and I have to say, you're an eclectic bunch.'

'Yeah?'

The only other friend of Dee's who Jono had met was Chelsea, who seemed a fairly typical character at the time.

'Well, leaving aside the local gang culture she's been mixing with of late, we've got a handsome young man in a wheelchair, a nearing 60, mega bad-ass biker and a middle-aged hippy lady, for starters,' Derek said.

'D..d..don't forget the s..st..stuttering n..nerd.'

Derek laughed and clapped Blink on the back.

'Not a chance, that's a major role.'

Watching the pair, Jono smiled his first genuine smile of the day and felt the tension in his shoulders ease. There was more banter as they set up the chess board on the dining table, cleared chairs away and put crisps in a bowl. The game was light-hearted, with Derek asking questions designed to let Blink show off his knowledge and slipping Jono the odd, surreptitious wink. The lad's stutter was much less pronounced when he was on confident ground.

Apart from several loud thumps from above – Delilah's room, according to Blink - Jono almost forgot that she was upstairs, until Derek excused himself to go to the loo. The second he was gone, Blink's entire demeanour changed and the game was abandoned.

'L..look, Derek might n..not be able to t..tell you anything, b..but I can. Delilah got m..m..mixed up with some h..horrible men and n..now she's p..p..pregnant. The police kn..know all ab..bout it and s..someone b..beat them up anyway, b..but Delilah is g..getting really d..d..depressed. Y..you're her b..best friend, but I th..think she's too emb..barrassed to tell you.'

Jesus. What a smack in the chops. Jono wanted Blink to repeat it, but there wasn't time. It certainly made sense of Dee's silence…and the social worker's caution.

'She won't reply to my texts mate, and she hasn't come downstairs, even though I'm here. What do you want me to do?'

'She'll be r..really m..mad about t..today, but i..i..if you could c..come back, I th..think she'd s..see you n..next time.'

Not if she thought Blink had blown her trust she wouldn't. What was he supposed to *do* with this information? Apart from get very angry in the small hours of the morning.

'Are you going to tell her you've told me?'

'Yes. She'll a..a..ask and I'm a c..crap l..liar.'

'She'll flip.'

'I kn..know.'

Jono couldn't help but smile at Blink and as he did, an idea popped into his head. It wasn't a good idea, but it might save Blink from a near-death experience.

'Alright, tell Dee I was fine about it, just a bit worried, and then tell her I need her help, not the other way round.'

Derek came back in and examined the board for a moment.

'I haven't missed much then,' he said, sitting down and raising his eyebrows.

Blink went red.

'We got gassing,' Jono said, 'and I was just telling Blink that I need Dee's help, or advice at least. I've messed up, big-time, with a girl I've been talking to online. Dee tried to warn me early on, but

I didn't listen. Now I want to know how she would go about fixing it.'

Jono concentrated on Blink's surprise and not Derek's ill-disguised smile.

'W..will she kn..know what I m..mean, if I j..just tell her th..that?'

'I reckon so. Tell her to text me when she's ready and that I'll be coming back next Saturday anyway.'

'C..cool.'

There were several more thumps and a loud bang from upstairs.

'Let's hope Delilah hasn't destroyed her room and everything in it before then,' Derek said. 'Come on, I want to see who makes check-mate first.'

~ ~ ~

The day shift on a Saturday was Derek's least favourite time to work. His whole family was at home, full of glee at reaching the weekend and hectic with all the small tasks that built up over the week. Talia always turned it into a party; playing music, singing along, rewarding the cleaning of each room with tea and snacks. The boys loved mucking in, even if they tended to create more mess than they cleared.

This Saturday however, he drove to Sunny Bank with a sense of anticipation. Whilst trying not to expect too much, Derek hoped that Jono's second visit would lighten the miserable atmosphere, currently permeating every corner of house. As per his secret expectations, Blink had told Jono about Delilah's present situation, confessing all to Dee, later that night. Her reaction was cataclysmic and her paranoia such, that every member of staff was considered part of the betrayal.

Not satisfied with shredding a number of Blink's favourite books, stamping on his phone and throwing coffee all over his duvet, Dee's rage continued throughout the week. Even Blink's stoicism was starting to wane, though he made Derek promise not to tell anyone, when he found him crying in the garden after school, unable to face entering the house.

Reading up on the logs from the previous two days when he arrived, Derek was pleased to see that Dee had gone to visit Shona on Thursday night. At least there was one peaceful evening and Gareth would have made the most of it with Blink. He went through to the kitchen to make coffee for him and Lisa, surprised to hear the shower running upstairs. It was only 8am. Blink must be sticking to the body-weight training routine, which Derek gave up on weeks ago. Good on him.

He was still in the kitchen when Blink appeared, wet-haired and buzzing with energy.

'I did f..fifty of everything this m..morning!' he said. 'In r..reps of ten, b..but it's getting easier.'

'Wow! You've got more staying power than me, that's for sure. Have you moved on to any of the more interesting exercises yet?'

'I've b..been trying h..handstands against the w..wall. I've got n..no chance on m..my own yet th..though.'

'It'll come.'

Blink chattered all the way through his breakfast, also cheered by the imminent arrival of Jono. There was every chance that Delilah would take the opportunity to kick off again, but that was left unsaid. Having fetched his homework, Blink stayed in the kitchen, working at the table until Jono arrived, half an hour early. The news that Dee still hadn't replied to any of his texts was disappointing, but unsurprising. This was going to be a big one for her to get over.

'I guess she did flip then, when you told her about our conversation?' Jono asked.

'F..flip is p..probably the u..u..under-s..statement of the y..ear,' Blink said, but did not elaborate.

Jono looked at Derek.

'I'll second that and this fellow deserves a medal.'

'She's b..been through so m..much though,' Blink said, his tone defensive, 'and she's s..still p..p..pregnant.'

There was a pause, which started to develop into an uncomfortable silence.

'Are you getting the chess board out again?' Derek said, for something to say.

'We c..can do, b..but I was g..going to ask you ab..bout your tr..training r..regime,' Blink turned to Jono. 'You o..obviously do w..weights or something.'

Jono looked pleased at the turn of conversation, so Derek left them to it and returned to the office.

'Everything quiet out there?' Lisa asked. 'Delilah still in bed?'

'Yes, for now. I have to say I'm glad. Jono and Blink are getting on like a house on fire and I can't think of a better role-model for him.'

Lisa's eyebrows questioned that statement.

'I really do think so,' Derek said. 'They might be facing completely different adversities, but I get the impression they tackle them the same way. A friendship like this could be the making of Blink.'

That opinion was reinforced when, returning to the kitchen, he found them engrossed in a discussion on the finer points of computer programming. They didn't even stop to acknowledge his presence. Jono stayed for lunch, not leaving until late afternoon. Delilah was a no-show, but further plans were made for the following Saturday. Blink and Jono seemed determined to out-stubborn her.

Talia pulled a face, but did not complain, when Derek swapped his shift to work again the next Saturday. He arranged a baby-sitter for the Saturday night, so they could go out on their own later and vowed to plan a family trip out the following weekend. He usually put his own children first, but in his experience, the '3rd time lucky' rule often worked, so he would give the Blink-Delilah-Jono triangle one more try.

The week leading up to it was calmer and quieter, but not in a good way. Delilah was morose when she did leave her room and still wouldn't talk to Blink, who struggled to maintain his cheerful façade. She ate in her room and only spoke to staff when necessary, the sole positive being her staying in. Her mother was back in hospital, so even visiting Shona was a less regular occurrence. Becky brought several people to try and talk to her, but Dee refused to see any of them.

Having talked to Becky about Jono's visits, there was an unrealistic amount of hope riding on today and a frightening lack of options in the wings. Derek wasn't going to tell Jono that, but he waited for him to arrive with an almost nervous tension. Blink was doing his homework in the kitchen again, but kept popping through to check the drive for Jono's car, alerting Derek with a squawk just before a door slammed outside.

'Go and let him in, I'll stick the kettle on,' Derek said.

Blink and Jono joined him in the kitchen less than a minute later.

'I've sent Dee several texts this morning, trying to get her to come and have a drink, or at least say hello, but she hasn't replied,' Jono said. 'Is she seeing a psychologist or a counsellor or anything? Cos I'm really getting quite worried.'

'We've tried and so has her social worker, but she's refusing to see anyone.'

'She's s..still n..not even t..talking to m..me.'

'Well I'm pretty much out of ideas…bar one,' Jono said.

His expression didn't inspire Derek with confidence.

'And the problem with that is….?'

'It'll break every health and safety rule in your policy and I don't like it much anyway.'

'So try giving her a shout first. You never know.'

Jono went back out into the hall and yelled up the stairs.

'Come on Dee. I don't know what I've done to upset you, but you're doing my head in now. Please come down, just for a second or two. I haven't seen you for months…I'll forget what you look like!'

There was no response.

'J..jono's brought a m..massive chocolate c..cake,' Blink shouted.

He received a 'so fucking what' in reply. Derek shook his head and poured milk into the mugs of tea as the pair returned, despondent.

'N..now what?' Blink said.

'Now we have a cup of tea and a piece of this cake,' Jono pulled it out of his bag and plonked it on the table, 'while you two work out if you can get me up those stairs.'

'That chair looks pretty heavy duty to me,' Derek said, hoping this wasn't the one idea.

'I'm not on about the chair, we'd all end up in hospital if you tried that, I'm just on about me.'

'What, like c..carry you?'

Jono grimaced.

'Yes. A piggy back's easiest on the level, but I'm thinking an arm around each of you to tackle stairs.'

'W..what about your l..legs?'

'They'll have to drag.'

Imagining how that would work, Derek winced. If Julie was in, it would be a definite 'no' and he wasn't at all sure that Sandra would go with it. He took a sip of tea, waving away the slice of cake that Blink offered.

'I can't skip training *and* eat cake mate. Let me go and run this by Sandra. I don't want her freaking out when she discovers us half way up.'

He could have predicted her response, when he went through to the office.

'But what if you drop him? What if Blink puts his back out trying? Derek, this is a ridiculous idea.'

'It's a ridiculous situation, Sandra. Do you have a better one?'

She didn't, and looked quite cross about it.

'Well at least let me knock up some sort of disclaimer, so that Jono can't sue us when he ends up paralysed from the neck down, instead of from the waist.'

'Ok, you do that,' Derek said.

It might keep her busy for long enough to stay out of the way. He went back to the kitchen. Shit or bust.

'Are we going to give this a go then?'

At first, it was easier than he expected. Jono's grip on their shoulders was fierce and with their arms around his waist, they made a secure unit, powering steadily up the first eight steps. Blink's training must be having an effect and Derek was beginning to feel it was a lot of fuss about nothing, until he heard a gasp from below.

'You! But...'

316

'Too late Sandra and please don't distract us now,' he said, trying not to grunt with the effort of the ninth and tenth steps.

'But his legs!'

She stopped talking again and Derek hoped she wasn't taking photographic evidence of his irresponsible behaviour. He couldn't look to check and was surprised when Jono's weight lessened and the thump, thump, thump of his feet knocking against the stairs stopped. Sandra was a lot cooler than she made out.

They all collapsed on the floor outside Delilah's room, getting their breath back. Jono manoeuvred himself to lean against the wall and grinned at them.

'Well done team, and thanks for saving my shins from a battering,' he said to Sandra.

She tried to look disapproving, but couldn't help returning his smile. Jono banged on Delilah's door.

'Oi! If you're not going to join the party, then the party's going to come to you. Open the flippin' door, Dee.'

'No!'

Her reply was muffled. It sounded like she had her head under her duvet.

'Look, no-one's expecting you to come out singing and dancing, but you're not going to feel any better staying holed up in there.'

'Don't care.'

Jono let his head flop to one side and Derek prayed that all this effort hadn't been in vain. Sandra excused herself and went back down to the office.

'Ok. Do you remember the only time I ever said the 'f' word in front of you?' There was silence from behind the door, so Jono carried on. 'I was talking about missing the old haunts and you asked why my climbing mates couldn't take me. I said...'

'Because I fucking hate being carried.'

She sounded a lot closer to the door now.

'Yeah. Well, how the hell do you think I got up here? Sometimes we have to do things we hate, to achieve something we want. So will you open the....'

317

The door opened a few inches. A smell of stale food and unwashed clothes wafted out, but Jono stuck his arm through the gap.'

'Are you going to break my arm, or are you going to come and have some tea and cake....and help me get back down these bloody stairs?'

The door opened wider and Dee appeared. Her hair was lank, her top stained and her face sulky. She looked down at the three of them, crashed out and panting on the floor. Derek wanted to shout for joy when her mouth twisted into the 'I will not smile' pout.

20

Three stops into the journey, the only other person in her section of the carriage got off, so Shona decided to call Jim. She pulled the letter with his new phone number from her bag and tapped in the digits. He answered on the third ring.

'Hello?'

'Jim, it's Shona. I got your letter this morning and thought I'd call for a catch up. Is it a good time?'

'Perfect, it's great to hear from you. How are things?'

'Oh fine, interesting and busy, but how are you?'

'Good, pretty damned good, all things considered. It's very quiet over here. McGrath came to see me again, but it didn't sound like they were making much progress.'

'So what did he want with you?'

'Just checking on a few things. In fact, it was a friendly visit; he slapped my right arm in greeting and my left as a farewell.'

'That sounds like an ulterior motive.'

'Perhaps, but he should have been a bit quicker if he wanted a reaction. Honey and a few cotton stitches work faster than he does. You haven't heard anything, have you? That was last month and they've not been back since, although he didn't seem too anxious for information. I spent more time debating the relative merits of whisky than answering questions.'

'Not a thing, and I was expecting a tougher interrogation too. He's got a soft spot for Dee though, that one. Shame there aren't a few more like him.'

'You're not wrong there. Speaking of Dee, have you seen much of her? Is she ok?'

'She was laid pretty low for a while, but seems to be bouncing back now. She's keeping the baby, although you can hardly tell that she's four months gone. That Jono chap is back on the scene and boosting morale. He was all she talked about when I saw her last week. Apparently she's sorting out his love life.'

'Bloody hell, he must be a desperate man.'

'More of a kind, conscientious one, I think. He dropped her off here with a huge bunch of flowers when Kelly came out of hospital. Oh, hang on a sec.'

She put her hand over the phone while the tinny voice announced the next stop.

'Sorry, back now.'

'Shona, you're not seriously talking to me on a train, are you?'

'There's no-one anywhere near me, don't worry. I don't know when I'll get another opportunity. I'm going up to Manchester to see Laura again.'

'Paulie's girl? What's happening there then?'

'Oh, it's such a mess. Laura seems quite pleasant, but her mother won't let her go and Social Services are adamant they'll take the baby if it's born at home.'

'At least she's got a mother who cares I suppose.'

'No, she's got a mother who doesn't want to lose her cook, cleaner and baby-sitter. She doesn't give a damn about Laura, or the baby.'

'Ah.'

'Yes. There's not a lot I can do really, but at least it was Laura who called me this time and not her social worker. We're meeting for lunch.'

'Sounds promising.'

The train pulled into a station and Shona could see a large crowd waiting to board.

'Bugger. It looks like that train's about to fill up. So you're sure you're ok? And Crank's alright, is he?'

'I'm fine. Crank's a bit stiff these days, but he's not lost his dignity yet. Good luck with lunch.'

'Thanks. It's been lovely to talk to you and I'll call again as soon as I get chance.'

'You too. Take care, Shona.'

A babbling horde of teenage girls surrounded her and Shona hit the red button. She pinned a polite smile to her face, but none of them gave her a second glance. That was just fine. She wanted to think of a few, neutral subjects to talk to Laura about, in case conversation was stilted. They were meeting in McDonald's, but Shona would rather pay over the odds for decent food, than eat that salted pap.

She felt better educated on the life and times of a modern 17 year old when she disembarked, if a little shocked. But then, who was she to judge? It must be age, creeping up on her. Following the directions she had printed off at the library, Shona felt quite the seasoned traveller when she waltzed up to McDonald's without the smallest difficulty. Perhaps she should explore further afield, now she had the time, inclination and her finances were in better order.

Laura wasn't there yet, so Shona bought a coffee and sat by the window. Trying to dismiss the idea – which she hadn't considered up until now – that Laura might not show up, she imagined booking a holiday to Spain, or Portugal, seeing a bit of Europe and having adventures again. She was so lost in the idea, that she didn't notice Laura arrive, until the girl tapped her on the shoulder.

'Oh! Hello love, sorry, I was miles away. Can I get you anything? I bought a coffee so I could wait inside.'

'If we're getting food, I'll have a cheeseburger Happy Meal with Coke, please.'

'A what?'

Shona knew what a Big Mac was, thanks to her visits with Delilah, but that was as far as her knowledge stretched. Maybe a 'Happy Meal' earned its name by including some vegetables and they could stay here after all.

'A cheeseburger Happy Meal. It's for kids, so it's only £2.49 for a burger, fries and a drink.'

'Oh.' Back to Plan A then. 'Well you're eating for two now and I'm not a big fan of burgers, so I was thinking we could go somewhere else to eat...a café, or a pub or something. Do you know anywhere?'

The girl shrugged her thin shoulders. She was due next month and ought to have some meat on her bones and an enormous belly, but one of Shona's dresses would drown her.

'Well, if you've got the energy, we could have a little wander up the road, see if there's anything that looks inviting.'

Laura shrugged again, which Shona decided to interpret as acquiescence. She took a last sip of coffee and stood up.

'Right then, we'll go and have a quick look, but we'll come back here if we don't find anything within a ten minute walk. Ok?'

'Ok.'

Shona was relieved to spot a Wetherspoons within minutes of setting off and steered Laura towards it, putting an arm through hers. The girl was stiff and awkward for a moment, but her arm soon relaxed and she flashed Shona a smile.

'I've seen people walking like this, but I never tried it.'

Shona bit her lip, glad that Laura was now looking at the pub and not at her. She was so like Delilah. What chance did these children stand of becoming mothers, when they had never been mothered themselves? She went through the doors first, pleased to see the pub only half full. Spotting a free table in a booth against the far wall, she led Laura towards it.

'You order whatever you fancy, love.'

Shona went for the lasagne, disappointed that Laura still opted for a burger and chips. The conversation was sparse and mundane throughout lunch, but Shona felt there was more to Laura's nervous behaviour than just the unfamiliar situation. She waited for the puddings to arrive before pressing her.

'Well this is quite lovely. I'm so glad you asked me to come and see you. I hope you know you can call me, any time you want to talk?'

Laura looked up at her and then away again, chewing her lip. She sliced off a piece of chocolate fudge cake with her fork and pushed it around the pool of cream, but didn't answer.

'Look, I can't help thinking there's something you want to say, or ask me, Laura. I won't be cross and I doubt you could shock me. I brought up Paulie, remember?'

Laura nodded, still toying with the cake. Shona let the silence stretch, watching the fork move faster, until at last Laura spoke.

'You can say no, I'll totally get it.'

'No to what, exactly?'

There was another silence, but Shona held firm.

'The Social want to take my baby away.'

'I thought that was only if you stayed at your mum's? Isn't your social worker trying to find you a place of your own?'

'There in't none. Well, there was a shitty flat, but she don't think I'll manage and I haven't got no baby stuff or nothing.'

'So what's she suggesting?'

'Nothin'. If there in't somewhere decent I can stay, they're gonna take the baby.'

Shona's heart sank.

'But that's terrible, surely there's...'

Then she realised what the girl was asking, and her heart sank several feet further.

~ ~ ~

For the first time in weeks, Becky wanted a cigarette. Almost enough to go and buy a pack, but not quite. It was so much easier to resist with the baby now a physical presence, a wriggling being, sharing her body. Instead, she parked up around the corner from Sunny Bank and sat in her car for twenty minutes, doing the breathing exercises and thinking. Not that there was any choice; six months into her pregnancy it was obvious to most people, including the staff at Sunny Bank, so Delilah must be told. It was the 'how' that was problematic.

The turnaround over the last month had astounded them all, Dee's progress outstripping even her key-workers' expectations, which Becky had thought over-hopeful to begin with. She was pleased to be wrong and terrified that the imminent news of her year's maternity leave would upset Dee's fragile, emotional balance. It was only two weeks since her return to the catering course and Becky so wanted her to experience some academic achievement before having the baby. With a taste of success,

323

there would be more chance of her returning to education afterwards.

But, it couldn't be put off any longer. After a couple of light bleeds, Simon was insisting she start her maternity leave early and Becky knew he was right. This was her last week at work and if she did it today, there were still a couple of days to try and make amends, if Delilah reacted badly. She stopped thinking, threw her coat over her lap-top and stepped out into the muggy July heat. She would walk the few hundred yards to Sunny Bank.

Delilah was supposed to be cooking in the kitchen with Sandra this morning. The college were allowing her to undertake certain tasks at home to catch up, if she provided photographic evidence. Derek had warned of a personality clash, but reports suggested it was working so far. Becky prepared to revise that thought, as she signed in to a soundtrack of Delilah shouting.

'I whisked the fucking thing for hours and it's still flat!'

There was the crash of a pan being slammed down. Becky poked her head around the kitchen door with caution and saw Dee, red in the face, scraping something that might have been an omelette into the bin. Sandra was sitting at the table, a patient smile on her face. It was the kind of smile guaranteed to incense a frustrated Delilah, but happily, her back was turned.

'I'm so glad it's not just me who can't get things to rise,' Becky said, walking into the kitchen. 'You should have seen my last sponge cake – it looked more like a cookie.'

'Huh,' Dee said, without turning around. 'You weren't getting marked on it though.'

'No, it was worse than that; I had my mother-in-law coming round. I ended up dashing to Sainsbury's for a replacement, which she assumed I'd cooked. Now she thinks I'm a baking expert and will be sorely disappointed at some point in the future. That's why it's never good to lie.'

A grin broke through Delilah's angry frown, but fell away again when Sandra proposed a second attempt.

'Actually Sandra, I was hoping I could steal Dee for half an hour,' Becky said quickly.

Sandra looked like she was going to argue the point, but Dee jumped at the chance of escape.

'Yeah, and I need a break anyway. The nurse said I can't get too stressed.'

'Alright then, but there's nothing stressful about washing up. If you don't want to do any more cooking today, you can at least tidy up the mess while you talk to Becky.'

'Yeah, whatever. I'm having a fag first.'

Sandra raised her eyebrows, but left them to it.

'I'll be back in a minute,' Dee said, heading for the patio doors.

'I might come with you, if that's ok.'

Dee shrugged, so Becky followed her outside, to a bench shaded by a large tree. There were several sparrows scratching about in one of the flowerbeds, chirruping and chasing each other around. It was the most relaxed meeting with one of her wards Becky had ever experienced. There was almost an air of companionship, unless she was just being fanciful; or wistful, or an over-emotional pregnant heifer. Now was not the time to get all wishy-washy.

'So have you managed to do much catching up, or is Sandra driving you crazy?' she said, still watching the sparrows.

Dee took a couple more pulls on the cigarette before answering. It smelled delicious.

'She's alright...it just does my head in when things don't come out right. It's loads of time and work for nothing and I get pissed off.'

'I'm sure no-one else gets it right first time, every time. I know I don't.'

'Doesn't stop it pissing me off though. And trying to smoke less just makes me want to smoke more, and that pisses me off too.'

Becky smiled, wondering whether to confess just how much sympathy she felt on that score. Better not.

'I'm dead serious,' Dee said. 'Even the nurse said it'd be better for the baby if I just have one or two a day, when I *really* need one, cos my blood pressure got so high.'

Becky supressed another smile, but it slid away on its own when she realised that Delilah was talking more freely, in fact had probably said more already, than in any previous conversation between them. To have finally gained her trust and formed a positive relationship to work from, after all that work, it was more than she could bear to say goodbye.

'Have they given you any stress-busting techniques to try? When I stopped smoking, I used breathing exercises. Boring, but quite effective,' she said.

Delilah turned to look at her, eyes wide.

'You used to smoke? What, when you were young, like? I wouldn't have guessed.'

'No, well, I would never have let you guess. As you now see for yourself, it's an evil habit that hooks its claws in deep. You'll get there in the end though, if you keep trying.'

'I won't have any bloody choice, with Blink around.'

'I'm glad you're friends again, he's a nice lad.'

Delilah pulled a face.

'He's soft.'

'It's a good job he is, or he wouldn't put up with so much grief off you. How's Jono?'

Delilah lurched around to face her, flapping her hand with excitement.

'Shit! I nearly forgot! I need to ask you if I can go to uni with him, on Thursday. I need to help him with something.

'Really? Well I think that's brilliant. You'll be able to have a look around while you're there, see if it's something you might like to do in the future. As long as it doesn't interfere with attending your course and the staff here are ok with it. So what are you helping him with?'

'Girlfriend problems. He pissed her off and now she won't talk to him. I'm going to explain to her what he's really like.'

Oh God.

'Er…right. That's not quite what I had in mind.'

'Oh for fuck's sake, everyone's been like that. I'm not stupid. I won't swear or nothing, Jono'd kill me if I did. I've just got to be nice to her, that's all.'

But what was Delilah's idea of being *nice* to someone?! Still, Jono wasn't daft, although he must be desperate.

'Well, just try not to cause a scene, and promise to have a look around with a view to going there yourself someday.'

'With a baby? No chance.'

'People do, you don't have to give up on anything.'

'Hmm.'

She was swinging her foot against the dirt underneath the bench, rolling the pouch of tobacco between her hands and Becky would lose her in a minute. The pause extended into a silence. She had to do it now.

'Dee, there's something else I need to talk to you about; something to do with me, not you.'

She didn't look up.

'Can I have another fag then?'

'That's your choice, not mine.'

'I'll roll a really skinny one, with hardly any bacca in it.'

Maybe it wasn't such a bad idea.

'Ok. Dee, I'm actually pregnant too.'

The face that turned to look her up and down was open-mouthed with shock.

'No WAY! I thought you were just getting fat!'

'Yes, thank you for that. Unlike you, who look no different apart from a swollen belly, I have put on equal amounts of weight, everywhere. I'm sure I'm going to look like a sumo wrestler in the end.'

'Yeah, probably. How far gone are you?'

'Six months.'

'But that's only a month more than me!'

'I know. It's been killing me, not telling you, but there didn't seem to be a right time.'

'But you'll be ENORMOUS! Aren't you too old to have a baby though?'

'What?! You cheeky mare. I'm thirty-four, so there's time to have a few more yet, if this one doesn't put me off.'

Dee regarded her with raised eyebrows while she licked the cigarette paper, uttering another 'wow' before lighting it. Her incredulity was quite demoralising.

'Unfortunately, what this means, is that I'll be going off on maternity soon and you'll have a different social worker.'

'Who?'

'Her name's Denise. She'd like to come and meet you later, if that's alright?'

Dee shrugged.

'I'm not going out.'

'I'll be taking a year off, but if you're happy and settled with Denise when I come back, you can stay with her.'

'I'll see if she's a bitch or not.'

'Well you can still call me until the end of the week.'

'Cool.' Dee took a last drag and then stood up, stamping out the smouldering cigarette end. 'I'm going to do another omelette.'

'Oh, ok. Well good luck with it.'

'Yeah. Good luck with the baby.'

Dee turned on her heel and went back inside. Becky sat for a moment, sapped of energy. Was that it? Her work mobile started ringing in her bag and she fumbled for it, pleased to see 'Bill' on the screen.

'Hi Becky. Everything alright over there?'

'Uh, yes, I suppose so. Delilah was fine, not bothered at all.'

'That's great. No attachment issues then. Are you coming back to the office? Something's come up with one of your case transfers, but it can wait another half hour if you are.'

'Um, yes, nothing more to do here.'

'You sound strange. Are you still at Sunny Bank?'

'Yes, in the garden. Delilah's just gone back inside.'

'Are you ok?'

'I'm gutted.'

Her eyes filled with tears. She ought to move, before any of the staff came out. She could sneak around the side of the house and call them in a minute, explain that she forgot to sign out.

'Becky, why are you gutted?'

She had almost forgotten Bill.

'We had our best conversation, ever. Really chatty and relaxed. She trusts me Bill, I could really make some progress with her now.' Her lip was starting to go too, and her voice wobbled. 'But then, even after all that work and energy, she doesn't care. She wasn't upset at all, it means nothing to her.'

'Hey, hey, listen to yourself. You're describing the perfect scenario, the dream ending that we hardly ever achieve. You're her social worker, so you can't be her friend, you can't ever be her friend. It's the optimum time to part company and the fact that you can do so, with so little trauma, shows how ready she is and what a great job you've done. Delilah is independent Becky, she's learning how to manage social relationships and this *is* what you've worked for.'

He was right. The human side of her would miss the angry, damaged girl she had come to care for, that was natural, but the social worker should be planning a celebratory dinner...or takeaway. She sighed.

'Thanks Bill. You do talk good sense.'

'I'm glad you think so. Now come back here and tick another one off your list.'

He hung up and Becky took a deep breath. She would go back through the patio doors, shout goodbye to Delilah and sign out in a professional manner.

~ ~ ~

It was hot, but Jono wasn't prepared for the minimalism with which Dee had dressed. Her shorts were tiny and her vest top comprised barely more material than a bra. Her bare, swollen belly glistened with sun cream, drawing the eye in a disconcerting way. Dee seemed to have moved from complete denial, to pregnant and proud, within a very short space of time. Jono was relieved to see Gareth running out after her, brandishing a shirt.

'Dee! This is fresh off the clean washing pile, please take it. I suppose you could wander around the campus like that, but do cover up a bit if you go inside.'

'Why?' Dee said, snatching the shirt from him and opening the back passenger door at the same time.

'Well, there is a lot of you on display, and you don't want to embarrass Jono, do you?'

329

She peered inside the car.

'Am I embarrassing?'

Jono grinned at her.

'Not embarrassing as such, but the shirt might save a lot of questions, from people wanting to know who you are and whether I'm the father.'

'Fine.'

She got in and slammed the door.

'Hey, be nice to my car.' He wound down the passenger window. 'Bye Gareth, we'll be back in a couple of hours.'

Gareth bent down and waved at them.

'See you later, have a nice time,' he said.

'Jesus, it's no big deal. Can we just get out of here?'

'Only if you stop being so grumpy,' Jono said, but he put the car into drive and pulled away from the still-waving Gareth.

Delilah was quiet on the journey and Jono suspected that she was more nervous than she was letting on. However nervous that was, it couldn't come close to the trepidation he was feeling. When he first made the suggestion, it was a joke, and he should have tried a lot harder to explain that at the time, instead of going along with her crazy scheme. In persuading himself that it couldn't make things worse, he hadn't factored in the wider university audience.

'Is it in a park?' Dee said, as they turned into the wide drive.

'Sort of. The grounds are quite nice, I thought we could have a walk around before we go in. The wheelchair access is good and you can have a fag. There might not even be a good opportunity for you to talk to Trudy, because she needs to be on her own, not with a bunch of mates.'

'But isn't that what we're here for?'

'Well, partly, but we can always come back another day.'

'Whatever.'

She was looking at him in the rear-view mirror, but Jono avoided meeting her eyes. He was starting to feel sick.

'Are you bottling it?' she said.

'No! Not totally, but the time's got to be right. You can't rugby-tackle her in the cafeteria or chase her across the lawn.'

'As if I would. You're being paranoid anyway, I don't even know what she looks like.'

'Ah, of course you don't.'

He wanted to laugh with relief and found a new enthusiasm for the outing. He was still in control, mostly. Dee jumped out and then stuck her head back in.

'If I'm supposed to be your carer, shall I get your chair out and bring it round?'

Jono opened his mouth to decline the offer and then reconsidered. It would be easier than dragging it across his lap and perhaps having another purpose would distract Dee from her main goal.

'Yeah, that'd be cool.'

It took much more effort to coach Delilah through reconstructing the chair than it would have to do it himself, but following instructions was a good precedent to set. They set off to explore the grounds first, but after a few hundred yards, Dee was complaining of her ever-decreasing bladder capacity.

'Unbelievable. I need a piss again, already. What's it gonna be like when I'm seven or eight months gone? I'll have to wear bloody nappies. I'll nip behind this bush, back in a sec.'

'Er, we could just go in, find the loos and then get lunch? We can always come for another walk afterwards.'

'All the way up there? I'll never make it.'

'But...'

She disappeared before he could protest further. Jono didn't dare look up at the terrace above to see if anyone was watching and spun his chair instead, wheeling away to draw attention from the bush. There was a rustling behind him.

'Hang on, I'm not bloody running,' she shouted.

Catching up with him, she took a few steps further, scanning the path ahead.

'Doesn't look like there's much up there and I'm not that bothered about plants. Can we go in and get some food? I'm starving.'

'Fine, we'll turn around.'

It could only be about 11.15, so the cafeteria shouldn't be busy. They walked back to the drive and turned left, heading for the main building. Jono scanned the small groups of students scattered around for any of Trudy's course-mates, but he didn't see anyone familiar and their passing only drew a few curious glances. Once inside, they found a table and Jono gave Dee a tenner to go and buy two coffees.

'If you see anything you fancy food-wise, just grab it. They do paninis and toasties at the coffee bar, and cake of course. I'm not hungry yet.'

Dee looked dubious and shuffled off slowly. He watched her stand back, observing other people buying things for several minutes, before she ventured up to the counter. It was a miracle that she was this socially functional really, considering the small amount of time spent in school and the large amount of time spent with God-knows-who as role models.

He stopped watching as Dee returned, spurning a tray and pressing together two paper cups of scalding liquid, right above her bump, a sandwich tucked under her arm and a flapjack sticking out of the pocket of her shorts. Looking over at the stairs, he saw a group of five people making their way down, two of the girls staring at Dee with real alarm. His breath caught in his throat when he realised that one of them was Trudy.

Dee was almost at the table now and Trudy's eyes moved from her to him, before flicking away. Jono wrenched his eyes away too, reaching out to help balance the cups as Dee put them down.

'Blimey Dee, you've just brought several people, including me, to the edge of cardiac arrest, carrying those like that. You'd be in a mess if you spilled the tiniest bit on your bump you know.'

She just shrugged and tore open the sandwich.

'I didn't though, did I, and you can't arrest people for shit like that, just cos they're pregnant. Pouring water out of a kettle is almost as bad.'

He was still trying to process that, when he became aware of several people, very close by. A large, dark-haired woman leaned across him, with such rude deliberation that she must be one of Trudy's friends.

'Hey lady, I'm all for celebrating womanhood and new life, and you do look amazing, but watching you carry those drinks was really scary,' she said to Dee. 'I don't doubt you'll take care of your baby, but if you'd slipped, or someone bumped into you, there wouldn't *be* a baby. Aren't you kind of young for motherhood anyway?'

Jono couldn't see Dee beyond the interfering cow and was so terrified of her imminent response, he didn't bother trying to locate Trudy.

'Stay cool, Dee,' he called. 'She's only saying what I just said and trying to be helpful, apart from the bit about being young, which you don't have to answer.'

The broad back reared up and away from him, a gigantic bosom presenting itself inches from his face, but Jono was intent on preventing a scene and ignored the woman. He could now see Dee, pale and scowling, two red spots of colour on her cheeks and clenched fists pressed into the table. She glared at him.

'Just tell me this stupid bitch isn't Trudy,' she said. 'Cos I'm not fucking talking to her, even if she is.'

'I don't know who she is and I get why you're mad, but please don't kick off in here. We can leave if you like.'

Dee's mouth screwed up a little tighter. There was a murmuring from the people standing around them, who Jono now looked up at. They were the same five he'd watched coming down the stairs. Four of them walked off in animated discussion, leaving just one girl standing next to their table. She pulled out an empty chair and sat down, angling herself away from him and addressing Dee.

'So, I'm guessing Dee is short for Delilah. I'm Trudy and it sounds like you want to talk to me?'

Dee's eyes widened for a second and then she scowled, going bright red and ducking her head. Jono's throat seized tight. He couldn't speak, even if he did have the faintest idea what to say.

'I'm sorry about my friend,' Trudy said. 'She's one of those Earth Mother types, who wants to look after everybody and fix all their problems, which can be quite annoying if you don't think you have a problem, or don't want it fixing.'

'I haven't got a problem,' Dee said.

'No, I'm not saying you have, in fact, I suspect you're here to try and fix someone else's problem.' Trudy still didn't look at him. 'You were right about that girl in the photo though, she was a complete bitch.'

Dee looked up at that and the two girls grinned at each other. Jono breathed out, happy to be excluded from the conversation, for now.

21

The look on Shona's face was crazy. It was happy and stressed and manic, all at the same time. Maybe she was going mad, like old people did, like her mum was getting.

'Dee! Hi! Wow, lots going on. Er...do you want to come in?'

She wouldn't have knocked on the door if she didn't.

'Doesn't matter, I can go straight round to Mum's, I was just gonna ask how she's doing first. She doesn't really text much any more.'

'No, no no, come in for a minute. Your mum's a bit under the weather right now and there's someone you need to meet.'

Great. She wasn't in the mood for new people. She wasn't in the mood to talk to people she *did* know, which is why she'd gone out in the first place. Jono was on his first date with Trudy, which should be a good thing. It *was* a good thing and she was happy for him, but it still made her feel miserable and lonely.

She started to protest, but Shona took her arm and pulled her inside. The kitchen was rammed with stuff and Dee began to notice that most of it was baby-related, when a girl appeared in the doorway from the front room.

'Hi,' the girl said.

Dee stared at her huge stomach. It probably wasn't that massive, but the girl was so skinny, it looked that way. Looking back at her face, Dee guessed she was about 18 or 19 and then registered that the smile had gone and she was staring back with an almost scared expression. She ought to say something.

'Hi. Are you Paulie's girlfriend?'

'Yeah. I'm Laura. You must be Delilah.'

She spoke with a strong Manchester accent, but was smiling again.

'Yeah, but call me Dee. How far gone are you?'

'Thirty-eight weeks. What about you?'

'Twenty-two weeks. Are you living here now?'

'Um…yeah, for a bit at least. Shona's been fab.'

'Why don't you two go and sit down and I'll be even fabber and bring you both a cup of tea,' Shona said.

'Thanks,' they said together.

Laura turned into the lounge. Dee followed, curious now, and sat down beside her on the settee.

'So it could be any time then…are you scared?' she asked.

Derek and Blink were trying to get her to go to ante-natal classes, but she didn't even want to think about giving birth yet, it just didn't seem possible, not through…eugh…just, not.

'I was, still am a bit, but I'm just so tired, and uncomfortable, and sick of carrying this weight around, I'm actually looking forward to it now. The maternity suite at the hospital is nice. We went to have a look yesterday. Have you been yet?'

'Nah,' Dee shook her head. 'I've not even done any of the ante-natal stuff. Did you go to classes?'

'A few. I felt stupid at first, like they were all judging me cos I was on me own, but they were mostly nice and it was dead useful. You should try it. Isn't your boyfriend interested then?'

'No, and he's a total fucking wanker anyway. I don't want anything to do with him and he isn't coming near the baby, even if he wants to. He might be in prison though, when he gets out of hospital.'

The cold, angry ball was in her chest again and Dee gritted her teeth. She didn't want to talk about shitty fucking bastard Gaz, especially when she wasn't even sure he *was* the father.

'God, that sounds pretty hardcore, but I suppose it was illegal, getting you pregnant in the first place. Yeah, Paulie was a total wanker too, although Shona reckons he's a lot better now. He told me to get rid of it, first off. I haven't been to see him yet…it'd be well shit if I went into labour at the prison. I might take the baby though, in a few months, if he's still into it and if I feel like it. I dunno yet, it's all such a mess.'

The anger vanished as fast as it arrived. Laura wasn't surprised, or freaked out, and her situation wasn't that much different. It was nice talking to someone who wasn't a nurse, or a key-worker, or a social worker, or a policewoman; someone who talked because she wanted to, not because she was being paid to.

'When's Paulie coming out?'

'I dunno that either. He got two years, so the earliest he'll be out is January, but only if he keeps his head down inside.'

Dee opened her mouth and then shut it again. She was only talking to Derek about that yesterday. Josh should have been coming out next week, but now they were keeping him in because he kept getting into fights. No need to tell Laura that though. Shona came in with mugs of tea and a plate of biscuits.

'Well, Paulie's doing ok so far,' she said. 'He even did some exams a few weeks ago and he might be able to do an electrician's course. He says he wants to make everything right, get a job, look after you and the baby when he comes out, but we'll see.'

'Don't you think he will?' Dee said.

'Who knows? What people say, and what people do, are different things. Sometimes it's best not to get your hopes up too high. You and Laura both need to look out for yourselves, then any surprise help will be a bonus.'

Nobody said anything for a minute and Dee thought about Blink, who was still acting like he was the baby's father. He wanted to go to the ante-natal classes with her. She took a biscuit and ate it, without noticing she was dropping crumbs all over the carpet.

'I could come with you, to the next ante-natal class, if I haven't gone into labour,' Laura said.

Dee looked at her, still thinking about Blink and confused by the offer.

'But why, if you've already done them?'

Laura shrugged.

'Just to give you a bit of support, so you don't have to go alone. I know what it feels like and I know what they'll be talking about, so I can explain anything you don't get. Only if you want to though.'

Dee swallowed a part-chewed lump of biscuit. Her stupid eyes went all hot and her throat started hurting. That was one of the other shitty things about being pregnant that no-one told you; it wasn't just always needing a piss, she also cried loads more, and she hated crying.

'Uh…cool, thanks. I'll find out when it is.'

'Wicked. Give me your mobile number then and you can let me know. Even if it doesn't happen, you can still come round and we can moan at each other about stupid men and aching backs.' Laura smiled at Shona while Dee fumbled with her phone. 'I feel a million times better than I did this morning Shona. I've got two whole friends in Derbyshire now, and me and Dee'll be able to go shopping, and go to Mother and Toddlers together and allsorts.'

Dee couldn't believe her ears. Laura wanted to be her friend, a proper girl-friend, and they were in the same boat and everything. She lost her battle with the tears that were now boiling behind her eyes, but Laura just laughed and squeezed her hand.

'Hahaha…and we can sit and cry about fuck all, and then laugh at ourselves too.'

Even Shona was bawling now. It was stupid, but nice at the same time.

Dee had face-ache from grinning on the walk home and wanted to run and jump and shout, even if her legs weren't up for it. Laura was her friend and she could go and practise changing nappies and feeding her baby, before she had to do it for her own. Even the classes and the hospital visit and giving birth weren't so scary now…she knew Laura would tell her everything.

She was still grinning went she walked into Sunny Bank and Sandra gave her a dodgy look when she met her in the hall.

'Hi Dee. You look a lot happier than when you left.'

'Yeah. Where's Blink?'

'In the lounge with Derek. Are you sure you're ok? You haven't been taking anything, have you?'

'Oh fuck off Sandra.'

Dee headed for the lounge.

'Language!' Sandra called after her. 'That wasn't necessary, I...'

Dee shut the lounge door behind her and cut off whatever Sandra was saying. The furniture was shoved aside to make room for Derek and Blink to do press-ups on the floor, although they were both collapsed and sweating. Blink snatched his glasses off the settee and put them on, squinting up at her.

'Delilah! Wh..where've you b..been?'

'Shona's. I met Laura, who's having Paulie's baby. She's moved in with Shona and she's going to come to an ante-natal class with me. She's really nice.'

'That's g..great,' Blink said, but his face went all mardy.

'Well don't look so fucking miserable about it then. She'll only be able to come to one anyway, cos she's nearly due. If I like it, you can come to the rest. It doesn't mean you're my boyfriend though, even if you pretend you are when we're there.' His mouth fell open, making him look proper gormless. 'And only if you promise not to pull stupid faces like that.'

~ ~ ~

Crank seemed chuffed at the prospect of a walk. His wagging tail and excited whine lifted Jim's spirits and gave him the necessary kick up the arse to get moving.

'Alright fella, let's go do it. Just a short one around the village though.'

Bob was out on his veranda and hailed him as he passed.

'Alright Jim? Not a bad bit of sunshine for September, is it? Don't suppose you fancy a game tonight?

He didn't. He wanted to distance himself, prepare for the necessary break, but if it was imminent, then some sort of farewell might ease the wrench.

'Can do. I'll give you a shout when we're back from our walk.'

'I wish I could join you, but my hip's acting up again.'

'Crank's too. Damned age is playing havoc with us all.'

'If you could pick up a cigar on the quiet, I'd much appreciate it. Just a cheapo one'll do.'

Jim smiled and nodded.

'I will. See you later.'

They received several more greetings and waves on their way out of the site. If only these innocent old folk knew what he could bring down on them, at any minute. He headed for the alchie's park and was pleased to find The Indian, alone, stretched out on the bench, basking in the sunshine.

'Is there room for a little un?' Jim said.

The Indian smiled and sat up, without opening his eyes.

'I hear a very large person, but there is always room.'

He swung his legs down and Jim sat beside him, pulling Crank's back end between his knees and massaging the offending hip. The Indian watched, still smiling.

'I almost feel my own aches being soothed away. Ah, for a young Aphrodite to tend me in my ailing years.'

Jim snorted.

'I don't fancy your chances now mate, but I'm sure you've spent a few nights with Aphrodite in your time.'

'She and others. Freya visited for a while and I was truly blessed when Venus bestowed a night of passion upon me. If only Hebe had stayed a little longer...her elixir would bring fire to my heart and eternal blossom to the trees.'

'Well they're all out of elixir at the offee I'm afraid,' Jim said, not wanting to further encourage this flight of fancy. The Indian could be lost to the gods for days at a time. 'Have you seen anything of Dicko? I haven't noticed him around for a few days.'

The beatific smile on The Indian's face vanished. His whole body seemed to wither and contract as the positive energy left him. Jim felt bad for bursting his bubble, but he needed to know.

'He has gone to the Place of the Dying.'

'The hospital? Most folks get fixed up and leave you know.'

'Not he, and not I. It is my darkness, my living hell, the door to Hades. To think, that in this modern world of joy and evil, one can catch a bus to the Underworld.'

Bloody hell. If he hung around here too long, he'd be slitting his own wrists and saving everyone a lot of bother.

'You'll find your own place of dying, mate, I'm quite sure of that. We can steer fate, if we try hard enough.'

The Indian's eyes slid around to meet his and the intensity of his gaze gave Jim a peculiar feeling of transparency.

'You believe that.'

It wasn't a question, but he felt the need to reply.

'I do.'

'You do not lie. Some are powerful enough to take Destiny by the throat and bend her to their will. You are one. But beware...she has teeth.'

Jim was glad he hadn't smoked any pot for a day or two. The edges of reality were blurred around The Indian and it would be easy to get sucked into the vague sanity of his madness.

'I'll be careful, I promise.' He stood up, moving to one side to prevent his shadow falling over The Indian. 'You take care, friend.'

'I wish you great strength in your endeavours. Farewell.'

The Indian's eyes were closed. The goodbye was final. Whether he was a true seer or just a canny old bastard, the warmth Jim felt towards him was genuine. He would like to explore that intricate mind further, but with Dicko out of the way, there was a window of opportunity for one last move. He wasn't aware of any other resident spies, so it could buy him a good few months of anonymity. Tonight would be another silent farewell, which would need masking with good whisky, so his next stop was the offee.

With a bottle of Glenfiddich under his arm, Jim was about to leave the shop, when a thought occurred to him. He turned back to the counter.

'Do you know The Indian, Raju?'

'Indian like me?' Raju said, a bemused smile on his face.

'Sorry, no, Indian like an American Indian. He isn't, but he looks like one. I don't know his name, but he probably comes in here. Long grey hair, parted in the middle, very thin and a bit...well, mad.'

'I know the man you speak of. We call him 'Garuda', the messenger between gods and men.'

'That's him. Can I leave some cash here, to cover his next few shopping bills?'

'Gladly. He will maybe take more than just rice and vegetables, if his purchase is pre-paid.'

Jim left £50 with Raju and on impulse, bought a couple of Cornettos to take with him. He and Crank walked down to the beach, which was a little busier than usual, with people enjoying the last taste of summer. They carried on until the excited shrieks of children were a muted soundtrack to the view and Jim found a spot in the dunes that gave shelter from the gritty wind. He took the Cornettos from his pocket and unwrapped one for Crank.

'Don't think we need to worry about your chops now old pal,' he said. 'Your legs'll pack up before your teeth fall out.'

The ice cream was melted to slop, so he gave Crank the second Cornetto too and rolled a fag for himself. Watching the twists and turns of a dragon kite, he wondered how Shona was getting on with her new lodgers. The last time he'd called, he could barely hear her for the wails of an angry baby in the background, although Shona sounded happy enough to be a grandma.

The sprog might have chilled out in the three weeks since, unless it was trying to deal with a lack of Class A's in its system. He took his phone out and rang her.

'Hello?'

'It's Jim.'

'On another new number. Is it worth me saving this one?'

'Yes, for now. You good to talk?'

'It's perfect timing actually, Laura has just taken Jacob to the park.'

'Isn't he a bit young for the swings?'

'For a walk to the park, in his pram, you daft sod. How are you?'

'Alright. The sun's out here, so me and Crank are sitting in the dunes, eating ice cream. Have things settled at your place?'

'Well, we have a routine, of sorts. I'm still trying to adjust from being a lonely old woman to having a permanent houseful.

Delilah's here most days too. She's thick as thieves with Laura and getting a lot of practice in with Jacob.'

'That's good to hear. I wasn't sure if that bunch of scrotes would play the sympathy card to get her back on board.'

'Not much chance of that. They put a picture of her boyfriend in the paper, she showed it to me. He looks like Freddy Krueger now.'

'Like who?'

'A monster. There was an article about the attacker still being at large, but the following week, they printed another article, saying that an un-named source in the police had confirmed that the 'victim' was exploiting young girls for sex. Without being too direct, they suggested that the attacker was a vigilante hero.'

'Nice.'

'Certainly helpful, and he'll have to move out of the area altogether now. Look I'm sorry Jim, but the phone keeps beeping in my ear, and the only other people likely to call are Paulie and Laura. Can I ring you back?'

'Don't worry, it was only for a chat. We'll catch up again soon.'

'Ok. Thanks Jim. Bye.'

The line went dead. He scrolled through the few contacts on his phone, until he found the number of the farmer he had spoken to a few weeks back. He was a reticent chap, who wasn't interested in Jim, beyond the £50 a week he was prepared to pay for sticking a caravan in a farthest corner of his land. With the delivery approved, he called the caravan dealer he'd visited yesterday. Satisfied to hear the van he most liked was still for sale, he gave instructions to drop it, with a full gas bottle, at the farmer's address tomorrow afternoon, promising the cash would be left at the sales office in the morning.

'We're all set, Crank,' he said, ruffling the dog's neck. 'I'd better go and let Bob beat me at cards and ruin himself on this Glenfiddich, before I tell him we're off.'

He was about to get to his feet, when the roar of several Harleys became audible, getting louder by the second. Jim sank back into the sand.

'On second thoughts, we'll hang out here a bit longer. It's a lovely view.'

Rolling another fag, Jim decided that Dicko's phone had been unanswered one too many times and alarm bells were ringing. It might already be too late, or perhaps they would ask around, discover Dicko's hospital stay was of his own doing, and give it another day or two. Either way, he had to leave tonight.

~ ~ ~

Sandra came in, pulling the office door shut behind her with unnecessary force. Derek saved the report he was writing and looked up.

'Everything ok?'

'Well, it's quiet I suppose, but it does wind me up to see Delilah treating Robert like a slave.'

'Why, what are they up to?'

'She's lying on the settee, watching tv and he's sitting on the floor, giving her a foot massage.'

'Well Dee's nearly eight months pregnant, so she's allowed to lie down, and Blink has been reading up on ways to keep expectant mothers calm and happy. You have to admit, it could be an awful lot worse.'

'That's not the full extent of it, and you know it.'

He sighed. She did have a point.

'She's as straight with Blink as you could hope any 14 year old would be; she doesn't lead him on and I've heard her tell him, more than once, that whatever he's doing won't make her fancy him. You can't expect her not to waver, Sandra, when she's gone from no attention at all, to Blink treating her like a princess.'

'Oh, I know that really, it's just that Robert's worth more than this and he could really make something of himself.'

'Perhaps being a good Dad and keeping Delilah on the straight and narrow is all the fulfilment he needs for now. On the plus side, he'd probably be doing the same thing with someone else, someone less deserving and more manipulative than Dee, if she wasn't around. And you're quite right to call him Robert and I should try harder, he just begs me not to.'

'Hmmn...we should be grateful for small mercies I suppose. Delilah will be 15 in just over a week by the way.'

Derek shook his head. Where had the last year gone? Even the long summer holidays had flown by, at home and at work. Were it not for the week away in Wales, he would hardly have seen any more of his boys than usual, with their endless sleepovers and days out. Delilah had spent every hour possible with Laura and Jacob and in response, Blink had taken up running. It made for an easy life on shift, but there was no satisfaction in it.

Since the start of the new academic year, some degree of normality had returned, but with the progression of Dee's pregnancy there was a variable air of expectancy and dread. Dee refused to acknowledge that the baby might be taken from her if she didn't cope well with motherhood, but Blink was well aware of how closely she would be watched and was bearing that pressure himself.

'It'll get worse you know, once the baby is born,' Sandra said.

She wasn't going to let it drop.

'That depends on your definition of 'worse'.'

'Robert will be the one changing nappies and getting up in the night. The saddest thing is, it won't help her cause, not when the baby's social worker reads through our logs.'

'You're missing quite a major point, Sandra. Blink wants to do this; he's planning to be a father to the child and to share equal responsibility with Dee. If a married couple have a baby then the father is expected to help out, so why should Dee have to do it all alone, when she has a willing partner?'

'With regard to 'wants', Delilah 'wants' to eat chips for every meal and smoke cigarettes all day, but we encourage her not to, because it's not good for her. Robert may 'want' to be a father, but he isn't, and shouldn't have to be at his age. His social worker is very unhappy with Delilah and the baby staying here.'

'Well he's the only one who is and I'm sorry, but I don't have a magic wand to wave and resolve the situation. I've spoken to Blink, on a very personal level, on several occasions. We've talked about how difficult Delilah will be to live with, we've talked about how draining and demanding babies are and we've talked about what a negative impact the situation will have on his employment prospects. I can't control his decisions and I wouldn't want to. All I can do is offer advice and guidance, which I've done to the best of my abilities.' She was managing to wind him up now. He needed to not be sharing a small room with her. 'Talk to him yourself, Sandra, you've got a couple more weeks to change his mind. See if you can make him think logically and not listen to his heart. I'm going to see if they want a drink before bed.'

Derek got up and left the room, without looking at her pouting face. She might mean well, but these kids were heading for the real world, where ideals weren't a feature, never mind achievable. Still, it kept a balance between the staff he supposed. Aware that years of working with young people in care had warped his definition of 'ordinary', Derek made a conscious effort not to let it affect his aspirations for them. That didn't mean he was successful and having Sandra around stopped his expectations sliding too far.

The tv was on in the lounge, but both Dee and Blink were asleep, she still lying on the settee and he sitting at the far end, her feet in his lap and his head flopping forwards. Without the background script, they looked the epitome of sweet innocence. If only they could capture this moment and suspend time, just for a little while. He leaned against the doorway, reluctant to disturb them, watching, smiling, praying to someone or something in his head.

Blink's head drooped again and then jerked up so sharply that he woke in surprise.

'Hey dude,' Derek said in a loud whisper, 'you need to get to bed. You'll wreck your neck if you keep nodding off like that.'

Blink directed a sleepy, half-smile towards him, but was not going to move whilst being allowed to cradle Dee's feet. She stirred too, frowning in her sleep and uttering an irritable moan. Blink stroked the top of her foot and her features smoothed, but a spasm jerked her body and the frown returned, her mouth opening in a grimace of pain.

'Delilah,' Blink said, squeezing her ankle. 'Delilah, w..wake up. Are you a..alright?'

Derek moved into the room as she opened her eyes, her face still contorted.

'Ah...shit...I need a piss, I think, like...half an hour ago...aahh...'

Dee struggled to sit up and hauled on Blink's hand, rolling her legs sideways off the settee. She managed to stand, but doubled up, clutching her stomach.

'Oh fuck. I need the bog, right now. Derek, help me.'

'Ok, no problem,' he said and then shouted Sandra, who would need to take over once they made it to the bathroom. 'Do you want me to pick you up, or will an arm do?'

'Don't...know...'

She clutched his forearm with fingers of steel and Derek swallowed. His own stomach was tightening now and his pulse began to hammer. This seemed like rather more than needing a wee, but it was too early, weeks too early. Sandra appeared in the doorway and Derek heard her gasp, as Dee dug her nails into his arm again.

'Shit, sorry, shit...I've pissed myself. Oh, fucking gross.'

'Delilah, that wasn't urine, that was your waters breaking. Please get back on the settee,' Sandra said, in a tone that brooked no objection. She looked at Derek, her eyes wide, but her mouth a firm line. 'Derek, I'm calling an ambulance, then I'll fetch towels and hot water. It's perfectly natural and we all need to stay calm.'

She disappeared, leaving him far from calm. His job description was broad, but at no point included gynaecology.

'Er, ok guys. Blink, can you take Dee's other arm and we'll lower her onto the settee. Dee, you're doing great, just try to relax and don't push...yet.'

'Push?! You've got be fucking joking. I am so NOT having the baby in here. I'm...aaaahhhh...'

Her face screwed up again, baring gritted teeth. It was only minutes since the last contraction, not even that, maybe just the one minute. Oh, Christ Almighty.

'Dee, that's talking, not relaxing. Getting stressed out won't help. The ambulance will be here any minute and they'll get you to hospital, but only if you lie still and relax.

'Yeah right,' she gasped, letting him ease her back onto the settee. 'I'd like to see you relax, with a baby trying to dive out of your fanny.'

Derek let out a shout of laughter and then got a grip. Hysteria was hovering close and he couldn't afford to lose it now.

'Blink, I'm sorry mate, but you might need to get out of the way pretty soon.'

'No! I want Blink here,' Dee said

Blink squatted down and took her hand, pale, but looking more in control than Derek felt.

'I'm not g..going anyw..where.'

Sandra came in and dropped several towels on the armchair. She threw a flannel to Blink and put a jug of water on the coffee table.

'Bathe her forehead, Robert,' she said and turned to Derek. 'Julie and the ambulance are on their way. Gareth is coming back from the shop right now. They should all be here in minutes, but the operator said we should still prepare. It's lucky we're less than a mile from the hospital, but if the labour continues to progress at this speed, they might not want to move her.'

'Ok. Shouldn't we swap? I'm not too hot with this kind of thing...and I'm a bloke.'

'Soon, I just need to fetch a few more things. You need to time the contractions, see how far apart they are. Do you have a bag packed, Delilah?'

'Yeah,' Dee said between pants, 'Laura made me. It's next to my bed, but I need my phone.'

'Your phone isn't important right now,' Sandra said, and hurried out of the room again.

'It bloody fucking is,' Dee said, heaving herself upright.

'It's f..fine, I'll f..fetch it,' Blink said.

Time froze for a second as she squeezed his hand in thanks, Derek almost felt the pressure in his own hand, then Blink was mobile again, running from the room, his feet hammering up the stairs. Dee flopped backwards and looked up at Derek, giving a gurgle of laughter.

'You look shit-scared,' she said, before her face creased again.

Derek looked at his watch: 22:47.

'Not scared, just nervous. You've got to hold on til the ambulance gets here you know, cos I don't want to deliver this baby. It's not my speciality.'

'Not unless it wants a hot chocolate,' Dee gasped.

The contraction passed and her face relaxed again, but there were beads of sweat on her forehead. Blink returned with the phone and snatched up the flannel.

'Can we s..swap places?' he said.

'Sure.'

Derek moved aside, relief washing over him as he heard Sandra letting the paramedics in. It all happened in a blur from there. Bodies everywhere, a stretcher, terse instructions to get out of the way, louder cries from Delilah. In less than ten minutes they were gone, Sandra riding in the ambulance with Dee, Blink and Derek left in the sudden void.

'We h..have to g..go. I need to b..be there,' Blink said, almost frantic.

'We will, just as soon as Julie gets here. You won't be allowed near her for a while anyway mate. Why don't you call Laura, like Dee asked you to?'

'Y..yeah. I'll d..do that first.'

Derek went to the kitchen and put the kettle on, just for something to do. He didn't know what to think and tried hard not to think of anything, going through the motions of tea-making on automatic pilot until Blink came into the kitchen.

'L..laura's going to the hospital,' he said, sounding even more desperate now. 'It's t..too early, isn't it? She sh..sh..shouldn't be having it y..yet.'

'It is a bit, but I don't think it's too terrible. Some babies are born earlier than this.'

'B..but she's so y..young…and it's her f..first. W..what if something goes wr..wrong?'

'She'll be fine. You heard her, cracking jokes and swearing like a trooper. Nothing's going to go wrong.'

A shiver went down his neck as he said it and he gripped the wooden leg of the table, where Blink couldn't see his hand.

22

The insistent ringing of a phone drew Shona through layers of sleep, until her eyes snapped open. Annoyance and alarm engaged in a brief duel, alarm winning the bout, when she looked at her bedside clock: 23.04. So much for her early night. Who was calling Laura at this time and why wasn't she answering? Footsteps ran across the landing, from the bathroom to Paulie's old room. With one question answered, Shona lay back on her pillow, listening to Laura's muffled voice, which grew suddenly loud, an excited squeal urging Shona to sit up again. Delilah.

She threw off the covers and grabbed her dressing gown, opening the bedroom door to find Laura on the other side, about to knock.

'Dee's gone into labour!' the girl said, beaming at her.

'Oh Lord, that's not so great, is it? I thought she was six weeks off!'

'Yeah, but thirty-eight weeks is as good as forty, and she wasn't dead sure of the time anyway. It's probably only a week or two premature. I've got to get to the hospital.'

'Is Jacob asleep?'

'Nah, he wouldn't settle. I've just fed him and changed his nappy, so I'll take him with me.'

'Well give me five minutes and we'll all go, then I can bring Jacob home if he gets grizzly. You call a taxi and I'll get dressed.'

Pulling on the clothes she'd not long taken off, Shona wondered whether to ring Kelly, but decided against it. Whether she was conscious or not, Kelly would slow everything down and be no help whatsoever. Vodka was still a higher priority than her daughter.

She ran downstairs, checked there was enough money in her purse, shoved that and the baby clothes she'd bought into a bag and started lacing her boots.

Laura appeared carrying Jacob, a bulging rucksack slung over her shoulder.

'Me and Dee packed our hospital bags last week. Good timing, eh? Taxi'll be here in five minutes.'

'Smashing love, well done.'

Although Laura was young, ditzy and woefully uneducated in certain areas, Shona was impressed by her practical skills and obvious experience in dealing with babies. There were some small advantages to being born eldest in a large family, with a needy, incapable mother.

'It were that Blink who rang me,' she said. 'He's got a terrible stutter, but he sounds really sweet. I reckon there'll be quite a party at the hospital.'

'They might not let us see Dee 'til she's had the baby, so be prepared for a long wait.'

Laura rolled her eyes and lifted the rucksack with a shrug.

'What do you think this is? I've spent plenty of time hanging around hospitals.'

The sound of a car pulling up outside ended the conversation. Laura shot out, Shona pausing only to lock the door. She noted on the way down the path that there was still a light on at Kelly's and felt a pang of guilt. Once in the taxi, she took out her mobile and rang Kelly's number. She was preparing a message in her head, when it was answered on the last ring.

''Lo?'

'Kelly, it's Shona. I thought you should know, Dee's gone into labour. Laura and I are on our way to the hospital.'

There was a long pause.

'Dee? D'lilah?'

'Yes Kelly, your daughter. She's having a baby.'

Another long pause.

'Baby? She can't be avin' a f'ckin baby, she's jus' a baby.'

Oh, dear God. How did you forget something like that?

352

'Well she is Kelly, and you did know about it. I'll call again when there's any news.'

She put the phone back in her bag and shook her head.

'We'll just tell Dee that her mum's asleep, eh?' Laura said. 'She'll remember in the morning.'

Shona nodded and patted her knee, unable to speak. They were at the hospital in fifteen minutes and the taxi dropped them off right outside the main entrance. It wasn't long since the two of them had made the same journey for Jacob's arrival and they went straight to the maternity ward reception desk.

'We're here for Delilah McClafferty,' Laura said, shifting Jacob to her other hip and kissing his forehead, as he screwed his eyes up against the bright lights.

The nurse checked her computer with a frown and then smiled at them.

'She's just arrived. We're expecting her at any moment. You two must have been quick off the mark!'

'Had to be,' Laura said. 'She wants me in with her.'

'We'll see how she's doing. I believe it's a little earlier than expected, so we'll need to make sure there are no complications. If you take a seat, I'll keep you updated.'

'Alright, thanks.'

Shona followed Laura over to a corner filled with toys, feeling a little redundant. Laura dumped her bag and dropped to the floor, managing to engage a fretful Jacob with a large teddy bear within seconds. Shona watched, smiling, hoping Paulie would prove as interested in his son as he claimed. They would be meeting for the first time next week, assuming the visit went ahead.

A small commotion down the corridor made them both stand up, but the nurse behind reception raised a hand.

'The doctor's going in now to make an assessment. We'll know more in just a few minutes, so please be patient.'

'Huh. They'd let me in if I was her fella,' Laura grumbled, but she sat back down.

'I might grab a couple of coffees, while we have the chance,' Shona said.

353

The second cup was still filling when the nice black guy from Sunny Bank walked in, followed by a tall, well-muscled white lad, with blond hair and glasses.

'Hey Shona,' Derek said. 'You beat us to it. Any news yet?'

'I'm afraid not. They're doing an assessment now. I take it you two have had quite a stressful evening?'

She smiled at the young man, waiting for an introduction.

'It was a pretty short burst of excitement really…Dee went from being asleep on the settee, to having regular contractions, within a couple of minutes. This is Robert, by the way.'

Shona held out her hand.

'Pleased to meet you, Robert,' she said, noting a burst of rapid blinks behind the glasses. 'You wouldn't be the chap Dee's always banging on about would you? She calls him Blink.'

'That's m..me,' he said, a grin lighting up his face. 'I p..prefer Blink to R..robert. Does Delilah r..really talk about m..me?'

'Oh yes, and it's all complimentary…in a Delilah kind of way. Come and meet Laura.' She led them to the corner, taking in Laura's quizzical expression and hoping she wasn't going to drop Dee in it. 'Laura, this is Derek, Dee's key-worker and this is Blink.'

Laura stood up, holding Jacob in her arms, her forehead creased, but her lips curving upwards.

'*You're* Blink?' she said, ignoring Derek for the moment.

'Y..yeah, I s..spoke to you on the ph..phone.'

'Right, yeah, nice one for calling me. Pleased to meet you at last. I wasn't expecting…well…'

Shona was about to interrupt, but Derek beat her to it.

'Thanks for getting Dee to pack a bag Laura, it made things a lot smoother.'

She dragged her eyes away from Blink and smiled at him.

'No worries. I've just been through it all with this little man, so I knew what was coming. This is Jacob.'

Derek took a pudgy hand between his fingers and was about to say something, when the reception nurse called out to them.

'Delilah is doing well and a natural birth is still planned. She's asking for Laura and Shona, if that's you two?'

Shona wasn't expecting to be on hand-holding duty. The recent and traumatic arrival of Jacob was more than enough experience of young girls in childbirth to last a lifetime.

'What about Jacob?' she said, but Laura grinned back at her.

'These guys aren't going anywhere and Blink's been doing all the ante-natal classes. Do you mind?' she said, passing Jacob to Blink, who took him from her with open-mouthed astonishment. 'There's a bottle in the bag and a towel if he gets sicky. His nappy should be fine for a bit, but I'll pop back as soon as I can.'

Shona glanced at Blink, holding Jacob like a ticking bomb and Derek, who looked half amused, half horrified. Oh well, they couldn't go too far wrong in a maternity ward and there was no other option. She followed Laura down the corridor before either of them could protest.

Dee looked pale and exhausted, her hair plastered to her head with sweat, but she managed half a smile as they approached the bed. A woman Shona recognised as also from Sunny Bank stood up, squeezed Dee's shoulder, wished her luck and left the room.

'Where's Jacob?' Dee asked.

'I've left him with Blink,' Laura said, 'who is WELL fit! You said he was a geeky nerd!'

'He is.'

Dee wheezed and her face creased in pain. A midwife stepped forward and took her shoulder.

'You're fully dilated Delilah and things seem to be progressing quite quickly. It's a while since your waters broke, so you need to start pushing now.'

Laura grabbed her hand.

'Squeeze as hard as you like mate, it doesn't matter if you break my fingers, I can get em sorted out straight away in here.'

Dee clenched her teeth, her body tensing as she let out a long moan, pushing hard. The midwife stepped back and indicated that Shona should take her place. Her proffered hand was snatched up.

'Stop pushing when the contraction ends,' the midwife said. 'Take some good deep breaths and there's gas and air here if you need it.'

355

Dee slumped back into her pillow and said 'gas' in a faint voice. The midwife passed her a mask and she drew on it a few times, then let her hand fall back onto the sheet.

'I can't do this, it's too hard.'

Laura laughed, still holding Dee's other hand.

'It's not like you've got a choice. I felt like that too, but you *can* do it and Jacob's new best friend will be out and in your arms before you know it. Anyway, back to Blink.'

'He's not fit,' Dee said, sounding a little more like her usual self.

'He bloody well is. It's only his glasses that make him look geeky, but he's got a right nice bod.'

Another contraction wracked Dee's body and she cried out this time, a raw sound that ripped at Shona's chest. She felt so helpless, trying hard to fight back tears and think of something encouraging to say. She was amazed when Laura resumed the conversation, as if nothing had happened.

'He's like Clark Kent, you know, Superman, who looks all straight but is an amazing bloke underneath. He was probably a right ugly kid, but I'm telling you, he's gonna be gorgeous in a couple of years.'

'Bullshit,' Dee said.

Shona looked at the midwife, expecting a frown of disapproval, but she was smiling as she wrote something on the board at the end of the bed. The pattern of violent contractions, alternating with inane debate over how attractive Blink was, continued for over ninety minutes. The only change was when Dee's moans progressed to howls and then screams of pain.

Laura did not let up the stream of banter for a second, but Shona was exhausted and struggling to stand. At the end of the next contraction she suggested she go to check on Jacob.

'Go and sit down for a bit, you look knackered,' Laura said. 'You can send Blink in instead.'

Shona raised her eyebrows and looked at Dee, who just gave a weak nod. She found Sandra and Blink still in the kid's corner. Blink was sitting on the floor, Jacob fast asleep on his lap. Sandra was looking on, displeasure written across her face and she got up to meet Shona half way across the waiting room.

'This is outrageous,' she said in a loud whisper. 'That girl can't dump her baby on Robert like that, she should have sorted out some alternative care.'

Shona was too drained to think of an appropriate response, so she just pushed past Sandra and carried on towards the corner.

'Seems like you've been doing a fine job,' she said to Blink, who looked up with a tear-streaked face.

'H..h..how's Delilah? I h..heard her s..s..screaming.'

'She's ok, nearly there now. I've come to take Jacob so you can go and be with her for the final push.'

'I hardly think…' Sandra started to say, but Derek came up and put a hand on her shoulder, his other hand clasping a phone to his ear.

'If it's what Blink wants and what Delilah wants too, then I can't see a problem. Are you ok with Blink seeing the birth Julie?' he directed the question down the mouthpiece. 'Great. The boss says yes, Sandra.'

Blink stood up, still holding Jacob, fresh tears pouring down his face.

'Does she r..really w..want m..me in there?' he said, his face alive with hope.

'Oh sweetheart,' Shona took the sleeping baby from him and patted his cheek with one hand. 'You've been the only subject of conversation in there, with those two bickering about how 'fit' you are between every contraction, so don't worry if the midwife gives you funny looks.'

For a second Blink stared at her, his mouth hanging open, then he gave a strangled shout and shot off down the corridor.

'You sit down and I'll get you a drink. Tea or coffee?' Derek said.

'Coffee please.'

Shona smiled her thanks and sank into a chair, cradling Jacob. She ought to get him home to bed, but he might not settle without his mum and Dee was so close. She watched Derek returning with the drinks, trying to block out the muted screams when they started again. Sandra got up and began pacing, not as cool and collected as she made out. The screams rose to a crescendo that made them all freeze, before they were cut off abruptly.

They waited in agonized silence for long minutes. It was Laura who appeared, with shining eyes, to break the news.

'James Andrew McClafferty has just weighed in at five pounds and two ounces. He's healthy and has a fine pair of lungs on him.' She came over and kissed her sleeping son, without trying to take him from Shona. 'Are you ok for another ten minutes?'

'Absolutely. How's Dee?'

'Knackered and a bit torn up down there, but happy she popped him out so fast...she knew I was in for a whole day. She's blown away by her baby and has a strong pair of arms around her.'

She winked and gave Shona a wicked grin, before returning to her friend's side.

~ ~ ~

Lying in bed on Sunday morning, Jono smiled at the ceiling, his belly still full of pizza from the night before. Trudy was out surveying plants, on an inaccessible hillside in the White Peak, but he was confident that next Sunday she would be here, next to him, filling his senses with her soft, sweet-smelling warmth. They'd been through the tears, confessions and admissions of insecurities, on both sides. Last night had marked a return to the easy conversation of the early days, the excitement over how many interests they shared, the thrill of mounting trust.

There was a bizarre level of coincidence in their journey to this point. Trudy had chanced upon one of his basketball matches whilst waiting to meet a friend at Sheffield Uni, enjoying it enough to become a regular supporter. She'd signed up to the quirky, low-key chat-room just days after him, and spotted his profile picture within minutes. His enrolment at the same university as her should have been the final nudge and Jono cringed inwardly, for the hundredth time, at the thought of how obtuse he'd been. Still, things seemed to be back on course now.

He was remembering the gentle kiss with which they'd parted, when the phone on his bedside table pinged. Thinking it might be

Trudy he snatched it up, but found instead a text from Dee, asking if he'd like to visit Sunny Bank to meet Jamie this afternoon. Jono still found it difficult to imagine Dee, the angry kid, with a baby of her own and was hoping to garner Trudy's support for his initial visit to Dee, the mother.

He spent several minutes composing his response. He hadn't mentioned it to Trudy yet, but he thought she'd go for it…if she was free. If she wasn't, he would have to go and see Dee anyway.

Hey D. Glad to hear you're up for visitors ☺ I was actually thinking of coming over on Thursday, for your birthday…unless you're going out? J.

Her reply was several minutes in coming, by which time he was up and dressed, with the kettle on.

Thats cool. Going anywere is a nitemare now so will b here. Dx

She wasn't embracing the joys of motherhood then. Or maybe she was and the grumpiness was her trying not to smoke. One could hope. Jono wondered how Blink was faring and realised that he was rather looking forward to seeing him again. There was no official declaration yet, but, according to the first few garbled texts on the morning Jamie was born, Blink had been at the birth. If he and Dee became an item, Jono would be much more confident about the future prospects of mother and baby.

He spent over an hour trying to find suitable presents online. There was a vast array of cool baby gear and he spent a stupid amount on a teddy bear suit with paws for feet, but Dee's birthday gift should be something not baby-related. In the end, he opted for a basic e-reader, with a £10 voucher to cover her first few books and a daft chocolate machine, which dispensed mini Dairy Milks. That would do. He was about to log off, when his chat icon flashed.

Ugh. Walked 4 miles and STILL full of pizza! I think you might be bad for my health… Having a nice, lazy morning? ;) x

Ha. He'd rather be out in the hills with her.

No. It's been very productive, although I can't say I saw the sun rise. Pleased it's stayed dry for you, but I bet it's freezing

up there. Fancy coming to see Dee and her baby with me on Thursday evening? X

Oh pleeeease say yes.

Freezing? I'm roasting! It's a hard climb. Yes, I'm up for Thursday. I like Delilah and I might have a few things to thank her for. Going to be out of signal for the next hour or so. Call you later. xx

He couldn't wait. He really, couldn't wait to speak to her. And he'd never felt like this about any of his former girlfriends, even the very first one. Deciding to spend the afternoon catching up on his coursework, Jono realised that it wasn't just a general lift in positivity, but a hope for the future. His goal-posts had shifted.

Trudy drove over Thursday afternoon and wandered around the flat while he made tea.

'You know, I like the lack of doors,' she said. 'It's so open and airy, it feels more like a cave than a house. I've always wanted to live in a cave.'

'Really? Tallow candles, drafts and all?'

'Eugh, no, not tallow. The drafts I can work around.'

He smiled. Trudy was a vegetarian, which didn't seem to be a problem, yet. She hadn't tried to lecture him over his pepperoni pizza anyway.

'We could compromise on a log cabin,' he said, wanting to feed this fantasy of a shared home.

'That would be equally awesome. In fact, a log cabin does feature in my long-term dream.'

'Which is?'

'Running a plant nursery, selling all the usual stock, but also specialising in herbs and preserving rare species. If it's open to the public, you need on-site toilets and an office, then it's only a small step to living quarters. If we built out of wood, we wouldn't even need full planning consent. It's the only way I can imagine affording a house, but I like the idea on its own merits too.'

'Sounds pretty cool,' he said, though he could see several flaws from his own perspective.

She had collapsed onto the bean-bag, so he took the drinks over to the coffee table and looked down at her, eyes shut, a broad smile lifting her cheeks. Hearing the clank of cups, she sat up and looked straight at him, the smile shrinking to a small, tentative lift of the lips.

'It would be, and I don't want to freak you out, but I have, you know, thought it all through. It would be totally possible.'

His heart began to beat a little faster.

'With me and the chair, you mean.'

She nodded and then tore her eyes away.

'But it's way too heavy yet, I know.' She picked up one of the mugs and took a big sip, which must have burnt her mouth. 'So what time have we got be there?'

'Uh...' he fought to readjust his thoughts. 'Half an hour-ish. We'll drink these and go, eh?'

'Fine. Do you want to go in your car or mine? My boot's empty, so I can put your chair in the back, otherwise, I'll have to move it. I'm afraid I've blocked you in.'

He smiled, touched by her nervousness at having said too much.

'We'll go in yours, and I like you thinking things through.'

'That's really good news,' she said, her pink cheeks turning a shade darker.

Jono was prepared for a good hour of awkwardness on their arrival, but Trudy's immediate delight in Jamie seemed to bypass all barriers. There was another girl there called Laura, also with a baby, and the women went into a cooing huddle on the settee, Trudy happily ensconced in the middle. A haggard-looking Blink seemed pleased to get Jono to himself for a while.

'You've not been doing the night shift with the little un have you?' Jono said.

'N..not really, Delilah's t..trying to b..breast-feed, but when he c..cries, I'm aw..wake instantly. I..instinct I sup..pose.'

'I dunno about that. I doubt I'd wake up if he was screaming next to my head. Once I'm asleep, I'm out like a light.'

'I b..bet you w..would, if it was y..yours.'

Jono had been trying to dismiss thoughts on that theme since Trudy first picked up Jamie.

'So how're the A-levels going?

'Er...w..well, I was ahead b..before, so not too b..bad. W..we're very b..busy with J..jamie though and n..now there's the Ch..christening to or..organise.'

'Christening?'

Jono said it loud enough to include Dee in the question and she looked over at him.

'Yeah, probably, we've been talking about it anyway.'

'But I've never heard you mention religion, in any context whatsoever,' Jono said, dubious as to the motives behind it.

'M..me and Delilah don't even kn..know if we w..were Christened,' Blink said. 'B..but it can't hurt and w..we want to give Jamie the b.best start p..possible.'

'Fair play.'

That sounded quite reasonable.

'And that includes not letting any opportunity for presents pass him by,' Laura said. 'We're gonna have a joint Christening for Jacob and Jamie.'

Which made a lot more sense. He looked at Trudy, whose rolling expressions forced him to stifle a smile.

'What about the part where you agree to bring the child up as a Christian?' she asked. 'I think you'd have to convince the vicar that you at least know what that means. You might even have to attend Church for a while.'

Laura shrugged.

'Free wine on tap though, isn't there. Can't be that boring.'

Her light tone and complete frankness took the sting out of the statement. Jono was no believer, but found such a spectacular lack of respect rather at odds with the intention. He wanted to disapprove of Dee's close friendship with Laura, but couldn't help liking the girl.

'Talking of presents, don't you want yours?' he said to Dee. 'We brought one for Jamie too.'

He pulled the parcel with the baby suit from his bag.

'You open it,' she said to Blink.

Jono was gratified by Blink's excitement.

'Wow! I l..looked at this, b..but it was r..really expensive. Th..thanks Jono.'

He held out his hand, which Jono shook with slow deliberation. He really was a cracking lad. He pulled two more parcels and a card from the bag.

'These are yours,' he said, lobbing them over to Dee's end of the settee.

She opened the card first, reading each word with care before turning the voucher around in her hand.

'What's this for?'

'Open your presents and you'll see.'

She opened the chocolate machine first and he was pleased to see a return of her happy grin. She was less sure about the e-reader.

'Thanks, but you already bought me a tablet.'

'Oh cool!' Laura said. 'That's not a tablet; it's for books, so you can download them instead of carrying them around. I've wanted one for ages. And you'll be able to buy a few with that voucher.'

Jono started to revise his opinion of her influence over Dee, until she suggested downloading 50 Shades of Grey. He was grateful for Blink's simultaneous squawk of protest. There followed a debate about suitable books, which made his head spin. Trudy only laughed once, managing to adjust her mind-set swiftly. He was impressed with her handling of the odd situation and very relieved that she was prepared to make the effort.

All in all, it was a pleasant and entertaining visit and they only left when one of the Sunny Bank staff pointed out that it was an hour past Jamie's usual bath time.

'That was a very different evening, but I enjoyed it,' Trudy said on the way home. 'They're kind of 'old kids' aren't they, who know too much about some things and not enough about others.'

'And then some. You wouldn't believe how much Dee has changed since she moved in there. She was barely literate, but Blink got her into reading when she was laid up with a broken ankle.'

'He seems lovely.'

'He is, it's just a shame Dee doesn't think so.'

'I thought they were a couple? Isn't it his baby?'

'No, but that's a very long story.'

He didn't want to spend the rest of the night talking about Dee. There was something more important stamped across his mind right now and it would be an easier conversation to have side by side in the car, than face to face at home.

'You looked like a natural with Jamie. Do you want kids of your own?'

She didn't reply for several, long seconds and Jono was glad he wasn't driving.

'I suppose I can't get away with saying I haven't thought about it,' she said, leaving another pause. 'Yes, I've always imagined having kids, someday, but it's not a desperate urge. Without knowing where you broke your back, I couldn't look that up, but I know it's not straightforward.'

It didn't feel like the right time for a full explanation, but he'd started the conversation, so he shouldn't make her ask.

'Ok, well, I broke my back at T12. It's not quite a complete break, but as good as. I can't usually get a natural erection, but I have found ways around that in terms of sex. According to the consultant I'll still produce sperm, but I've only ejaculated twice since the accident and like me, they're healthy enough, but not strong swimmers. I should be able to father children, but I'd probably need a bit of medical assistance.'

She didn't say anything, but reached across the gear stick and laid a hand on his thigh. Jono couldn't feel the fingers, but seeing them there sent a tingle up the back of his neck. He laid his hand lightly over hers and was awed by the response in his chest to just that minimal contact. It was magic.

'Um...that's lovely, but I'm going to have to move my hand before I drive off the road,' she said, pink but laughing.

He let go and grinned.

'Alright, but only if you promise to put it right back when we stop.'

'I'd be quite happy to leave it there all night, just not when I'm steering a ton of steel.'

All night. She said *all* night.
'So you'll stay then?'
'Yes.'
Jono had to work hard not to yell with delight.

~ ~ ~

The fourth cup of coffee did the trick. Lucy was still grizzling, but Becky was now at a level of consciousness that meant she could operate the shower. And she was a master of the two-minute rinse. She took Lucy from the high chair and put her in the carry-cot.

'Are you going to come to the bathroom with Mummy? The steam might clear a bit of that snot.' Lucy screwed up her face and wailed. 'Yes, if you're feeling half as crap as I am on so little sleep, I'm not surprised you're grumpy.'

The blast of hot water cleared her head sufficiently to allow full recall of yesterday's Sunday dinner with the in-laws. It wasn't a mood-boosting memory, although the fresh indignation did result in a spike of energy. Given her time again, Becky would introduce strict vetting procedures for the parents of prospective suitors. Simon was living up to every one of his promises, but good God, his mother was horrific.

'They're pompous asses, Luce,' she said, sticking her head around the shower curtain. 'I bet you don't want dunking in a stone font, by some vicar in fusty old robes, do you?'

It wasn't the idea of a Christening that offended her so much, as the outrage she faced after admitting it wasn't a consideration. She and Simon hadn't been into a church since their wedding and his parents weren't regular attenders. It wasn't a moral issue, or even anything to do with religion, it was about his mother being able to spout about it at her bloody coffee mornings. She towelled off and dressed for a walk.

'We're going to be good, domesticated ladies and go and post those Christmas cards we wrote last night Lucy, a good ten days earlier than we've ever posted cards before. It might be cold, but the sun is shining and in that snuggly pram, you might even sleep for another hour. What do you think?'

The gurgle was a more enthusiastic response than the previous wailing. Becky was surprised by her own patience - thus far - with the incoherent demands of a new baby, but then her whole focus was on doing this well and it was a full-time occupation. On the occasions when she considered her return to work, she was not so blasé.

Less than a hundred yards from the house, her phone started ringing. Seeing it was Simon, Becky hesitated before answering. He hadn't tried to rebuke her for the anti-religious rant at the dinner table, but was very quiet on the way home and through the rest of the evening. She hoped he wasn't going to ask her to apologise.

'Hello.'

'Hi Sweetheart. What are you up to?'

The endearment boded well.

'We're just out for a little walk. Lucy isn't settling and I'm hoping a stint in the pushchair will either distract her or send her to sleep. How's your day going?'

'Steady, thank God, I'm shattered. And if I'm shattered, you must be completely worn out. I was just calling to say don't worry about tea, or not for us anyway, I'll get us a takeaway.'

'Oh that's lovely, thank you.'

She felt bad now. The days of subtle sarcasm and snide comments were long gone, his thoughtfulness and consideration so consistent since Lucy's birth, that Becky could not think how or why she had ever questioned their relationship.

'You're not actually going to post those Christmas cards, are you?' he said.

'Ha! Yes I am. This new leaf of mine is going to grow into a sturdy branch, I'm telling you.'

'I'm starting to believe you. Hey, I've got to go. Take it steady and I'll see you in a few hours.'

'Ok my love, thanks for calling.'

If he kept this up, she might be persuaded to try for a second child after all. Becky smiled as she put the phone away and then looked up, startled to see how far she'd walked without noticing.

366

The church spire towered above the houses ahead, a beacon of gentle admonishment, challenging her blasphemy of yesterday. The smile broadened into a grin, as she acknowledged that some perversities of her nature still ran unchecked. Perhaps she would call in and, if anyone was about, ask a few questions about the possibility of arranging a Christening.

The big doors were propped open, despite the cold, so Becky wandered inside. There was no service underway, just three ladies wrestling with a vast flower arrangement at the far end of the church. They turned around when Lucy made one of her random noises of interest and Becky was surprised to see that the one in jeans was also wearing a dog collar. Not an old man in fusty robes then.

'Hello,' the be-jeaned lady vicar said, walking down the aisle towards them. 'Can I help you, or are you after a little peace and quiet?'

The woman's smile was so warm and welcoming, Becky found her shoulders dropping.

'That would be nice, but there's not much chance with this one in tow. I was actually wondering how I'd go about booking a Christening.'

'Well, there are a few things we would need to discuss, but before I go into any of that I'll fetch the diary. There's been quite a flurry of Christenings recently and I don't want to bore you with details if we don't have a suitable date. I'll be back in a second.'

Becky looked around as she waited, admiring several further flower arrangements and a display of photos from a twinned Church in Kenya. Continuing her rotation, she found herself face to face with an image of Jesus on the cross and the bubble of tranquillity ruptured. Amongst her many doubts, she'd always found the repetition of that image contrary to the bit about not worshipping an idol. Plus which, she was quite sure that Jesus would not have wished to be remembered in that way.

'Here we are,' the vicar said, returning with a large book. 'When were you thinking of?'

'Um...February,' she said, regretting the visit already.

Resting the book on a nearby table, the vicar began leafing through the pages. Becky leaned in to feign polite interest.

'Right, here we are. We only perform Christenings on the first Sunday of the month and it looks like we already have two in February, although three isn't a problem, if you don't mind sharing the ceremony.'

Incapable of replying, Becky continued to stare at the name 'McClafferty, James Andrew', printed across the page in front of her. That could not be a coincidental muster. But...really?

'You don't have to decide now. Go home, discuss it with your family and pop back sometime in the next week. We can have a longer chat then.'

'I'm sorry, I think I already have my answer. This James McClafferty...is his mother very young?'

The vicar eyed her warily, but seemed to find reassurance in whatever she saw.

'Yes, very, and her friend, the mother of the other child, does not appear to be too much older. They were honest though, and keen enough to agree to the various conditions.'

'As in, they'll be attending a few services?'

'Yes, amongst other things.'

'Gosh. Well, I've had some professional involvement with that young lady, so I'm afraid it wouldn't be appropriate for me to socialise with her on a personal level, but I'm pleased that she's been to see you.'

The vicar's eyes narrowed, but the suspicion had a mischievous edge.

'Is there anything I should be aware of?'

An endless list of things.

'Er...I'm extremely limited in what I can say, but Ms McClafferty is not familiar with mainstream family values, her language may not be decorous and she will have little idea of how to conduct herself in church. However, she is honest, straight-talking and won't be eying up the collection plate.'

'It sounds like she's lacking in role models and not moral fortitude, so I think we should be able to handle the odd slip of the tongue. Thank you for the forewarning though, and I will make allowances for whatever you weren't able to disclose.'

They shook hands and Becky found the eye-meet intense, but not intimidating. Whatever her beliefs, this was a good woman, who tried to do good things. She couldn't help smiling on the way home though, as she imagined Delilah trying to sit through a church service. Perhaps this new friend was a born again angel, gathering the vulnerable into the arms of the Church, but Becky thought it more likely that she was encouraging Delilah to take advantage of an authority-funded party.

Good on them and hurrah for Delilah having a proper, girly friend. The smiles turned into giggles, as Becky imagined the congregation in uproar over a whole host of potential scenarios involving Dee's mouth. She was laughing so much, that she walked straight past the post box without seeing it.

~ ~ ~

Already in a bad mood, McGrath was gutted to see Delilah leaving through the main doors of the station. He'd been confident that with those scum-bags out of the way and a baby to look after, she wouldn't have the time, opportunity, or inclination to get into any further trouble. How could one teenager have such an impact on his working life? The cause of his current ill temper was the refusal of his senior officer, that morning, to let him reclassify the case regarding the assaults on Gascoine & Co as unsolved.

Having popped out to buy a sandwich, he was going to return by the back door, but changed course to stop by the main desk. The reason for Delilah's presence would irritate him all afternoon otherwise. It was the 22nd of December - she should be Christmas shopping, not answering bail, or whatever she was doing. The duty clerk looked up in surprise as he pushed through the heavy glass doors.

'Sir! There's a letter here for you. It's just been dropped off by a young girl. Does it need processing?'

'No, it's fine, thank you. I saw her leaving. I know the girl and have no concerns about potential content. I can call her social worker direct if it contains anything of import.'

McGrath opened the letter on his way up the stairs and stopped dead in his tracks. He was invited to the Christening of James Andrew McClafferty, in early February. Andrew! Of course, she might know another Andrew who was important to her, although there wasn't one in her list of known family and associates. Either way, he couldn't accept the invitation, but the gesture went a long way towards restoring his happiness.

Almost at the top of the stairs he stopped again, as another thought dropped heavily into place. If he was invited to the Christening, then Jim would be too. Jim Travis, who was still at the top of his list - if not the official list - of main suspects in the Gascoine case. Perhaps he would be able to attend the Christening after all, in an unofficially official capacity.

23

Used to being alone and never bothering much with Christmas or the New Year, Jim found enforced solitude a different kettle of fish. The lack of drunken idiots was a bonus and all the commercial bollocks drove him crazy, but here there was nothing and nobody to avoid. He picked up his phone, registered that it was now 00:07 on the 1st of January and took a slug of whisky.

'Happy New Year, old fella,' he said to Crank, who opened his eyes and thumped his tail, once.

He could ring Shona and wish her a Happy New Year, though when he'd called at Christmas, there'd been too much shrieking and whooping in the background to have much of a conversation. Her house was full of young folk again, but of that he wasn't envious, just pleased that now Delilah had a friend and Shona a purpose. As long as that weasel Paulie didn't get out early and ruin everything.

Was that really a whole year ago? Refilling his glass, Jim mused over whether the confusion of old people was due to the phenomenon of variable time-lapse. If it got to this dizzying pace in middle age, then it must be like existing in a constant whirlwind in your eighties. Unless you reached the eye of the storm and found peace and stillness, but that would have a lot to do with circumstances. His soul would be staked out where the vortex was at its wildest, regardless.

'Oh cheer up, you maudlin twat,' he said aloud, the tone causing Crank to lift his head. Jim grinned at him. 'I'm glad you're listening mate, cos otherwise, I'd be talking to myself and that's not a good sign.'

He looked at his phone again: 00:21. If he was going to call Shona it ought to be soon, before she went to bed and he got any more pissed. He wasn't much in the mood for conversation, but a human voice would be good to hear. He hit dial, but regretted it when Shona's 'hello' morphed into a huge yawn.

'Oh shit, you weren't asleep were you?'

'No, no, don't worry. Jacob's teething, so sleep is a rare luxury at the moment. But hey, Happy New Year, Jim.'

'And to you. It sounds quiet. No party at yours tonight?'

'No, Laura's gone over to Sunny Bank and I volunteered to baby-sit. Two parties in a week is a bit much for me these days. I'm not convinced I want to celebrate another year passing me by anyway.'

'I was just thinking something similar. The clock seems to tick a lot faster now.'

'It does, but at least it means Paulie will be able to apply for parole soon. I think he and Laura are planning to make a go of it.'

'Right. That's good news, I suppose.'

With a mountain of support from Shona of course. Sly little bastard.

'It is, but don't worry, Jim, I know prisons don't work miracles or perform personality transplants. I'll be careful and try to be strong, I promise.'

'You'd better. Was Dee ok about the god-father thing? I'm still made up about it, but there's just no way...'

'She was fine. You were first choice, but there was another candidate hot on your tail.'

'As long as it's not McGrath.'

'Ha! No, I think you'll be pleasantly surprised...assuming you're still coming?'

'Yeah. Churches aren't my favourite places, but the kid's come a long way and I'd like to support her. Can I come to yours first? I don't want to leave Crank here all day.'

'Of course. Look, I'm going to have to go, Laura's just come back. I'll see you in a month and we'll talk before then anyway. Thanks for calling!'

'Good to talk to you. Take care, Shona.'

The glass was empty again, so he filled it. If he was going to show his face back in the old territory, he might as well sort a few bits of business out too. He could stay over at Shona's and leave Crank with her, while he went into Nottingham on the Monday. Assuming the solicitor he had in mind was still in business. Digging out an old envelope and a pen, he started to make notes on the several plans now forming in his head.

~ ~ ~

Shona was impressed with Laura keeping her word and doing the lion's share of the preparation work. Jacob, content in his door bouncer, watched the activity with interest. He was the most chilled out and happy baby she had ever met, which not only made him blissful to have around, but eased her worries about how Paulie was going to adapt to fatherhood. He would be living here in just a few weeks and Laura, unaware of the debts he had passed to his mother, never mind the assault, assumed that Shona was looking forward to it as much as she was.

This Christening party would have been a vast imposition, had the last year not already brought such intense involvement with Social Services. The initial suggestion that it should be held at her house filled her with horror, but, in spite of the bizarre mix of guests, there were few who had not already drunk tea in her kitchen. And it wouldn't be appropriate for a 15 year old to hold a Christening party in a pub, nor could Sunny Bank open its doors. The way Laura put it, there was no other option.

The only real concern was how Laura's mother would handle herself in such company, but she had cried off just yesterday. Now the last worry knocked on the back door with a huge fist. Laura was in the kitchen, so Shona scooped up Jacob, not convinced his equanimity would stretch to this next encounter. She smiled as she walked through, seeing Laura take several steps back from the door and Jim's bulk filling the space beyond.

'Hello!' she said. 'I was beginning to think you'd changed your mind.'

'Yeah, sorry, I struggled to find somewhere to stash the bike, with the kennel-trailer in tow,' he said and looked at Laura, who was gazing at him with wide eyes. 'Hi. You must be Paulie's girl.'

Laura just nodded and took another step back. Jacob's expression conveyed similar uncertainty, but when Crank followed Jim inside, his mouth opened and his eyes gleamed, one chubby little arm jerking in the dog's direction.

'Crank will be ok with Jacob, won't he?' Shona said, squatting down so the child could have a closer look.

'Fine, he loves kids. Just watch his back end...the journey here won't have helped his hips.'

'Er...'

The sight of her baby, almost face to face with a very wolf-like dog, seemed to galvanize Laura.

'Don't worry, he's soft as butter,' Shona said. 'Could you put the kettle on, love? Jim must be gasping.'

Laura nodded slowly and turned to the sink. Jacob giggled, grabbing a fistful of fur as Crank licked the side of his face.

'Shall we show Crank where he's sleeping tonight?' Shona asked him, hoisting the squirming child onto her hip. 'Bring your stuff through, Jim. You'll have to stick it behind the settee until later. I'm sorry there isn't a bed, but this old thing is still comfy and long enough, even for you.'

'What time have we got to go to the church?'

'The taxi's booked in forty minutes. There's room for you too, although Crank will have to stay here. He won't nick the sausage rolls will he?'

'No. He's not up to traversing worktops these days.'

'I'm half pleased to hear that. Will you keep an eye on him and Jacob while I fetch your tea?'

She put Jacob on the floor again, amused by the brief expression of fear on Jim's face. Laura had gone upstairs to get ready, but there were two mugs of tea on the side which Shona carried back to the living room. She paused in the doorway to watch Jim, who was squatting on the floor with the baby and the dog. What a shame he wasn't Paulie's father.

'Perhaps you should have said yes to being Jamie's god-father after all,' she said. 'Looks like you're not too bad at this baby lark.'

'Huh,' Jim's grunt was full of wry amusement, but when he looked up, Shona was startled to see real pain in his eyes. 'I'd still fail on the longevity bit. What's this Jono like anyway? I never did get to meet him.'

Shona stared at him for a moment, but knew better than to pry.

'He's lovely, but you'll find out for yourself soon.'

Their conversation centred on the various attendees, delving no deeper than a vague concern about McGrath's presence, which didn't seem to bother Jim too much. Maybe he would open up later, when the whole event was done and dusted and the visitors gone. She found herself looking forward to that far more than the rest of the afternoon.

The taxi pulled up outside and now there was a panic to find shoes and bags and Jacob's coat. Jim settled Crank on his blanket and went to wait outside.

'Laura? We've really got to go, love!' Shona shouted up the stairs.

'Coming!' The girl came rushing down, under-dressed, but without enough time for it to be worth pointing out. 'I'll bring Jacob. You two go and get in the taxi and I'll be there in a sec.'

Shona went out and ushered Jim down the path. He opened the back door of the taxi and then climbed in behind her.

'Why don't you get in the front, you daft apeth? You'll put your back out.'

'She'll need the space, with the baby and bags. Don't whittle, woman.'

Shona smiled and shook her head, patting the knee that was almost on a level with her chin. Jim squeezed her hand, but let go of it again, so she put it back in her lap. Apologising to the driver, she hoped that Laura would hurry up. Sharing the back seat with Jim was already proving claustrophobic, if in a fairly pleasant way.

At last, Laura came tottering down the path in terrifying shoes, on the verge of losing her hold on Jacob at every step. The taxi driver sensed the urgency and tried to make up for the minutes lost, but as they pulled up level with the church, Shona could see

Jono and Trudy outside, and the backs of several people disappearing through the main door.

'We need to get a wriggle on folks,' she said, throwing the door open on the traffic side, rather than wait for Jim to unfold himself.

She took her purse from her handbag, but as Jim climbed out, the car drew off.

'On me,' he said and stretched. 'Hey, hang on, isn't Dee's mother coming?'

'She's back in hospital, but as Dee said, it's probably for the best, as she'd have necked all the Communion wine. Do you want me to take Jacob?'

Laura was struggling with him, a large bag and the awful shoes.

'Would you? Just for a minute...'

She moved to pass the baby to Shona, but Jacob reached out for Jim's beard on the way past. His arms lifting automatically, Jim took the child from her. Laura's eyes widened a little, but Shona grinned.

'Excellent. We need to run up these steps and he'll weigh nothing more than a fly to Jim. Laura, why don't you take off your shoes and put them back on before we go in.'

'I'll ladder me tights!'

Shona sighed and shook her head.

'Well, take your time then. Better to be late than break your leg. I'm going to see if things have started yet.'

She hurried up the steps, Jim close behind her. They couldn't be too tardy, as Jono and Trudy hadn't moved.

'Who's the dude in the chair?' Jim asked in a low voice.

'That's Jono,' Shona said, wishing she could see his face.

Hers was burning by the time she reached the top step and she had to stop for air, surprised when Jim strode straight past her, still carrying Jacob. Jono's grin faded into a less confident smile, as the sheer size of the man mountain heading straight for him became apparent. Pressing a hand to her heaving chest Shona followed, catching up just as Jim stretched out a giant paw.

'Alright mate? You must be Jono. I'm Jim.'

Jono started to laugh as they shook hands, but another hand touched Shona's sleeve, drawing her attention away. She turned, expecting to see Laura but finding an unfamiliar, nervous-looking young woman, standing very close to her.

'Hi...are you Shona? I'm Debs, Blake's wife.'

Blake? A scream from the top of the steps distracted her further and she didn't know whether to laugh or cry, when she saw Laura sprawling on the grass between two headstones. Oh God.

'Is that Laura?' the woman asked.

'Yes and I need to go and sort her out, sorry,' Shona said, still confused.

'I'll help.'

Shona's addled memory pulled itself together, at last. Of course. Blake. Paulie's pad-mate, Jacob's god-father. Debs was here by proxy.

'Ah, Debs. Sorry, I'm all over the shop today and thank you, all help will be appreciated. It already is - your husband has done more for my Paulie than anyone else ever has.'

'Well, I'm pleased that something positive has come from him getting banged up,' she said as they hurried over to the now-sniffling Laura.

She didn't sound all that pleased and Shona hoped she wasn't going to off-load right now. She could already feel her blood-pressure rising.

'Don't worry, Dee's not even here yet,' Jono called, his voice full of amusement.

Shona snatched a glance at the group and saw Jim was also grinning, Jacob still engrossed in his beard. She began to smile, but Laura let out another wail.

'I've got grass-stains on me arse!'

Two cars pulled up beside the pavement below and doors slammed. An audible argument spilled out, with Dee's voice the loudest. She was yelling at someone about 'fucking shit shoes'. Debs was now winding her beautiful scarf around Laura's green bottom, so Shona decided to give in and join the calmer bunch outside the doors. She found that 'calm' was not quite the right adjective however, with Jono suffering from mild hysteria, not quelled in any way by Delilah appearing at the top of the steps, dressed in a purple party dress and black boots.

'I can't do this!' he gasped. 'It's more like a comedy sketch than a Christening...the vicar's going to be in bits. What the hell has Dee got on her feet?!'

Blink was trotting behind her, waving a pair of purple, sparkly, high heeled shoes which, half way up the path, Delilah took from him and threw across the church yard. Derek and three other adults, presumably from Sunny Bank, lagged behind the pair, varying degrees of exasperation on their faces. The closer they got, the more thunderous Dee's expression grew and she glowered at the floor, rather than look at them.

'Don't you dare wind her up any further,' Trudy said, poking Jono's shoulder.

'Would I?'

'Yes.'

'You're a braver man than me then,' Jim said. He held Jacob out to Shona. 'Yours, I believe.'

'Not for long.'

The three groups converged, Dee and Laura both cheered by the presence and tarnished appearance of the other. Shona handed Jacob back to his mother and entered the church with Jim, taking a seat half way down the aisles of pews. There were mutterings throughout the congregation as the motley Christening crew made their way inside, but the female vicar gave them a warm welcome, betraying only the tiniest flicker of shock at the young mothers' strange attire.

The service was quicker than Shona was anticipating, although she suspected, from some of the murmurings around her, that the vicar was taking deliberate short-cuts. She remained calm though and was very patient with both the girls' fumblings and Jono's poorly concealed amusement. The atmosphere afterwards was almost carnival, with evident relief from the care staff that all parties had survived the ordeal.

Laura had accepted a lift in one of their cars and was staying for more photos, but Jim and Shona didn't linger, wanting to get back for ten minutes' peace and quiet, before the horde arrived. They were waiting on the pavement for the taxi when McGrath ran down the steps towards them.

'Oh, hello,' Shona said. 'I thought you hadn't made it.'

'I stayed at the back, where I could chuckle without causing offence,' he said, shaking his head. 'What a wonderful experience.'

He held a hand out to Jim, who took it without reluctance.

'Jim. Good to see you here. Are you around for a few days?'

'Nope. I'm heading back tomorrow.'

'Ah, I could just do with talking to you again, about the Gascoine and Co. case.'

'Not got that wrapped up yet?'

'No. I tried to shelve it, but apparently, I have to try harder.'

Shona's happiness drained away as she watched the two men, eyes locked in silent communication.

'No worries. Looks like you'll get another jolly to the seaside then,' Jim said, 'unless you're coming to the Christening party?'

Shona could see in McGrath's face that he wanted to and prayed fervently that he wouldn't.

'No. No, I'll leave you to it, but I'll be in touch soon. Are you on the same number I took last time?'

'Yep.'

'Alright, well, have a good afternoon.'

He headed off up the road and Shona stared after him.

'Oh Jim, I thought that was all over.'

'Don't worry, he's got nothing on me. Bloke's got to do his job, even though I don't reckon he wants to.'

But she did worry. All through the afternoon she watched him, cuddling Jamie under Dee's supervision, gently prising Jacob's fingers out of Crank's ears, talking to Blink for over an hour, huddled in a corner with Derek for almost as long, laughing, actually laughing, with Jono and Trudy. She'd imagined he would spend most of the party smoking in the garden, out of the way. It would be unbearable if he went back inside for facilitating all of this. They might have been gathered for Delilah's wake, if he hadn't sorted those scum-bags out.

By 6pm they were all gone. Even Laura was out, she and Debs having taken Jacob to the park, with a picnic from the remains of the buffet. There wasn't half the mess she'd feared and when she

379

went into the kitchen, she found that one of the women from Sunny Bank had done most of the washing up.

'Sit down woman and let me pour you a whisky. You deserve it after playing hostess all afternoon,' Jim said.

'That sounds nice, although you've done more of the polite conversation than I have.'

Shona collapsed onto the settee, only opening her eyes again when Jim sat down beside her. He handed her a glass of amber liquid and she took a sip, revelling in the warmth that glided down her throat.

'Gosh, that tastes a bit special.'

'It is, but it's a special occasion. Seems like Dee's pretty sorted now.' Jim took a sip from his own glass, savoured it for a second. 'So how do you feel about Paulie coming out?'

'Oh, mostly pleased and quite excited. Laura's not as ditzy as I first thought and Paulie seems a changed man, I just worry that he'll slip back into his old ways. He's saying all the right things though and if this Blake chap is going to be on the scene, then he might help keep Paulie on the straight and narrow. If he's happy, then I'll be happy and whatever happens, I've got Laura and Jacob. But what about you? What about this Gascoine thing?'

Jim sighed and said nothing for several minutes. Shona was on the point of prompting him when he spoke.

'To be honest, that's the least of my worries. I sit here, after a day in the company of decent folk, with the most pleasant, chilled out woman I've ever met, and I imagine that there is a second chance, another life I can make my own, but it's a dream, Shona. I can't escape the past. It keeps catching up with me and I'm getting tired of running.'

'Oh Jim.' The tears gave no warning and she gave them no heed, taking his big hand in both of hers. 'There has to be a way, even if it's going abroad or something. People can't hold grudges forever. You could change your identity...or...buy a cottage in the Highlands.'

Jim stared at her for a moment and then smiled.

380

'You're right, I'm just being morbid. Look, I won't have much time tomorrow - I'll be out all morning and then I need to get back in the afternoon. Why don't we go out for dinner tonight?'

She would rather order a takeaway and stay on the settee, but Laura would be back soon, with Debs and Jacob, and the house would be full again.

'Ok, but only if it's a dark, quiet pub…not a restaurant.'

'Deal.'

He stood up and held out his hand.

~ ~ ~

It must be an hour since she got into bed, but Dee didn't feel any nearer to sleep. The events of the day kept tumbling around her head, interspersed with other, heavier thoughts that she didn't want to think about right now. Every time she returned to the Christening, she remembered fresh snatches of conversation and snap-shots, like McGrath's face, when she told him that Jamie's middle name was for him. That memory made her smile in the darkness, but then she recalled him saying something about Blink being a wise choice of father and all her frustration returned.

Throwing the covers off, she felt her way over to the chair where her jacket was hanging and took the pouch of tobacco from the pocket. Having pulled back the curtains, she could see enough to roll a fag and then opened the window, leaning out as far as possible before lighting up. It was an even bigger no-no, now that Jamie was living in the house, but she'd been good for months and no-one was going to moan at her tonight. Hopefully.

Blink, Blink, bloody fucking Blink. Sometimes, it felt like they were married or something, now he was driving and took her loads of places. It was good to get out, but he usually picked boring things to do. And he reckoned he loved her, but the one time she'd tried it on, behind a wall in some wrecked castle, he'd gone bright red and literally run off. He said he wanted to do it properly, when she was 16, but she would be in ten months and like, der, she had a baby.

She still didn't know if she even fancied Blink or not. Laura's ranting had forced her to admit that he was pretty fit, since he'd done all that training. And however annoying and boring he could be, he wasn't an arsehole. When she'd heard Blink and Derek talking about him being able to get a flat next month, when he was 18, she'd flipped out about it, but then when he said she could move in when she was 16, she didn't know if she liked that idea either. How could you think about moving in with someone you hadn't even snogged?!

But Laura was marrying Paulie, even though he'd been a total wanker about Jacob and got sent down. Dee had thought that meant losing her best friend, but Laura refused to move the Christening and wait for Paulie to come out, even though he asked her to. She was going to be a bridesmaid and in on all the wedding plans and now she was Jacob's god-mother too, like Laura was Jamie's. Laura wouldn't let Paulie stop them being friends.

Then there was Jono, who was always with Trudy now. It sounded like they were proper serious. He'd even got a job, a really good one. Some bloke on his course told him about it, moaning that they wanted applications from disabled people cos they didn't have enough or something and that it wasn't fair. Nob-head.

Jono hadn't even finished his course, but he still passed the interview and was going to earn loads of money. He said he'd take her and Jamie out for dinner with his first month's pay...and Blink. Even Jono was trying to get them together and Trudy just treated them like a couple anyway. The vicar called him Jamie's father in church.

But they weren't a couple, not really, and how could she tell if she wanted to be, if he wouldn't even get off with her? Bloody idiot. She was contemplating rolling a second fag when she heard a faint cry. Shit. She'd stink of smoke. Leaving the window open, she closed the curtains and flicked the light on, whipping off the baggy t-shirt and grabbing another top from the chair. She took a swig of water and then pulled the top over her head with one hand, opening the door with the other.

She was half way across the landing before she realised that the top didn't reach her hips, never mind cover the thong she was wearing. Oh well, Jamie didn't care and the staff would only come up if he yelled for ages. Pushing open the nursery door, she found Blink already feeding him a bottle, Jamie guzzling contentedly in his arms. He was only wearing pyjama bottoms and his chest looked lush. She hadn't even heard the microwave in the corner ping.

'You got here quick,' she said in a whisper.

'I didn't have my h..head out of the window s..smoking,' he whispered back.

He didn't stutter so much when he whispered. Or maybe he didn't stutter so much now anyway, not with her at least.

'Don't moan at me, I couldn't sleep, it was boring.'

'Me n..neither. It's been a p..pretty amazing day, hasn't it?'

'Yeah.'

She went and sprawled out on the single bed, where she'd slept when Jamie was first born and could still if he was poorly. Blink didn't look up, concentrating on holding the bottle at the right angle and keeping Jamie's head up. Dee watched them for a while, then remembered him sitting with Jim for ages at Shona's.

'Hey, what were you talking about with Jim?' she said, unable to imagine what they had in common.

'Uh...all sorts of s..stuff.'

Even in the dim illumination of the night light, she could see his face go red. When he looked up at her, it went even darker.

'Delilah! You've got no pants on!'

'Ssh!' She giggled and rolled on to her side. 'I have look, it's just a thong.'

'Oh.'

He stared at her for several more seconds, until Jamie blew a raspberry, pulling away from the bottle. Blink put the bottle down and used Jamie's soft bib to wipe his face, before lifting him to his shoulder.

'Delilah, you could b..burp Jamie, now I've f..fed him. C..come and t..take him, I n..need to go b..back to b..bed.'

Freak. He said he couldn't sleep a minute ago.

383

'It'll wake him up. You might as well carry on now, he'll go down soon.'

'Delilah, p..p..please.'

He tried to cross his legs and then half turned away from her. He sounded desperate. Then she got it. Blink's fingers fluttered over Jamie's back and her awesome little boy let out a series of burps, dribbling milky spit over Blink's bare shoulder. Dee picked up a towel from the end of the bed and went over, taking longer to wipe away the goo than she needed to and pressing her leg against his.

Blink made a squeaky noise and his leg started to shake. Jamie let out another burp and Dee wiped the bare shoulder again, even though he didn't sick anything up, breathing in Blink's deodorant, which was proper tasty. He squirmed around further in the chair, so she pressed herself against his back. This time, he made a strangled kind of sound.

'I think Jamie's ready to go down now,' she said, near his ear.

'Y..y..yes. Y..y..you go b..b..back to b..bed. I'll p..p..put him d..down in a s..s..second.'

'I don't want to. I want to talk to you.'

She backed off a bit and Blink stood up, both his legs shaking now. He tried to keep his back to her, but Dee sidled around him to get a better view and saw a gigantic boner pushing out the front of his pyjamas, like a tent. It looked crazy and she only just stopped herself laughing. She watched him stoop to lay Jamie down and didn't want to laugh any more. The fact that he wanted her so badly gave her those feelings in her stomach at last, like when she was first with Gaz. She wanted Blink too. Now.

He stood up but didn't turn around, so she went over and put her hands on his waist. Goose bumps came up all over his back and he shivered. Dee watched the reaction, fascinated. Blink turned and put his hands on her shoulders, so she reached out to touch the source of the tent.

'No!' he gasped. 'N..not in here, w..with Jamie.'

'Well come on then.'

Dee took his hand and led him across the landing to her own room. She opened the door and pulled him inside. Blink let go of her to close it carefully behind them and Dee snatched off her top, so that when he turned back, she was standing in just the thong. His mouth fell open and he gazed at her, not moving except for the tent growing a little taller, which she didn't think possible.

Blink took a step towards her, but looked scared now. She took one of his hands and put it on her tit, the fingers squeezed by themselves.

'We c..can't,' Blink said, his voice hoarse now. 'I h..haven't g..g..got a c..c..'

'I've got an implant.'

He hesitated for a second longer and then it changed. Dee found herself lifted in his arms, pressed close to his chest, being kissed more fiercely than she'd ever known. She wrapped her legs around his waist to stop them dangling and Blink walked them over to the bed. Dee wondered how he would get the pyjamas off and couldn't prevent a giggle escaping. Blink froze.

'W..what's f..f..unny?'

'Nothing, I'm just happy,' she said and kissed him again.

He kissed her back for a few seconds, then laid her gently on the bed. The pyjamas weren't a problem after all and Dee was glad to be rid of the thong, but it was over too soon after that. Or maybe not. Blink continued to kiss and caress her, telling her he loved her, asking what she liked best, stroking her face, her belly, wanting to touch every bit of her, as much as she wanted him to. It wasn't exciting like the best times with Gaz, although that could have been the drugs, but it was warm, and satisfying, and safe.

~ ~ ~

Crank was flaked out on the bench seat, his ears drooping. Jim didn't feel much more cheerful, but put a hand out to comfort his friend, stroking the loose ruff of his neck.

'I'm sorry old man,' Jim said. 'It's been a hectic couple of days for you, especially with those long rides, but you were definitely a hit with the kids.'

The ears didn't rise, but Crank's tail flopped a little.

'Shona said Jacob fell asleep on you while I was out this morning and you didn't move a muscle for over an hour. That probably hasn't helped, but it was an honourable deed.'

The tail flopped again. Jim gave a dry laugh and took another slug of whisky from the bottle. Honourable deeds. There hadn't been many of those in his life, but he had made some attempt to compensate. Too little, too late. The emotions wrought in him yesterday - among the highest and lowest in his life - now left him hollow and drained. But at least he'd experienced them.

If he did get to sleep tonight, he would drift off dreaming of his recent revelation; of what a life with Shona could be like, with Jacob as a grandson, to teach all the things he had been forced to learn the hard way. To be accepted as an equal by those people who had always lived in another world to him, to have earned the respect of a man like McGrath.

That 'if', he knew, was a million to one bet. The black transit that tailed him on the journey home, staying a long way back and only visible on long straights, suggested otherwise. Still, he now knew his stance on the old 'would you rather know or not' debate. The list of regrets was long, but significantly shorter than it could have been. He'd paid the farmer three months' rent in advance on his return, to cover any ensuing hassle, all his meagre affairs were in order and he was as prepared as he could be. There was even an element of peace – there would be no more running, no more farewells.

The whisky bottle was two thirds empty and midnight a thing of the past, when the sound of throaty engines roused him from his pre-planned reverie. Jim was instantly alert. With most of his body protected by the steel plate screwed to the wall, he peered through the purposeful slash in the curtain and saw three vehicles. That was that then. He took the gun from inside his jacket, went back to the bench seat and knelt down, resting his forehead against Crank's and wrapping an arm around his neck.

'Well old friend, there'll be no time to reload, so there's one for you, one for me and four for them.' Crank licked his face as he flicked off the safety. 'I'll catch you up.'

He straightened, pulled the cushion between the gun and the trusting eyes, and pulled the trigger. There were shouts from outside, but they were swiftly drowned out by the raging fire burning up from his chest. Kicking open the door of the caravan, Jim shot the nearest figure, then the next. Somewhere amidst the flames, he registered a pull to the side, a kink in his aim; he was taking out shoulders, not chests. He didn't want to kill, didn't want to leave yet more fatherless children, didn't need to use all the bullets.

There was a sickening impact in his gut, then another in his left arm. Lifting the gun to his temple, Jim paused only to recall Shona's warm smile, before pulling the trigger for the last time.

Epilogue

Sitting at the breakfast table with a cold mug of tea, McGrath re-read the letter that had arrived the day before, delivered to his home, addressed to 'Mr A. McGrath'. It threw up many more questions than it answered, but his main concern was how to attend the appointment without compromising himself professionally. He was invited to meet a solicitor of dubious reputation called Smith, in Nottingham, at 10.30am this morning, regarding the estate of Jim Travis, deceased.

The easy option would be to request compassionate leave, to arrange the affairs of a dead relative, but it was mostly untrue and easy to disprove. He shook his head, grimly amused that Travis still had the power to corrupt him, even from the other side. Abandoning the tea, McGrath decided to head in to work early and see how hectic things were after his two days off. It might not be possible at all.

Any hope of casting off the somewhat haunted feel was dashed, when he found a letter written in the same spiky hand waiting in his office, this time addressed to 'Detective Inspector McGrath'. The content was the same – an appointment, at 10.30am this morning – though there was a further line, saying that crucial evidence regarding the Gascoine and Co. case would be made available to him. Bingo.

He took Robson with him for the sake of protocol, confident that his Sergeant would wait outside the solicitor's office without question and glad of his presence when they entered the musty Victorian building. The whole thing was reminiscent of a Sherlock

Holmes tale and finding an old-fashioned bell system inside, rather than an intercom, only served to reinforce that impression.

McGrath half expected a wizened character, in crow-like garb, to be waiting for him on the third floor and was a little disappointed to find that Smith was a smartly dressed man in his early sixties.

'Detective Inspector, do take a seat.'

'I'd rather stand, thank you.'

'I'd rather you sat. This is both a civil and legal affair and may take some time.'

The impasse lasted long enough to satisfy form. McGrath was very aware that there were no cards in his hand and pulled out the leather-backed chair without further complaint. The personal bequest was to be dealt with first, taking the form of a sealed letter which he signed for with some discomfort.

'Your signature does not commit you to any action, sir, it simply asserts that you received the document. Would you like a coffee?'

'No, thank you.'

McGrath moved to slide the letter inside his jacket, but the solicitor raised a hand.

'It was Mr Travis' wish that you read it before we move on to the second bequest.'

His lips pressed into a tight line, McGrath gave a curt nod and tore open the envelope. Three paragraphs in, he was forced to rest his wrists on the desk, to stop the paper shaking in his hands.

'I'll go and fetch that coffee.'

McGrath ground his teeth, but was glad to be alone for a few minutes. He didn't understand why people wanted to read the harrowing life stories that seemed to fill the best-sellers lists these days, and to be forced to do so in a strange environment, with a known subject, was almost more than he could bear. When Smith returned with fresh, strong filter coffee, McGrath's antagonism waned. Having moved on to a section describing – in oblique terms that could not be used as evidence – the initial assault upon Shona, McGrath had also regained his composure.

He was not surprised to read that Paulie was the perpetrator and Jim's subsequent involvement brought a smile to his lips. The request to keep an eye on the situation - with Paulie's outstanding drug debts in mind - made him wince, but Jim asked nothing more. There were no specifics. The final paragraph, thanking McGrath for his time and respect in reading to the end, brought on a dry cough. Smith also cleared his throat.

'Can we move on to the second bequest?'

'Yes, although I have a question first,' McGrath said. 'Was it necessary to contact me with two separate letters? I'm not altogether happy that you were able to obtain my home address.'

Smith smiled, enjoying the upper hand.

'There was a dual purpose behind that, Detective Inspector. The first and main purpose, was to allow you to complete an honest inventory of your formal bequest. The second and *secondary* purpose, was to demonstrate how easy it is to acquire someone's personal details when they are recorded on a computer system. The licence conditions of Mr Travis ensured that he could never gain anonymity, or escape those who pursued him.'

McGrath was quite sure the weighted silence which followed this statement would have lasted much longer, had not time been money.

'Let us move on. I will require your signature again, for the second document.'

There was no hesitation this time. McGrath's hopes regarding the content were higher now and rewarded the moment he opened the envelope. The first sheet was a signed confession to the assaults on Gascoine & Co, giving full details of means, method and motive. Behind that was a second confession, relating to a gang-land manslaughter some twelve years ago, for which someone else was still serving time.

The third sheet he scanned, but returned to the envelope without reading fully. It contained further information, including names and contacts that Jim had dug up when looking into sexual exploitation and porn franchises. That could go straight over to Vice.

'There is just one matter remaining,' Smith said, as McGrath made to stand up. 'The funeral. Mr Travis asked that you attend.'

'Yes, he mentioned it in his letter.'

'That may be, but I doubt he was aware of the date at that time. It's next week, Thursday.'

Smith handed him a photocopy of the notice from the funeral directors, which McGrath took from him with ill-concealed irritation. It was an effort to shake the man's hand, a fact that Smith acknowledged with a sly smile. McGrath shot over to the door, before the obsequious shit could open it for him.

Those in attendance were an eclectic bunch and fewer in number than McGrath expected. He spotted Shona, her eyes red and swollen, standing with a small group by the entrance to the crematorium. Despite his lack of uniform, there were several heavy stares coming his way from a bunch of biker-types, but McGrath merely nodded at them and made his way towards the familiar face.

'Hello. How nice of you to come,' Shona said as he approached.

'There's nothing nice about it, I just needed to be here. Strange as it may seem, I had a lot of respect for Jim.'

'I know that. I mean you could have...well you probably...oh ignore me, I can't think straight at the moment.'

Her blush suggested otherwise and McGrath gave her a wry smile. He bent towards her ear, speaking in a low voice.

'It may make you a little more comfortable, to know that Jim left a full confession regarding his most recent activities with a solicitor, addressed to me.'

Shona's eyes grew wide.

'As in...Dee...'

'Yes, *those* activities.'

She let out a long breath, but her lip crumpled at the same time.

'He was such a good man. Do you know he left £2,000 in a trust fund for Jacob, the same for Jamie, and £2,000 each for Dee and Blink, with another £3,000 if they get married! I don't know if they'll go for it and she's not even 16 yet, but it's a good incentive.' Trying to smile through her tears, she hiccoughed instead. 'I've got the motorbike. He left it with the farmer.'

McGrath took the paper from under his arm and passed it to her.

'Yes, he was a good man, and this is small comfort I know, but I have tried to spread the word.'

He'd folded the paper open at the Obituary pages and watched as Shona's eyes flicked over the sheet, starting with surprise when she found the entry.

Obituary – Jim Travis

I, the author, am a man of middle years and have worked in law enforcement for almost thirty of those. My depth of experience led to an arrogance in assuming myself an accurate judge of others. Jim Travis - a convicted criminal, who spent much of his adult life in prison - taught me otherwise.

He taught me to disregard my preconceptions and evaluate actions on an individual basis. He taught me that good and bad are not contrasting in stance, but rather a shifting kaleidoscope of perspective. He taught me that, on occasion, the law protects the evil-doer and fails the vulnerable; a travesty that should be exposed, not shied away from. He taught me that we all have malicious potential, and that the course we take is as much about education and circumstance, as about choice.

Here, I salute the strength, courage and bravery of Jim Travis and offer my very greatest respects. His passing will be grieved in some circles and rejoiced in others, but he leaves a legacy in several hearts, including my own, which I believe will continue to inspire change for the better, for years to come.

Regretfully Anonymous

Shona put a hand to her mouth and the tears flowed in earnest for a few seconds. Still crying, she also began to laugh.

'Oh, he'll be having a hoot up there, to think he has such a fine obituary…and written by a policeman!'

McGrath smiled, hoping for a moment that if there was an 'up there', Jim would be pleased to see that the next appointment in his diary was regarding his retirement plan; to work as a counsellor with young offenders.

~ ~ ~

Driving home from Sunny Bank for the last time, Derek experienced a nauseating blend of sorrow and excitement. It washed over him in waves until he was forced to pull over. Eleven years was a long time, but he wasn't leaving that much behind; he wasn't a key-worker for either of the two new girls and didn't know them well at all. He would miss a couple of the staff, but not too much, as they'd never mixed socially.

What he would miss was already gone - that genuine sense of 'family' created by Blink and Delilah and little Jamie. The day of their formal departure had caused such devastation that Julie gave everyone the rest of the shift off. It was a success story, but upsetting nonetheless. That was part of the attraction of the new job – forming positive relationships that didn't run too deep. It also fulfilled his two greatest passions in one hit; working with needy kids and playing music. Being in an education setting, he would even have school holidays off, to spend with his own children.

It was a no-brainer. He shouldn't be feeling any sadness at all. Looking across the street, he realised he was only half a mile from Blink and Delilah's flat. Perhaps one last goodbye was needed to seal the deal. He checked his mirrors before doing a u-turn, half hoping they would be in, half hoping they would not. Talia was cooking a celebratory dinner.

The flats were not inspiring and he tried not to look around as he waited for the buzzer to be answered. He gave it one last press and was about to walk away when Blink's breathless voice came from the speaker.

'Hello?'

'Hey, it's Derek. I've just dropped round to see how you're doing.'

'Great! C..come up.'

The door clunked and Derek pushed through it, wrinkling his nose at the smell in the hallway. Their flat was on the first floor and he ran up the stairs, the quicker to escape its cloying pissiness. Blink let him in with a broad smile.

'Sorry, I was just s..seeing to Jamie when you buzzed. He's got a c..cold, but hopefully he'll s..stay asleep now. Come through.'

Apart from a pile of washing waiting to be put away and a few pots in the sink, the place was absurdly tidy and every surface shone.

'Wow. You're doing a proper job here mate,' Derek said. 'It's a damn site smarter than my first flat. You guys must be working really hard to keep it this nice.'

Blink's non-committal 'hmmn' suggested the effort was mostly his, but he looked pleased with the praise.

'So what's Dee up to?'

'She's out.'

'Ah.'

She was out the last time he'd called round too.

'It's ok, she's with L..laura and she's usually b..better for a bit when she's seen her.'

'Better?'

Blink paused while he filled the kettle, keeping his back to Derek while he messed with mugs and tea-bags.

'She gets f..frustrated, you know, with having to w..work around Jamie all the time, and then she feels b..bad because she really loves him too.'

'It's always difficult when they're this age, but it will get easier, when he starts going to nursery and then school.'

'I know, it just seems a l..long way off to Delilah.'

But not to him? Blink seemed a lot more cheerful about the situation than most mature, experienced guys managed to be.

'Well I have to say, you don't look like it's getting you down.'

'Oh it d..does sometimes, and I h..hate it when Delilah goes out and th..then talks about l..lads she's met that I d..don't even know, but everything's c..cool now. I can't believe you've t..turned up actually.'

'I've just finished at Sunny Bank, for ever. I've got a new job in Nottingham, but it made me think of you guys. So what's happening?'

Blink turned around and passed him a mug of tea. His smile was back, with bells on.

'Delilah was r..ranting last week, about the smell of p..piss in the corridor and being s..skint. I said we could always get m..married and use the money from Jim as a b..bond on a new place, a house m..maybe, and still have some l..left over. She wasn't s..sure, but she said y..yes in the end.'

Derek whooped and clapped him on the shoulder, genuinely thrilled.

'That's awesome! No wonder you're happy.'

'That's not the b..best news,' Blink said, grinning now. 'I talked to my social worker, and a s..solicitor. I'll be able to adopt Jamie, be his r..real father and have equal r..rights. He'll n..never, ever end up in c..care.'

Derek hoped that shock wasn't over-shadowing the joy on his face. Blink had been utterly committed to Jamie from the moment he was born and this news was no surprise, but for it to take precedence over Delilah agreeing to marry him was unexpected.

'You moved on that pretty fast.'

'I had to. At the Ch..christening me and Jim were t..talking for ages, about growing up in c..care mostly. He said the s..same things as you, that Delilah would be h..hard work, that I w..wouldn't see Jamie if we split up, that Social Services would be a..all over us for y..years. He said people don't b..bother with marriage any more, but it's the b..best way to sort things legally. When we f..found out about his will, I knew that's what he m..m..meant me to do. Now everyone's h..happy, especially as Laura will be t..telling Delilah that it's a g..great idea. She likes me.'

He went pink and Derek grinned, but could not help shaking his head a little, awed by the young man in front of him and his humble aspirations. There was a wail from the bedroom.

'Daddeee!'

Derek drained the last of his tea and put the mug on the worktop.

'I'll get off and leave you to it,' he said, taking Blink's hand, then casting it away and grabbing him in a big hug. 'I am so bloody proud of you.'

Blink's eyes were moist when he let go, but he was still smiling...smiling and not blinking at all.

'Good l..luck with the new job.'

'Thanks. You take care. Say hi to Dee.'

'I will.'

Derek didn't notice the stink outside the flat and floated back to his car with a sense of detachment. *Now everyone is happy.* Blink's words rolled around his head throughout the journey, illuminating dim corners and drawing together stray thoughts.

Happiness was about understanding and accepting limitations. Happiness was about perspective. Happiness was a personal design. He was going home to work on his own pattern of happiness, to draw in his wife, his children and never take the love they shared for granted.

Cat Hextall is on Facebook and Twitter

Acknowledgements

These must go to Jed, again, for putting up with life in the land of Delilah so patiently, for so long.

A big shout out to the home editing crew – Jed Draper, Charlie Draper, Kate Turner, Sarah Francis, Cate Adams, Simon Day, Colin, Wendy and Richard Butt, Jonathan Cundey and Bev Llewellyn.

Massive thanks to Rob Kerr, for yet more awesome cover photography and Laura Bowlzer for being such a wonderful model.